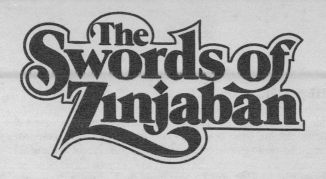

The Swords of Zinjaban

L. Sprague & Catherine Crook de Camp

BAEN FANTASY

THE SWORDS OF ZINJABAN

Copyright © 1991 by L. Sprague de Camp and Catherine Crook de Camp

A Baen Books Original

Baen Publishing Enterprises
P.O. Box 1403
Riverdale, N.Y. 10471

ISBN: 0-671-72039-2

Cover art by Tom Kidd

First printing, February 1991

Distributed by
SIMON & SCHUSTER
1230 Avenue of the Americas
New York, N.Y. 10020

Printed in the United States of America

Contents

That's Show Biz!

Reith pulled on the aya's reins and set the brake on the carriage. Across the road ahead shambled three huge Krishnan beasts: a female bishtar and two young. The adult bishtar was of elephantine size and build with six legs and a hide covered with glossy fur of purpled brown with cream-colored spots. The head resembled that of a tapir, though vastly larger, with small trumpet-shaped ears and a long muzzle ending in a pair of stubby, meter-long trunks.

"We ought to have one of those things in our movie," whispered White. "Do they have tame ones for rent?"

Reith replied, "The Dasht of Ruz has one in his zoo; but he'd never lease it. We'd have to go to Majbur to find one of the tame bishtars the Krishnans use to pull railroads."

"One good action shot of that animal would be worth a hundred meters of an animated model—" White began.

"Oh, hell!" said Ordway. "We can't run all over the planet on the budget they gave me!"

"But Cyril, don't you see—"

The two executives from Cosmic Productions had gradually raised their voices. Reith said, "Hey, pipe down! You're bothering the animals."

The female bishtar had turned to face the carriage and stood with ears twitching and trunks sniffing. Then it opened its vast maw, gave a thunderous snort, and began shuffling with appalling speed towards the travelers . . .

INTRODUCTION

The Swords of Zinjaban is the latest in our series laid on the planet Krishna, an Earthlike satellite of the star Tau Ceti. Krishna harbors an intelligent species of humanoids enough like Earthmen so that an enterprising member of one race can disguise himself as a member of the other. The Terrans who live on Krishna must cope with cultures that range from primitive to medieval and with an interplanetary organization that forbids the introduction of 22nd-century technology into this comparatively primitive world.

An earlier novel, *The Hostage of Zir*, introduces Fergus Reith, a travel agent who, though inexperienced, finds himself shepherding a dozen erratic sightseers on the first guided tour of Krishna. Along the way the Regent of Dur, a quasi-medieval state, traps Reith for political reasons into marriage with a native princess. From the clutches of the Regent and the embraces of his bride, Reith escapes and returns to Novorecife, the Terran spaceport and complex.

In the following novel, *The Prisoner of Zhamanak*, the Terran community is aroused by the news that a social scientist, Dr. Alicia Dyckman, has been imprisoned by a Krishnan ruler. Alicia, beautiful and brilliant but headstrong and hot-tempered, is rescued by Percy Mjipa, a Terran consular employee of African origin. When the fugitives finally reach Novorecife, Alicia meets Fergus Reith, and the two fall precipitately in love.

The Bones of Zora opens over a year later when, after a passionate but stormy marriage, Reith and Alicia are newly divorced. Reith undertakes to assist a French paleontologist on Krishna's first fossil-hunting expedition; while, unknown to Reith, Alicia is guiding a rival scientist to the same area. Thrown together, Reith and Alicia become lovers. Each contemplates remarriage; but Alicia's contentiousness causes so many quarrels and problems that in the end, Reith sadly decides that they would have no chance of happiness together. Grieving, Alicia departs for Earth, planning to undergo drastic 22nd-century psychotherapy to improve her tempestuous personality.

The present story begins twenty Terran years later. Reith, now a well-established tour manager, has aged but little, because medical science has tripled the human life span. Alicia, seeming not to have aged at all, returns to Krishna as a motion-picture executive, to assist in making the first feature film on the planet.

While the Terrans on Krishna are of various national origins, the official language of the Viagens Interplanetarias, the Brazilian-dominated interstellar transport system, is Portuguese. For those interested in pronunciation, we have placed a short scholium at the end of the novel, explaining our suggested renderings of some of the exotic names in the story.

—L. Sprague de Camp
Catherine Crook de Camp

1

FERGUS REITH

The *Pará* set down on a pillar of flame. Long, lean, and auburn-haired, Fergus Reith waited at the lower end of the ramp as the interstellar travelers straggled down to set foot on the soil of the planet Krishna. Beside him stood a stripling, with hair as carroty red as his own had been twenty Terran years ago.

A group consisting of two men and a woman emerged from the crowd. These, Reith decided, might be his new clients from Cosmic Productions. But as they came into full view, Reith's jaw went slack. The concrete of the spaceport seemed to vanish beneath his feet, leaving him in free-fall. For the woman in the lead was Dr. Alicia Dyckman, the eminent xenanthropologist—who, a score of years before, had been Mrs. Fergus Reith.

As she approached, lithe in a blue-and-gold-jumper that matched her sapphire eyes and smooth blond hair, Reith experienced a dizzying sense of time travel. He knew that he had aged during the intervening years. Despite the longevity pills that tripled the normal human life span, the passage of time had marked him. And here came Alicia, looking no older than the day when, twenty Terran years ago, she had mounted the ramp to the *Juruá*, weeping because Reith, the hus-

3

band whom she had deserted and divorced, would not take her back. She was the same tallish, slender, animated, golden woman, with delicate features and a tip-tilted nose. The illusion of fragility still clung to her; although Reith knew full well that, physically and mentally, she was as strong as a man and as tough as nails.

Reith also knew that the cause of this apparent anomaly in their ages lay in the relativistic effects of space travel. For two decades, Reith had plied his trade as a tour guide on Krishna; and for him, time had plodded by at its normal rate. Alicia, on the other hand, had spent most of that interval journeying between Krishna and their home planet Earth, at a velocity close to the speed of light. For her, time had slowed to a crawl, and the transit from planet to planet seemed little more than a fortnight.

As the trio completed their descent, Reith pulled himself together and stepped forward. "Hello, Alicia!" he said with a casualness that disguised the painful pounding of his heart. "Are you and these gentlemen my new clients from Cosmic Productions?"

Alicia's sky-blue eyes widened. "Fergus Reith! Is it really you?"

"I—I'm . . ."

"You look so different, somehow, in spectacles. And your hair's darker—a nice auburn instead of that fiery red."

A trifle self-consciously, they shook hands. With a self-deprecating grin, Reith murmured: "Well, I haven't gotten any younger in twenty years, Earth time." To avoid an awkward pause, he turned with forced cordiality to the two men. "Welcome to Krishna! I'm Fergus Reith, your guide, interpreter, and general troubleshooter."

With a visible effort, Alicia regained her composure. "This is Cyril Ordway, production manager for Cosmic Productions; and Jacob White, the location manager. I'm the assistant production manager."

Murmuring amenities, the newcomers shook hands with Reith. Ordway, he saw, was a pudgy individual with a sandy mustache and a mottled complexion. Little red veins gave his thick snub nose a roseate hue. White, slight of build, seemed a nervous person, who repeatedly combed his thinning black hair across a balding scalp. Glancing from Reith to Alicia, Ordway said, in a concise Londonese accent, "I take it you two know each other already?"

"Yes," said Reith shortly. "And this is my son Alister; Doctor Dyckman, Mr. Ordway, Mr. White. Let's move along to Baggage Claim, so as not to hold up the line."

As the youth pushed ahead, followed by Ordway and White, Alicia whispered: "Your son looks *so* like you! Your wife must be proud of him."

Reith shook his head. "No wife. I'll tell you about it later." Raising his voice, he said: "Here's Baggage Claim, gentlemen. When you've located your luggage, I'll take you through Customs and Security and help you get settled." He turned to his son and dropped his voice again. "I'll see you back home in time for dinner, String. Tell Kardir to set an extra place."

Young Alister disappeared. An hour later, Reith and his party headed for the Visitors' Building in the Novorecife compound, behind a burly Krishnan who wheeled a laden baggage cart. They traversed an aggregation of massive concrete structures, their starkness slightly relieved by touches of ornamentation in Krishnan style on roofs and doorways.

Reith stowed his clients and their baggage in their respective rooms, leaving Alicia and her possessions to the last. When the porter had departed, Reith said: "Look, Lish, as soon as I arrange for your colleagues' dinners, why don't you come out to my place? My Krishnan cook makes meals at the Novo cafeteria look like cold slumgullion."

The term "Lish" evoked a fleeting smile from Alicia;

Reith had always called her that when they were on friendly terms. "Where is your place?" she asked.

"Two or three *hoda* out of Novo. It's a small ranch, with enough hectares to raise a few shaihans. How about it? We have a lot to talk about, and here the walls have ears."

"Sounds tempting. But we can't just desert poor Cyril and Jack!"

"They will be taken care of." In the Portuguese of the Viagens Interplanetarias, Reith spoke crisply into the room communicator. "*Zero cinco*. . . . Herculeu? Do me the favor of taking two of my clients to dinner, will you please?"

"*¿E a dama deleitosa?*" rasped the machine in the same language.

"She has other plans," said Reith.

"*Bem.*" Herculeu Castanhoso's snicker resounded over the communicator. An hour earlier, at the immigration desk, the security officer had made a great fuss over Alicia. Like everyone else in the Terran community, Herculeu knew the bittersweet story of the long-ago romance between the social scientist and the professional tour guide.

Ignoring Herculeu's chuckle, Reith turned back to Alicia. "All fixed!"

"Well, if you're sure—"

"Of course, wear your outdoor clothes, and bring overnight essentials."

She looked sharply at him. "What sort of quarters are you putting me in?"

"Fear not," he said with a mischievous grin. "You'll have your own room, with a bolt on the door big enough to stop a bishtar. And Alister—"

A knock announced Ordway, who plaintively asked: "I say, Reith! When do we get something to drink? I haven't had a bloody drop in a fortnight, and I'm tripping over my tongue."

"In a few minutes," replied Reith. "The Nova Iorque

doesn't open till the ninth hour, Krishnan time. Lish, want to wassail with us?"

"No, thanks. I need to clean up. Come back when you're through."

In the cocktail lounge, Reith and White sipped light falat wine. Ordway took a generous draft of the kvad he had ordered. "Not bad," he said, staring into his mug.

"Be careful," said Reith. "It's deceptively smooth, but it runs up to 35 percent alcohol."

"Don't worry," said Ordway, gulping another swig. He glanced about at the other patrons, staring at the Krishnans among them. These were, for extraterrestrials, remarkably humanoid in appearance, save for their pointed ears, olfactory antennae, and faintly greenish complexions. Ordway said, "Tell me about these wogs. I thought they had no hair on their faces, but those two seem to have beards."

"It's a fad among Krishnans," said Reith. "False beards in imitation of Earthmen."

Ordway laughed so loudly that heads turned, and White looked worried. "By God's foreskin!" cried Ordway. "That's a hell of a thing! Thank the Lord, we human beings haven't started trying to look like Krishnans —yet. What are those feathery things above their eyebrows, like a moth's feelers?"

"Organs of smell," said Reith, lowering his voice in an attempt to warn his brash companion. "Some Krishnans have an olfactory sense much keener than ours—like a hound's."

For half a Krishnan hour, Reith answered questions about the planet and its inhabitants. Ordway asked: "They do look jolly human, except for those feelers. Tell me, how do they—ah—go about making little Krishnans?"

Reith grinned. "Much the same way we do. But they're oviparious."

"Eh?" Ordway looked blank.

"They lay eggs."

"Oh. How about Krishnans and people? I mean, if you put a he of one species with a she of the other, could they—ah—"

"Yes, they could. Their organs look different, but they're still compatible."

"Like British and American lighting fixtures?"

"Exactly. As far as I know, they're the only extraterrestrials you can say that of."

"Is there any—ah—interracial frigadoon around here?"

Reith shrugged. "Some; mostly male Terrans mating with female Krishnans. The other combination is rare."

"Why is that?"

"For one thing, Terran males outnumber Terran females, so the girls can easily get human husbands. For another, Terran women say they don't enjoy sex with Krishnans; it's over too quickly."

Ordway's round, ruddy face took a sly look. "Have you ever—ah—rogered a Krishnan female?"

Bristling, Reith began: "None of—" Then he checked himself, not wishing to get relations with these new clients off to a bad start.

"Sorry!" said Ordway. "No offense intended; but one can't help being curious."

"That's okay," said Reith. "Matter of fact, I was once married to a native princess."

"I say, that could be the basis for a script! What happened? I mean, what was the upshot?"

"Annulment on grounds of coercion."

"Who did the coercing?"

"I'll tell you the story someday, maybe," said Reith firmly.

Ordway looked disappointed but forbore to pursue the matter. He asked: "How about offspring? I mean, are there little half-Krishnans mucking about?"

"No. Their organs may be compatible with ours, but their genetic systems are not. It would be easier to cross a man with a geranium."

"I've known men who'd been crossed with pansies," smirked Ordway.

White interjected: "Cyril is a man of strong prejudices."

"I know what's normal, that's all," said Ordway. "Look here, how about another round? I'm as dry as your American Death Valley."

Reith signaled to Yang. He and White drank only falat; but Ordway laid heavily into the much stronger kvad. Whereas drinking made Ordway boisterously cheerful, it seemed to depress White. Reith asked: "What's the matter, Mr. White? Don't you like the prospect of shooting a picture here?"

White smiled weakly. "Call me Jack. To tell the truth, I don't. I didn't want to leave Terra, but Stavrakos—"

"Who?"

"Kostis Stavrakos, my boss; he insisted. He knew I had no dependents at the moment, so I didn't have an excuse for backing out."

"You haven't suffered so far, have you?"

"That's not it. I don't mind travel, at least on Earth; but, you see, I'm an observant Jew. God knows how I'll obey the dietary laws here, or keep track of the holy days."

"I understand," said Reith. "We get Muslims who can't figure out how to pray towards Mecca. As for the holy days, we have our own clocks and calendars, since our day and year are longer than Earth's, while the moon—that is, one revolution of Karrim—is shorter than the Terran month. But the boys in Space Control can tell you what day it is on Earth. As to the food, you'll just have to become a vegetarian, since we have nothing here exactly corresponding to a Terran ruminant."

Lugubriously, White nodded. "I feel this will be my unlucky trip. And another thing . . . I follow my horoscope at home—"

"Damned superstitious nonsense," growled Ordway.

Reith asked: "Isn't there something in the Old Testament about astrologers being burned with fire?"

"Yes, in Forty-seventh Isaiah," said White. "But in Judges it says the stars in their courses fought against Sisera. So there must be something to astrology after all."

"You can stop worrying about that, at least," said Reith. "The official religion of the Gozashtando Empire is a kind of home-grown astrology. It's exactly as scientific as the Terran variety. You'll see when we get there."

As talk continued, Reith uneasily noted that Ordway's voice grew louder and that his speech, less guarded, developed a touch of Cockney. As his voice became harsh, his words waxed offensive.

"Look at that twee bloke with the sword!" boomed Ordway. "Oo the hell does the bloody wog think he is? For ten bob I'd pull his goddam beard off!"

"Shut up!" snapped Reith. "That's Prince Ferrian of Sotaspé, a big shot around here. He's also a dangerous fighter and an old friend of mine."

"I don't give a shi' if he's the bloody emperor. I say no fuckin' greenie 'as any business in a white man's bar. I'll pull the twit's bleeding beard off—"

"That's about the quickest way of getting yourself killed that I know of," barked Reith. "Jack, can't you do something with this ass before he starts a brawl?"

The object of Ordway's vulgarisms, a tall Krishnan wearing a purple tunic aglitter with golden spangles, rose, stared coldly at Ordway, and stalked out of the bar.

White shrugged helplessly. "I'll try! But when liquor gets into him—"

"Oo you calling a hass?" said Ordway. "I don't let no fuckin' Yank—"

"Shut up, Goddamn it! Here comes Herculeu to take the two of you to dinner. You met him in Customs and Security, remember?"

The small, squirrel-like security officer approached. White plaintively asked: "Aren't you coming with us, Fergus?"

"Sorry; I've got another engagement."

"Oho!" chortled Ordway. " 'E's gonna have a tryst wiv the fair Alicia. I can tell you, mate, it's no good asking her to 'oist her skirt—"

"One more crack out of you," said Reith, rising, "and I'll show you what you can do with your movie. . . ."

"Cyril!" bleated White. "For Christ's sake, pull yourself together! Help me to get him out, Fergus."

White and Reith hauled Ordway to his feet and, with Castanhoso pushing from behind, started for the door. As they passed a table at which sat a Terran and a Krishnan, the latter wearing a false beard of purplish hue, Ordway wrenched loose, reached down, and yanked off the hairpiece.

"*Hishkako baghan!*" shouted the Krishnan, bounding to his feet. Instantly they were trading punches, while other patrons scrambled out of the way. A chair went over; glass shattered. Yang the bartender yelled: "Stop! *Pare! Quitez! Bù huì! Ostanovityes'!*"

Round and round they went, stumbling over broken glass and slipping on spilled liquids, flailing at each other with more vim than accuracy. Then the Krishnan kicked Ordway in the belly. As the Englishman doubled over, Castanhoso and the Krishnan's companion, a large, blond man who seemed to Reith vaguely familiar, seized the Krishnan's arms and pulled him back. Reith caught one of Ordway's wrists, while White grabbed the other.

For a moment the fighters glared and panted. Then Ordway, strong despite his dissipated look, wrenched his arm loose from White, throwing the slight location manager back against a table, which went over with a crash. With a yell of: "No fuckin' wog can kick me!" Ordway aimed a roundhouse swing at the Krishnan. He

landed instead on the head of the Krishnan's companion, who released the Krishnan to roar: *"Du Scheisskerl!
Ich bringe dich um!"*

The German swung at Ordway but instead connected
with the side of Reith's head. Reith staggered and almost fell, but managed to retain his grip on Ordway's
arm.

Yang, the bartender, pushed forward holding a si-
phon bottle. He aimed the nozzle at Ordway's face,
pulled the trigger, and discharged a stream of carbonated
water. The stream flowed until Ordway, half-drowned,
raised his free arm in surrender. While others hustled
the Krishnan out, a dripping Ordway stood coughing
and choking.

Castanhoso looked at Reith and spoke in Portuguese:
"Senhor Dom Fergus, I perceive that you are involved
with one of those who may make trouble for us all if
allowed to run loose. If you wish to file an expulsion
request, I will put him back on the *Pará* for return to
Terra as an undesirable."

Reith frowned. "Not just yet, Herculeu. This film job
he's here for is too big and involves too much *caixa* for
me to upset it lightly."

They hauled Ordway to the men's room and wiped
him down. Ordway grumbled: "Oo the 'ell you fink you
are? Don't nobody stand up for a white man's rights?"

Reith grabbed the slack of Ordway's jacket and thrust
his face close to that of the drunken production manager. He snarled: "Look, you stupid bastard, I could
have you put back on the *Pará* and shipped to Terra,
and your half-billion movie would go down the drain.
One more yelp out of you and I'll do it; understand?"

Ordway stared at the floor, clenched and unclenched
his fists, swore under his breath, and finally muttered:
"Okye, Reith, I guess I did rather let myself go. You've
got me by the prick."

"Furthermore," said Reith, "if I take you out in the

field, the first time I see you under the influence, back you go to Novo. Get it?"

Ordway mumbled what might have been an assent. Reith said: "All right, you two can go to dinner now with Herculeu."

Castanhoso whispered: "You really should come with us, Fergus. You know more about the project of these clowns than I."

Reith grinned. *"Desculpe, mas tenho uma entrevista."*

Castanhoso sighed. "With such a woman, I cannot blame you. Enjoy yourself!"

As Reith left the Nova Iorque, he felt a tap on his shoulder. Turning, he found the large blond German. "Mr. Reith, not so?"

"Yes."

"The blow was unintentional, I assure you. There is, *dennoch*, another matter." The man brought his heels sharply together, gave a stiff little bow, and handed Reith a calling card reading:

Herr Enrique v. Schlegel
Kultursachverständiger

Reith stiffened. "Hello, Schlegel. I didn't know you without your whiskers."

The man bowed again. "If you will inform me of where you are staying, my seconds will call upon you to make arrangements. It must be outside of Novorecife, to comply with the law, and it must be early, because tomorrow leave I for Qirib."

"What on earth are you talking about?" said Reith. "Are you proposing a duel?"

"Naturally; honor demands it."

"Oh, grow up, Schlegel! Anyway, since I'm the one who was hit, it's up to me to demand satisfaction."

"I refer not to the accidental blow this afternoon, for which I apologize; but to the foul stroke you gave me in Mishé two years ago."

"Are you serious?"

"I am always serious. Will swords be satisfactory, or prefer you some other weapon?"

"Don't be silly! I don't fight duels; if I did, I'd pick the Novo cafeteria's rolls at ten paces. They're hard enough. But we're not living in the Middle Ages."

"Ah, but we *are!* Most Krishnans are in that stage of culture. That is the true *Heldenalter*. Will you fight, or are you a decadent coward?"

"I don't duel; but if you attack me, I'll defend myself. Several have tried, but they're no longer with us. Good night!"

Reith strode off, uncomfortably aware of his weapon-less state. But nothing struck him in the back.

As red Roqir hung in a greenish sky amid the spires of ancient trees, like a beach ball impaled on a picket fence, Reith handed Alicia into the gig. She asked, "Where's your son?"

"I sent him ahead to tell my people to get dinner ready."

"You sound like landed gentry."

"Not really. I have just a cook, and a couple for general work, plus a few shaihan-herds and my secretary Minyev."

"Minyev? That's a Khaldoni name. Would it by any chance be my old factotum in the Khaldoni lands?"

"Yep; same one."

"What a coincidence!"

"Not really," said Reith. "Although he ran out on you, he still wanted to work for Terrans. He's got his eye on a diplomatic career. So our would-be Krishnan Talleyrand beat his way here, picking up odd jobs. A few years ago, he got my name from somebody who'd known us both and applied for the post when I needed someone to handle the bookkeeping."

"A clever little fellow," said Alicia.

"Right. In fact he can imitate my handwriting so

perfectly he makes me nervous, lest he some day forge my name to a check."

Reith flicked the single aya with his whip, and the horned, six-legged beast trotted smartly out through the compound gate. In the open country, Reith turned towards his onetime wife for the simple, sensuous pleasure of looking at a beautiful woman, smiling in the ruddy light of the setting primary.

He saw Alicia's eyes widen with concern. "Fergus! where did you get that horrid great bruise on your cheek?"

"Your colleague Ordway drank not wisely but too well in the Nova Iorque and started a brawl. I got in the way of a roundhouse meant for him."

"Oh, dear! I was afraid of something like that. Cyril couldn't booze up on the *Pará*, so I guess he was making up for lost time. Would a drop of cologne help?"

"No, thanks; the skin's not broken."

"What happened in the bar?" she queried.

Reith summarized Ordway's behavior and Schlegel's subsequent challenge, adding: "Like all my tourists, they brought up Topic A."

"Krishnan sex?"

"Sure; who does what with what. I've gotten used to explaining about the bees and the flowers, as if we had bees and flowers here."

"I hope you don't tell them about *us*," she said.

"I haven't mentioned it. Why, don't they know?"

"No, though I suppose they'll find out sooner or later. I hope it's later."

"What's the difference? It's not as if we'd robbed the bank at Novo."

"The whole location crew would pry into my history, or try to match me up, or . . . All movie people are gossips or romantic busybodies."

"My dear Alicia, they're bound to hear. The next *Novo News* will be out in a few days with the story. You can bet Meilung's checking the passenger list against the morgue right now—"

"Who's Meilung?"

"Meilung Guan—or Guan Meilung, if you prefer—is the reporter for the *News*. She was at the landing. I thought she'd buttonhole you people; but instead she got involved with that Balkan politician."

"I did see a cute little Chinese-looking girl with a camera; but mostly I was looking for you. I thought everybody would have forgotten me by now."

Reith chuckled. "Forgetting you, my dear, is about as easy as forgetting the Los Angeles earthquake. When word gets around, every Terran will have his psychic antennae quivering with curiosity about us. Novo's just a small town, where gossip is the leading sport."

Alicia sighed. "Anyway, let's not tell Cyril and Jack anything unless we must."

"I'll be as silent as Dejanai's tomb, as long as possible. As they say in Zamba, sooner recall a shaft that has left the bow than a word that has passed the lips."

For a while they rode silently, hearing the rhythmic beat of the aya's six hooves and watching Roqir's last rays cast a rainbow across the bright-hued vegetation. "Funny," said Alicia at last. "I feel as if I were coming home."

"Do you intend to become a Krishnander after your present job?" Reith asked.

"What's a Krishnander?"

"That's what nowadays we call a Terran permanently domiciled on Krishna. I wondered if you planned to stay here."

Alicia smiled enigmatically. "I don't know. It depends. . . ."

Maybe she thinks it depends on me, Reith reflected, and briskly changed the subject. "Here's my property line."

The aya quickened its pace. Soon the gig drew up at a rambling, one-story building, designed in a hybrid

Krishnan-Terran style, half-timbered with a wide veranda. Reith handed Alicia down and showed her to her room as his groundsman carried in her overnight bag and led the aya away.

"It's a fine evening," said Reith. "Let's have drinks on the terrace. What'll you have?"

"Just a little light falat, please. My, what a handsome, well-kept place! Some of these Krishnan things are beautiful!"

Reith grinned. "The fruits of my tourists' gratitude. My geese often get together to give me a draft or a gift certificate. Luckily, Sivird at the Outfitting Shop has good taste; he's helped me with the furnishings."

As an aproned Krishnan appeared in the corridor, Reith called out in Gozashtandou: "Oh, Kardir! Falat of Mishdákh on the veranda, please; and dinner in half an hour!"

Alicia cautiously sipped her wine. "Excellent! I haven't tasted Krishnan drinks since . . ." After an awkward pause, she said: "Were you expecting me, Fergus?"

"No! You were a complete surprise a shock you could have registered on the Richter scale. You haven't grown a day older, while I'm settling into middle age."

"I must say you're looking splendid; just as fit as ever."

Reith ignored the compliment. "Did you expect me at the ramp?"

"I thought you might be there. You see, I sold Kostis Stavrakos the idea of hiring you as our guide."

"So that's how a fat, juicy contract fell out of interstellar space into my lap! Thanks a lot, Lish; I can use the *fric*."

"Be sure to demand at least half your money at the start. The movie industry's full of fairy gold, and I don't mean sexual deviation."

"Advice noted. Who's this Stav—whatever his name is?"

"Kostis Stavrakos is the producer, the man in overall charge of the film project. You'll meet him when the shooting crew arrives." Alicia studied the long shadows across the meadow. "Tell me how you come to have a son when you're not married?"

Reith gave a sour smile, almost a grimace. "I wondered when you'd get around to asking." Soberly he explained: "I married one of my tourists, a girl named Elizabeth. A couple of years after Alister's birth, she left and got a divorce. Then she died; that's all."

With more tact than had been her former wont, Alicia forbore to quiz Reith for details. She said: "I wonder that no nice girl has lassoed you during the last fifteen years or so."

Reith smiled. "Ever try to rope a crafty old bull shaihan? A few local ladies have sent me signals, but I haven't followed them up. After two divorces and an annulment, I realize I'm not cut out for spousehood."

"Nonsense, Fergus! Any woman with the sense of a retarded flatworm would be glad of a fine man like you." She reached over and gave his hand a little squeeze.

But you weren't, he thought. Aloud he said: "Nope. Three tries; no brass ring. I'm no gambler, and I've given up that kind of roulette. 'Down to Gehenna or up to the throne, he travels the fastest who travels alone.' "

"Perhaps; but then he has nothing to do when he gets there."

Reith chuckled. "Kipling never thought of that angle, not having your X-ray insight." He heaved a small sigh. "At least I have Alister."

"You poor thing! And it's all my fault."

"No, it's not. You did what you were programmed for, and so did I. So stop feeling guilty!"

"The spouse who leaves normally feels guilt, while the one who's left loses self-esteem. I'll get rid of my guilt when you get back your self-esteem!"

Reith laughed gently. "It's a deal, though I don't know that one can do these things on order. Anyway, it's all behind us now. Tell me how the world's been treating you. Any adventures?"

Alicia shrugged. "I have no tale to tell. Since I left Krishna, I've been chased often enough, but nobody's caught me."

"Chased but chaste, eh? Have you turned back into the little blond icicle you once were?"

"Not really. But my psychotherapy took most of a year, leaving no time for romance."

"What's it like, this Moritzian treatment?"

"Like a surgical operation without anesthetic. And after it was over, I had to cram for my new job."

"How did you come to be hired by Cosmic?"

"Some exec there had read one of my books, and they got in touch with me. Stavrakos was looking for someone with Krishnan expertise to ride herd on his movie. My joining the team caused a fist fight between Stavrakos and Fodor."

Reith asked: "Who's Fodor?"

"Attila Fodor is the director, who thinks he's a reincarnation of Attila the Hun. They say he's so tough he holds his socks up with thumbtacks. Thinks he knows all he needs to about Krishna, and resents outside advice, especially from a woman."

"Who won the fight?"

"Neither; people pulled them apart. Those human canker sores heartily dislike each other, but they make better pictures together than separately. So they stick."

"Like Gilbert and Sullivan?"

"Precisely. Kostis thinks he's a great artist as well as a financial wizard; so he tampers with the scripts and sets, and that makes Fodor furious. Actually, Kostis has all the esthetic sensitivity of Paddy's pig. He admires me; I guess that proves I'm no great shakes."

"Come on, Lish!" said Reith. "You've never lacked admirers, honorable or otherwise."

"Sure; I gather propositions the way garbage does flies. People assume a divorcée is good for high diddle any time of day or night."

"It's lust that makes the world go round."

"Perhaps; but I'd want a good husband or nobody at all."

"Well, Krishna's the place to look, for demographic reasons." Reith's imp of perversity tricked him into adding, with a wry smile: "I tried to be a good husband." He instantly regretted the remark.

"Fergus, if you say another word about that, you'll make me cry. You were a *splendid* husband until I spoiled it all." She blew her nose.

Reith quickly changed the subject. "Tell me, what does an assistant production manager *do*?"

"Oh, I'm just a glorified gofer, handling matters the production manager can't or won't.

"What I don't understand," said Reith, "is how a company can send its people off on a project for which they won't see results for twenty years."

"Big corporations can afford to take the long view; like raising trees commercially or building a fusion-power plant. They want to find out if shooting on another planet can be profitable despite the long lead time."

"Isn't Stavrakos afraid someone will steal his job while he's away?"

She smiled. "They say he's a sharp man with a contract; so I'm sure he's taken precautions."

"Let's hope we don't have trouble with that nut Schlegel. His last flimflam scheme—"

The cook appeared to say in Gozashtandou, "Sir and Madam, dinner is served."

When Alister Reith joined Fergus and his guest at dinner, Alicia drew the young man out with the skill of an experienced interviewer.

"I go to school in Novo, Miss—I mean Doctor

Dyckman," he said. "But what I really like is working the shaihans with the Krishnans."

With paternal pride, Reith said: "Here's a rancher in the making. I'm also breaking him in as a tour guide; he'll be good at that, too, I hope."

After dinner, they sat around a crackling wood fire; for Krishnan nights, as a result of the slower rotation of the planet, became quite cold even in low latitudes. Throughout the evening, Alicia eagerly asked for news of people she had known, and Reith gave long, gossipy replies. She inquired: "Where's Ken Strachan nowadays?"

Reith chuckled. "Poor Ken! The great apostle of love 'em and leave 'em fell hook, line, and sinker for one of the secretaries, Juanita Rincón."

"Juana's daughter?"

"The same. The last I heard, Ken was in Rosid, building mechanical toys for the Dasht of Ruz. When he's away from home, they say . . ." Reith glanced at his son's eager face. "Hey, String! Isn't it about time you hit the books?"

Looking disappointed, Alister said good night and vanished. Reith remarked: "There's a problem with Alister, which I share with other local parents."

"What problem?"

"Higher education. I'm sure he's college material; but I don't want to send him to Terra and not see him again for a quarter-century, if ever. As for Krishnan universities—well, you know what they teach. Some of us are trying to start a Novorecife College."

"Splendid!" said Alicia. "Maybe you could use me on your faculty."

"Hey, that's an idea! If you decide to stay, that is. I'll bring the matter up the next time the committee meets. . . ."

The talk trailed off; at last, by wordless consent, Reith and Alicia rose. Reith said: "If you want anything, Lish, that's my room down the hall."

For several heartbeats, Reith and Alicia stared silently, as if wondering what to say next. Reith was tempted to invite her to share his bed. But, although in his profession a decisive, quick-thinking, resourceful man, he hesitated. For one thing, her posture was not encouraging: back straight, head up, arms folded. Slightly raised lower eyelids implied wary suspicion, belying her friendly smile. To Reith her stance said "Let's be friends, but *only* friends!"

He took refuge in a change of subject. "Lish, shouldn't I read the script of the movie, to find out where to take your people? I'm new to this—"

"Fergus dear, I'm way ahead of you. While you were reveling in the Nova Iorque, I ran off a copy." She darted into her room and, returning, thrust a bulky envelope into his hands. "Here you are!"

Reith said: "Good night, Lish. Remember, my door is never locked against you."

He watched to see if she would react to the hint; but all she said was: "Good night, Fergus." She gave him a brief, cousinly kiss and vanished into her room; Reith heard the snick of the bolt.

Reith tried to sleep; but the harder he tried, the more memories tumbled into his brain. He recalled events he had not thought about in years: the narrow escapes with Alicia; the times he and she had saved each other's lives; the nights of passion. . . . He also remembered their quarrels and Alicia's shrieking tantrums; her stunning him with a frying pan during their last dispute. . . .

Questions whirled through his brain. Had she changed? She did seem different—less aggressive and argumentative; more reserved and self-controlled.

What did he want? Wife, mistress, light love, platonic friend, or capable business associate? What were her expectations? Might she lead him on to enjoy the revenge of refusing him, as he had refused her? Could anyone retain strong feelings, pro or contra, towards another for twenty years, despite a complete lack of contact? Could there still be a spark of mutual love, waiting to be fanned into flame? No, no! Old hostilities had surely quenched that fire for good. . . .

To calm his emotions, Reith turned up the oil lamp, hauled out the script, and settled himself to read. The script stirred him up almost as much as thoughts of Alicia. It enraged him that anyone should be paid handsomely to write such bilge. The scenario was false to the character and ways of life of the Krishnan hominoids. Worse, it bored. Before the final scene, Reith fell asleep with the lamp still lit.

II

ALICIA DYCKMAN

Fergus Reith arrived at the dining table to find Alister tucking away an enormous adolescent breakfast. "Hello, String!" said Reith.

"Hi, Dad. Say, is this Doctor Dyckman the girl you were married to before you met Mom?"

"Yes. How did you know?"

"I've heard talk, and she seemed to fit. Are you going to marry her again?"

Reith choked on his fried bijar egg. "Great Bákh! Please, Alister! Till yesterday, we hadn't seen each other in eighteen Krishnan years. Would you object if I did?"

Alister frowned. "I've always wondered what it would be like to have a mother. Doctor Dyckman seems nice, and she's certainly swell-looking. But I've heard stories about how badly she treated you before; makes me mad every time I think of them."

"She's supposed to have had a big personality lift on Torra," said Reith. "We'd have to see if it worked."

"Besides," said Alister, "you'd have to get rid of that native girlfriend you've got upriver."

"*Gluk*," sputtered Reith, disconcerted for the second time. "You know about her?"

"Oh, sure. These things get around."

"Just what do you know?"

"She's at Rimbid; her name is something like 'sorry,' and you stop off there about once a moon."

"She's just a young Krishnan widow I'm sorry for, that's all," said Reith stiffly, hoping against hope that his words carried conviction. "I'll give the matter the most careful consideration. Meanwhile, the less said about Alicia and me, or Sári and me, the better."

Alicia came in, looking as fresh as springtime. While Kardir served her breakfast, Reith said, "Did you sleep well?"

"Just fine. Have you read *Swords Beneath Three Moons?*" When Reith, his mouth full, nodded, she added: "And what did you think?"

"Bloody awful, as our old friend Percy Mjipa would say."

She sighed. "I was afraid of that. Fodor and his stooge Motilal wouldn't hear a word of advice." She stared at the window. "What's that going *bop-bop* outside? Sounds as if someone's playing tennis."

"Good guess," smiled Reith. "I've built a court behind the house, and a couple of my neighbors are knocking off a set."

"Marvelous! We must play when we can find the time."

"Me, play an intercollegiate champion? You'd sweep me off the court."

"My game has gone down dreadfully from lack of practice."

"Well, mine was never much to begin with; but we'll give it a try. Some Krishnans, even, are taking up the game."

Alicia laughed lightly. "My movie people had better shoot their medieval scenes soon, or all the Krishnans will be playing golf and tennis and going to work with briefcase in hand and bowler on head."

"That's not so farfetched. Last time I was in Majbur, some merchants asked my advice on setting up a Chamber of Commerce on the Terran model."

A small, slight Krishnan, with antennae of exceptional length and luxuriance, came in. In fluent but accented English, he said: "Good morning, Mr. Reit'. What do you—" His glance alighted on Alicia, and his eyes widened. "M-madam!" he stammered. "Fuf-forgive my forwardness, but are you not de Doctor Dyckman, wiz who—wiz whom I once traveled in de Khaldoni lands?"

"Why, Minyev!" cried Alicia. "What a pleasant surprise! Fergus said you were working for him."

"Oh, madam!" cried Minyev, falling to his knees and touching his forehead to the floor. In the Khaldoni language he reverently added: "Thou art a goddess to me! Thou shouldst have been a queen!"

"Come," she said, smiling indulgently. "Do get up!"

Reith turned to his secretary. "Minyev, Doctor Dyckman and I are going in to Novo. You're to start bringing my card files up to date."

Back at Novorecife, Reith stabled his trap. Alicia said: "My charges won't be up for an hour or two. Let's look around." As they strolled, she remarked, "My goodness! With all these new buildings, I'd hardly know the place. What is this one?"

"Our Athletic Club."

"Who are those people in front of it?"

Three Terrans were pacing back and forth before the entrance, bearing signs. All wore transmundanes, the semi-safari suits favored by Terrans on planets with Earthlike climates and atmospheres. Their headgear, however, varied. One, who combined a clerical collar with his suit, wore a black felt hat. His sign read: FORA AS INDECÊNCIAS—AWAY WITH INDECENCY!

Another, swarthy and black-bearded, wore a kaffiyyah or Arab head cloth. His sign bore a sentence in the

fishhooks of Arabic script, and beneath them the words
À BAS L'IMPUDEUR!

The third, darker yet and gray-bearded, wore a turban. He carried a sign painted with the flat-topped characters of India's Devenagari alphabet and below it: THE SHAME OF THY NAKEDNESS, Rev. iii, 18.

"What on earth?" said Alicia.

"They're campaigning for compulsory bathing suits in the A.C. pool. Most of the time the Christian, Muslim, and Hindu missionaries hate and intrigue against one another; but for this campaign they've formed a united front." Reith lowered his voice as they neared the demonstrators. "They asked the new Comandante, Planquette, to issue an order, but he just laughed. And Judge Keshavachandra wouldn't help."

"Is old Ram Keshavachandra still your magistrate?"

"Yep; he and Herculeu are the only officials left over from when—when you lived here before."

"I'd like to see the Club."

"Okay," said Reith as he approached the demonstrators. "Alicia, these are the Reverends Hafiz Misri, Arjuna Ghosh, and Gaspar Corvo. Gentlemen, Dr. Alicia Dyckman."

Ghosh, the Indian, frowned. "*The* Alicia Dyckman, who worked here years ago?"

"Yes. Let's go in, Fergus."

"A minute, please!" said Ghosh. "Are you thinking of taking a swim?"

Alicia's eyes narrowed ominously. "I might, if I feel like it."

"With a proper bathing suit?"

"With what *I* consider a proper bathing suit."

"May I see your suit, please?"

"You're looking at some of it now. My skin."

"We cannot permit that!" said Misri the Arab. The three missionaries clustered in front of the entrance and all began speaking at once: "It is a sin against God!"

"Thou shalt not uncover . . ." ". . . example to the
young . . ." ". . . promoting immorality . . ."

"Lish!" said Reith. "If you want to swim, I'll take you
elsewhere."

Alicia ignored him. "Stand aside!" she snapped at the
clerics. Passersby stopped to watch.

The demonstrators continued: "Please, we are only
doing our duty. . . ." ". . . our consciences compel
us . . ." ". . . we act in love. . . ."

"Out of my way if you don't want to be hurt!" grated
Alicia, swinging her handbag by its chain.

"We cannot!" said Misri. "God will not permit us!"
He feinted at her with his sign.

"Hey!" said Reith. "If you hit her with that thing, I'll
make a grease spot of you!"

"Guard my back, Fergus," said Alicia. "I'll handle
these—"

Reith glanced around. A small East Asian young
woman pushed forward and aimed a camera. "Oh-oh,"
said Reith, "Here's Meilung!"

"I'll give her a story," said Alicia. Turning back to the
missionaries, she said: "We'll put on a counterdemon-
stration for the paper. I'll model my idea of a bathing
suit, and the reporter can shoot the four of us together." She handed Reith her handbag, peeled off her
khaki shirt, and called: "Closer, Meilung!"

"Walla!" cried Hafiz Misri. "You cannot do this thing.
Our reputations—"

"I'll stand between two of you, with an arm around
each," Alicia said, dropping her trousers and stepping
out of them. She fumbled with the fastening of her
brassière.

"God help us all!" cried Ghosh, backing away. Father
Corvo, muttering Latin, put down his sign and melted
into the crowd. In a matter of seconds, the other two
missionaries had likewise vanished. Most of the spectators roared with laughter, although Reith heard a few
murmurs of sympathy for the discomfited preachers.

Pulling her outer garments back on, Alicia asked: "Get some good pictures, Meilung?"

"I d-don't know," sputtered the reporter. "I was laughing so I could hardly aim the camera."

The pool contained only a handful of swimmers. Reith said: "Later in the day, the pool's so popular you always find someone's knee or elbow in your eye. Shall we give it a try?"

Alicia looked at her watch. "Too late, I'm afraid. I've got to visit the Outfitting Shop for this safari."

As they left the building, Reith said: "Anyway, I prefer a swimming hole a couple of hoda west of my house. Glad to show it to you."

"I'll take you up on that. Coming with me?"

"Thanks, but I have to drop in on Herculeu to check up on the countries where we'll be working. Pick you up at the shop in an hour, eh?"

Reith found Castanhoso comparing photographs of troublesome Terrans. "*Olhe!*" said the security officer. "Here's that *trapaceiro* Enrique Schlegel. Wasn't he in last night's fracas?"

"Yes," said Reith. "After the fight, he challenged me to a duel."

"He did? If I'd known, I'd have jailed him. Now he has left Novo for Qirib. Did you strike him in the confusion?"

"No, he struck me. He's angry over something that happened a couple of years ago. I was showing my tourists around Mishé, when he came up and began haranguing about his new religion—or rather, the worship of the old Roman gods, which he said was better suited to Krishna than newfangled theologies like Christianity."

"It might be, at that," mused Castanhoso.

"He claimed to be an incarnation of Mars—the god, not the planet. He was dressed as Mars in a helmet with a scrubbing-brush crest and a ball-baring kilt. After he'd rattled on, I asked him politely to go away. He took a swing, and I conked him with my dagger pommel. Now he's calling himself a 'culture expert' and adds a 'von' to his name for instant gentility. What's his game?"

Castanhoso explained. "He's started a Society for the Preservation of Krishnan Culture and has quite a following in Suruskand. His gangs roam the streets; when they find a woman wearing clothes of Terran style, they tear the garments off."

"Wow! Imagine their stripping a party of my middle-aged tourists! What are you doing?"

"I have advised President Da'mir to expel this *malvado* as a subversive. What strange characters get passports to Krishna!" He eyed Reith sharply. "And that includes those two cinematic persons you fobbed off on me last night. This morning I sent my deputy to say they could come peaceably to settle damages or face arrest and deportation. They came meekly enough. The fat one seems to have had some sort of accident.

"By the way, rumors are flying of a campaign of conquest by the nomads of Qaath. Have you heard anything?"

Reith shrugged. "Not I; but then, you know rumors. May I have some new maps of Ruz and Mikardand? Mine are *gastado*."

Reith and Alicia hastened to the Conference Room to keep their appointment with the other clients. At the sight of Ordway, Reith exclaimed, "Good lord, what happened to you?"

Ordway, with purple discolorations outlining the bandages on his face, groaned. "You tell him, Jack."

White said, "We were walking back from breakfast when we passed that Krishnan with the false beard and the fancy clothes—the one you called Prince Fairy or something."

"Ferrian of Sotaspé," said Reith. "Go on."

"Well, this guy stopped Cyril and said, in perfect English: 'Sir, last night you made disparaging remarks about me in the presence of others. A man in my position does not brawl in public; but now you are here alone but for your fellow Terran. I think he will have the wisdom not to interfere.'

"Then he took off his sword belt and coat, laid them down neatly, and beat the goddam stuffing out of Cyril. When he'd knocked Cyril cold, he wiped his hands on Cyril's suit, calmly gathered up his coat and sword, and walked away."

"You ought to do something, Reith," groaned Ordway. "What good are you if you can't protect us from these bloodthirsty natives?"

"Damn it!" exclaimed Reith. "If you pick fights the way you did last night, you'll get in trouble no matter what I do. You're lucky Ferrian knows Terran customs. Another Krishnan might have let daylight into you with his sticker."

"He's right, Cyril," said White. "Don't make things worse."

"Oh, very well, very well," said Ordway penitently. "I suppose I did go off the reservation a bit. We've been to the boss rozzer's office, paying fines and damages." After a moment's pause, he glanced from Reith to Alicia with a smirk that showed despite his bandages. "I'll wager you two had a jolly good night!"

Reith restrained an urge to punch Ordway's battered face. "You see, Lish," he growled, "one might as well be hanged for a sheep as a lamb." He turned his coldly steady regard on the production manager. "About your godawful script, I can tell you you've got a dud. Whoever wrote it doesn't know beans about Krishna. He merely cobbles together a couple of Arthurian legends, glues false antennae and ear points on some actors, and dyes their hair and skin—"

"Look here," said Ordway. "You may be right as rain, but it don't make a blasted bit of difference. Attila says this is how he wants it, so that's how it's going to be."

"Can't somebody tell the boss that this silly plot is risking your investment? It put me to sleep."

White spoke up diffidently. "Excuse my saying so, Mr. Reith; but it wouldn't do a bit of good. Even if you're right, you don't have any screen credits to give weight to your words."

Ordway added: "Just forget it, will you, like a good bloke?"

Reith began an angry retort, but a look from Alicia silenced him. "Fergus, I've dealt with these paranoid egomaniacs, and authenticity is the last thing they worry about. Stavrakos and Fodor made one historical in which Abraham Lincoln married Queen Victoria."

"Didn't he?" asked Ordway innocently.

"Hell, no!" said White. "Even I know that. Lincoln was the man who liberated the Jews from slavery."

Alicia winked at Reith. "So, Fergus, my advice is: do your job, take your money, and run."

Reith drew a long breath. "Okay. I'm here to take you to shooting sites and help you recruit Krishnan extras." He unfolded a map. "You'll need a castle, unless you'd rather build your own."

"Let's see some real castles first," said Ordway.

Reith continued: "You'll find good castles in Ruz, here." He pointed a long finger. "So our first trip had better be to Rosid, the capital. I know the Dasht of Ruz—"

"The who of what?" interrupted Ordway.

"The Dasht of Ruz, a vassal of the Dour—Emperor, if you prefer—of Gozashtand. You could call the Dasht a count or baron. Dasht Gilan's raised one of the best units of armored cavalry around; but maintaining first-class cavalry is costly, so Gilan's always short. You could probably hire his lancers; how many would you need?"

Ordway answered. "About a thousand—five hundred on a side. What sort of country is this Ruz?"

"Hilly, with farms along little narrow valleys. Like Kentucky."

White shook his head. "We want a wide, flat area, so we can put up towers and shoot the whole scene from above."

Reith frowned in thought. "Much of Mikardand, south of here, is flat. But the area near Mishé, the capital, is all farmed, and you can bet the landowners won't allow cavalry charges across their crops.

"There's an arid section in the West, Zinjaban Province. The hardscrabble farmers there might let you trample their crops if you made it worth their while."

"How far is this Zinjaban?" asked Ordway.

"Over three hundred kilometers from Mishé. That's six to ten days' travel."

"How do we get our people from here to there?" said Ordway. "You can't expect the shooting crew to bounce all the way on the backs of those oversized six-legged gnus."

"How many in the crew?" asked Reith.

"We're trimming them to an absolute minimum—say thirty, including deadheads. For hewers of wood and drawers of water, we count on hiring locals."

"What are deadheads?"

"Our top people always have a dependent or two they insist on bringing. We try to find them jobs, in case the ruddy stockholders raise a stink. For example, Fodor will bring his wife *and* his mistress. Then, Cassie—"

"Who?"

"Cassie Norris, our leading lady—originally Kasimira Naruszewicz. She always wants both her husband and her current lover. Luckily, the lover this time is our leading man, Randal Fairweather. He at least will be earning his brass.

"Then, we shall need vehicles for equipment, which will require at least as much space as the people."

Reith said: "I'll tell you. Mishé has an omnibus system of buckboards seating twelve. If we could rent them, we could carry your people in three or four, plus a couple of wagons for equipment."

"Makes sense," said Ordway. "You know," he added plaintively, "I work my arse off trying to keep costs inside the budget. Then Fodor or Stavrakos gets a case of ego and says: 'Why be cheapskates, Cyril? Let's do the job right, with twice as much of everything!' Then they wonder why some of their flicks lose money.

"I'd have skipped this battle scene, and have some chap run in to announce a glorious victory, like those Russian plays where a cove wanders in to say that Uncle Ivan just hanged himself in the barn. But no, Attila must have his battle, with simulated gore and severed heads scattered about." He sighed. "Ho for the Middle Ages!"

Reith said, "Consider yourselves lucky to shoot medieval Krishna before it disappears."

"I thought," said White, "the Interplanetary Council kept out advanced technology."

"They try," said Reith. "But blockades leak, and the Krishnans invent on their own. A couple of Krishnan armies have a few crude muskets, something like a Renaissance arquebus. They create more noise and smoke than damage—so far."

"We shan't want guns," said Ordway. "They'd spoil the romance, like Romeo calculating his income tax. Are there castles in Zinjaban?"

"Mikardand isn't a feudal state," said Reith, "but there's a big government fortress across the Khoruz. If the Knights cooperate, you might use it as your castle. . . ."

At last Reith looked at the wall clock. "Enough planning for one day. I've got to round up a carriage for Rosid, get you two outfitted, and give you a date with Heggstad."

"Who's he?" said White.

"Ivar Heggstad's our athletic trainer. You'll need some exercise to toughen you and some practice at sword fighting, aya riding, and other Krishnan skills."

White and Ordway groaned in unison.

Sinking Roqir saw Fergus Reith and Alicia Dyckman facing each other across the terrace of Reith's ranch house. Padded and masked, they were whacking and thrusting with qong-wood, basket-hilted single sticks. When they drew back after a touch, Reith said: "No, no, Lish! I've told you a parry in seconde is suicide if the other party knows the double."

"My fencing has gone downhill," she said, pulling off the wire mask. "Enough for today; I'm soft. I see you've kept in practice."

"I try, since I want to stay alive. You take first crack at the tub." With a small curl of his lip, he added: "It's only big enough for one, alas."

"You leer most attractively, Mr. Reith," she said with a departing laugh.

After dinner for three, counting Alister, Reith suggested: "Why don't you stay over again? We've got so much to talk about."

"Wish I could, Fergus; but I don't dare leave Cyril and Jack to their own devices. I shouldn't have left the compound last night, except it's not often one finds one's long lost—uh—"

"Amorex?" said Reith, cocking a sardonic eyebrow. The term meant "a lover of one's former spouse."

"Ex-amorex would fit better, but it sounds like some medicine. Oh, before I forget!" She dug into her carry-all and handed Reith a book. "Remember urging me to write up my Krishnan adventures? Here they are!"

"By Bákh's toenails!" said Reith. "A real Terran book!" He read the title: *Pirates, Priests, and Potentates*, by Alicia Dyckman Reith. "Oh, boy! I won't get much sleep tonight. . . . Say, if this has been published, wouldn't White and Ordway know—ah . . ."

She shook her head. "It hadn't yet appeared when we left Terra. So please don't show it to them, at least not soon. Your demon reporter's been after me, but I refused to discuss personal matters."

Minyev brought the gig around the corner and handed Reith the reins. With a backward glance at the ranch house in the moonlight, Alicia asked, "When do we leave for Rosid?"

"In a few days." Reith clucked the aya to its six-legged trot. "I'll send someone ahead to warn the Dasht."

At the Visitors' Building in the Novorecife compound, he dropped Alicia off with the perfunctory kiss that was becoming their regular ritual.

Back at the ranch, Reith settled himself to read in bed. He started on *Pirates, Priests, and Potentates.* Although fascinating, the book proved slow going. Every sentence so flooded his mind with memories that he had to stop reading every few paragraphs and stare at the wall as image after image paraded by.

When Alicia had spoken of writing a popular book instead of a sociological treatise on Krishna, she had promised to dedicate the book to him. Reith looked in vain for a dedication. Then he noticed that the page following the title page had been snipped out, leaving a centimeter-wide strip. He suspected that the missing sheet had borne the dedication. Had she dedicated it to another? Had the sheet borne some embarrassingly personal sentiment?

The more Reith read, the more absorbed he became. He found himself appalled by the candor with which she set forth the details of their checkered relationship. She accepted the entire blame for their breakup and pictured him much more saintly and heroic than he knew himself to be. Without actually saying so, the work was a book-length love letter.

On the other hand, the incident of the three clerics, that morning, suggested that Alicia the termagant was not dead but sleeping, easily roused to fury. Although his sympathies had lain with her in that confrontation, he firmly resolved thenceforth to treat her as a quasi-sister and to shun the slightest hint of anything closer.

He was also taken aback by her precise, unabashed accounts of her liasons with other males on Krishna, two natives and a Terran, before and after her marriage to Reith. Although in each case she had been more or less coerced, the last of these intrigues had played a part in her final rupture with Reith.

Throughout, Doctor Dyckman the social scientist was in evidence. Using her own experience, she told in baldly physical terms what copulation with a Krishnan male was like. Reith was shaken and embarrassed. Even honesty, he thought, could be overdone.

Reith had assumed that all his feelings towards Alicia Dyckman had faded away, that he had put their stormy romance behind him. Now he was alarmed to find himself bubbling with contradictory emotions. He wanted both to treat her with wary reserve and to offer the ultimate intimacy; to share his every thought and feeling and to retire into a shell of isolation; to be lovingly warm and coldly indifferent; to kiss and cuddle and to shake and slap her.

Despite all that had happened, Alicia had not lost the capacity to arouse an emotional tornado in Fergus MacDonald Reith. The sky was paling when at last he fell asleep, the book open on his lap.

At Avord, the halfway point from Novorecife to Rosid, Reith's party drew up at Asteratun's Inn, identified by an animal skull above the front door.

The carriage that Reith had rented was a barouche, with two facing double seats in the body, another seat in front for the driver, and a collapsible top. A pair of Reith's ayas drew the vehicle. Alicia, Ordway, and White rode in the carriage. Reith was driving; but sometimes he turned the reins over to Timásh, his assistant, and either sat with his clients or rode one of the spare animals. Now Timásh, wearing one of the broad-brimmed, floppy straw hats favored by Krishnan shaihan-herds, rode one spare aya and led the other two.

Alicia also took an occasional turn in the saddle, she said, to get her riding muscles back in trim. When Reith suggested that White and Ordway do likewise, White groaned. Ordway, now clean-shaven, growled: "Not on your life, cobber! I'm so stiff from the workouts that displaced Viking of yours gave me that I can scarcely climb into your rattletrap."

Reith led them into the inn, where he greeted a stout, wrinkled Krishnan with ragged antennae. The innkeeper cried in Gozashtandou: "God den, Master Reef! Your herdsman told me to expect you. Be these your latest batch of Terran tourists?"

"They are businesspersons," said Reith, introducing them. When he presented Alicia as "Doctor Dyckman," Asteratun peered at her dusty riding clothes and said: "Excuse my curiosity, my good sir, but this lady bears an astonishing resemblance to one ye brought hither, it must be nigh unto twenty years past, the one ye called wife. Could this fair young maid be the daughter of you twain? I know not how long it takes you Terrans to grow up."

Reith pursed his lips, frowning at this reminder of a stormy past, while Alicia's classic features revealed only her rigid self-control. "It's a long story; I'll tell you sometime. Meanwhile, what about quarters? The lady requires a private room."

"'Twill cost you fifty karda the night, sir, counting the stabling for your beasts."

"Your price has risen," said Reith.

"Aye, so it hath. With this new paper money His Awesomeness in Hershid doth issue, all prices have soared."

Reith shrugged; Cosmic Productions would pay. After a wearisome day on the road, all were glad to retire after dinner. In the hall upstairs, Reith glimpsed Ordway in low-voiced conversation at Alicia's door. Then Alicia entered her room and closed the door in a marked manner.

Reith guessed that Ordway had renewed his importunities. Turning into his own room, Reith was fighting down his rising wrath when Ordway called: "I say! Reith! Fergus!"

"Yes?"

"May I speak to you for half a mo'?"

"What is it?"

Coming close, Ordway spoke softly. "About Alicia: first, I've been watching you two. I'd wager that you and she, although old acquaintances, aren't lovers. Am I right?"

"Gods of Krishna, what a question! Now look here—"

"I know; you're going to tell me it's none of my damned business. But it is in a way. You see, old boy, I love her, too."

"Indeed?"

"Rather! Been jolly well smashed on the sheila since I first met her in Montecito. I might even ask her to marry me, if it weren't that I may still have a wife kicking around somewhere."

"And what," said Reith with ice in his voice, "has that got to do with me?"

"Well, you see—ah—I thought that you, knowing her from way back, might be able to tell me what brings her round. Might even put in a good word for me. I can guarantee her a first-class roll in the hay. Ask any of the gels I've rogered if I don't give satisfaction. I can also help her to a career in Montecito. So, how can I get her to give it a try?"

Reith stared poker-faced. At last he said: "I can tell you one thing: if she says no, she means it. No blustering or wheedling will get you anywhere; and if you try any rough stuff, she might kill or cripple you. She knows how."

Ordway stared at the floor. "But Goddamn it, man, I'm so bloody horny it's driving me crackers!"

"Ask Asteratun if his barmaid will entertain a straight commercial proposal. He knows a little English. Good night!" Reith closed his own door sharply behind him.

As setting Roqir touched the gilded onion domes of Rosid with crimson, Reith's party wound through the crooked streets, the carriage wheels bumping over cobblestones. Krishnans crowded the roadway; some walked, some pushed along on scooters, some rode or drove the planet's saddle and draft animals.

When Reith signed his party in a Khenamos's Inn, Ordway said: "I say, Fergus, two days on these dusty roads have put a layer of dirt on me you could plow and plant. I was brought up to take a bath once a week whether I needed it or not."

"When we're settled," said Reith, "we'll walk to the bathhouse."

The bathhouse door, identified by the ornate shell of some marine organism, bore a placard with several words in a curly script. As they took their places in a shuffling line of patrons, White asked: "Fergus, what does the sign say?"

" 'Genuine soap,' " Reith translated. "Soap making is one of the few bits of Terran technology the Interplanetary Council has allowed into Krishna."

"Do you mean," asked White, "that they're trying to keep these people stuck in the Middle Ages, for fear they'll learn too much and blow up their planet?"

"That's the idea. But in practice, the Krishnans either smuggle in the technology they want or invent things themselves." As the bathhouse proprietor waved Reith's party in, Reith said in Gozashtandou: "Hail, good Master Himmash! How goes your business?"

"Well enough," said the stout Krishnan who stood behind the counter, handing out towels and collecting fees. In a lower voice he added: "Were't not for this new rule His Altitude would foist upon me, I had no complaint."

"What rule?"

"He ordains that I shall divide my establishment into two, sundered by a wall, and admit males only to one pool and females to t'other. 'Tis said those Terran holy ones who infest the court have persuaded him to their ninnyish alien notions of modesty. How many *Ertsuma* bring ye this time?"

"Just these three." Reith dug out a small silver coin, then led his party into a locker room crowded with Krishnans of both sexes and all stages of undress. All were talking at once in their rolling, rhythmic speech, punctuated by oratorical gestures. The pungent Krishnan body odor saturated the air.

Reith spoke to an attendant, who handed him four keys on necklaces of string. As he distributed keys to White and Ordway, he said, pointing: "Yours are numbers nine and twenty-four. Just match the squiggles on the keys with those on the doors of your lockers, and be sure to lock up all your gear."

Ordway, who had been staring bemused at the Krishnans, began in an absentminded way to strip. White, looking appalled, said: "Fergus, I can't! If it was just men—I mean, males of both species—but . . ."

"Do you want a bath or not?" rasped Reith, wrestling off one of Alicia's boots. "That's how we get clean on this world."

"Oh, no!" said White. "It's just too indecent for someone with my strict, Conservative Jewish upbringing. . . ."

"What ails your Terran?" said Himmash, who had poked his head and antennae into the locker-room doorway. "Doth he suffer some *Ertso* infirmity?"

"In a way," said Reith. "His religion forbids him to undress in mixed company."

"We can easily remedy that," said the bathhouse proprietor as he bustled away. Returning with a large square of cloth with a hole in the middle, he continued:

"There's a cult in the distant North that have a similar rule. I keep this sheet for the seldom-seen patron from those purlieus." He deftly lowered the sheet over White.

When Reith and Alicia had stowed their clothes, they turned to see Ordway, sitting on a bench with a forgotten sock in his hand, staring goggle-eyed at Alicia. Reith scowled like a berserker until Ordway looked away.

"Come on!" he said calmly. "We'll miss dinner if we don't hop along."

He chivvied his Terrans down a hall past several small chambers. In one, four mature Krishnans, three males and a female, sat around a small pool smoking cigars. Reith caught a sentence about a rise in the price of *tunest*. In the next room, a virile young Krishnan grunted as he heaved a barbell aloft. In the next, a masseur was busily slapping and thumping his voluntary victim.

The travelers emerged into a room containing a row of basins full of soapy water. A pair of Krishnan attendants slathered the bathers with suds, using spongelike objects, which were a kind of fungus. Being old Krishnan hands, Reith and Alicia turned slowly to present all sides to be lathered. Ordway submitted uneasily to this ritual, while White huddled unhappily in his sheet until an attendant handed him a fungus and let him soap himself beneath the flapping poncho.

Clad from neck to foot in a thick layer of suds, Reith and Alicia led the way to the next room. From a large pool of water, plumes of vapor rose like indolent ghosts. The pool was full of Krishnans, standing, floating, or resting against the walls of the tank in torpid ecstasy.

"Ouch!" said Ordway, inching his way down the marble steps. "Any hotter and you could jolly well serve me up for dinner." White gingerly followed, his sheet billowing out around him.

Reith and Alicia swam leisurely to a corner of the pool, where they rested their feet on the nether tiles of the tank. The sight of Alicia, rising in pink and golden glory from the rippling water like some goddess of ancient myth, brought the whole heartbreaking tale of their ill-starred romance rushing into Reith's mind. He unexpectedly felt his eyes watering but hoped that any actual tears would be mistaken for drops of pool water. In myths, he vaguely remembered, mortals who mated with goddesses came to sticky ends.

Suddenly Reith caught sight of a tiny metallic gleam against Alicia's ivory skin, which had before been hidden by suds. Suspended on a slender chain, a simple ring of gold reposed between her breasts. As Reith bent forward to scrutinize the ring, Alicia flinched back; then she quietly submitted to his inspection.

"What's this?" said Reith, turning the ring. "Without my glasses I can't read the initials; but it sure looks like—"

"Same old ring," said Alicia. "I ought to have left it in the innkeeper's strongbox. But when I thought of it, we were here, and I don't trust these lockers."

"You've kept our ring all these years?"

"Not so many for me, remember."

"But—uh—why . . ."

"Oh, I'm just a sentimental idiot. We did have some good times together, didn't we?" She sharply changed the subject. "Let's swim some more!"

Next to Ordway, a Krishnan said: "You Earsman is?"

"Yes, old boy, I am."

The Krishnan puzzled over this. "I sa-tudy ze English. I sink 'boy' mean young he-Earsman. How can 'boy' old be?"

"Just a manner of speaking," grunted Ordway.

"'Manner' mean 'polite,' yes?"

"I suppose so," said Ordway, looking around for Reith. But Reith and Alicia were standing at the far end of the tank, talking in low tones. The Krishnan persisted: "Zen you say 'old boy' to be polite, yes?"

"Look here, my friend—"

"Look where? Look at you? And is you friend?"

"I'm trying to tell you, I don't speak your bloody language."

After a few seconds of silence, the Krishnan said:
" 'Bloody' mean has blood on, yes? How can words—"

"Oh, God!" breathed Ordway. "Let me relax and enjoy my bath, will you like a good chap?"

"Chap. 'Chap' mean part of face, no? Zen how—"

"I don't know, Goddamn it! Will you please for sweet Jesus's sake shut your face and leave me alone?"

"Jesus not my god is, and you cannot alone in a crowd be." After more silence, the Krishnan pointed to White. "Ozzer Earsman zere. Why him have shit all over?"

"Now see here, I don't let no bloody greenie insult an associate of mine! You natives are getting too much cheek—"

" 'Cheek' mean same as 'chap,' yes?"

"Shut up!" screamed Ordway. Putting his pudgy hands against the Krishnan's bony chest, he shoved. The Krishnan fell backwards; all but the ends of his olfactory antennae disappeared beneath the ripples.

The Krishnan reappeared, sputtering: "*Hishkako baghan!*" Then he shot out long arms and seized Ordway's throat. Other bathers crowded round. Some yelled advice and encouragement; others offered bets. A female shrieked: "Out with these filthy aliens! These vile barbarians trample the rights of us human beings!"

Attendants scrambled into the pool, pushed through the crowd, and laid hands on the struggling pair; but they did not succeed in separating the combatants until Reith hooked an arm around Ordway's thick neck and began to strangle him.

"G-Goddamn you, Reith," guggled Ordway, "letting these wogs call us full of shit! I'm not afraid of—"

"He meant Jack's sheet, you ass!" said Reith. "The two of you, come on out. It's time for the warm pool before you get us into further trouble." Reith turned to the assaulted Krishnan and spoke a few private words.

"Nay," growled the Krishnan in his own language. "I crave no legal contentions with Terrans; ye are too clever for us honest human beings. Take your unmannerly aliens away."

The next pool was larger, less crowded, and filled with lukewarm water. Reith and Alicia swam slowly side by side around the perimeter. Ordway floated, his belly making a red-furred dome above the surface. White stood looking unhappy. Reith murmured to Alicia: "Tell me, what flat rock did you find Cyril under? If that one-man pestilence goes around making bigoted remarks and picking fights, he'll get his throat cut and ours, too."

"Cyril's strange," she replied. "Most of the time he presents the persona of a competent, self-controlled English executive. But get a few drinks into him, and he turns into an East End larrikin. Every few weeks or months he goes on a tear."

"Has he been—uh—troublesome in other ways?" asked Reith diffidently.

"You mean, has he propositioned me? Oh, sure. He pestered me the whole time on the *Pará*, stalking me like a lion after a wart hog—"

Reith chortled. "The prettiest woman on Krishna, calling herself a wart hog? Ha!"

"Who, me—a beat-up, washed-out divorcée, past her first youth? I like praise from you, Fergus; but I don't take such flatteries—"

"Okay, okay," Reith laughed. "But you can't deny that, as wart hogs go, you're the prettiest one in captivity. I'll call you 'Wart Hog' just to remind you. But go on about Ordway on the *Pará*."

"After I used a judo trip on him and he bumped his head on the deck, he kept his hands, at least, to himself."

Reith felt a visceral stir of jealous anger. He told himself not to be silly; it was no business of his if a former wife, whom he had not seen in eighteen Krishnan years, accepted or rejected another's advances. He asked: "If he's such a blug, how did he get an important job with a big, rich company?"

"He's not a boor all the time; and he's really expert at his job. He can carry an amazing lot of details in his head and fit them together like a jigsaw puzzle. And if you think Cyril's a character, you ought to see some of the others in the movie business! They remind you of the nameless creeping things you see in a drop of swamp water under the microscope."

"How about White?"

"Jack's only known vice is gambling. He's a bit of a twerp but otherwise not a bad sort. Speaking of whom, the poor squit just stands there looking miserable. Let's see if we can ginger him up."

As they beckoned White to join them, he mumbled: "I'm sorry, but I don't know how to swim."

"I'll teach you!" said Alicia brightly. "First lesson: lie back with your arms raised above your head. Don't be afraid; I won't duck you."

While Alicia bullied the reluctant White into his first swimming lesson, Reith continued his swim. After another lap, he noticed that Ordway now stood in waist-deep water very close to a Krishnan female. Reith heard the woman coo: ". . . oh, I *loov* ze Terrans. I weesh I could know one ca-lose—you know, antim—intam—"

"Intimately?" prompted Ordway.

"Zat iss it, antamcctly—Aiee!" Her words ended in a shriek.

A large Krishnan came plowing through the water towards the pair. Reith was awakened from his blissful lethargy just as Ordway scrambled out of the pool, followed by the formidable Krishnan roaring threats. Ordway began to run around the pool; the Krishnan ran after him, reaching with hooked fingers.

The two had completed their first lap when they

plowed into a knot of newcomers. Feet slipped on the smooth, wet flagstones; naked bodies went sprawling. A couple made a resounding splash as they struck the water.

Reith thrust himself between Ordway and his pursuer, who howled: "Beshrew me an I slay not this unspeakable mass of ordure!"

"Easy, easy," soothed Reith. "What has Master Ordway done?"

"He hath grossly insulted my wife!"

"How?"

"She engaged him in converse, meaning but to practice her English and thus to amplify friendly intercourse betwixt our far-flung worlds. This *zeft* laid lustful hands upon her blameless person!"

"I'm sure it was a misunderstanding," said Reith.

This Krishnan, however, proved less easily pacified than the other. "I care naught!" he cried. "The stain upon mine honor cannot be washed away, save only by blood! I will meet this stinking alien with swords or crossbows or whatever weapons—"

"Master Ordway is not permitted to fight duels," said Reith. "He will, however, compensate you for any injury done to your dignity."

"Honor cannot be bought with vulgar coin! How much hath the *dazg* with him?" Among Krishnans *dazg*, applied to Terrans, was an ethnic pejorative, as were words like "gook" and "wog" used by Earthmen of the crasser sort.

"We shall see," said Reith. "Come, all! We'll skip the cold plunge."

In the locker room, Reith made Ordway turn out the contents of the large coin purse he carried and handed the money to the angry Krishnan.

"You're leaving me flat skint!" groaned Ordway.

"Serves you right, idiot!" snarled Reith, turning away. When the aggrieved Krishnan had departed and the Terrans were dressing, Reith said: "Now, Cyril, give me the straight goods about that encounter, or you can stick your movie where the sun never shines!"

"I was enjoying the water, Fergus, when this bird comes up and commences to practice her English. When she starts rubbing up against me, I couldn't help getting a—you know—well, after seeing Alicia without her—anyway, I don't care what this dame says; I know what she wanted. So to help matters along, I gave her a gentle little pinch on the arse. 'Ow was I to know that big bloke was her husband? The Eyetalians do it, and it gets 'em a quick go in the bushes any time."

Reith sighed. "I don't care for your excuses. The next Donnybrook you stir up will be your last on this planet. And I mean it!"

An officer in a silvered cuirass led Reith and his protégés into the audience room of the Dasht's palace, where tapestries of battle scenes hung behind statues of raging warriors and ravishing women. As they marched in, with Alicia walking in step with Reith and the other two trailing, Ordway craned his neck to peer at the Krishnan females in marble, muttering, "They're not quite like us—proportions different somehow—but I'd like to give one a try. . . ."

"Hush up and keep your mind on the business at hand," murmured Reith.

As they entered the room, four trumpeters in medieval-looking tabards, like those of playing-card jacks, raised silver trumpets and blew a long flourish. On the opposite side, four drummer boys burst into a deafening ruffle.

The officer leading them strode forward, dropped to one knee before a seated figure, and banged a fist against his gleaming breastplate, intoning, "Your Supreme Altitude, I have the honor to present visitors from the world called Terra, namely: Master Reith, Master Ordway, Master White, and Doctor Dyckman."

With the hand behind his back, the officer motioned to the four Terrans to approach.

Ordway muttered: "Blast you, Fergus! You made me shave off my mustache, and now look at that comic-opera brighter in the dixie!"

The person referred to rose from his throne to acknowledge the Terrans' bows with a condescending nod. Gilan the Third, or Gilan bad-Jám, Dasht of Ruz, was a tall, slim Krishnan with a nose more prominent than usual among his flat-faced countrymen. He wore shiny black jackboots, tight scarlet breeches, an argent breastplate ablaze with medals, and a silver helmet whence sprouted a pair of aqebat wings. The Dasht's most arresting feature was a large, obviously false mustache, the ends of which turned up like the tusks of a Terran wild boar.

"My Altitude is pleased to greet the visitors from another world," said Gilan in a high, rasping voice, speaking English with only the slightest trace of accent. "Mr. Reith, have I not had the pleasure before?"

"Indeed so, Your Altitude," said Reith. "Twice, when I have brought parties of Terrans through your splendid city, you have graciously condescended to greet us in person."

"Indeed, *my* memory never fails," said the Dasht. "But tell me, is the person the usher called 'Doctor' the female Terran I see?"

"Yes, sir. She is a learned student of the societies of your planet."

The Dasht wagged his head. "I should not have thought that one so youthful, and a female at that, were capable of such distinction; but perhaps it is different with your species." He stepped forward and held out his hand, palm down, to be kissed.

Ordway grabbed the proffered hand, gave it a hearty squeeze, and pumped it several times. When the Dasht recovered his appendage, he rubbed his fingers to restore circulation. The flash of anger that flickered across his features was quickly replaced by a glimmer of amusement. He proffered his hand to Reith, who ceremoniously kissed it. Alicia and White followed suit, while Ordway looked uncomfortable. The Dasht spoke: "My good Terrans, you come at an auspicious time. Tomorrow begins the year's Rosido Fair, with a parade and a concert. Tonight I bid you to a banquet heralding the opening of the fair. Afterwards our talented Earth-born engineer, Mr. Strachan, will demonstrate the wonders of science. Until the tenth hour, then, farewell!"

III

PRINCESS VÁZNI

"Bloody wog tribal chief!" muttered Ordway. "Must think he's the Pope."

"You're just an ethnocentric bigot," said White. "I thought he treated us well enough. Not his fault you didn't know the rules."

"Don't be fooled," said Reith as their carriage rolled back to the inn. "He can put on the gracious manner, and he speaks the best English of any Krishnan I know after Ferrian. He's done some good things; but he's got a terminal case of the ruler's disease."

"What's that?" asked Ordway.

"Megalomania. He's unpredictable and quite ruthless with anyone who gets in his way. If you're keen to know what having your head cut off feels like, try pulling off *those* false whiskers."

At the inn, they washed up and changed into their best finery. When Alicia appeared, Reith stared, White gulped, and Ordway whistled. Reith asked: "Lish, could that dress be a copy of the one we bought together in Majbur, years ago?"

"It's the original," she said. "I've guarded it with my life, all the way to Terra and back. Is it still in style?" As Alicia paused to twirl like a model, the filmy violet gown, cut down to midriff level in front, swirled around her like a lilac mist.

Reith smiled fondly. "I haven't been to any Krishnan parties lately, but a gorgeous girl in a gown like that should set the styles, not follow them. I ought to remind you, though, that in the outback, some missionaries have persuaded the local rulers to forbid such—uh—displays of personal resources."

"What a shame!" laughed Alicia. "Every woman should be allowed to make the most of her assets. Are we ready to go?"

At the palace, the Terran guests found themselves on a receiving line that stretched through the anteroom and out into the hall. Everyone waited patiently for a quarter-hour, while the line failed to move. Reith asked the cause.

"His Altitude's betrothed is late, as usual," grumbled the courtier ahead of him. Behind Reith, Alicia whispered: "Fergus, I think the missionaries have been hitting the shaihan's eyes here. Not one woman is wearing a dress like mine."

Reith glanced up and down the lengthening line. "You kid me not! Not a tit in the tatting. It's not just fickle fashion, either; dames wear dresses like yours in other cities."

"I see I'll have to buy a new evening dress. Do you know where I might find one?"

"I don't think ready-mades can be bought in a town of this size. You'd have to hunt up a dressmaker." With a slightly shamefaced grin, Reith added: "I know, because I've had to take my women tourists shopping."

Alicia suppressed a snicker. "Poor Fergus, who always hated shopping so!"

The line began to move, like a sun-warmed serpent. As the Terrans inched forward, Reith saw that, inside the salon door, Dasht Gilan stood smiling the distinctive Krishnan smile at the head of a string of beaming officials. The Dasht, splendid in a flashing cuirass of gilded metal scales and scarlet tights, stood beside a handsome, mature Krishnan woman wearing an emerald gown and a gem-encrusted tiara in her dark-green hair. To Reith she looked uneasily familiar.

As each guest approached, a servitor repeated his name to the Dasht, who proffered his bejeweled hand to be kissed. The guests bowed to the Dasht's companion and greeted the remaining notables with the usual Krishnan thumb-grasping handshake. When at last the Terrans approached, the Dasht beamed. In English he cried: "Dear friends! It is good of you and your clients to honor our small gathering on such short notice! Permit me to present my affianced bride, the widow Vázni bad-Dushta'en. My dear, these visitors from across the nighted gulfs of space are Mr. Reith . . . Doctor Dyckman. . . ."

As White and Ordway filed past, bowed stiffly, and were likewise named, Gilan's bride-to-be scarcely noticed; she and Reith were staring at each other in tardy recognition. Alicia looked sharply at both, her azure eyes widening.

"Are you in sooth Sir Fergus Reese?" said the fiancée in accented Cozashtandou. "My Fergus?" She pronounced it "fair-goss."

"That is my name," said Reith, struggling to control his features. "And you are . . ."

The smile of the Dasht evaporated, and his face became intent. To his betrothed he said: "Meanst that this Terran be he to whom you once—I had forgot—" Nearby officials stared, and a susurration of murmurs spread outwards like ripples in a pond.

"May it please Your Altitude!" interrupted Alicia in English. "Permit me to suggest that such matters were better discussed in private."

With a sigh of relief, Gilan drew himself up and forced a smile. "Your quickness of wit, dear madam, testifies to your right to the honorable title of 'doctor.' I withdraw my remark of this afternoon; even I have been known to err." With the aplomb of a practiced courtier, he spoke graciously to the Terrans. "Mr. Ordway, Mr. White! I have reserved the third hour tomorrow for our conference. It shall take place upon the drill field, where later a parade and other entertainment will mark the opening of the fair."

The Dasht nodded a dismissal and turned to his next guest. Reith and Alicia continued down the reception line, grasping thumbs with the Dasht's treasurer; with the commander of the army, a weather-beaten old officer called Sir Bobir; and with several minor bureaucrats, who stared at Alicia with ill-concealed curiosity about this alien female of such evident if unexplained importance.

At the end of the line, Reith and Alicia found a handsome, powerfully-built Earthman with wavy brown hair, wearing a tartan kilt complete with sporran. As Reith gave him a Terran handshake, he cried: "Haw, Fergus! And do ma een deceive me? If it isna ma ault jo, Alicia Dyckman!" He seized Alicia and gave her a hearty kiss. "Now how in Hishkak did you come to fall out of the sky?"

Reith introduced White and Ordway to Kenneth Strachan, old Krishnan hand, professional Scotsman, mighty lover of women of both species, and engineer now turned toymaker for the Dasht. "How goes it, Ken?"

Strachan lowered his voice. "As well as with any hired clown. That's all this building of mechanical beasts for His Altitude's amusement amounts to. Man, what I could do with modern technics!"

Reith shepherded his party towards the buffet. Ordway said: "What was that all about, Fergus, between you and Big Bwana's girl friend?"

"It seems," said Reith, picking his words with the care of a bomb-disposal expert disarming a thousand-pounder, "that the Dasht's fiancée and I knew each other long ago. Let's move on; we're blocking the way."

Reith and Alicia, each carrying a drink and a snack, found an empty spot behind a potted plant. Alicia giggled. "Poor Fearless, cornered by two ex-wives at once! First you looked as if you'd seen a headless woman walking in a graveyard at midnight. Then you turned red as a beet!"

"Can you blame me?" muttered Reith, draining his goblet of falat. "You'd be aghast, too, if a pair of ex-husbands popped out of a trapdoor at you, like the Devil in that opera. The etiquette books don't cover the situation."

"Not having two ex-husbands, I wouldn't know. One ex is one too many."

Reith's eyebrows rose. "You mean you'd rather not have me around?"

"No, no, of course not! I love having you with me. I'm delighted that you're here. I just mean—oh, never mind."

Reith glanced towards Ordway, preparing to act if the production manager got drunk and made a disturbance. But Ordway, talking to the Dasht, seemed on his best behavior. Reith said: "I hope Cilan doesn't decide to cut off my head—or some other important part—lest Vázni be lured back to my lecherous embraces."

"You poor darling! If he tried that, I'd offer him my virtue to save you."

Reith swallowed his arthropod on a stick and gave Alicia's arm a little squeeze. "You're the best friend I've ever had," he said, feeling his eyes watering.

"And always will be," said Alicia. "You're the only ex-husband I'm ever likely to have, so I've got to take care of you. Here comes the trumpet call for dinner!" She set down her goblet and clapped hands over her ears.

Reith was directed by an usher to a seat along the horseshoe-shaped table. He found himself between two Terrans, a middle-aged man and woman, in decent but sober Terran dress. The Dasht had placed Vázni on his right and Alicia on his left, and Reith observed that Alicia now had a gauzy scarf tucked into her bosom to cover her breasts.

White and Ordway sat among Krishnans, with whom they could communicate but little for want of a common language. Pulling himself together, Reith donned a glassy smile and a synthetic suavity, and introduced himself to his dinner partners.

"I'm Trask," said the male. "Edmund Trask; or, if you must be formal, the Reverend Edmund Trask. This is my wife, Melissa. We are pleased to meet you, Mr. Reith. We have heard of your exploits."

"The tales exaggerate," said Reith. "You are missionaries?"

"So they call us. We think of ourselves as friends of those in need."

Reith nodded. "What denomination, if I may ask?"

Trask made a deprecating motion. "We set no great store by denominational differences. All are brothers in Christ. But if you really wish to know, we are Polyecumenal Baptists."

"Oh. What success have you had in Ruz?"

"Less than we'd like, but more than we might have. Fortunately, the Dasht protects us from the malice of the misguided."

"Who are they?"

Trask lowered his voice. "The priests of this benighted astrological cult, like that fellow over yonder." He nodded towards an elderly Krishnan wearing a purple robe embellished with symbols embroidered in gold thread. "They try to stir up the fears of the ignorant against us; but that is to be expected. I assure you, Mr. Reith, we do not dwell in idle parasitism."

"Have you converted the Dasht?"

Trask chuckled. "Not quite. He tries to carry water on both shoulders. I suspect his plan is to wait until he is old and infirm and submit to a deathbed conversion, just in time to avoid the flames of Hell. Of course, the sainted Constantine—or so some call him—did much the same."

"Tell me more," said Reith. The Trasks launched into a voluble account of starvelings fed, abandoned infants rescued, and other virtuous deeds. By their lights, at least, the Trasks were the salt of their adopted planet.

"We also persuaded the Dasht," said Melissa Trask, "to abolish that barbarous method of executing criminals, by putting them in a pit and releasing a yeki or other predatory beast to devour them, the way the Romans did with lions and Krishnans—I mean Christians. Now he hangs or beheads them before just a few witnesses. We should prefer no death penalty at all, but in this medieval world I daresay that's too much to expect."

While digesting this information, Reith ate his crisped unha skin with small *nánashu* or Krishnan pancakes, served with a sour-sweet sauce. This was followed by a fungus stuffed with arthropod paste; and that by the shredded roots of the *sha'pir* herb, detoxified, with slices of fried *máru*, a small relative of the semi-reptilian 'avval. At last he said, "Did you have anything to do with the change in women's fashions? I notice the ladies no longer wear dresses like those of my associate Doctor Dyckman, the blond Terran woman beside the Dasht—that is, before she improvised a small change in it."

"Indeed," said Melissa Trask. "We told the Dasht we considered that bare-bosomed fashion indecent. He hasn't actually forbidden it; but he's let it be known that women so clad will not be welcome in the castle. He is a person of austere tastes; you will notice that he drinks only fruit juice, as Edmund and I do.

"But tell me, is that Doctor Dyckman the same lady who had a reputation on Krishna, before we arrived, for research in the social sciences? I believe her first name was something like 'Alice.' "

"It's Alicia," said Reith. "Yes, she's the same."

"I should have expected an older-looking person."

"She's been back to Earth, and you know what space travel does to the normal passage of time."

"Dear me, yes!" said Melissa Trask. "Though I've never understood it. We heard she was always involved in some controversy or adventure."

Reith smiled. "Her story is more fantastic than anything you can imagine."

"Oh, really? And such a pretty woman, too! Do tell me the story."

Reith said: "Some other time, perhaps. Why do you consider the traditional Krishnan style of dress indecent?"

"Isn't it obvious, Mr. Reith? The sight of the bare female bosom arouses carnal thoughts in the male. Such emotions are to be expected between a wedded pair; but public displays of nudity lead to sinful conduct with drastic social consequences. One of our converts told us a horrifying story, that recently in Novo one of our brothers in Christ—though of the Romish persuasion— was pursued down the street by a naked Terran woman, menacing him with a sign on a pole. Do you know anything of this?"

"No," said Reith, keeping his face straight by sheer willpower. "But you know how rumors exaggerate."

Leaning towards Reith with eyes aglow, the Reverend Trask ran off with the conversation like a football player intercepting a pass. "First, Mr. Reith, there are the social diseases. Every time the medical profession thinks it has one of them under control, a new epidemic appears—by mutation, I think they call it. Providence works in wondrous ways. Then there are the countless homicides and family tragedies arising from adulteries. We know—and I'm sure Doctor Dyckman would agree— that it's better for a child to grow up with both its biological parents than with only one, as so often results from sexual laxity. You've heard, I'm sure, of the broken-home syndrome, with its delinquency, addictions, crime, and suicide."

As Trask paused for breath, Melissa Trask seized the thread of of the discourse. "So you see, dear, dear Mr. Reith, even if you don't believe that Moses literally came down from Mount Sinai carrying a slab of stone engraved with 'Thou shalt not commit adultery,' the ancients still had good reasons for imposing strict rules on sex."

"Did you and the Reverend urge the Dasht to order modification of the bathhouses?"

The Reverend Trask clasped his hands, looking saintly. "The Dasht asked our opinion, and we gave it. We compel nobody. As it is, the bathhouse proprietors find one excuse after another for putting off the change."

Reith's imp of perversity tempted him to launch a harangue on the destructive effects on native populations of missionary meddling; but his common sense asserted itself. "Tell me more about your good works," he said.

While the Trasks prattled guilelessly on, Reith worked his way through the rest of the repast: boiled *burind*, an animal resembling a winged monkey, stuffed with an omelet of bijar eggs; a cut of roast shaihan smothered in a piscoid sauce. . . . A glance down the long table showed that White had given up trying to follow Judaic dietary rules. He was at least sampling everything.

When food and drink were finished, the Dasht stood up in his glittering mail and rapped for silence. The chatter died a quick death.

"Friends!" shouted Gilan III in Gozashtandou. "We have eaten and drunk and enjoyed ourselves. My Altitude hopes that my hospitality hath not displeased you.

"Tonight I shall speak of the defense of our homeland. Harken closely, for *I* am never wrong! It hath come to mine ears that some do grumble at the taxes required to defend the realm against its foes within and without. A nation that be not prepared to don its shining armor and sharpen its gleaming sword doth live at hazard!

"We have witnessed all too many examples of the tragic effects of such cowardice. Once Jo'ol was independent; what is Jo'ol today save a sphere of the barbarous nomads of Qaath? But fear nought, my friends. *I* shall be your shining armor; *I* shall be your invincible sword. . . ."

The speech rambled on for half a Krishnan hour. Trask whispered to Reith: "I wish we could convince him to follow the Christian way: 'Whosoever shall smite thee on thy right cheek . . .' "

"Wouldn't work on the Kamoran of Qaath," grunted Reith. "He'd not only smite thy left cheek but take thy head for good measure."

When the speech was over, the glittering company trooped into a large chamber filled with seats that faced a stage. Here Strachan displayed his automata: a mechanical yeki, which stalked and pounced on a wild unha; ayas and shomals, which leaped fences; bijars and aqebats, which flew in circles on the ends of wires; a pair of puppets, a Qaathian and a Gozashtando warrior, who fought, circling and whacking. The show concluded with the eruption of a miniature volcano, which sent a fountain of smoke and a spray of sparks to the ceiling.

Afterwards, when the guests had cracked their thumb joints and rose to chat, Reith congratulated Strachan. The Scot glanced about before muttering in English: "Ye know I dinna care burha-shit for these gadgets. All their principles are already known to the Krishnans, or I cudna use them. As soon as ma contract's up and I'm paid off, I'll be out of here faster than Maibud left Bákh's treasure vault when the god caught him stealing. How's ma little Jenny and ma wee house?"

"Juanita was all right the last time I saw her," said Reith. "Where did you find that new Highland getup?"

"Had it made in Majbur. The sporran, noo, is of burha hide in place of badger." Strachan chuckled, fingering the furry purse that hung from the waistband of his kilt. "Mrs. Trask, the missionary's wife, asked me what a Scot carried in his scrotum. I tried to explain athoot embarrassing the dear lady; but not, I fear, wi' complete success."

"What's funny?" asked Alicia, seeing Reith convulsed.

"I'll tell you later," he said. "Where are Jack and Cyril?"

At the inn, Reith bade his companions good night and entered his room. As he started to close the door behind him, the sound of a scuffle, followed by the thud of a heavy fall, brought him round. He looked out, saw Ordway sitting on the floor, and glimpsed Alicia's door slamming shut.

Reith hurried to the fallen production manager, who was dazedly shaking his head. Blood ran from his roseate nose and spread out over his lips.

"Now what the devil!" exclaimed Reith.

Ordway groaned. "You were right, Fergus," he mumbled, "and I was a silly ass. Help me up, will you like a good bloke?"

Ordway lurched to his feet. "What happened?" snapped Reith.

"Well, you see, she was going into her room when I came up behind her. She wasn't wearing that scarf thing she'd borrowed earlier, and I merely tried to slide my arms affectionately around her—you know what normal man could resist a perfectly ripping pair of tits like—ah—"

"Get on with it!"

Ordway dabbed at his face with a handkerchief. "She's every bit as deadly as you said. First she snapped her head back and smashed my poor nose. Then she kicked me in the shins. When I let go of her, she turned and hit me in the neck, I don't quite know how, and down I went. Must be one of those tricky oriental self-defense things."

Reith said, "Cyril, you'd better understand something. Twenty of your years ago, during her first stay on Krishna, Alicia and I were husband and wife."

"Uh-oo!" said Ordway, putting a hand to his mouth. "Bit of a floater, what?"

"You may well say 'oh,' " growled Reith, glowering down like an avenging deity. "I won't go into details, but we're still very fond of each other. So shelve your Alicia project, at least on Krishna. If she decides to go back to Earth, what you two do thereafter is your own affair. But for here and now—well, I advise you not to bother her again."

"What would you do if I did?" said Ordway belligerently.

"You'd find out soon enough. Somebody just might end up dead. Your head would look swell over my fireplace."

Ordway clenched and unclenched his fists, cursing under his breath. Then he smote one palm with the other fist. "Don't suppose I can blame you for feeling strongly. I shan't hold a grudge. Common sense tells me that if you want this she-cobra, you're welcome to her. I never was much for rough-and-tumble. Good night!"

After Ordway disappeared with his bloodsoaked handkerchief pressed to his face, Reith knocked gently on Alicia's door. "Lish! Are you okay?"

The door opened a crack, and Alicia said: "Just a skinned knuckle—nothing that needs attention. Go to bed, Fergus dear!" The door closed.

Back in his room, Reith was laying out the contents of his pockets when he heard a discreet knock and a high, muffled voice, saying in Gozashtandou: "Fergus! Let me in, forthwith!"

Reith's heart leaped up at the thought that it was Alicia, but then it struck him that she would have spoken English. He opened the door to find the Princess Vázni, who pushed her way in. She wore a hooded black cloak, which she tossed on the bed, uncovering the emerald gown she had worn at the banquet.

"Vázni!" he exclaimed. "What in the world—"

"Hush! I had to see you."

"Sit down, my dear."

"Oh, Fergus, it hath been so long. . . ."

"Yes, yes, but what is it? Aren't you running a risk, coming here alone?"

"Aye, but it cannot be helped. I had Dupulán's own time, evading my servants and those of the Dasht. When mean you to return to Novo?"

"That depends on my clients' business. In a few days, Bákh willing."

"Canst take me with you? If Terrans can disguise themselves as human beings, I can to the converse. I'll tape down my antennae—"

"Good gods, what an idea! Why are you so eager to flee your betrothed? Don't you like him?"

Vázni made the Krishnan negative head motion. "Gilan's a little mad. When he wrote the Dour of Gozashtand, inviting my husband and me to remove to Rosid and enjoy unlimited credit, methought 'twas noble generosity; but when I came to know him—"

"The Dasht called you a widow. What happened?"

"My husband was Aslehán bad-Khar, a knight of Dur. After you so cruelly deserted me, he consoled my grief. The Regent, hoping to lure you back to Dur, would not hear of ending my marriage to you so that I might wed Aslehán. To paint our union with the color of legality, we fled by stealth and took refuge at Dour Eqrar's court.

"Then, when we'd served our purpose as bargaining counters in Eqrar's chaffer with my cousin Tashian, the Dour lost interest in us. So we came to Rosid."

"Had you any offspring?"

"Aye; we'd hatched a daughter in Hershid. She's lately wed and gone to distant Suruskand. Then last year, poor Aslehán was slain in a tournament. Gilan was so sympathetic that my liver was touched, and I accepted his proposal. But after that . . ."

"But what?" Reith prompted.

"A rumor reached mine ears that Gilan had compassed my husband's untimely cease. He'd caused a regular fighting lance to be used by Aslehán's antagonist instead of the tilting lance. This fell device was disguised by a bogus coronal, with prongs of strengthless paper. The lance pierced my dear man through.

"I also saw that Gilan's proposal was but a move in his game political. He'd put away his first wife, the lady Farudi. She then wished to wed Sir Shost; but Gilan forbade, calling it unworthy that any woman who had enjoyed his embraces should ever belong to another. When his spies caught the pair in a tryst, he had Sir Shost beheaded on a trumped-up charge and imprisoned Farudi.

"I went to her cell and learned much. The Dasht had discarded her hoping to wed me, thinking that as my consort he'd prevail upon Tashian to name him Dour of Dur—or, failing that, to change the law and name me Douri, whilst he enjoyed the power of my rank."

Reith asked: "Did Gilan figure on begetting a male egg on you, who'd hatch and grow up to become Dour?"

"Doubtless he entertained such a whimsey. But if Farudi spake true, methinks he'd never succeed. He's all but impotent."

Reith chuckled. "Good gods! In spite of all his bluster and warlike posturing?"

"Verily. She said that, in six years of wedlock, he'd gone in unto her fewer than a dozen meager times, and then had discharged but little seed. Now you know why I'm fain to flee from Dur. I've learned a deal since you and I were—"

Alicia, still wearing her bare-breasted gown, tapped on the door and opened it, saying: "I heard voices, Fergus, and—oh!" In Gozashtandou she added: "Are you not the Princess Vázni?"

"Aye; and you are that Mistress—ah—Dackman, was it?"

"Dyckman," corrected Alicia. "We met once, long

ago, at Regent Tashian's court, when I was doing research in Dur."

"Well, Mistress Dyckman, any friend of Sir Fergus is a friend of mine. But I must tell you, madam," added Vázni with a touch of hauteur, "that you come at a time untimely. Sir Fergus and I have personal matters to discuss—in private."

"Whatever you say to him you may say to me," replied Alicia, a dangerous glint in her eye. "We are old friends and business associates, and there are no secrets between us. I shall leave only after you."

Vázni looked down her nose and spoke in glacial tones: "You understand not, my good woman. This is an intimate matter, and I shall linger after you depart. As Sir Fergus's former wife, I have a right to a private conversation—"

"I am likewise his former wife," said Alicia sharply. "So I have every bit as much right—"

"You, too?" cried Vázni. "By the divine stars, here's a Ziadian knot to untangle! I'd heard Sir Fergus had wedded again but not to whom. Did he desert you as he so callously abandoned me?"

"No. It was the other way round."

"What a fool you were, to leave so fine a man!"

"I agree. But that's not all; Fergus married once again."

Vázni's feathery antennae shot erect. "Doth he remain conjoined to this third spouse?"

"No. She died."

Vázni relaxed with a slight Krishnan smile. "Meanst that he's fair game for her who can sniggle him?"

"Ladies!" interrupted Reith. "I am *not* a prize up for grabs. I'm not a superior man. I'm a competent tour guide and a fair swordsman, but I'm a flat failure as a husband."

"Pay no attention," said Alicia. "He likes to talk about himself that way."

Vázni turned to Reith. "Fergus, for twenty years I've

yearned to ask: Why didst you leave me in such thwart fashion? Was I not a good and loving wife?"

Reith sighed. "I never meant to hurt you, Vázni. But I never wanted to marry you in the first place. I was forced to do so, literally at sword's point."

"Aye, after you'd robbed me of the jewel of maidenhood!"

"Oh, come off it! I didn't rob you; you were just as ready, willing, and eager as I. Nobody's to blame but your cousin the Regent. He planned the whole thing, knowing you and I could never produce a legitimate heir to threaten his position.

"Now let's get to the point. Excuse me, Vázni, if I speak to Alicia in our Terran tongue; it'll go faster." He gave Alicia a quick résumé of the princess's tale.

"She can't possibly come with us," said Alicia. "No telling what this crazy baron would do if he found her missing. If he didn't arrest us on our way out of Ruz, he'd at least refuse cooperation on the movie." She turned to Vázni with a forced smile. "My dear Princess, Strachan leaves Ruz soon. I'm sure you could persuade him to smuggle you out; he's harum-scarum enough."

Alicia walked to the door with the firmness of a practiced interviewer ending a session. With a hand on the doorknob, she said brightly: "It's been pleasant meeting you, Princess. Some other time we must—"

"Oh, I mean not to depart!" said Vázni, resolutely sitting down on the bed. "Let us compare our recollections of Sir Fergus. When you were intimate with him, were his lectual powers as great as those I enjoyed? He could perform—"

Reith broke in. "Vázni, please! This is most embarrassing. If you must dissect me—"

" 'Tis no more than you merit," said Vázni, turning to Alicia. "Tell me, fellow ex-wife, did he—"

"Really, Princess," said Alicia, "it's not the sort of thing—"

Reith raised his voice. "Enough nonsense! It's late, and we must be on site early tomorrow. Good night to both of you!"

"I'll not go until she doth!" exclaimed Vázni, eyeing her rival coldly.

"Nor will I leave until she goes!" retorted Alicia with a steely stare.

Reith scratched his scalp. "Well, I'm going to bed, right now. If you want to see a male strip act—"

Vázni gave the Krishnan equivalent of a shrug. "Proceed, and sprackly, husband-that-was! Bákh knows I've seen you naked often enough, and I doubt not that Mistress Dyckman hath, too. I shall relish the spectacle."

"Very well," said Reith, red-faced but determined. "You asked for it."

As he shed his underwear, Vázni remarked: "He's still as lean as ever, save in the belly. There he doth bulge a trifle."

"He's in marvelous shape for a man of his age!" said Alicia defensively. "He keeps in trim by constant exercise."

"Good night, dear ex spouses!" said Reith, sliding into bed and pulling the covers over his head.

For a while he lay, hearing the verbal fencing between his visitors and hoping that it would not escalate to hair-pulling. If it came to physical combat, he was sure that Alicia knew enough of the martial arts to make mincemeat of the Krishnan woman.

At last Reith faked a gentle snore. Soon he felt the weight of Vázni's cloak removed from the blanket above him and heard his door open and close. When he turned the blanket down, he found that the two women had tiptoed away. With a sigh of relief, he put out the lamp and fell asleep.

IV

KENNETH STRACHAN

The third hour of the next day saw Reith, with Timásh at the reins, driving Alicia and her associates to the drill field beyond the city walls. The adjacent fairgrounds dozed in the morning sun; multicolored pennants hung limply from the poles of tents, as a few of the fair folk moved sleepily about, feeding and watering their animals. Even the guard eshuna lay somnolent with heads on outstretched paws.

In contrast, the parade ground seethed with activity. Liveried flunkeys from the palace were briskly setting out rows of light chairs as an assortment of Ruzuma, from rich to ragged, scrambled for choice locations.

A drumming of aya hooves heralded the arrival of the Dasht. A splendid rider, flanked by several henchmen, the Dasht galloped across the field in still another martial costume. Over a long coat of silvered mail he wore a linenlike surcoat like that of a Terran Crusader, save that instead of the cross, the garment was embellished with astrological symbols in red and yellow and blue. Reith recognized one of the entourage as a bodyguard and another as a minor bureaucrat from the Treasury.

While Timásh secured Reith's ayas to a hitching post,

Reith led his clients to the edge of the drill field. The riders drew up sharply before them.

"Good morning!" barked Gilan, leaning down, "You passed a comfortable night, I trust? As soon as we are mounted, we shall commence our discussion."

"Mounted?" muttered Ordway. "Oh, God!" he exclaimed, as grooms appeared with four saddled ayas.

Reith and Alicia swung easily into their saddles, but the others had more difficulty. A groom had to boost the pudgy Ordway up. White waved aside an offer of similar assistance; Reith could see him biting his lip, visibly working up his courage to mount as he rehearsed the steps that Heggstad the trainer had taught him.

White's aya craned its long neck to stare at its hesitant rider. Then it rolled its eyes, uttered a bleating cry, shifted its feet, and lunged at White in an effort to hook him with a horn.

"Damn you, hold still!" cried White in a voice cracking with tension.

"He doesn't understand," Reith called out. "The word is *urám!*"

"*Urám!*" yelled White. The aya paused in its tarantellic dance long enough for the location manager to get a toehold in the stirrup and swing into the saddle.

"Let us go!" cried the Dasht, urging his aya to a fast walk. The others followed. When they were out of earshot of servitors and spectators, the Dasht said: "You see, my friends, *I* do things efficiently. I think best when mounted; so I combine my business of state with my morning's ride.

"Now, let us address your proposal to rent one of my castles and hire my aya-men for this living picture. To get right down to numbers: how many soldiers will you need, and for how long? How much will you pay them? Some think it base for a nobleman to concern himself with crass commercial matters; but *I* am a modern noble, who comprehends that money is the bloodstream of the state. . . ."

Thus began an hour's chaffering, at which Ordway showed himself an able negotiator despite his physical discomfort. From time to time the Dasht, also a shrewd bargainer, forced the mounts into a fast trot. At these times, White and Ordway, gasping for breath, were unable to say a word. The aya's trot was especially jarring, because the saddle was placed over the middle pair of legs.

At length Gilan and Ordway reached a tentative agreement. Since the Dasht refused to release a thousand of his men-at-arms from duty, it was agreed that five hundred should be enlisted whenever they were needed. He would not permit his palace in Rosid to be used as a movie set; but he made Castle Shaght, an abandoned fortlet in the hills, available to the shooting crew.

"It is time for a gallop!" cried Dasht Gilan. *"Ziddav!"* His aya broke into a canter. Ordway and White, ashen with fear, bounced along clutching their saddles as the group rode the length of the field and circled back towards their starting point.

As they neared the spectators' seats, Gilan reined to a sudden stop. All the other animals obediently pulled up save White's. This aya, with a defiant bleat, broke into a full gallop, pounding towards the far end of the field.

"Hey!" said Reith. "We've got to stop that critter!" He kicked his mount into a run, and Alicia galloped beside him. The Dasht followed, shouting orders to the grooms.

As they neared the end of the drill field, Timásh, who had been left with the carriage, ran out shouting and waving his big straw hat. The Krishnan shaihan-herd intercepted the runaway.

Instead of stopping, White's aya wheeled and headed back towards the other end of the field. Reith expected to see White hurled from the saddle like a flung slingstone by the centrifugal force of the turn. But White, with the strength of terror, retained a death grip on his saddle.

The turn allowed Reith and Alicia to gain on the runaway; but the sound of the sextuple hoofbeats behind it spurred the uncontrolled animal to go faster than ever. They reached the end of the field with Reith and Alicia a length behind White, and the Dasht a like distance behind them.

Between the drill field and the city wall, a kilometer away, lay a sprawling suburb of narrow streets and crowded markets. "If—he gets into that tangle, he'll—kill somebody!" gasped Reith.

"Can you—bulldog an aya?" asked Alicia.

"Don't—know; never—tried. You stay back!"

White's aya thundered into the main road, heading for a massive cart drawn by a pair of shaihans.

"Jack!" yelled Reith. "Say *'ast!* That's 'stop.' "

White shouted something, but amid the thunder of hooves and the cries of alarmed Krishnans scrambling out of the way, Reith could not tell what was said. Just as a head-on collision with the cart seemed inevitable, White's aya wheeled into a narrower street, where displays of divers markets spilled out into the street in a mosaic of reds and yellows and greens.

The turn allowed Reith to gain on the runaway. With a fierce kick he forced his aya to bound forward until it was abreast of White's, although upset bins of fruits and vegetables and the yells of outraged proprietors told him that he lacked proper space for the maneuver. Then he saw that Alicia had drawn abreast of White on the left. She was leaning forward in the saddle and extending an arm towards the aya's nearer horn.

"Back, Lish!" screamed Reith. "You'll be killed!"

Instead of obeying, Alicia hurled herself out of the saddle and caught the horn. Instead of stopping, the aya plunged on, dragging Alicia's boots through the mud.

A second later, Reith in turn leaned over, gripped the beast's right horn, and swung himself out of his saddle. He came down with his feet braced, his heels plowing through the mud. The combined pull brought the aya to a sudden halt. White pitched over its head, turned a half-somersault, and landed on his back in a large tub of plumlike Krishnan fruit.

Behind them, Dasht Gilan shouted orders from his saddle. In response, the bodyguard dismounted and pushed past White's aya, still held by Reith and Alicia, and bent over the fallen man.

"My Altitude greatly regrets your accident!" cried Gilan. "Are you hurt?"

White, covered with purple *ilá* juice, sat up and rubbed a shoulder. "Nothing seems to be broken," he mumbled.

The bodyguard extended a hand and hauled White to his feet in the remains of the shattered bin. Around them, the clustering Krishnans had begun to cry: "The alien hath ruined my stock!" "I demand repayment!" "Justice, my lord! I seek justice!"

Dasht Gilan barked: "Later, goodmen! Who hath a cloth?"

At last someone produced a towel, with which the guard solicitously wiped the smashed fruit from White's transmundane.

Ordway appeared, still mounted and accompanied by two grooms. "I say, Jack, you are a sight! What the devil happened?"

Gilan turned to Reith and Alicia. "Are you all right? Any damages?"

"None, except for my poor scuffed boots," replied Alicia.

"Any harm done to you or your garments shall be remedied." He addressed a groom. "The Terran gentleman hath need of a strong drink!"

The attendant produced a flask. With shaking hand, White took a swig, coughed, and drank some more.

"Now," proclaimed the Dasht, "back into the saddle with you! It is the only way to avoid a fear of riding." As White looked at his aya with an expression of horror, Gilan added: "Not that fractious beast, but—let me see—ah, *Kul* there. The name means an herb. She's so well-mannered, she could walk on eggs without cracking a shell."

At a signal from the Dasht, the groom riding the mount in question got down and turned the animal over to White. The Dasht led the party at a stately walk to the main street and thence to the drill field. The errant aya, with its sides heaving and held by two stalwart grooms, brought up the rear.

On the field, the Dasht gathered his minions around him, speaking sternly. "The Terran's mount looked strangely familiar. Could it be the one we called Flighty?"

"Aye, my lord," mumbled a groom. "The horsemaster commanded us to give Flighty to one of the Terrans— either one."

"He said he had received a message from Your Lordship," added another groom with a worried air. "We thought ye wished to jest at the expense of the alien beings."

"This mystery shall be unraveled," growled Gilan, "if need be, with rack and pincers." The grooms paled beneath their greenish-tan complexions. Gilan faced the Terrans. "Some villain has tried to play a more than cruel joke upon you, my friends. When I find him, he shall regret his perverted humor."

"I wonder who did it and why?" mused Reith.

The Dasht gave the Krishnan version of a shrug. "Perhaps it was a spy of the Kamoran of Qaath. Those ferocious barbarians are always up to something. Or it could be a follower of your fellow Terran, the cult leader Shel—Shneg—he of the Society for Cultural Preservation."

"Schlegel?" murmured Reith.

"That is he. I hear that he aims to sever all communication between my world and yours. He holds that, with each contact, we Krishnans borrow the worst ideas and manners—the vices—of your culture. In this he may not be altogether wrong. But, knowing cultural exchanges to be inevitable, I deem it better to control these borrowings, encouraging those of benefit to us and discouraging the others.

"But enough of lecturing. Mr. White, when you return to your inn, my servants will carry forth your stained garments for washing and repair. You have spares to wear meanwhile, I trust? Mr. Ordway, once I have ascertained the extent of my people's losses, you will, without doubt, make good the damage to their stalls and merchandise?"

"Surely, surely," mumbled Ordway, looking glum.

"And now," barked Gilan, "you must stay to enjoy the parade and concert. Choice seats have been reserved for you. Farewell!"

With a genial wave, the Dasht galloped off, followed by his troop of attendants.

The Terrans straggled towards the reserved seats, from which they watched with disaffected eyes as the band marched up and burst into a cacophany of tunes, mostly crudely-rendered Terran marches. After suffering through their version of Ganne's *Marche Lorraine*, the empurpled White whispered to Keith: "I've got to get out of here; I've been scared cross-eyed and battered to mush. Watching a parade in this mucked-up suit would finish me off for sure!"

Ordway added his plea to that of the dejected location manager. "I need some rest, too. After this morning's workout, I ache all over."

"Let's all go," said Alicia. "His Pomposity is nowhere in sight, and the locals will fill up our chairs."

As the band struck up the march from Victor Herbert's *Babes in Toyland*, the Terrans scuttled away.

The journey to Castle Shaght was made the following day on aya back, because the road was too narrow and overgrown for carriages. The Dasht did not accompany them, but sent a score of attendants to minister to their comfort and safety. Ordway chaffed: "Fergus, are you plotting to kill Jack and me by running us ragged, to leave you a clear field with Alicia?"

Reith grinned. "I hadn't thought of that. Fear not; I'll take good care of you, at least till I'm paid off."

Ordway looked from Reith to Alicia and shook his head. "You two must be made of steel and india rubber. You both seem as lively as ever."

"Just practice," said Reith.

"And we love our jobs," Alicia added.

They reached the abandoned castle, towering over a ridge in the forest. They found it ruinous, with crumbling walls and holes in the roof. White and Ordway prowled, stepping over fallen blocks and conferring in undertones. When they had completed their inspection, White told Reith: "I'm afraid this won't do at all."

"Jack's right, you know," said Ordway. "It would cost almost as much to restore this tumbledown pesthole as to build a new one." He glanced at the attendants, unpacking foodstuffs and supplies. "Must we stay the night here?"

"Afraid so," said Reith. "If we started home now, night would catch us on the road."

As darkness descended, White uttered a shrill squeak from where he stood arranging his bedding. "My God, what's that?" He pointed to a pair of luminous spots near the ground at the margin of the lantern light. The spots were joined by another pair, and another.

"Just some of the present tenants," said Reith. "They're harmless; those big enough to be dangerous have been frightened away."

"Come on, Jack!" said Ordway. "Where's your courage? Summon up the sinews, stiffen the blood!" As rain began to fall, he sighed. "Remind me to strike Cosmic for combat pay."

*   *   *

Reith's bedraggled party reached Rosid late the following morning. In sight of the capital, the rain ceased and Roqir broke through the clouds, gleaming against the gilded onion domes of the temples. Reith announced: "We've got time to rest a bit and clean up before lunch. Afterwards, if you like, we can take in the fair."

"The way I feel now, old boy," said Ordway, "it takes all my self-control not to tell you where to stick your bloody fair."

Later, however, the motion-picture executives felt better. Ordway volunteered: "I say, Fergus, when do we visit the fairgrounds?"

"I'll have Timásh hitch up the carriage."

They found the fair athrong with gaping visitors. On one side of the Midway, three jugglers tossed their sharp-honed knives and hatchets. Beyond, a pair of acrobats in red-and-white loin cloths balanced on a wire stretched between two poles. The male leaped into the air, turned a somersault, and landed with his feet on the wire. The impact threw the female into the air, to come down in her partner's arms. Then the pair bounded to the ground while the crowd shouted and cracked thumb joints.

Across the way, hidden puppeteers manipulated the strings of their marionettes. "By Jove!" said Ordway. "A Punch-and-Judy show, with caricatures of us!"

In the act, a villainous Earthman, identified by blond hair and a huge nose, was dragging off a Krishnan maiden, saying in Gozashtandou: "Come with me, my love! I'll show you pleasures beyond the compass of your degenerate race—"

Then a Krishnan hero appeared to belabor the Terran with a slapstick, crying: "Take that, ye alien scoundrel!" while the Earthman begged for mercy.

Reith and his clients pushed past mountebanks hawking nostrums. They dodged reeling drunkards and side-stepped harlots displaying blue-green nipples. Alicia whispered: "Fergus, I see low-cut dresses are still worn in Ruz—but considering the class of women who wear them, no wonder people stared at me at the banquet!"

On they went, their noses assailed by strong Krishnan body odors and the pungent smell of Krishnan cigars. The people running the concessions were mostly Gavehona —members of a nomadic ethnos that wandered (some said infested) the Varasto nations. They lived by handiwork, petty trade, fortune-telling, and less reputable occupations.

Passing a booth, White exclaimed: "Hey, that's for me!" He pointed to an astrologer's sign, beneath which sat a wrinkled old Krishnan with ragged antennae. The sign advertised his wisdom in Gozashtandou, Portuguese, and English. The English version read:

ALL-KNOWING STARGAZER GHAMIR OF MENZAL SHALL READ FOR-
TUNE IN STAR FOR TROUBLED MORTAL. RATE VERY GOOD. CLIENTS
SHALL BE EXECUTED IN ORDER OF INCOME.

White said: "You go on; I'll catch—hey, wait a minute! Does that sign say what I think it does? Is he going to slice off my head for his fee?"

Reith laughed. "Just his fractured English. He means first come, first served."

Looking apprehensive but determined, White vanished into the astrologer's tent. Alicia said: "Fergus, I want to talk to that young Gavehon over there! I mean to study their culture for a book I have in mind. You and Cyril go on; we'll meet at the flagpole."

Reith and Ordway strolled on until a whore sidled up to the Briton and spoke in Gavehonou.

"Eh, what?" said Ordway. "Don't you speak English?"

The whore said in Gozashtandou: "Would my Terran lord be fain for pleasure?" She gave a sensuous wriggle.

Ordway caught the drift. "Yes! *Oui!* Fergus, what the hell's the right word for 'yes'?"

"*Irrá.*" Reith chuckled. "Want me to come along and translate?"

"Thanks, but no thanks. Lend me the going fee, will you like a good bloke? I'll pay you back in Novo. . . . Thanks a million! *Irrá!*" Ordway and the female disappeared.

Later, Reith found Alicia still interviewing the Gavehon youth. As they walked away, Alicia said: "After we got friendly, I twitted him on his people's reputation for theft. Know what he said?" She rapped her own chest with her knuckles. " 'A Gavehon who does not steal is not a real man!' "

Reith smiled. They strolled towards a clump of Krishnans, swiftly growing into a crowd, who stood around an orator esconsed on a cask. As they neared, they made out his words.

". . . never, never trust these aliens from across the black depths of space! Believe not their protestations of friendship and non-aggression! Their own history shows their beguiling words to be but a pack of crafty lies. Their annals drip with the scarlet of their alien blood!

"On their own world, whenever a nation with mightier machines meets another with lesser, the former sends in explorers, traders, teachers, and preachers, who subtly undermine the faiths and traditions of the weaker folk. When the victims seek to expel these subversives, the more mechanized state sends armies with death-dealing weapons, to crush the people and make them slaves. And so it will be here, if ye heed not my warnings. . . ."

Reith felt Alicia stiffen. She said: "I'd like to get up beside that fellow and demand equal time. I'd show him—"

"No, you won't!" said Reith sharply. "He'd set a mob on us—"

"But, Fergus, someone has to—"

"Lish!" exclaimed Reith, taking a firm grip on her arm. "You know how volatile these folk are, and they're a hundred to one of us. It's lucky nobody's noticed you and me. Now come along!"

Reith forcibly swung Alicia away from the orator and started marching her back toward the tent that had swallowed White. He braced himself for an explosion of temper or even a physical assault, like that by which Alicia had felled Ordway. In a fight, she was a hundred-and-seventy-centimeter stick of dynamite.

Instead, after a few long breaths, she said: "You may release my arm, Fergus. You were right and I was wrong."

Reith drew a deep breath. "You've certainly changed, my darling Wart Hog!"

"I try not to make the same mistake twice, that's all."

"If that's what the Moritzian therapy accomplished—"

"Look, Gilan's men are taking an interest in the proceedings!"

Reith turned back. A squad of mailed fairwardens with quarterstaves were moving in on the crowd. The orator cut short his speech, hopped down from his cask, and vanished in the dispersing throng. The fairwardens grabbed one auditor after another, barking questions; but each fairgoer so seized wrapped himself in a cloak of innocence. Soon the area was clear save for gaping passersby.

"That fellow may have been one of Schlegel's boys," said Reith, "though I hear there are several anti-Terran cults and societies working—"

White hurried up, crying: "Fergus, I've been robbed!"

"How so?" asked the tour guide, frowning.

"The astrologer said I ought to try a booth down the way, where you throw darts at a spinning wheel. The wheel's divided into sectors with different values. But no matter how carefully I threw, I could never get a winning combination. The thing must be rigged."

"What are you crabbing about?" retorted Reith. "You've had your fun and paid for it—probably less than Cyril will pay for his."

"What's Cyril up to?"

"Don't ask; a lady is present." Reith grinned as he

caught Alicia suppressing a laugh. When she felt like it, he knew, she was capable of language that would make a longshoreman blush. "And by the way, the Dasht wants us to see another castle tomorrow. His people must have told him you weren't ecstatic over Shaght."

"Where is this other castle?"

"A day's journey north. It's an active fortress, so at least it'll be in good repair."

As they mounted the stairs at the inn, the taverner's potboy touched Reith's arm. "A man from the castle commanded me to give you this missive, my lord. Strictly confidential, he said."

"Thank you," said Reith. In his room he unfolded a sheet of Krishnan paper and frowned as he read the spidery hooks and curls of Gozashtando longhand:

Dearest F: Show no surprise if a strange Terran youth joins you on your return journey.

Opening his door with a haste born of apprehension, Reith called: "Lish! Come here and look at this!"

Alicia studied the script and nodded. "It's Vázni, all right. Seems she's determined to go to Novo with us."

"We must stop her somehow!" exclaimed Reith.

Alicia eyed him sympathetically. "Easier said than done. If I'm any guesser, she'll make herself scarce until departure time. Then, if you try to turn her over to the Dasht—"

"I couldn't do that! He'd kill her."

"It's nice to know you feel that way about ex-wives. But if we tried to stop her some other way, she'd run to the guy with a fanciful tale of rape or mayhem. Then you'd find Gilan's gleaming sword more than a figure of speech."

"I'm not afraid of the pompous ass—"

"Don't be silly, darling! He's got armed men all over

the place, and we—Cyril, Jack, and I—are hostages for your good behavior."

"You're right, damn it. It's your most irritating quality, Lish. So what should we do?"

"Look, you don't need me at Castle Mikkim. I want to stay here anyway for a little shopping. While I'm about it, I'll see what can be done about this other thing."

"Got a plan?"

"Let's just say, I'm hatching one."

Reith heaved a sigh. "Okay, superwoman. You've sprung me out of durance vile before; so I guess you'll find the key to this one."

Three days later, Reith, White, and Ordway returned to Rosid. As Reith drove his carriage through the streets, he sensed an undercurrent of bustle and excitement. When he drew up at the inn and turned the reins over to Timásh, Alicia burst out the door to seize Reith and give him a kiss that was anything but cousinly.

"How was your trip?" she asked with one of her dazzling smiles.

"So-so. Jack likes Castle Mikkim better than Shaght but hopes to do better still. The fort's pretty far out in the boonies—"

"That's not the main objection," said White, animated now by the discussion of his specialty. "It's lighting. Castle Mikkim stands on the banks of a river, with steep cliffs on both sides. So it's always in deep shadow. Since we can't bring in good artificial lights, we need the sun, and it strikes Mikkim for only a few minutes each day."

"I thought," said Alicia, "with that super-sensitive film they have nowadays, you could shoot in pitch darkness."

"We could, but you can't fake the chiaroscuro you get from full sunlight. Some of our scenes demand it. An overcast could tie up production completely."

"I hadn't seen Mikkim before," said Reith with a travel agent's enthusiasm. "It has the kind of wild, romantic beauty that will appeal to my tourists. What's been happening here? Is something going on?"

Alicia smiled like a satisfied cat. "Only that the Dasht, his fiancee, and a small army of attendants take off tomorrow for Hershid."

Reith gasped: "How come?"

"It seems that Tashian wrote to King Eqrar of Gozashtand—"

"Who's Tashian?" asked White.

"The Regent of Dur, up north, and a cousin of Princess Vázni. Anyway, the Regent sent a letter to his fellow ruler King Eqrar at Hershid, saying that it was time to consider the future government of Dur. Vázni is the late King Dushta'en's only surviving legitimate offspring, and their constitution doesn't allow for the succession of females to the throne. In this connection, he trusts King Eqrar will receive Vázni at his court when she comes to Hershid to discuss the matter of succession with the ambassador from Dur.

"So, after you left, Eqrar's secretary dispatched a messenger inviting Princess Vázni to sojourn at the palace while visiting the capital of Gozashtand. Although the letter invited only Vázni, you can just bet Gilan won't stay home while his betrothed goes off to become heir to a throne or something. He'll be there, presenting his plans, in his usual modest fashion, for becoming the real ruler of Dur.

"Thank goodness, we'll be on the move tomorrow, too. By the way, Gilan has invited us to a farewell banquet this evening. So get washed and shaved, the lot of you!"

"I'm going to let my whiskers grow," said Ordway. "If the wogs can put on false beards, I can wear a real one."

When they were alone, Reith looked narrowly at Alicia. "How did you work it?"

"Who, me? I had nothing to do with it—unless a little prayer to Dashmok helped."

Reith grinned. "If I believed that, I'd also believe in Prince Bourujird's flying chariot."

When they gathered for the drive to the palace, Reith gazed at Alicia with significant intentness. "New gown, in the Rosido high-necked fashion?"

Alicia smiled. "New dress, new style. I spent half of yesterday at the dressmaker's being measured and fitted and poked like a pincushion."

Grinning, Reith quoted:

"Let never maiden think, however, fair,
She is not fairer in new clothes than old!"

"Who wrote that " asked Alicia. "Byron or one of those other old-timers?"

"Tennyson. Just a fragment remembered from my schoolteaching days."

The onion domes of Rosid emerged from the sun-shredded morning mists and then disappeared behind the coach at a bend in the road. The four travelers settled themselves comfortably for the journey to Novorecife. The barouche moved briskly along the wide road south, the hooves of the ayas crunching on the gravel with Timásh at the reins. Zerré, the shaihan-herd whom Reith had dispatched ahead on the journey to Rosid, followed with baggage loaded on spare ayas.

The farewell banquet had kept them all up most of the night. Ordway and White, after patting yawns, fell into a doze. When they seemed dead to the world, Reith quietly requested: "Lish, now that we're clear of the city, give me the straight goods on this excursion of our lordlings to Hershid."

She chortled. "I forged a letter from King Eqrar and hired the Gavehon I interviewed to deliver it. I figured Vázni would choose a chance to become queen of Dur over a flight with us to Novo."

"How did you get a suit of King Eqrar's livery for the fake messenger to wear?"

"I made it."

"*What?*" Reith's exclamation snapped White and Ordway out of their doze.

"I've told you," said Alicia, "sewing is my one domestic accomplishment. I found a picture book of costumes in Gilan's library, bought the fabric in Rosid, and sat up the night before last stitching the thing. It didn't fit very well, but nobody noticed. By the way, Cyril, Cosmic owes me a thousand karda for expenses. No arguments, now! It took most of that just to bribe the Gavehon to deliver the letter and then disappear."

"What'll happen," Ordway asked, "when Gilan and company get to Hershid and find it's all a hoax?"

Alicia shrugged. "That will be interesting to see— preferably from a safe distance."

Reith chuckled and winked at White and Ordway. "Gentlemen, you'd better take Doctor Dyckman back to Earth with you. If you leave her here, she'll soon be running the whole damned planet."

Alicia raised a defiant chin. "And the whole damned planet could do a lot worse than that!"

Back at Novorecife, the travelers renewed their wardrobes, submitted to Heggstad's exhausting athletic drills and torturous massages, studied maps, and sought news of the Republic of Mikardand.

"We don't want to arrive in the middle of a revolution," said Reith at the end of several days of preparation for the next journey.

"If it's already a republic," asked Ordway, "what's their peeve?"

"It's a peculiar kind of republic. The power's in the hands of a military caste, the Garma Qararuma or Knights of Qarar. Among themselves, the Knights practice a kind of communism, sharing everything, including sex."

"That I must see!" said Ordway. "That's the kind of communism I approve of."

Ignoring the comment, Reith continued. "They promote the most gifted commoners to knighthood, to nip the buds of disaffection; but sometimes the less fortunate Mikardanduma get restless. Will you and Jack be ready to set out early tomorrow?"

"Certainly, mate," said Ordway.

"Okay; then I'll send Zerré on ahead with a letter to the Grand Master. The Knights have just elected a new one, and I don't know how he feels about Terrans."

As Reith strolled out into the sunny afternoon, a yell of "Haw, Fergus!" made him turn.

"Ken!" he cried as the engineer approached, a smaller companion in tow. "Who's your new—good gods, it's Vázni!"

"The goddess Varzai blast your keen eyesight, Fergus!" said Vázni. "You're the first whom my masquerade hath not befooled."

She was dressed as a Terran youth, with her antennae taped down and freshly-bleached hair arranged to hide her ears. Grease paint and powder had tinted the faintly olive-green hue of her skin to a ruddy pink. Reith said: "Let's step into the Nova Iorque. Have you two just arrived?"

"Aye," said Strachan. "I've been stabling ma ayas and finding quarters for the princess."

In the bar, Strachan took a wall seat. Vázni insisted on sitting beside him, snuggling up close. Reith formed his own opinion as to how these two had amused themselves on the way from Hershid. He said: "Now talk!"

"Weel," said Strachan, "I wanted to go to Hershid wi' the Dasht and the princess, to make sure I received the last instalment on ma contract. I wudna have put it past Gilan to hare off to become regent of Dur, leaving me to whistle for ma siller."

Strachan glanced around the barroom and switched

to the Duro language, either out of courtesy to Vázni or to baffle eavesdroppers. "I put it up to the Dasht, who said: 'Surely, my lad, come along.' But when we reached Hershid, we found the Dour saying he knew of no such missive to Vázni, and Tashian's ambassador denying he'd received such a word from the Regent, and the Dour's secretary professing equal ignorance. Know you aught of this Fergus?"

Reith shook his head, and Strachan continued: "Seeing that the party would return to Rosid disappointed, I took the Dasht to task about my money. But he was in a fury, threatening to have whoever had perpetrated this jape stepped on by a bishtar from the baronial menagerie. When I spoke of the contract, he said: 'Are ye involved in this unmannerly jest, Strachan? If I discover that ye be . . .' And he drew a finger across his throat.

"So I said to myself, Kenneth my lad, you'd better hie you hence before His Self-Importance sets his headsman on you with rack and thumbscrews. I was saddling up when along came the princess, disguised as you see, demanding to be taken, too. Since there's no crown awaiting her in Baianch, it was either flee, with her jewels in a little bag in her bosom, or return to Rosid to be Gilan's blushing bride—if these greenish folk can blush. So here we are."

Thoughtfully, Reith said: "Gillan may soon test Novo's right to grant asylum. I, luckily, shall be far away. What are your plans, Princess?"

She glanced appealing from one Terran to the other. "I truly know not. What are yours, Fergus?"

"I leave tomorrow for Mishé with my people."

"And you, Kennet'?"

The Scot grinned. "I'll bide at home a while; then who knows? I hear the Krishnans have made a botch of the Majbur-Mishé railroad. Perhaps they could use a good Terran engineer."

Vázni sighed. "There's nought left for me, save to

join my daughter in Suruskand. She hath invited me. I shall have to find trusty bodyguards, who'll not murder me for my gems along the way."

"I'll ask Castanhoso to help," said Reith. "Now I'm bound for the ranch. Can I give you a lift, Ken?"

Before dropping Strachan off at his house, Reith brought the Scot up to date on the movie project. Strachan said: "Aside from your business, how about you and your onetime kimmer, Alicia? What's the status, if ye dinna mind? You two were my favorite people, and I wudna wish to put my foot in it."

"We're just good old friends, that's all."

"Hmph!" Strachan snorted. "I dinna ken about you, Fergus; but if I were unattached, I cudna be 'just friends' with such a lovely woman for very long. Something would have to give."

Reith grinned. "Something or somebody, eh? Just give us a while to find out."

V

LADY GASHIGI

Its folding top up against a drizzling rain, the barouche rolled briskly down the river road to Qou. On their left, the country sometimes opened out into cultivated farmland, then closed in again behind a crowded wall of temperate-zone forest. Gaudy trunks of bright-hued trees lined the roadside, like billboards along a busy Terran highway.

Timásh, riding ahead on a spare aya, threw up a warning hand. Reith pulled up his pair of ayas and set the brake.

"What's up?" demanded Ordway.

"You'll see," said Reith. "Just be quiet."

Across the road, a score of meters beyond, shambled three huge beasts: a female bishtar and two young, one half-grown and one a new calf. The cow was of elephantine size and build, with six columnar legs supporting a long-barreled body. Its hide was covered with glossy fur of purpled brown, spangled with constellations of small cream-colored spots, as if a demented painter had flapped his brushes at the animal. The head resembled that of a Terran tapir, though vastly larger, with small, trumpet-shaped ears and a long muzzle ending in a pair of stubby, meter-long trunks.

"Wish I had an elephant gun," breathed Ordway. "There's no hunting for sport on Earth any more; all the wildlife's in parks and preserves."

"We ought to have one of those things in our movie," whispered White. "Do they have tame ones for rent?"

Reith replied: "The Dasht of Ruz has one in his zoo; but I daresay he'd never lease it. We'd have to go to Majbur to find one, at the end of the coastal railroad lines."

"They've got *railroads* here?" exclaimed White.

"Hush! Yes, they do, with tame bishtars for locomotives."

"We've really got to get one into the picture!" said White. "One good action shot of that animal would be worth a hundred meters of an animated model—"

"Oh, hell!" said Ordway. "We can't run all over the planet on the budget they gave me!"

"But Cyril, don't you see—"

The two executives had gradually raised their voices. Reith said, "Hey, pipe down! You're bothering the animals."

Timásh, pulling up beside the carriage, mumbled: "Ye had best turn and flee, Master Reit'. Yon cow hath taken an ill will to you."

The female bishtar had turned to face the carriage. Now she stood with little ears twitching and stumpy trunks sniffing.

"Help me wheel these ayas round," grated Reith, releasing the brake and hauling on the reins.

The road proved too narrow for easy turning. Reith had to back the vehicle so that its rear wheels crunched into the vegetation. Batting his big straw hat at the ayas' heads, Timásh turned them partly around; but then, rolling their eyes in terror, they balked. Out of control, they danced about nervously, unmindful of threat or encouragement.

Alicia slipped out of the carriage, seized the horns of the nearer animal, and hauled its head around by main force. Reith called: "Fine, Lish! Get up on a spare aya; it'll be safer for you."

Timásh threw Alicia the reins of one of the spares. She caught the strap and vaulted on to the back of the unsaddled beast.

Just then, the cow bishtar opened its vast maw, gave a thunderous snort, and began shuffling with appalling speed towards the travelers. Reith, having at last turned the animals and carriage, cracked his whip and shouted "*Byant-hao!*"

All the ayas broke into a gallop. Ordway, glancing back from his seat in the swaying barouche, cried: "My God, Fergus, that damned thing's gaining on us!"

The bishtar's pounding sextuple footfalls had indeed begun to close the gap. Ordway's ruddy face paled to a livid hue, and his jowls quivered like rolls of jelly.

"I think we're gaining," said White in a strangled voice that lacked conviction. But even as he spoke, the bishtar slowed to a stop, sides heaving, and shook its ponderous head. Reith let his team slow down. When the bishtar was almost out of sight beyond a slight bend in the road, Reith pulled to a halt and looked back.

"There she goes," he murmured at last, as the cow began plodding back the way she had come. When the beast was wholly out of sight, Reith turned the carriage again and cautiously resumed the journey.

"I say!" said Ordway, mopping his forehead. "That'll be something to tell the shooting crew about. Were we in real danger?"

Reith shrugged. "If she'd caught you, she'd have squashed you like a grape. But once we turned, I knew we had enough of a start to get away, unless we lost a wheel or something. Bishtars can move pretty fast, but they soon run out of breath. I once got away from one on foot."

"You *did?*" said White.

"Sure you're not pulling my leg?" added Ordway.

"No; straight goods; tell you some time. There's nothing like being chased by an angry bishtar to bring out the best in a runner. But next time I say to keep your voices down, do it!"

By midafternoon they had reached the Qou ferry landing, where they waited an hour for the ferry. At last a broad-beamed scow, propelled by a dozen oars, crawled like a water insect out of the drizzle. The oarsmen were Krishnans of the tailed species, naked and hairy, who under the ferrymaster's direction swarmed chattering ashore. While Reith and Timásh led their nervous ayas out on the deck of the scow, the tailed ones manhandled the carriage aboard. White remarked: "Cyril, I've got a great idea! Couldn't we get Attila to write in a scene with these monkey-men?"

Ordway raised a skeptical eyebrow. "You know script writers."

When at last they were settled in Qou, Reith and his charges strolled about the slatternly village, staring at the tailed primitives. Scarcely assimilated into such civilization as the town possessed, they lived in a clump of circular reed huts and toiled at menial tasks.

White disappeared into another astrologer's shack. Alicia became engrossed in conversing, in a tongue full of grunts and clicks, with a group of idle primitives. Amazed that any tailless being could address them in their own language, the tailed ones crowded round, grinning and chattering.

"Look at her!" said Ordway, whose round face bore a stubble of reddish-gold beard. "She can do *anything*, that gel. Makes one feel flat-out inadequate, just to watch her. I say, Fergus!"

"Yes?"

"Don't take this wrong; but are you and she—ah— contemplating . . ."

"Damn it, Cyril—"

"Please, old boy, don't get off your bike! You know my reason for asking. Here am I, with a peg you could hang a fur coat on, while you two dance a kind of hesitation waltz, circling round and round. I want the gel, and you're driving me loopy!"

Reith's expression did not change; experience had taught him to hide his emotions. After a pause, he coolly replied: "I'm afraid you'll have to put up with our dance a while longer. We're just living from day to day, enjoying life and promising nothing." He glanced at the setting sun, intermittently visible through tattered clouds. "We'd better get back; these people dine early."

Dinner, served by the innkeeper's wife and buxom daughter, looked like a kind of shrimp stew and tasted like spiced rubber. Reith entertained his companions with Krishnan tales.

"A French adventurer, Felix Borel, once worked the perfect swindle. He sold the Knights of Qarar the rights to a perpetual-motion machine. He'd have made a good thing of this flimflam, only he got into a duel with a Knight over a female. Being no fighter, he had to run for it—yes?" he said in Mikardandou. The innkeeper's half-grown son was plucking at his sleeve.

"Pray, Master Terran," said the boy, "hast seen my bozmaj?"

"No, my lad I have not. I'll watch for it."

"What's that?" asked Ordway.

"The boy's lost his pet, a small relative of the shan. To get back to Borel's sad tale—"

White, staring at Reith's plate, made a strangled sound. Reith looked down to see one of the "shrimps" stagger to its eight feet and now, dripping gravy, wander off the plate. It plodded across the table top, leaving a double row of little brown spots where its feet had touched the wood.

Ordway, his blue eyes wide, said: "Good God, what's that? I thought the live spaghetti we've been eating was pretty revolting; but at least it didn't walk away on a lot of legs!"

"Oh, that's all right," said Reith. "Lots of lower Krishnan organisms still move after being boiled. Something in their proteins." He deftly skewered the creature with one of his eating spears and held it up. It arched its body and rhythmically waved its eight legs.

White clapped a hand to his mouth, rose, and bolted out the door. Reith called: "Madam Nirizi! Kindly take my little friend here back and boil him for another quarter-hour!"

Ordway sighed. "You two seem not only to be made of piano wires and india-rubber bands, but to have stainless-steel insides as well!"

"We've adapted," said Reith. "Actually, a Terran can eat most Krishnan foods. A few would upset or even kill you; but I see to it that my clients don't get them."

Alicia added sweetly: "So whenever a visitor acts obnoxious, all we have to do is to slip him the wrong kind of eats."

Ordway shuddered. "I assure you I shall sprout wings! And never let it be said that a plucky British lad funked out at the sight of strange food. I've faced up to worse hazards on dear old Terra." He bravely attacked his pseudo-shrimp. Later he said: "Alicia, you haven't eaten half your dinner. Has that live prawn zapped your appetite, too?"

"No," she replied. "I eat what's good for me, no more."

Ordway sighed. "Wish I had your self-discipline."

"Suffering is the price of sylphishness."

Ordway frowned. "What's selfishness got to do with it?"

"I said 'sylphishness.' You know, like a sylph."

"What's that?"

"A kind of fairy."

"D'you mean the kind that flits through the woods on gauzy wings, or the kind that swishes along on Piccadilly?"

"The former," said Alicia, adding severely: "You shouldn't ridicule the handicapped, Cyril."

"Sorry. What beats me is that we still have 'em, when I'm told they can easily be cured nowadays."

Alicia shrugged. "It's like Jack's gambling; some people don't *want* to be cured."

"Ah, well," said Ordway, "at least I've never had to worry about it myself. I'd gladly show you my capabilities—"

"I saw them in the bathhouse at Avord," said Alicia dryly, "and they looked much like other men's. Just keep your mind above my belt!"

Ordway sighed. "Easier said than done, with a bonzer bird like you."

After dinner, Ordway fell into halting conversation with the innkeeper's daughter, who spoke a little English. Reith and Alicia strolled down a muddy street to the rickety ferry pier. The overcast had rolled away, leaving a clear sky ruled by all three Krishnan moons: big Karrim, middle-sized Golnaz, and little Sheb. Their radiance cast pyramidal shadows that turned the shabby village into a tenebrous fairyland. Above, the satin sky was diamonded with shimmering stars, faint in the overwhelming moonlight.

"What a night for love!" breathed Alicia as she stood with chin up, gazing at the celestial display.

Reith gave a faint grunt, forced by the inner turmoil that intimate converse with Alicia aroused. "Poor Cyril's suffering from unrequited lust. He's even asked me when we'll end our tango, so he can make passes at you again."

"Fergus, are you trying to tell me to give him my all?"

"Gods, no! I'm just gossiping."

"Well, that's a relief. I really don't like him, you know."

"I'm glad of that. It wouldn't commend your taste in men."

"I once showed excellent ta—" She stopped in confusion. To cover an awkward pause, Reith said: "You know, Lish, I look back with pleasure on a tour I guided about five years ago."

"Why?"

"Because that was my one group with no sexual complications for anyone. No falling in or out of love; no domestic quarrels, infidelities, deviations, or involvement with Krishnans."

Alicia, who had been holding Reith's arm, released it and stiffened. "Do you mean I'm just a sexual complication?"

"Eh? No—of course—I don't—you're just—oh, hell!" He gathered her in for a long, fervent kiss. As they resumed their walk, Reith explained. "I was thinking of a tour of the other kind, with a highly visible case of adultery and an outraged husband brandishing a souvenir sword. I saved that Don Juan's gore at the cost of a cut on the arm, but relations were pretty strained all around for the rest of the trip. The etiquette books don't cover situations like that." He smothered a yawn. "Time to turn in; we have a long drive tomorrow."

Alicia looked wistfully up at the triple moons. "But it's so nice. . . ."

Reith regarded her classic features, heartbreakingly beautiful in the moonlight. "Listen, girl, you'd better do as I say if you don't want splinters in your backside!"

"Oh." She glanced down at the rough planking of the pier and giggled. "I see the point—or points. Besides it *is* getting chilly. I'll race you to the inn!"

Alicia won the race. As they flung open the door and staggered in, laughing, the taverner cried in alarm: "What is't? Are the wild Koloftuma attacking?"

It took some minutes to convince the apprehensive innkeeper that foot-racing was just a zany Terran form of amusement.

At Alicia's door, Reith prolonged the good-night kiss. Then they were embracing with the intensity of mutual passion. He was sure that if he stepped into her room . . .

A hideous scream tore them apart. Down the hall galloped Cyril Ordway in his underwear, eyes staring and short legs pumping.

"Help!" he shrieked as he raced past. "It's got me!"

After him scuttled the bozmaj, the pet of the inn-keeper's son, hissing angrily. It was a scaly animal, as long as a man is tall but mostly neck and tail. From time to time the lizardlike jaws on the end of its serpentine neck snapped a centimeter from Ordway's rear.

As the beast passed, Reith shot out a hand, caught it just behind the head, and hoisted it into the air. He held it away from his body so that the claws of the six thrashing legs could not gouge him as 'he bellowed: "Master Fangchu!"

As Reith stood holding the bozmaj, Ordway clattered down the stair. Reith heard him pounding on the locked front door, shouting: "Let me out! Let me out!"

Down the hallway whence Ordway had come, Reith glimpsed the innkeeper's daughter, leaning out of her door and staring like one bewitched. Then the innkeeper's son appeared at the head of the stairs crying: "Master Terran, that is my pet! I pray you, give it me!"

"Gladly," said Reith, handing over the bozmaj. The boy embraced the creature, which wound its neck and tail around him and flicked out a forked tongue to lick his ear.

Reith and Alicia hurried down to the entranceway, where Ordway stood frantically trying to push open the door.

"Calm down, Cyril!" said Reith. "The kid has his lizard back. What happened?"

"Well—ah—I'd rather not discuss it in front of Alicia."

Reith grinned. "Go to bed, Lish, I'll tell you all about it tomorrow."

"Huh!" she said. "As if I didn't know already!" But she went.

"Well," said Ordway, "you saw me passing the time of night with Fangchu's gel. After you left the inn, we sort of wandered into her room. She wanted to practice her English, and she soon made it plain that she'd entertain a proposition. So we were sitting on her bed, and I was demonstrating the earthly custom of kissing, which she'd asked me about. Then this junior nightmare stuck its long neck out from under the bed and stared me in the eye. Never did like snakes."

"This isn't a snake," said Reith. "It has legs."

"It's a cross between a snake and a centipede, which is worse. It scared the hell out of me, so I jumped up and threw a shoe at it. That tore it. Look at my arm!"

Ordway's arm bore a dozen parallel scratches, oozing tiny ruby droplets. Reith said, "Alicia has the first-aid kit. Come on up."

"Damn!" growled Ordway. "That bloody beast spoiled a perfectly good firkin o' luck before it even got started."

You're not the only one, thought Reith. Ordway continued mournfully, "Why do these things keep happening to a nice, warm-hearted chap like me?"

"Because you don't seem to learn from experience," said Reith.

Ordway grunted. After a pause, he said: "Fergus, I should like an agreement. I won't make any more passes at Alicia, if you'll keep quiet about this lizard episode. I shouldn't care to have the shooting crew learn of it when they arrive."

"Okay," said Reith. "It's a deal."

Three days later, Reith's ayas clopped towards the huge, buff-gray wall of sprawling Mishé. From a distance, upthrust above the scowling wall, the Earthlings could see the central Citadel, a mesalike acropolis whose vertical sides were revetted with massive stone blocks. Over the Citadel's parapet loomed the upper stories of huge, boxlike, elephant-gray buildings, where the Guardians, the knightly ruling caste, dwelt and ruled.

During the journey, White, using a traveler's phrase book, had begun to learn spoken Mikardandou. Reith drilled him in simple phrases. When Reith suggested that Ordway do likewise, the Londoner said: "No, Fergus. Let the bloody wogs learn to speak English, like civilized people, if they want to talk to me."

Near the city gates, the carriage rumbled past an exercise field. There, knights and men-at-arms practiced martial arts. Afoot, they chopped at pells with swords and axes; mounted, they charged with leveled lances at a suspended ring.

Passing a rack of spikes decorated with the rotting heads of malefactors, the carriage drew up at the sentry box outside the gate. The travelers showed their papers to armored guards, who waved them through. Soon their vehicle was rattling over the cobblestones of the main thoroughfare. Ordway asked: "Are you taking us to another inn, Fergus?"

Reith said: "We're first going to see the consul. He's a reformed Englishman named Fallon."

"Reformed? You sound as if being English were a criminal offense."

"No, I merely meant that he's English, like you; and that he's also given up being a drunken drifter."

"Hm. I'm skeptical of reformed characters."

Reith leaned out, looking along the avenue. At last he said to the driver: "Stop here, Timásh!"

The Krishnan halted the ayas before a modest edifice. To one side of the door, the red white and blue medallion of the Terran World Federation was affixed to the beige stucco of the wall.

The passengers climbed down, wearily stretching cramped limbs; and a Krishnan servant admitted them to a long, dark hall. As they passed a stand bearing an open registry book, Reith paused to sign. "Now the rest of you sign, too, please!" he said, handing the pen to Alicia.

"Hey there, Fergus!" came a shout from the far end of the hall. "I thought I recognized that voice."

Footsteps signaled the man's approach. The newcomer proved a tall Terran who looked much older than Reith, although in fact the years that separated them were few. His wavy hair was gray and his face, once handsome, was lined and pouched from years of hard, dissipated living; yet Anthony Fallon stood militarily straight and moved with the spring of a younger man. He shook hands heartily with Reith and cheerfully acknowledged the round of introductions.

"What quarters did you get us?" Reith asked.

"A VIP suite in the Citadel. It looks as if your project should go through without a hitch."

"In my experience," said Reith, "when things seem too good to be true, they usually are."

"We shall see; we shall see. Can I give you all a drink?"

As Fallon waved his guests into the consular office, he touched Reith's arm and whispered: "I say, Fergus! Isn't she the gal you once—umm—"

Reith nodded silently and passed through the door. The travelers took seats and watched Fallon pour light falat wine into four goblets. Instead of pouring a fifth for himself, he filled his own vessel from a pitcher of water.

"Ordway can't believe you've reformed, Tony," said Reith. "Working in the movie industry has made him cynical. Tell him your tale."

"Very well; if you're sure it won't bore you," said Fallon. "I've led a pretty full life: been everything from king to drunken swagman, including along the way policeman for the World Fed, hippopotamus farmer, wild-life photographer, actor, professional cricketer, and spy. By the way," Fallon addressed Reith, "speaking of my kingship days, I got a letter from my ex."

"And how is the onetime Queen of Zamba?"

"Not that ex, the previous one, Alexandra—the one who married that Canadian—ah—Hasselborg, the chap who killed the then Dasht of Ruz. Alex was bubbling over because the Genetics Board on Terra had given them permission to have a third child. Thank the Lord, here we don't have to ask permission to beget our kind."

"Are they happy?"

"Apparently. I'm glad they're doing well, but you know how it is. Unhappy marriages are full of mixed emotions, conflict, and tragedy—the stuff of drama—so they're interesting. But as for happy ones—"

"What about your reformation?" interrupted Ordway.

"Certainly. It was about fifteen years ago, after the fall of Balhib, when Ishimoto was consul in Mishé. I was living here by my wits, indulging in futile dreams of getting my throne back and drinking myself to death.

"Then I pulled myself together, went back to Novo, and got the doc there to give me the treatment developed by that Indian chap. Now I can't abide anything alcoholic. Next, I persuaded the brass to make me acting consul here when the job opened up. Later I passed the qualifying tests; and here I am, an excruciatingly respectable civil servant, a bloody bureaucrat. I sometimes miss the old, irregular days; but to quote some ancient bloke: 'We live not as we wish but as we can.' By the way, Fergus, do you know a man named Enrique Schlegel?"

"Slightly, and not to my pleasure. What about him?"

"He was in Mishé a few days ago, campaigning for his Society for the Preservation of Krishnan Culture. In the past half-moon, his followers have smashed up a shop selling Terran-style women's clothes. Before that, they rioted at a concert where the orchestra played Rozanov's Second Symphony. Not that Rozanov would have known his piece by the time the Krishnan band got through with it."

"Why haven't the Knights kicked him out? Or better yet, put his head on a spike?"

"He has a following. Grand Master Juvain was ultra-conservative, and a lot of his admirers are still around."

"Was Schlegel disguised as a Krishnan?"

"Absolutely; a first-class cosmetic job. I talked with him, as I do with all such characters. When I mentioned you, he began to roar curses and threats. Seems you once knocked him down."

"So I did, when he disrupted one of my tours."

"Said he was leaving shortly for Mikardand, drumming up support for his cult, and you'd better look to your sword if he ran into you. He'd been kicked out of Suruskand and blames you."

"That was Herculeu's idea," said Reith. "Not that I didn't agree! But Herculeu wrote Dámir while I was away with my clients here, so I knew nothing about it at the time."

"I tried to gentle him down," said Fallon, "but he's a real paranoiac, sure all Terrans on the planet are out to get him. So keep your sword handy."

As the visitors filed out, Fallon touched Reith's arm to detain him, murmuring: "How the devil does it happen that you're knocking about with your former spouse?"

"I told you," said Reith. "She's an executive with these movie people, and she got me this guiding contract."

"Doesn't it make things a bit awkward?"

"Not a bit," said Reith, avoiding Fallon's eye. "We're friends, and neither of us is now married. We're—well, sort of like brother and sister."

"Good! Then I can be friends with both. You know, keeping up with both halves of an ex-couple is something to be done the way porcupines make love—carefully." Fallon shook his head. "I say, have you two any—ah—plans?"

Sternly, Reith said: "You're about the tenth person who's asked me that. The next will be eaten by my pet yeki."

"I didn't know you had a pet yeki."

"I don't; but I'll get one."

Fallon frowned. "Rum thing about exes; one doesn't get over them as easily as expected. You think it's long since done with, that you have no more feelings one way or the other, that there have been others since, and that you're both better off. But then something brings your former spouse into the foreground again. You see her, or hear from her, like this letter from Alexandra. And suddenly you're all of a twitter emotionally, as if you were still . . ." He broke off, staring wistfully.

"I know," said Reith. "Old man, I know."

The new Grand Master, Sir Yazman bad-Esb, proved unexpectedly young. It was hard to judge the age of a Krishnan, but Reith guessed this one to be under forty, a third of the normal Krishnan life span.

Sir Yazman cut a handsome figure save for a prominent scar on one side of his face. Because of the frequent duels and tournaments, such scars were almost as common among the Knights of Qarar as the blue-and-orange tunics and hose that formed their uniform. To indicate his rank, the Grand Master's tunic bore cryptic symbols worked in golden thread.

Fallon made introductions. The Grand Master looked uncertainly at the consul before he came around his desk with outstretched hand, saying in halting, mangled Portuguese: "¿Possa—poderei—dar um apêrto de mão?"

"He wants to shake hands," said Reith, "the way we do."

As the ceremony proceeded, Ordway muttered: "Dashed different from the other, eh?"

The Grand Master asked shyly in Mikardandou: "Said I that right, Master Reith? I essay to study the Ertso tongue for future dealings with your kind."

Reith bowed to hide a smile. "I am gratified that

Your Superiority takes such a lively interest in our Terran languages."

"I thank you. My Treasurer, meanwhile, hath set herself to master the English. It were expedient to prepare ourselves to address Terrans in any of their tongues. Pray, state how many such languages there be?"

"The last I heard, sir, about three thousand."

The Grand Master flinched. "Great Bákh! We shall never live to learn so vast a number!"

"Fear not, Your Superiority. Most Terran languages are spoken by small groups only. If you master a few leading ones besides Portuguese—say, English, French, Spanish, and Chinese—you'll be able to communicate with any Terrans you will meet. I note you referred to the Treasurer as 'herself.' What has befallen my friend Sir Kubanan?"

"He hath retired to the home for superannuated Knights. My lady Treasurer now handles all the business of the Republic; and you, of course, will make your financial arrangements with her." The Grand Master beckoned his secretary. "Dáest, kindly fetch Her Sagacity."

After the secretary departed, the Grand Master exchanged pleasantries with the movie executives, Reith and Alicia interpreting. At last the secretary ushered in a handsome Krishnan female, not quite middle-aged, whose breast-baring gown of sky-blue and orange was confined by a winking bejeweled girdle. At the sight of Reith, her antennae quivered.

"Ah, Far-goose!" she cried in tones of arch reproach. "How cruel you are, to pass again and again through Mishé without paying me a visit! It hath been a score of years since we had intimate converse; albeit the memory thereof still burns within my soul! I have had but a glimpse of you betimes, leading your bands of Terrans about our city, and rarely a hasty greeting; that's all. Art afeared of me, dear Far-goose?"

Flushing to the roots of his hair, Reith did not translate this speech. A glance showed that Alicia was struggling to suppress a burst of laughter. Ordway, with a sharp look, muttered: "What's funny, Alicia?"

She shook her head without replying. Mustering his dignity, Reith said: "Your Sagacity, I must watch my charges vigilantly, for they are often as foolish in their ways as Mikardand's commoners can be in theirs. Now permit me to present my associates. . . ."

As White and Ordway bowed awkwardly, Gashigi replied, in English as weird as the Grand Master's Portuguese: "Ah-ee am pa-lee-sed to mit ze guest-ess fa-rom ze Airf."

"Your Sagacity's English is coming along splendidly," said Reith. "But for serious business, it were better for each to speak his native tongue, while Doctor Dyckman and I interpret."

Gashigi made the Krishnan affirmative head motion. "Then let us begin our business forthwith. How soon will this making of a living picture start. . . ?"

Fallon excused himself and vanished. For two hours, Gashigi and Ordway verbally jousted, bandying times, sites, numbers of extras, rates of pay, and problems of logistics. As before, Ordway showed himself a master of complex calculation. Gashigi, equally able, did nearly all the talking on the Krishnan side, now and then turning to the Grand Master to ask: "Ye agree to that, sir, do ye not?"

Each time, Sir Yazman muttered a vague assent. Reith got the impression that the Treasurer had him firmly under her thumb.

By sunset, the negotiators had roughed out a tentative agreement. Gashigi said: "You understand, my noble *Ertsuma*, we must consult with our committees ere we can sign our compact. Neither you nor the Knights are bound as yet. Let us meet again tomorrow at the ninth hour. In the morn, rest and enjoy the sights of

Mishé, which Sir Fergus is well qualified to display for your edification."

The visitors bade farewell, again shaking hands in Terran fashion. The Grand Master said: "Had we known before of your arrival, we had staged a banquet in your honor. As 'tis, that must needs await the morrow. You will dine with us then?"

Assuring the Grand Master that they were delighted with his invitation, and bidding Gashigi a wary good night, Reith shepherded his party back to their quarters in the Citadel.

By prearrangement, the travelers met Anthony Fallon at a tavern in the lower city. This was an ill-lit place with a low ceiling of soot-blackened beams. The room was heavy with the odors of cookery, and the smoke made White cough.

The consul presented a buxom Krishnan female of middle-years, saying: "This is my wife, Paranji. She doesn't speak a word of English, so you can say what you like in that tongue."

Reith looked a question. Smiling, Fallon continued: "Oh, I was married by the most solemn, binding Krishnan rites and have a brace of stepchildren at home. You see, Fergus, it's all very well for the Knights to play at musical beds; but I live among the commoners, who adhere to a moral code that would make Savonarola look like a playboy."

"By Qondyor's toenails, you've certainly changed, Tony!"

"Don't we all—at least, those who get sense with the passing of years? How did your meeting go?"

Reith gave a résumé. "I got the impression that Gashigi rules *that* roost."

Fallon grinned. "You can jolly well say that again! Fact is, the Garma thought Yazman too young and inexperienced. There were a couple of stronger candidates for the office; but since each had about the same

number of partisans, they compromised and made
Yazman Grand Master. He was Gashigi's lover of the
moment, and she saw to it that he made her Treasurer.
Can't say she's not good at her job! Now tell me about
this cinema project of yours."

When Ordway had summarized the script, Fallon
wrinkled his face in distaste. "I might have guessed.
Knights in shiny armor galloping around on ayas; ladies
in bare-tit dresses leaning out of castle windows, and all
that feudal rot."

Ordway bridled. "Rot? Now look here—" He broke
off to cough from the smoke.

"What somebody ought to do," said Fallon firmly, "is
to picture the lives of ordinary Krishnans. You chaps
have no idea of what the lack of modern technology
means to the poor bastards. You pal around with a few
lords and get an entirely false picture of life on this
planet.

"For the vast majority here, life involves a perfectly
appalling amount of drudgery, which bears most heavily on the ordinary women. Your commoner Krishnan
and his wife work their arses off from dawn to dusk, just
trying to stay alive. If they accumulate any surplus, it's
taxed away to support the glittering courts of the dours
and dashts and the Chief Commissar up on the Citadel." Fallon jerked a thumb to indicate the Grand
Master. He continued: "You wonder why these people
stink? Well, if you had to lug all your bath water, a
bucketful at a time, from a well or a street tap or a
fountain, you'd stink, too. They don't read much, even
when they've been to school; why? Ever try to read by
the light of a taper, or one of those little pottery oil
lamps, which is all they can afford? After a quarter-
hour, your eyes smart so you can't go on.

"If you think the folk stink, you should have been
here thirty years ago, before the Interplanetary Council
let in soap technology. After talking about it for years,
the I.C. at last decided that the knowledge of soap and

eyeglasses would do the Krishnans more good than
harm, though Krishnan chauvinists like to claim the
Krishnans invented these things on their own. Things
will improve when the Krishnan Industrial Revolution
really takes off."

"And then," said Ordway, "their population will simply explode, so they'll end up with more poor, hungry
people."

Fallon shrugged. "Perhaps, unless they show better
sense about population control than Terrans did in the
past. They certainly won't become better off at their
present level of technics. So what you cinema wallahs
should do—"

"And who on Earth," snapped Ordway, "is going to
queue up to see a flick on the woes of a Krishnan
housewife who has to haul her dishwashing water from
the well? Most moviegoers want to forget sordid reality.
They want romance—adventure. Anyway, that's what
we're paid to give 'em, and by God's foreskin, that's
what they shall get!"

At the moment, dinner arrived. Reith was agreeably
surprised to find the meal simple but excellent; the
roast shaihan was done just right. Fallon's Krishnan
wife asked a question in Mikardandou. Turning to
Paranju, Fallon summarized the discussion. Then, with
a crafty smile, he turned back to Ordway, saying: "You
don't think there's romance in the lives of ordinary
Krishnans? I'll show you." From an inside pocket he
pulled and unfolded a mass of newsprint, which proved
to be a newspaper, printed on two large sheets.

"What's that?" asked Ordway.

"The Mishé *Defender* for the current ten-day. Let's
see: 'Headless Body Found.' 'Price of Meat Falls.' 'Mer-
chant Ghanum Knighted.' 'News of Royalty.' Ah, here
we are! This is Alvandi's personal-advice column. People write in about their problems—"

"Hey!" said Reith. "Isn't that the name of the last
Queen of Qirib? The one deposed and exiled?"

"Rather!"

"Is this the old she-yeki herself, or another of the same name? Or a pseudonym?"

"Wish I knew," said Fallon. "They're very secretive at the *Defender.* She's probably alive somewhere, because there's a movement in Qirib to restore her to the throne, as a figurehead constitutional monarch. Ever since Vizman made himself king—"

"Vizman's a king, now?" interrupted Alicia, staring.

"Why, yes. After he'd postponed the promised elections a dozen times, with the usual excuses—public unrest, the masses' political naïveté, etcetera—he announced that, to comply with the unanimous wish of the Qiribuma, he pronounced himself Dour. From what I hear, he's not doing badly as monarchs go; he's abolished slavery for one thing. But, I understand, lots of Qiribuma go about muttering that, if we've got to have a monarch, it should at least be a legitimate one. Hence the push to restore Alvandi.

"By the way, Alicia, you must certainly have made an impression on him. When he was here last year on a state visit, he asked me if I could round up any pictures of you. Seems he has a collection of old photographs, and he's having your portrait painted from them."

"Hasn't he taken a wife yet?"

"No; still unmarried. They tell me he spends time every day just looking at these photos of you. If you want to be a queen—"

"Let's not go into that," said Reith sharply, aware of the painful memories that mention of the former President Vizman of Qirib would evoke in Alicia. Her one-night liason with the Krishnan politician, though undertaken for idealistic reasons, had played a part in Reith's refusal to remarry her. "Do read us the questions and answers in Alvandi's column. They'll give us a window on the local culture and perhaps a laugh or two as well."

"Okay. Do your clients understand Mikardandou?"

"Practically speaking, no."

"Then I shall translate as I go." Slowly, pausing from time to time for the right word, Fallon read: " 'Dear Alvandi: My suitor wishes me to adopt that disgusting, perverted, unsanitary Terran custom called 'kissing.' He refuses to set our wedding date unless I do. How can I change his mind? Signed, Revolted.'

" 'Dear Revolted: You probably can't. Either learn to like the practice or find another suitor. The act doesn't seem to have hurt the Terrans.'

" 'Dear Alvandi: I am a tailor's apprentice, about to become journeyman; and I have stupidly plighted my troth to two young ladies at once. The first time, it was the night of the three moons; the second, I had a drop too much. Neither knows of the other. Both my fiancées' fathers have sharp swords. I have put off the dates of the weddings until one father muses aloud what parts he would amputate from any youth who trifled with his little girl's affections. The other father merely sits sharpening his sword and glaring when I come to call. What shall I do? Signed, Cornered.'

" 'Dear Cornered: I hear there are openings for journeymen tailors in Ghulindé, the capital of Qirib, now that some Qiribuma have taken to wearing tailored garments instead of the traditional shawl pinned over one shoulder. The alternative, perhaps impractical, would be to take your betrotheds to the Khaldoni lands, where bigamy is legal.' "

Alicia put in: "If he followed that last suggestion, he'd have to be careful to treat both wives equally. The Khaldonians are fussy about that. When I interviewed King Ainkhist's wives for *Women of a Khaldoni Harem*, their main complaint was that, being the nation's alpha male, he paid no attention to the law."

"Do you want to hear more?" Fallon asked. Assured of their lively interest, he continued: "Dear Alvandi: Eighty years ago, my husband wedded me. In those days, when I was in heat he could make love fifteen or twenty times a night. Now he can barely manage three or four. How can I strengthen his ability? Signed, Old but Still Ardent.'

" 'Dear Ardent: At his age, three or four times is phenomenal. Thank Bákh and stop grumbling.'

" 'Dear Alvandi: The other night, at a banquet, I sat between my present husband and my former spouse. Not having seen the latter for years, I was intensely curious as to how he had fared. Hence nearly all my conversation was with my ex-husband, while my present husband sat glowering. Afterwards my present husband was furious, saying I was free to leave him and return to the other, and similar indecencies. Now he sleeps apart. What should I do? I meant no harm. Signed, Well-intentioned.'

" 'Dear Well-intentioned: When he gets over his present snit, be sure hereafter, at gatherings, to give him at least equal time with any other male, including friends, lovers, and former husbands.' "

Reith muttered in Mikardandou to Alicia: "I could have used Alvandi's help in Rosid, when you and the princess had me up a tree."

Fallon resumed: " 'Dear Alvandi: Last year my husband left me for another, and I divorced him. Lately he has been coming round, saying he and the other woman have broken up for good. He takes me out, flatters me, and even makes love to me; but he does not say whether he wishes me to take him back. Secretly I still love him; besides, I've learned that good husbands are not easily come by. How can I discover his true intentions? Signed, Forlorn.'

" 'Dear Forlorn: Why not ask him?' "

Fallon glanced up, expecting another outburst of laughter. Instead, he perceived that Reith and Alicia were looking, not at him, but at each other with set faces. This last tale, though not quite a replay of his and Alicia's stormy marital history, hit Reith too close to home for comfort; and he guessed that it struck Alicia the same way.

"Oh!" said Fallon, sensitive to his listeners' mood. "I'm sorry—ah—"

"Marvelous evening, Tony," said Reith, rising in a determined manner. "But we must get back to our digs. It's been a long day, with another just ahead of us."

When Reith kissed Alicia good night and went to his room in the Citadel, he found a note tucked under the door. It read:

The Lady Gashigi wishes to see Sir Fergus at the third hour tomorrow, alone and in confidence. Come to Suite Twelve in the Domo Building. Destroy this paper.

After breakfast, Reith left the visitors' building and made his way to Gashigi's private quarters. He found her stretched out on a chaise-longue, wearing a filmy wrap of lavender gauze.

"Far-goose!" she cried, rising and spreading welcoming arms. "Come hither, you wretched alien!"

Reith submitted to her smothering embrace. It was plain to be seen that Gashigi had put on weight.

"Oh, Fergus!" she gushed. "I've had scores of lovers in the intervening years, but none hath erased the memory of our marvelous night. After a lusty Terran, all males of my species seem to lack . . ."

"Very kind of you," interrupted Reith, casting about for an idea to divert the proposal that he feared would come next. But, with the inexorability of an avalanche, it came. She said: "Could we not repeat our magical tryst, this very night?"

"I fear you'd be disappointed. After all, I'm twenty years older now—"

"Fiddle-faddle, good my sir! So forsooth am I, and I find my passions not a whit abated; and 'tis plain to see that your eye be as bright and your step as jaunty as ever. I'll wager you can pleasure a lady as featly as any wight."

"There are difficulties," he muttered, groping for an excuse. The thought of copulating with Gashigi had become repugnant to him.

"Is it that you and the yellow-haired doxy be lovers?"

"No, we are not. But . . ."

"Then what hinders? I can smooth your way to the Grand Master's approval."

"Isn't he your present lover?"

"Aye, but what thereof? He knows I seek pleasure elsewhere, and he'd better not cavil thereat!"

"How about Khabur, the fellow who was going to carve me up?"

"Dead. We parted at last, years agone, and he took up with another lady. He caught her in full futter with another knight and stabbed the libertine to death. Then a friend of the dead man challenged Khabur and slew him in a duel."

"Seems to me," said Reith dryly, "that with such a high mortality among the Garma, the Knights would have trouble keeping up their numbers."

"Aye, 'tis true. But you evade my question. I'll put it plain: Give me what I beg, and your clients shall make their living picture in Mikardand with our aid. Deny me, and Yazman shall refuse your simplest request. Grasp you the nub?"

"I understand and will give the matter thought."

"Think all you like, dear Fergus, but my promises stand. I shall expect you here within the hour that marks the close of tonight's entertainment. Unless you'd fain demonstrate now—"

"To my infinite regret, I've promised to take my people sightseeing. They await me below." Reith bowed himself out quickly, before Gashigi could seize him in another octopuslike embrace.

*   *   *

A sorely-tried travel guide showed his trio through the Citadel's miniature museum, translating the captions on the exhibits. Then he piled them into his carriage and drove them around the city. Ordway, little heeding the historic sights of Mishé, gazed fixedly at Alicia with the eyes of a hungry wolf. White craned his neck this way and that, from time to time exclaiming: "That street scene would make a splendid shot. . . . The place in the script where Attila has hero meet heroine at the vegetable stall: wouldn't that market over there be just right for it? Cyril, I'm talking to you!"

Back in the Citadel, White said, "I've got to write up some notes on what we've seen. Cyril, come along and help me remember."

When they had departed, Reith tapped on Alicia's door. "Lish, may I speak with you a minute?"

"Sure; come in. What's got you in a tizzy?"

Nervously cracking his joints, Reith paced about Alicia's two-room suite. "You know I was gone for an hour this morning? Well, I was paying a command visit on our Treasurer. . . . No, she didn't seduce me, though she tried. What happened was this. . . ." Reith summarized his talk with Gashigi.

Icily, Alicia asked: "Why are you telling me this?"

"Because I want to ask you, seriously: if I gave her what she wants, how would you feel about it?"

Alicia's sky-blue eyes widened, and she sniffed her displeasure. "Good heavens, what a question! It doesn't matter to me, which she-Krishnan you copulate with. I should think a man in your situation would leap at the chance. As I remember, you did it with her once before, after we . . . Go ahead and hump her till she yells, 'Enough!' "

"Lish, you haven't answered my question. Would you, deep down in, disapprove?"

"Fergus!" she said in a voice pregnant with exasperation. "Let's understand a few things. Once you and I were married. Later, when we were no longer married, we were lovers for a while. But all that's long ago and far away. Now we're not married; we're not engaged; we're not lovers. We're nothing but old friends—at least, I hope we are—and business associates.

"So your sex life is no affair of mine. I have no more right to object to your laying Gashigi than you'd have to stop me from inviting Cyril Ordway in for the night. So do what you want and just don't talk to me about it!"

"You still haven't given a straight answer to my question. *Would you mind?*"

"Would you mind if I didn't mind?"

Some of the tenseness went out of Reith, and he gave a sly chuckle. "Now you've put me on the spot! Let's say me ego would be chipped. So what's the answer to my question?"

Alicia brought her fist down on the night table, making the brass candlestick jump. "Damn it, stop badgering me! Go ahead and fuck your big, blowsy hominoid, and see if I care! You—you alpha male!"

Her lip trembled, and a tear ran down her cheek. Reith murmured: "Oh, darling!" and gathered her into his arms. After he had petted her and stroked her shining hair, Alicia shook herself free and wiped away the tears. She said: "Fergus Reith, sometimes I hate you for being the only person in the Galaxy who can make me cry. This is like a replay of my affair with Vizman, only with—" She broke off, clapping a hand to her mouth.

"With rôles reversed? Except that—"

She seized his arms and gave him a little shake. "Oh, please! Don't talk about it! I was a fool to mention it. . . ."

Reith enfolded her and held her silently for a few seconds. Then he bent down, saying: "Lish darling, please, give me some honest advice on handling this she-octopus. Right now, I no more want to frig her than if she were something that crawled out of the Great Koloft Swamp. I feel that if I so much as let her kiss me, I'd turn into an enchanted frog.

"Feeling that way, I doubt if I could give satisfaction in any event—even if I did it with your blessing—and there goes your movie. So what should I do? Weave a circle round her thrice and close my eyes in holy dread?"

Alicia looked up at him. "Fergus, I have a marvelous idea!"

He released her. "What's that?"

"To hear Cyril talk, you'd think he was Lothario, Don Juan, and Casanova all rolled into one. Of course we know better than to take such boasts seriously; but how would it be if you came down with a diplomatic illness and sent him to Gashigi in your place?"

"That's my brilliant superwoman! Even if he doesn't satisfy Gashigi, at least it'll stop him from stripping you with his eyes every time he looks at you!"

Next morning, Ordway did not appear for breakfast. Later, when Reith was in the courtyard directing the harnessing of the ayas and the stowage of baggage, Ordway came out; moving as if still half asleep. When he came close, Reith asked quietly: "How did it go?"

Ordway rolled his eyes. "God, man, the bloody popsie's insatiable! If my—uh—capacity hadn't given out, we should still be at it. I'm not that Spanish bloke they tell about, who could roger day and night without letup. What was his name? Something like Donald June."

"You mean Don Juan?"

"I suppose so. Anyway, I did my best." Grinning, Ordway dug an elbow into Reith's ribs. "Know what she said? That she preferred me to you, and not just for my beautiful whiskers. She's commanded me, on pain of flaying alive, to wait upon her whenever we pass through Mishé."

"Bully for you!" said Reith. "Are you packed to go?"

"Oh, hell, I'd forgot we're leaving! Half a mo' and I shall be with you." Ordway departed at a run.

Fallon appeared, saying, "Just dropped by to see you off."

"Keeping an Argus eye on all the Terrans in your bailiwick, eh?"

"I try, I say, old chap, when Alicia Dyckman was on Krishna before, she had the reputation of being a sort of female drill-sergeant."

"Who knows better than I?" said Reith.

"But yesterday she seemed pleasant enough; if anything, rather subdued. And still single after all these years—but I forgot; to her the lapse of time is only a fraction of what it is to us. Mark my words, Fergus: she won't stay unattached long!"

"Maybe not. Here she comes now. Give me your bag, Alicia."

VI

Cyril Ordway

On their second night out of Mishé, they stopped at Vasabád, the third largest city of Mikardand. Of Vasabád's three inns, Keith tried two before he found one where he could provide Alicia with a room of her own. After they had all settled in, he knocked on her door. "Hey, Wart Hog! I'm giving the boys a little walking tour. Like to come along?"

"You just bet!"

While more impressive than Qou, Vasabád was still a small town. Its sights were nearly exhausted when they came upon the little temple of Bákh. White said: "Fergus, let's have a look. Can we go in?"

"I think so. They're at vespers; but I know the priest, who won't mind if we're quiet."

They found the sparse congregation standing, there being no pews, while an elderly Krishnan priest recited the lesson and a pretty young Krishnan acolyte illustrated the recitation by manipulating a triad of symbolic objects: a mirror, a sword, and a vessel of water. These she lifted from the altar one by one and, with a dancer's grace, gazed at herself in the mirror, clove the air with the sword, and flicked droplets of water from the bowl in the four cardinal directions. Ordway whispered: "I say, do they sacrifice virgins here in the dark of the moons?"

Reith shook his head. "Neither in the light or the dark of the moons; though a cult in Balhib, I understand, went in for that sort of thing a few years back. I sometimes wish the Krishnans hadn't gotten quite so civilized; I know some people I'd like to sacrifice." He gave Ordway a stony stare.

"Our script calls for human sacrifice," Ordway went on, oblivious. "I always thought it a foolish waste of a perfectly serviceable woman."

Reith cocked an eyebrow. "What's your script got to do with the real Krishna? For that matter, what's any movie got to do with real life?"

Ordway sighed. "Fergus, if you were in the business, you might make first-class documentaries; but in entertainment you'd be an utter washout."

The priest finished his reading, covered the sacred objects, led a hymn, and dismissed his worshipers. As they straggled out, Reith brought his Terrans forward. He and the priest grasped thumbs, and Reith introduced his companions to the Reverend Vizram.

"I don't see anything here for our picture," muttered White, peering about. "Nice little temple, but the one in Mishé has it beat."

"A moment, I pray, Master Reef," said the priest. "As ye know, Sifad's comet attains its greatest brilliance tonight."

"I'd forgotten," confessed Reith. "The sky has been so overcast, I've never even seen this comet."

"The sky hath cleared as even veils the day. Tell me, pray, what opinion have ye learned Terrans anent comets? The astrologers make a great to-do thereof, saying they bear messages from the gods. Some predict this world's destruction; others, a thousand years of peace and plenty. What think ye?"

"Terran space ships," replied Reith, "have found comets to be nothing but stones, dust, and frozen water.

We consider them natural phenomena and not signals from the powers unseen." He paused as an idea struck him. "Isn't the platform atop your temple the highest structure in Vasabád?"

"Aye. The cult that owned the temple, ere we servants of Bákh acquired it, used the building for their astrological observations."

Smiling guilelessly, Reith asked: "Would you mind if we returned after dark to view the comet from the platform?"

"I shall be glad to unlock the temple doors, Master Reef," said the aged priest. "Pray, present yourselves within an hour of Roqir's setting, and knock thrice."

Reith did not translate this exchange for the benefit of his male clients. He was less interested in comet watching than he was in finding a moment alone with Alicia, although he was unsure of just what he meant to say. Walking back to the inn, he was so absorbed in composing and discarding little speeches that he was unaware of Ordway's absence until, nearing the inn, Alicia asked: "Where's Cyril?"

White explained. "He ducked back into the temple. Said for us to go on; he could find his own way back."

"Now what's that idiot up to?" growled Reith with foreboding.

"There he is!" exclaimed Alicia. "Somebody's chasing him!"

Ordway had appeared around a corner, his short legs pumping. Behind him rushed a crowd of Krishnans, waving clubs, brandishing knives, and yelling threats and curses. Ordway reached the trio of Terrans just ahead of the pursuers. He dodged behind Reith and seized the slack of Reith's jacket to use the guide as a shield.

Reith clapped a hand to his sword, but common sense told him not to draw it. While he might take one or two Krishnans with him, against such odds he stood no chance. Assuming a loftily commanding expression, he raised a hand.

"Quiet, please!" he shouted. The mob continued to scream: ". . . rape our maiden . . ."

". . . filthy *dazg* . . . flay the barbarian alive . . ."

As Reith called again, without effect, for quiet, the elderly priest of Bákh pushed forward, waving the sword the acolyte had used in the rituals. He tried to get at the cowering Ordway. White and Alicia hovered anxiously on the fringe of the mob, ignoring gibes.

Reith bent towards the Reverend Vizram's ear. "Tell them to quiet down, so I can find out what happened!"

The priest endeavored, with no more success. On a sudden inspiration, Reith called out: "Sing!" His voice rolled out in a familiar hymn:

> *"Trust Bákh, by whom all things were made;*
> *Hold fast thy faith; be not afraid. . . ."*

After the first line, the priest joined in. Then more and more of the mob added their voices, until all were singing. At the pause at the end of the stanza, Reith called out: "If all of you good people will be quiet, we shall get to the bottom of this. What happened, Father Vizram?"

The priest replied: "The fleshy Terran accosted my virgin daughter, who serves as acolyte. He made some obscene proposal in's Terran tongue. When she would have fled his lechery, he seized and would fain have distrained her; but I heard her cries for help."

Reith pulled Ordway out from behind him, the latter gasping: "What—what's the—the old padre saying?"

"Tell me your story."

Ordway's speech had become thick Cockney. "I saw this bonzer squid and remembered something I read, 'ow in ancient times the temples was combined viv 'ore 'ouses. Gels earned their dowries that way. So, bein' 'orny, I asks her, what's the price of a quick one? Since she didn't understand English, nor I 'er 'eathen speech,

I tried sign language. When she starts off, I grabs her arm, thinkin' she 'adn' got it. Then she shrieks, and her gov' and some other wogs comes runnin'."

With a forced-air composure, Reith said to the priest, "My client was so deeply impressed by your service that he wished to give all his money to the temple. Since he and your daughter had no speech in common, a regrettable misunderstanding arose." He turned to Ordway and said in English: "Give him all your cash—every last arzu. Don't argue, or I'll let 'em tear you to pieces!"

The priest accepted the money, thanked Ordway, and apologized for the contretemps. The crowd broke up and drifted away. As the Terrans reentered the inn, Alicia said: "Fergus, I want to apologize."

"What for?"

"Once, back when we—when I went on your tour, I scolded you soundly for mistranslating the talk between one of your tourists and a Krishnan. It was beastly of me, especially since I had to do the same thing when the reporter from the Mishé *Defender* interviewed us."

"Really? It's been so long, I'd forgotten."

"Not so long for me! Anyway, you were right. If you'd truthfully translated Cyril's words, we'd all be weltering in our gore."

"Lish, I believe you've changed more in two years than I have in twenty! In the old days, you never admitted you were wrong about anything."

"It's not the only thing I've been wrong about." She glanced around. "We'd better get to our table, before our host serves all the best cuts to the others!"

At dinner, Ordway grumbled: "I say: Fergus, couldn't you have at least bargained him down a bit? This leaves me stony until we get to Novo. It's not fair—"

Reith brought his fist down with a bang, making the goblets jump. "You fat-headed schmuck! You two-legged prick! God damn it, I thought you'd learned your lesson in the bathhouse at Rosid, but you never learn. If you're so stupid—"

"Now see here, I won't put up with—"

"Shut up, you blithering ass! If it weren't for the contract, I'd take the carriage and go off, leaving you on your own out here in the boonies. One more whine out of you, and I'll do it anyway, and to hell with your movie!"

Ordway subsided, staring morosely at his plate. The ensuing silence was finally broken by White: "Cyril, I can lend you some money till we get back to base." He turned towards Reith. "Fergus, I must say you showed steel nerves, standing up to that mob."

Reith shrugged. "Anything else would have been riskier."

"Were we in real danger?"

"Judge for yourself. A few years ago we had a gaggle of Russian tourists. The guide, Vera Yurieva, was a good kid; but some of her geese were real oafs. You know the temple of the mother goddess Varzai in Mishé? There's a basin outside for ritual hand-washing before going in to worship. A couple of these gloops mistook it for a public urinal. A mob chased them to the corner where Vera was lecturing the others, who ran for it. Vera stood her ground and tried to explain, but the mob beat her unconscious and left her for dead. She was moons recovering."

As Ordway and White ate in glum silence, a new group of diners entered and took a table near the doorway. Five were tough-looking Krishnans in divided kilts and uniform jackets of vaguely military appearance, which bore a cipher that Reith could not quite discern.

The sixth newcomer was a big, burly Earthman disguised as a Krishnan, with false antennae and ear points. So carefully had his makeup been applied that most Krishnans and Terrans, too, could have been deceived by it unless they scrutinized him closely. The man's

garb was like the others save that his jacket was covered
with glittering spangles and bore gold-braided epaulets.

Reith whispered, "Don't look now, Lish; but dip me
in guano if that isn't my old pal Enrique Schlegel."

"The man Tony Fallon mentioned, the one you had a
fight with!"

"The same."

"What do we do?"

"He hasn't made a hostile move yet. Let's eat quietly
and hope he doesn't notice us." After they had finished
and left the dining room, Reith sought out his Krishnan
assistants. "Doctor Dyckman and I are going to the
Temple of Bákh after dark. We want you two lads with
us."

"*Ohé!*" said Zerré in a disappointed tone. "Timásh
and I had an engagement after supper."

"How long will it take?"

"Belike an hour."

"It will still be light. Have your fun, but be sure to
join us here before dark. And come armed!"

"Master Fergus!" protested Timásh. "I am no swash-
buckler, but only a peaceful shaihan-herd."

"Bring those brush knives you two carry. They're as
good as half-swords." Reith turned back to Alicia and
muttered: "Our boys are going out whoring, but they
should be back in time."

Ordway asked: "What's all this mumbling in heathen
tongues?"

"Nothing," said Reith. "Alicia and I are going out this
evening. When you get to your room, bolt the door;
there are some bad characters about."

Reith and Alicia retired to Reith's room and locked
themselves in. For the next hour, Reith occupied himself with calculating expenses, while she organized her
sociological notes. Silence hung like a rain cloud. Finally Reith glanced at the window.

"It's dark outside," he said. "Our randy helpers should

be back by now." He stepped to the door, opened it carefully, and satisfied himself that the two Krishnans were not in their quarters.

Another half-hour passed, and Reith became restless. At last Alicia snapped her notebook shut. "Oh, for heaven's sake, Fearless, let's go! We can leave a message for your lads to follow when they arrive."

Scowling, Reith shook his head. "If it were just me, I'd say to hell with Schlegel and take my chances. But I can't take that risk with you."

"Don't be a timorous beastie! We've been in and out of a lot of tight places together, and I've never seen a comet. I'll take this along." She dug into her traveling bag and brought out a crossbow pistol. "Besides, if we just sit here, Schlegel's men could break down the door and come in for us. And if we wait much longer, Father Vizram will decide we're not coming and lock up again. Either we go now, or we check out and take to the road tonight!"

"I hate to cut and run," growled Reith.

"Then let's go templing!" She picked up her handbag and the crossbow pistol. "Sivird sold me this little beauty."

"All right," said Reith, with an uneasy feeling that, even though Alicia had discarded her former imperious, dictatorial manner, she still managed to get her way in most things. They went quietly downstairs and left word with the innkeeper to send Timásh and Zerré to the temple when the two Krishnans appeared. They saw no sign of Schlegel and his minions.

The observation platform atop the Temple of Bákh was a rectangular terrace, about two by eight meters, paved with flagstones and protected by a waist-high guard rail. Access to the structure was by a ladder and a trapdoor. At each end of the terrace, an ornamental spire rose from the slate roof for several meters more.

From the edges of the terrace, the roof sloped away on all sides.

Reith and Alicia arrived, breathing hard from the climb, as the last glow of twilight was vanishing. Above them, the boat-shaped crescent of huge Karrim illumined the landscape with the argentic brilliance of Terra's full moon. Golnaz, the second moon, was out of sight; while little Sheb, the most distant, appeared but slightly larger than Venus seen from Earth on a clear night. High in the northern sky hung the long, pallid whisk broom of Sifad's comet, named in honor of the Gozashtando astrologer who first recorded it.

Reith and Alicia gazed silently. At last Reith said: "Karrim sets in an hour. We ought to wait, because the comet will look much brighter without the competition."

They sat on a low stone bench with their backs against the masonry of one of the spires. For a while they were content to enjoy the heavenly spectacle of two moons, a comet, and the gleaming stars. Now and then a night-flying aqebat, pursuing arthropod prey, whirred overhead.

As Karrim neared the horizon, Reith slid an arm around Alicia, who responded warmly to a kiss. He cleared his throat and spoke hesitantly: "Lish—ah—I've been thinking."

"Yes?"

"Well—uh—I'd like to know more about your plans for the fut—"

"What's that?" said Alicia, suddenly straightening up as the clatter of people climbing the ladder broke the silence.

"Maybe it's the boys," said Reith.

"And maybe not!" She sprang to her feet. "We'd better hold the lid down till we know for sure!"

Alicia started for the trapdoor, with Reith a pace behind her. Before they reached it, the trapdoor flew up and Enrique Schlegel emerged, sword in hand. Four armed Krishnans followed him.

"You are Reith, are you not?" growled Schlegel in accented English.

Reith had drawn his own sword. "That's my name. What about it?"

"Is it true what I hear, that you are guiding representatives of a Terran cinema company, in order a motion picture on this world to make?"

"Yes. So what?"

"This I cannot allow."

"And who in hell—"

"I am the protector of native Krishnan culture! I know your cinema people. They will make a disgraceful burlesque of Krishnan life, giving Terrans a contempt for us. If the foul blow you struck me in Mishé were not enough reason . . ."

Schlegel threw himself forward, barking as he did so in Mikardandou: "Seize the strumpet! I will deal with the barbarian!"

Schlegel lunged at Reith, while the four Krishnans leaped towards Alicia. Her crossbow pistol twanged, and the foremost Krishnan doubled over with a howl.

Reith parried Schlegel's lunge and sent a quick counterthrust at Schlegel's broad chest. A mail shirt beneath the jacket stopped Reith's point.

Schlegel's three remaining followers sprang upon Alicia. Lacking time to recock the pistol, a task requiring muscle, she received the first assailant with a swing of the handbag. The bag struck the Krishnan's flattish face with a crunch. Krishnan blood, black in the moonlight, spattered as the blow flung the Krishnan back against the rail. His legs flew up, and he flipped over the railing. Then he slid rattling down the slates and off the roof. A shriek was followed by a solid thud.

The other two got their hands on Alicia before she could aim another swing. They wrenched away the handbag and pistol and pummeled and kicked her, while she fought like a wildcat.

Reith and Schlegel traded lunge for lunge, thrust for

thrust, and cut for cut. Reith found his opponent less skilled at fencing than himself but immensely strong. His strength, together with his light armor, evened the odds.

The swords whirled, flashed in the moonlight, struck sparks, and clashed with harsh resonance. The furious pace of the combat slowed as Reith and Schlegel both began to pant.

One of the Krishnans shouted: "Master! Give us leave to slay this she-demon! She hath kicked me in the crotch!"

"Do but hold her fast," panted Schlegel, who had never fully recovered his breath from the long climb to the platform.

"The *kargán* hath poked me in the eye!" shrilled the other Krishnan. "Methinks I'm half blinded!"

"Hold her whilst I account for this Terran!" snarled Schlegel. "Then shall she pay her just dues!"

For an instant Reith and Schlegel faced each other immobile, with their blades crossing but not touching. They gasped for breath. Schlegel's forehead sparkled with moonlit sweat, and Reith supposed that his did likewise.

"Someone comes!" cried one of the Krishnans.

Behind Schlegel, Reith glimpsed movement in the semidarkness, but he had no time for scrutiny. Schlegel threw himself forward, trying to beat down Reith's guard by the sheer weight and fury of his attack. Reith passed up openings on Schlegel's torso because of the mail shirt; but at last he homed a thrust at Schlegel's face, laying open one cheek.

"*Du Schurke!*" panted Schlegel as the whole side of his face became masked with blood.

From beyond Schlegel came the voices of Alicia, Timásh, and Zerré, and the meaty sound of brush knives biting into flesh. There were cries and groans and the thud of bodies. Simultaneously came a solid clank;

Schlegel reeled sideways, dropped his sword, and tumbled over the rail as the first Krishnan had done.

Alicia stood disheveled in the moonlight, holding her handbag by its strap. Behind her, Timásh and Zerré bent over the three Krishnan bodies, finishing off the one whom Alicia had wounded with a bolt from her crossbow pistol.

As Reith quickly perceived, when his herdsmen had emerged from the trapdoor, the two Krishnans holding Alicia had tried to defend themselves while retaining their grip on her. Hence they had readily been wounded. Wrenching free, Alicia had snatched up her handbag and struck Schlegel from behind on the side of the head.

Satisfying himself that his attackers were dead, Reith wiped his blade on a Krishnan's garments, sheathed his sword, and cradled Alicia in his arms. At last he glowered at his Krishnan employees.

"And where were you, my fine fellows, when we were in dire straits?"

Timásh and Zerré hung their heads and scuffed their feet. Zerré said: "A thousand pardons, Sir Fergus. 'Twas wrong of us, I know. We expected to be entertained by two ladies, but lo! We arrived to find but one. So we—ah—"

"Took turns," said Reith. "Now get to work. We've disposed of these rascals, but there were others. Doctor Dyckman knocked two off the roof."

"Terran women must be deadly creatures," muttered Timásh.

"Those whereof ye speak we saw not," said Zerré. "But we did find one standing guard at the temple door. When he would fain have barred our entry, we slew him like an unha for the stew pan."

Reith inspected the fallen Krishnans. "Pitch these bodies over yonder rail, so they shall fall in the street. Collect their weapons and follow me. I shall go down to see what happened to those two we knocked off the roof."

In the temple garden, they found the missing Krishnan groaning. Both legs lay twisted among the crushed shrubbery. The priest and his daughter fluttered helplessly about, wringing their hands.

"Sir Fergus!" cried the Reverend Vizram. "What tally of horror and bloodshed hath polluted my sacred fane?"

Reith recounted what he knew. Vizram said, "Pray, slay not this poor wight, villain though he be! There hath been enough of slaughter."

"I won't kill him," said Reith. "For one thing, we shall need him to testify tomorrow, lest we be charged with a crime. Help us to carry him in; I know enough first aid to set his legs. Then I'll send my men out to find the watch, to collect the bodies. Where is the *Ertsu* who led them? He, too, fell off."

A search of the grounds found no Schlegel, but only a smashed shrub into which the Terran had fallen. "Dupulán takes care of his own," grumped Reith. "Bet he didn't even sprain an ankle."

Back at the inn, as Reith and Alicia climbed the stairs, White and Ordway appeared. As they regarded the tour guide in the lamplight, White exclaimed: "Fergus, your hands are all bloody! What's happened?"

Ordway, peering at Alicia, said: "My God, what have you two been up to? Has Fergus been beating you up, Alicia? I'm no hero, but I won't stand by and let anyone mistreat a white woman—"

Reith interrupted. "Just a little difficulty. We had to kill a few people, that's all. Alicia took some bruises in the fight, but nothing's broken."

White and Ordway exchanged appalled glances. " 'Had to kill a few people,' just like that!" said Ordway. "Human or Krishnan?"

"Both; but the Terran got away. The casualties were

four Krishnans dead and one disabled. I won't even bother to notch my hilt for them."

"Cyril," said White, "I think we'd better be pretty damned careful how we speak to Mr. Reith henceforth. Fergus, what'll happen now?"

"We may be a day or two late getting back to Novo," said Reith. "I have to appear in court tomorrow, to convince the magistrate it was self-defense."

"Are we likely to be stuck here," asked White, "while you're in jail waiting for the guy with the mask and the ax?"

Reith shrugged. "You can never be sure, but it's not likely. Krishnans take a relaxed view of homicide among Terrans. They figure that if Earthmen kill other Earthmen, that's their problem. Excuse us; we've got to clean up."

In her room, Alicia dropped her handbag with a heavy thud, took off her shirt, and lugubriously examined her face and body in the mirror. "Oh, dear!" she sighed. "What horrible bruises! I can put makeup over the shiner; but this cut lip I can't disguise."

"It'll all be healed up by the time we get back to Novo," said Reith, picking up Alicia's handbag and hefting it. "What's in this, Lish? A flatiron?"

She opened the handbag and took out a spherical, tightly packed leather sack. Reith fingered the sack, saying, "Coins?"

She nodded. "It comes in handy with tumescent males."

"No wonder you knocked those guys off the roof! I'd better say good night before you decide to use it on me!"

Leisurely Krishnan legal proceedings put them two days behind schedule. As a result, they reached the village of Zinjaban, in the westerly province of the same name, seven days after leaving Mishé. Since rainfall hereabouts was less than in the central and eastern parts of Mikardand, the landscape was open, sparsely covered by many-colored Krishnan analogues of grass and herbs. Trees, with gaudy trunks of ruby and turquoise and amethyst, were confined to gallery forests along the streams, while elsewhere clumps of spiny bushes hugged the bare brown soil. As they traveled west, the riotous colors of the well-watered eastern provinces gradually faded to pastels and sober greenish grays.

The village boasted one tiny inn. Reith signed in for his party and then discovered that the second floor had only three bedrooms, a large one occupied by the innkeeper and his family, and two small guest chambers, each of which contained one double bed.

Before, Reith had always obtained a private room for Alicia. Now Timásh and Zerré made ready to stretch out in the common room below, while Ordway and White bore their belongings into one of the two available bedrooms.

Reith and Alicia halted at the door of the remaining room. She glanced in, then faced him with an enigmatic expression on her classic features. Reith thought she had gone pale under her light tan, but he could not tell whether her countenance betokened apprehension or anticipation, hope or fear.

For an instant, Reith was balanced on a knife edge of indecision. The male animal in him urged him one way, while his inbred caution, and suspicion that all of Alicia's fangs had not yet been drawn, pushed him in the other. His neo-Puritan conscience warned him that, the instant they bedded together, the brother-and-sister relationship he had been cultivating would not have the chance of a snowball in Hishkak.

Then Ordway, peering out of his doorway, gave a salacious smirk. Alicia looked at the production manager with distaste, then said coolly: "Fergus, we must have an understanding. . . ."

"I already understand," said Reith reading into her

tone an uncertainty like his own. "Don't worry about me. Hey, Zerré!"

"Aye, sir?" The Krishnan looked up from below stairs.

"Get out my sleeping bag and hand it up, will you please?"

Reith entered the other men's bedroom and threw his sleeping bag on the floor. Ordway said: "Good God, man, you're bunking in with *us?*"

"Yep."

Ordway shook his head. "Either you're out of your calabash, mate, or you're a bloody neo-Puritan."

"Call it a little of both," said Reith, stamping on a many-legged scuttler that raced across the floor.

Reith was already kicking himself for having ducked a chance to clarify his anomalous relationship with his former wife, his desire for whom waxed daily stronger. But he was too stubborn to reverse his snap decision and too protective of his dignity to present Ordway with ammunition for lewd jokes and innuendoes. Besides, he hated to give satisfaction to busybodies, like Strachan and Fallon, who were doubtless fantasizing about a romantic reunion between the ill-starred Reiths.

Next morning, Reith and White went location hunting. Alicia said she was tired and wanted to repair some clothes. Ordway also begged off on the ground that he could never learn to ride a six-legged gnu at his time of life. Reith told his Krishnans to saddle three ayas, so that Timásh could go along in case of accident.

The trio rode downstream along the Khoruz, circling about and examining landscapes that might serve as movie-sequence sites. In the afternoon, they worked upstream from the village.

The location manager, who made frequent notes and took pictures with his Hayashi ring camera, was becoming a passable aya rider. The Krishnan sun was fast turning his pale skin swarthy, and he could even exchange greetings in Mikardandou.

When they returned to the inn, White announced

that he had found several good sites. The next day, Alicia said to Reith: "Fergus, I'm coming with you. I don't care to be left alone with our resident sex maniac again."

"What! Has that dreg—"

"No, no, he hasn't laid a hand on me. But he fixes me with his glittering eye and says things like: 'If that skinny ex of yours hasn't got any balls, there are others who have!' or 'If that's all the enterprise he's got, no wonder you gave him the burlap!' "

Clenching a pair of knobby fists, Reith interrupted. "I'll punch his leering face in! I'll dance on his recumbent form with my climbing boots, the ones with hobnails!"

"No, no! He doesn't mean any harm. He's just a vulgar, pushy little gloop who thinks he's Bákh's gift to women and doesn't like to see them unf—going to waste, as he'd put it. So he drags the subject in by the hair of its crotch. I'm not afraid of him, but he's a bother. At least, don't hit him until the movie's been shot and you're paid off in full!"

"All right; but I still think he'd look better stuffed. I'd like to be the taxidermist, too."

They crossed the Khoruz at the ford near the village and followed the Balhib road, winding through the rugged Qe'bas, until they sighted Castle Kandakh, perched on its elephant-gray crag, with blue-and-orange pennants flying and drawbridge down. A trumpet brayed as the riders clattered into the courtyard. Reith, stiffly formal, presented the Grand Master's letter to the commanding officer, a Sir Litáhn.

To show the party around the fortress, Sir Litáhn called to him a knight with a false beard of a poisonous green. Reith turned to Alicia and quoted:

> *"But I was thinking of a plan*
> *To dye one's whiskers green,*
> *And always use so large a fan*
> *That they could not be seen."*

Viewing the arrow slits and other defensive measures, White became voluble with excitement. "Couldn't be better!" he cried. "Superbly photogenic! A cameraman's dream! Say, Fergus, the morning's not half over, with these long days they have here. Is there anything else we ought to see?"

Reith thought. "A Krishnan friend of mine lives a few hoda west of here. Let's ride down and say hello."

Under the blazing rays of the yellow primary, they trotted westward downgrade along the trans-Qe'ba road. When they walked the ayas to breathe them, Reith explained. "Yekar bad-Sehr is a cousin of the rancher Sainian, whose spread lies southeast of here. It was on his ranch that I helped to discover some kind of fossil reptile, which they say is an important evolutionary link. Remember, Lish?"

"How could I ever forget! What does this Yekar do?"

"Runs a shaihan ranch, like Sainian's, only smaller. I've thought he and I might go into dude ranching together. It would be quite an experience for rich Terran dudes.

"Yekar's spread lies in what used to be Balhibo territory; but when the Qaathians conquered Balhib, the late Grand Master seized the Qe'ba range. So one fine night, Yekar went to bed a Balhibo subject and woke up a Mikardandu."

West of the Qe'bas, the undulating plain wore a drab mantle of sparse vegetation in dull greens, browns, and grays. Yekar, who proved to be a younger cousin of Sainian's wife, welcomed the travelers warmly, and his mate served them a lunch big enough for a hungry yeki. When Reith asked him for news, the rancher replied: "Something is brewing with the Qaathians. Across the border on a clear, windless day, we see distant clouds of dust. I should guess cavalry maneuvers."

"Anything more definite?"

"Nay. For the past year, they've kept the border sealed, save for a few well-guarded crossing points.

They've put up new fences, bishtar-strong, shomal-high, and burha-tight. Their patrols gallop along these barriers day and night. Thus little news gets out."

Back in Zinjaban, Ordway greeted his dusty location team as they dismounted. "I'll wager you've all got sore buns. Any luck, Jack?"

"Absolutely!" said White. "The castle is splendid—very visual."

"D'you think we're finished here?"

"I believe so."

Ordway continued. "Obviously, this lousy little inn won't hold our shooting crew. We shall have to get tents, portable WCs, etcetera. I say, Fergus! Are we going back through Mishé?"

"No; it's quicker to follow the river road down the Khoruz to its junction with the Pichidé, then along the Pichidé to Novo. There's no point in going out of our way—through Mikardand—again until the whole crew's here."

"Damn! I wanted another go at the lady treasurer, the fair Gashigi."

"You'll have more chances later," said Reith dryly.

"How will our people keep clean in Zinjaban? Manshu's rotten little inn doesn't even have a tub."

"They'll have to use the river, as the natives do."

"But doesn't the river have those man-eating sea serpents—or I should say, river serpents? They call 'em evils or awfuls or something."

"Avvals? They're more like giant eels. I'm sure they don't range this far upstream; they prefer deeper waters."

Ordway sighed. "I see we shall have to face a cold plunge. Haven't had a bath since Vasabád. While I don't insist on one daily, like you Americans, we're all jolly ripe by now."

"Good idea," said Reith. "I'll tell Manshu to have dinner late, and I'll meet you all at the ford in a quarter-hour, with soap and towels."

Ordway looked sharply at Alicia, and the pupils of his eyes dilated. "You mean—her, too?"

"I'm an old Krishnan hand, Cyril," said Alicia severely. "We make nothing of it and expect you to do likewise."

The setting Roqir reddened the water as the travelers assembled at the ford, wearing raincoats in lieu of robes. White said nervously: "Shouldn't the men bathe in one place and Alicia in another, for decency?"

Reith snapped: "Alicia and I have taken more baths together than I can count. If it'll make you happy, wash below the ford, while she and I dunk ourselves above it."

"What about me?" said Ordway.

"Wherever you like."

"The water looks kind of muddy," said White.

"They had a heavy rain recently; so the river is high. We'll still come out cleaner than we went in." Reith and Alicia cast off their coats and strode resolutely into the ford, then upstream to deeper water. Behind them they heard low-voiced complaints of the cold.

Soaping himself, Reith found Ordway staring at him in a marked manner. With a mischievous smirk, Ordway said: "I see you've got 'em after all."

"Got what?"

"Oh, you know! For a while I wondered. . . ."

Reith pressed his lips together in an angry line. After manfully resisting his growing enchantment with Alicia, he did not need such gibes.

Oblivious of Reith's annoyance, Ordway persisted: "The trouble with you, old boy, is, you don't give your natural instincts a chance—assuming you've got—*yeeow!*"

With a scream, Ordway leaped almost clear of the water and splashed madly towards shore. He yelled, "An awful has got me! An awful bit me!"

A blond head emerged from the turbulent water, like a Rhine maiden rising to complain of the theft of the

Rheingold. Alicia stood up, spat water, and put her hands on Reith's shoulders to steady herself while she shook with laughter. Reith asked,

"Did you bite old Priapus in the leg?"

"You just bot! I won't have that that microörganism teasing you about your manhood; I could tell him a thing or two about *that!* I figured he couldn't see me under this muddy water."

"Darling!" said Reith, enfolding her. "There's nobody like you on two planets." After a hearty kiss, he drew back. "But we'd better finish and get out!"

Ordway had disappeared, though his yells of "Awful! Awful!" could still be heard. Soon a dozen Krishnans converged on the ford, carrying hunting spears, axes, and other improvised weapons. Ordway, shouting and pointing, hopped about among them, his belly bouncing. He ceased his antics when Reith and Alicia, hand in hand, waded out of the shallows towards the rescue party.

"It—it d-didn't bite you?" he stammered.

"There wasn't any," said Reith. "It was just your guilty conscience." In a few words of Mikardandou, he explained the contretemps to the Krishnans, who broke into the gobbling Krishnan laugh and walked off, shaking their heads.

Four days after leaving Zinjaban, the scouting party came to Rimbid, on the northern bank of the Pichidé. Reith looked furtively about in case they should encounter Sári, his local occasional sweetheart. Much to his relief, she failed to appear. Another confrontation like those with Vázni and Gashigi, he thought, would be just more than he could bear.

When they were settled, Alicia heaved a sigh. "Well, at least you won't have to sleep on the floor tonight."

"No," said Reith, his lips twitching in a secret smile. "The boys and I have the big room, with four beds. The only trouble is that they snore like thunder in the hills."

"Well, if we ever—" She broke off.

"Ever what?" said Reith with ill-concealed eagerness.

"Never mind. Maybe I'll tell you some day." As Reith opened his mouth to carry the conversation further, Alicia gave him a quick kiss and pushed him out her bedroom door.

Now why the hell, Reith asked himself as he walked to the big bedroom, *can't we make up our minds and speak them? Because, Fergus my lad, you're basically a coward. You're in a blue funk at the thought that she might turn you down in a scornful, humiliating way, to get even with your rejection of her. If she's watching for a chance to tell you off, her words would take the hide off a rhinoceros.*

But if you dillydally much longer, she'll either go back to Terra, take off on some scietific safari, or start looking around. There are plenty of mateless male Krishnanders who'd be delighted at the chance. If she really wanted to hurt me, she could even let Cyril . . .

Half an hour later Reith, filled with resolution, knocked on Alicia's door. "Yes?" she said, opening it a crack.

"Lish, we have a couple of hours before dinner. Like a little walk?"

"Oh, good! I've never seen Rimbid. Give me a minute to dress."

"Okay; I want to discuss something serious."

Another quarter-hour saw them strolling arm in arm along Rimbid's main avenue. After lingering before some shops, they came to a small park, where a gaggle of Krishnan children chased one another screaming. Reith said: "Lish, I want to ask you something."

"That makes two," she said, "because I want to ask something of you."

"Oh?" Reith felt a rising tension. "Go ahead."

"No, you spoke first. *You* ask."

"Absolutely not! By my honor as a male chauvinist, the lady gets first whack."

"Oh, all right. I want the whole story about you and Elizabeth. Don't think I was fooled by your dismissing the matter in a few words! Meilung hinted that the tale was dramatic."

"Hmm." Reith looked around. "Very well; you'll have to know some time. It's a long story, so how about sitting down?" He gestured towards a stone bench in the park. Seated, he said: "Here goes. Every so often, some nubile young tourist falls in love with her guide. It's a hazard of the profession. A smart man keeps them at arm's length; but this one sneaked into my bed and—well, the woman tempted me, and I did screw.

"The next I knew, Elizabeth was pregnant. Her old man, who was on the tour, was a director of the Magic Carpet Travel Bureau, and he'd have yanked the rug from under me, unless . . ." Reith smiled wryly. "So before you could count ten, I found myself with an adolescent bride."

"When did this happen? How long after I—we . . ."

"About three years after you left for Earthside. By then I'd stopped bleeding."

"Oh, dear Fergus. . . . Go on, please."

"We got along well enough until young Alister was a toddler. Then Elizabeth got itchy about my job and my absences on tours. She thought I was giving all the female tourists the extra service I'd given her, although I wasn't. She talked about a communal family—you know, couples to take turns with each other's spouses."

"That's been tried on Terra," said Alicia judicially. "The experiment nearly always ends in divorce."

Reith said: "Two couples tried it here, and it ended in murder. I'm sure some of my tourists have played such games, but usually they're discreet about it."

"What about Elizabeth?"

"I returned one day to find she'd gone off with a fat slob of a drug smuggler, a Terran, from the Hamda'.

Elizabeth got her divorce; but when she asked for custody of Alister, Judge Keshavachandra turned her down with some scorching remarks. Later, she told a friend she'd left because I was too sober and rational and predictable—in a word, dull."

"Any woman who found you dull," said Alicia, "should have her pulse checked to make sure she's alive."

"Thanks. Anyway, Elizabeth was one of those who, never having had a real adventure, imagines they're fun. They may be fun to tell about later; but whenever I've been caught in one—well, as the saying goes, on the whole I'd rather be in Philadelphia."

"I know," said Alicia.

"After I won the custody suit, Elizabeth's lover boy sent a couple of Krishnans to kidnap Alister."

"The poor baby! Were you living in your house at the time?"

"We'd just moved in. By pure luck, I came home from working the livestock to find these two bravos carrying my kid out, screaming. I let the sawdust out of one, and the other dropped the boy and ran.

"Later, Elizabeth showed up, begging me to take her back. I turned her down."

"I could have told her you would," said Alicia. "Do go on."

"The next thing, I learned that she had killed herself in the Hamda'. For a while I felt guilty as hell. Why was I such a resounding failure as a husband?"

"You're an *excellent* husband," said Alicia. "It's just that some women don't appreciate your virtues until it's too late. And now it's your turn to ask the question you had in mind."

Reith hesitated; the moment of truth had arrived at last. "Well—uh—I don't know quite how to put it. You know we've been through a lot together."

"So?" her face had gone blank.

Trying to keep his voice steady, Reith continued:

"We've had our troubles, but perhaps these are behind us. . . .

"What I mean," Reith stumbled on, "is, I think we should give serious thought to . . ."

"For-gass!" cried a high-pitched Krishnan voice, which went on in Gozashtandou: "I knew not that ye were in town. Why didst not let me know?"

Reith and Alicia looked up. A comely young female Krishnan stood before them, wearing a topless dress of sheer, shimmery fabric, through which her lithe body was visible.

"And who is the Terran lady?" continued the native girl. "I do perceive that she be a fair dame, even by our human standards."

In English, Reith muttered: "Gods of Krishna, not again! It must be a curse!" In Gozashtandou he said: "Mistress Sári bab-Khahir, I have the honor to present Doctor Alicia Dyckman, a learned lady who works for a Terran company. I am showing her about the country."

"I am honored to meet the learned Terran lady," said Sári, bending one knee almost to the ground and rising again.

"I am equally favored by the charming Mistress Sári," said Alicia, nodding.

"Oh!" cried Sári. "Ye speak our language? Ye must have spent much time in this world, to utter it so purely."

"I lived on this planet years ago," said Alicia.

"And did ye know Sir Forgass then? Hast known him well?"

"Fairly well." Alicia raised her delicate eyebrows. "And you?"

Sári clasped her hands. "Ah, words cannot describe my good fortune, to have so marvelous a friend amongst the Terrans. He hath bought me this beautiful dress!" She pirouetted.

"Really, Lish," said Reith in English, "I don't want to

sit through another discussion of my personal habits between two—uh—"

"How well have you known him?" Alicia persisted, ignoring Reith's complaint.

Sári rolled her eyes heavenward. "Ah, Doctor, how favored by the gods am I, to have the love of so magnificent a Terran gentleman! So brave! So kind! And *such* a lover! Why, compared to—"

"*Please,* Lish," said Reith. "I beg you—"

"Relax, Fergus," said Alicia. "This is a valuable sociological sidelight, and I mean to make the most of it."

Sári rushed on. "I have but two regrets. One is that he visits me no more than once a moon; the other, that he will not wed me. I understand his reasons—that he could never father an egg—"

Reith rose. "If you think I'm going to sit here turning pretty colors while you two analyze my sex life . . ."

Alicia smiled. "Tell me, Sári, why did you not force this *dezd* to marry you before giving yourself to him? Would that have improved your social standing?"

"You'll find me back at the inn in an hour or two," barked Reith, turning and striding away. Behind him, he heard Sári's high, sharp little voice.

"Oh, some old fogies still disparage the mistresses of Terrans, but . . ."

Hiking furiously, Reith worked off his anger. He marched down to the waterfront and back with so formidable an air that Krishnans, even if they could not read Terran facial expressions, shrank out of his way.

By the time he returned to the inn, he took a more indulgent view of his recent discomfiture. He knew Sári to be a garrulous, gushy young thing. He should have foreseen this meeting and, if he truly feared it, should have changed the schedule to avoid the stop in Rimbid. He should also have known that whenever Alicia scented some new fact in her field of xenanthropology, she would go for it like a terrier after a rat.

When they met at dinner with Ordway and White, the temperature between Reith and Alicia was noticeably lower. They were polite and friendly; but their exchanges were cooler, more impersonal and siblinglike, as if the undercurrent of sex had been washed out of them. After dinner they bade each other a prim goodnight, without a kiss.

This coolness persisted all next day, during the long drive to Novorecife. Reith spent most of the day either driving the carriage or riding one of the spare ayas, so time for conversation was limited. Upon reaching Novorecife, he drove into the compound, dropped all three passengers at the Visitors' Building, carried Alicia's bag in, and said: "Have a good night's sleep! I'll see you all in the morning."

Without further words, he returned to his box. Turning the carriage smartly, he slapped the ayas with the reins and headed for his ranch.

VII

ATTILA FODOR

Kardir the ranch cook answered the doorbell. Reith asked, "Where's Alister?"

"He hath gone to visit a friend, sir. I believe he left you a note, yonder." The cook indicated the mantelpiece, whereon lay a folded sheet of paper. Reith read:

Dear Dad:

I'm over at the Jemadaris' seeing Egbert. When are you two going to make up your minds? The suspense is killing me. Know what I'd like for Christmas? A mother!

Alister

Reith smiled as he thoughtfully folded the missive and put it away in his wallet. He asked Kardir: "Where's Minyev?"

"He said you owed him some leave, sir; so he went forth, soon after you departed."

"That's odd. Did he, too, leave a written message?"

"Nay, sir. Two men—of our kind—rode up one day and asked for you. After I explained your absence, they were fain to speak with your secretary. Minyev came forth, and the three walked away to the aya corral to talk beyond my hearing. Then Minyev came back, saying

149

he would take his leave now. Soon he carried out his
gear in a big sack and rode off on his own beast with the
other two. I have not seen him since."

Reith's suspicions stirred, like a snake uncoiling. With
half an ear he heard the cook ask: "Wilt have company
for dinner, sir?"

"Hmm—tomorrow, perhaps. What can you tell me
about the persons who took Minyev away?"

The cook shrugged. "They wore common shaihan-
herd's garb and spoke Mikardandou."

"That could mean they came from Mikardand, Qirib,
Suruskand, or the city of Majbur. Or it might not be
their native tongue. Could you learn anything from
their accents?"

"Nay, sir; how could I, who have never studied such
matters?"

Reith spent the evening in his office, recording expenses and straightening up his files, which Minyev,
surprisingly, had left in considerable confusion. The
following morning he saw to the management of his
modest ranch; then drove his gig to Novorecife. He
spent an hour picking up his mail, reading the latest
issue of the *Novo News*, consulting the space-ship schedule in the Space Control center, and discussing with
Castanhoso the rumors of wars and upheavals in the
nearby Krishnan countries. He also sought the security
officer's opinion of Minyev's sudden departure.

"Can't think of a reason for his taking off like that,"
mused Reith.

"Is there anything missing—silver or pictures, for
example?"

"Not so far as I can tell, except that my personal
papers were in something of a mess. Could it have
anything to do with these rumors of a Qaathian invasion?"

Castanhoso shrugged. "*Não sei.* Fallon tells me the
Kamoran has spies out; but I have heard nothing to
implicate your secretary."

Reith then visited the room occupied by White and

Ordway, saying: "The *São Paolo*, with your shooting crew, won't arrive for several days. What do you want me to do in the meantime?"

Ordway looked up from a paper-littered desk. "Matter of fact, old boy, Jack and I shall be so busy calculating times, costs, and distances that we really shan't have anything for you to do."

"Any objection if Alicia and I stay out at my ranch until the ship comes in?"

"Can't think of any. In fact, you might use the time to make up your shilly-shallying mind—if 'mind' is the word I want. You must be one of those prooks I've heard about."

"I beg your pardon?" said Reith, puzzled.

"Hey, what are you apologizing to me for?"

"I mean, Cyril, what's a prook?"

"You know, a prooks—a cavalier. One of those Johnnies who used to gallop around in stove piping, to save fair maidens from dragons and enchanters; like in that old flick, *Three Hearts and Three Lions*."

Reith laughed, forgetting the sharp retort he had meant to make to Ordway's all-too-accurate gibe. "Oh, you mean *preux*. It's French for 'gallant.'"

"Oh? What I'm trying to say is, you remind me of those old plays by that Russian chap with a name like Check-out. In his scripts there's always some bloke who most frightfully wants to get his gel between sheets; but every time he gets the beazel steamed up, the silly ass loses his nerve and backs away."

Reith grinned. "There may be something in what you say. But none of Chekhov's characters was ever in exactly our position."

"And why on earth do you call the gel 'Wart Hog'? If there's anything she's not, it's ugly."

"Just a private joke between us, like her calling me 'Fearless.' "

Ordway sighed. "When a couple start calling each other pet nemes, it means the cement's nearly set. Go on with your mating dance, and try not to be like the heroes in that fellow Checkout's plays. Cheer-o!"

"So long! If you want us, send someone after us."

Musing on Ordway's whimsical words of encouragement, Reith crossed the compound and found Alicia in her room. "Hey, Wart Hog! Ordway and White won't need us for a few days, until the *São Paolo* comes in with its load of nameless creeping things."

"You mean the Cosmic crew? Actually, some are almost human. So?"

"So why not come out to my place?"

"Well—ah—I might be needed. . . ."

"Oh, come on! Let me be your conscience. Then if anything happens, you can pin the blame on me. We can swim, play tennis, and fence; and you won't have our demon newsperson in your hair, trying to pry out a story about the star-crossed Reiths."

"Meilung will draw all the inferences she needs from my absence," said Alicia primly.

"So what? She'll draw them anyway. Under that hard-bitten exterior, she's a romantic little soul. Besides, at the ranch you won't have our own nameless creeping thing making passes all the time."

Alicia snorted. "That pimple on the face of mankind can think of more subtle little sexual suggestions . . ."

"Maybe I should take lessons—"

"You wouldn't need . . . Anyway, I'll come, if we can have the same arrangements as before."

"Whatever you say."

The following morning, as Reith bent to pick up tennis balls, Alicia said: "Your accuracy is coming up fast. You just need more practice."

"Huh! I was lucky to take one set out of ten. Trouble is, if I play with you only, you'll improve as fast as I. I'll never catch up."

Alicia laughed. "You'll get even at our fencing match this afternoon." She blew a puff of air at the golden bang that overlay her damp forehead. "Bákh! I've never seen it so hot and muggy. I'm drowning in sweat!"

"My dear Lish," said Reith, "men sweat; ladies glow. You glow, like a luminous Krishnan arthropod. Tell you what! I'll get Kardu to put us up a lunch, and we'll ride out into the country."

"Divine! Maybe we could try that swimming hole you—"

She broke off at the sound of hoofbeats. A mounted Krishnan trotted up the driveway, drew rein before the ranchhouse entry, and leaped out of the saddle. He wore a divided kilt and, about his upper body, a simple square of cloth pinned over one shoulder and passed beneath the other arm. Both garments bore a checkered pattern of emerald-green-and-purple squares. Reith said, "That—by Bákh! That's King Vizman's livery! What's he up to. . . ."

The Krishnan approached, bowed, and said in the Qiribo dialect of Mikardandou: "Have I the honor of addressing Doctor Alicia Dyckman?"

"Yes," said Alicia.

"I bear an epistle from my master, the great Dour of Balhib, to the noble Mistress Dyckman." He proffered a letter.

Alicia turned the envelope over. "Thank you, goodman." When the messenger did not move, she added, "Is there aught else?"

"My master hath commanded me to await your reply."

Alicia fingered the letter as if it might explode. "Fergus, may I borrow your knife?"

She pried off the seal and read. Reith said, "Well?"

"He's heard I'm back on Krishna and begs me to come visit him. He practically offers me all three moons if I'll come. Says he's carried out his promise about the slaves."

"That's true," said Reith. "But what's your answer?"

Alicia looked about like an animal caught in a trap. "I

ought to think it over. . . ." To the messenger she said,
"Speak you English, goodman?"

"Nay, mistress; of the Terran tongues, only a little
Portuguese."

She turned back to Reith. "At least, we can discuss
things in front of him. I don't want to write Vizman
without the most careful thought—certainly not with
this fellow fidgeting to begone. . . ." She turned back
to the messenger. "Tell your master—"

"One moment, my lady," said the courier. From his
belt pouch he brought out a notebook, made of a set of
cardboard-thin wooden sheets, strung together and
waxed. "Pray, speak slowly so that I can prick it down."

"Tell your master that, grateful as I am for his invitation, I am under a contract that will occupy all my time
for another moon or two. Ask him to communicate with
me again anon." The messenger scratched on his pad
with his stylus.

"Alicia!" said Reith. "After the movie's shot, you
wouldn't really go putting yourself into that character's
power, would you?"

With chin up, she defiantly met his eyes. "I don't
know. By then I may be on my way back to Terra, or I
may be looking for a job here. If nothing better turns
up, I'm sure Vizman would have work for me. I just
might . . ."

"But—but—" sputtered Reith.

The messenger bowed again. "I thank you, noble
madam. God den, good my sir." He put away his pad,
mounted, and trotted off. At the gate he broke into a
canter.

Reith chewed his lip. *She's putting me on notice,* he
thought. *If I don't get off dead center soon, she'll start
looking at other prospects.* With forced composure he
said: "How about our picnic and swim?" This time,
he resolved, they would settle matters once and for
all.

"Fine! We'll—"

Suddenly an earthshaking rumble quivered the ground beneath their feet. Reith looked up, startled. Alicia said: "Don't tell me a thunderstorm is coming up on a nice, fair day like this!"

"Thunder, hell! That's the *São Paolo*, coming in ahead of schedule! And we have to meet her. Hey, Simkash! Fetch the gig, *byant-hao!*"

They found White and Ordway among a crowd of Krishnanders milling about the waiting room of the Customs and Security Building. The *São Paolo* had already discharged its passengers, but none had yet come through the door from baggage inspection. A grinning Ordway said: "That fellow Kush—Kash—you know, the head copper—said he'd give 'em an exceptionally thorough screening, because everyone knows that Californians are crazy, and movie folk are a lot of drug smugglers and other delinquents."

The door opened, and the passengers began to file through. Most were from Cosmic Productions, and Ordway hailed them: "Hey there, Attila! Here we are, Kostis! Hi, Cassie!"

Ordway gathered his twenty-nine colleagues and began introductions in strict order of rank. Reith tried to fix each name and face in his mind. First Ordway introduced Kostis Stavrakos, the producer, a short, plump individual, well along in years.

Next came Attila Fodor, the script writer and director. This proved to be a huge man, half a head taller than the lanky Reith, and of rangy build. His craggy face bore a luxuriant mustache, whose ends hung down to his chin on either side of his mouth. In an age when a man could promote the growth of hair anywhere on himself that he wished, Fodor was bald. He had a bone-crushing handshake and a strong Magyar accent.

Cassie Norris, the leading lady, was a full-lipped,

bosomy platinum blonde, wearing a scarlet, high-style jacket and skirt better suited to the boulevards of Paris than to the austerely functional Customs and Security Building.

Randal Fairweather, the leading man, was tall and impossibly handsome, with a built-in seductive manner. His first words to Alicia were: "My dear, how I've been looking forward to seeing you again! How simply smashing you look, in that great-outdoors getup!"

He bent to kiss her. She did not exactly dodge, but turned her cheek towards him. Cassie Norris, Reith noticed, viewed the interplay without pleasure. Reith, too, felt a surge of jealousy.

The head grip or property man, Ernesto Valdez, was small, dark, and intense. Bennett Ames, his assistant, was introduced as Cassie's husband. He was a big man with a bewildered look on his blunt features.

Hari Motilal, assistant script writer and assistant director, proved small-boned and chocolate brown; he wore what seemed to be a permanent sneer on his aquiline Hindi visage. He looked Reith over with an uncordial stare and remarked: "So you, Mr. Reith, are the old Krishnan hand Doctor Dyckman has been telling us about! To judge from her remarks, you must be some sort of superman."

"You'll have to judge that for yourself," said Reith. Thereafter, names and faces began to blur. All seemed to talk at once, paying no heed to the remarks of anyone else.

"Excuse me, please!" said Reith. He rounded up Krishnan porters with hand trucks and directed the loading of the new arrivals' baggage.

Stavrakos said: "Mr. Reith, that security officer says he wants to keep our equipment here until tomorrow, to make sure it complies with the regulations. Can't you speed things up?"

"No," said Reith. "In such matters, what Castanhoso says, goes."

"Would a little . . ." The producer held out a hand, rubbing the thumb back and forth against the fingertips, ". . . help any?"

"Worst thing you could do. You may not believe it, but Herculeu is incorruptible."

"Hell of a place," muttered Stavrakos, turning away. "Can't even use an honest bribe."

Reith held up an arm and raised his voice. "Will everybody from Cosmic Productions please follow me?"

The next hour was spent in leading the movie crew to the Visitors' Building, assigning them rooms, sorting out hand luggage, and explaining the schedules of the cafeteria and the Nova Iorque bar and lounge.

When Reith's charges were disposed of, Alicia confronted him in the hallway. "Fergus," she said, "I hate to ask this of you; but will you go back to the ranch and fetch my things?"

"Why not come back yourself and change?"

"Oh, darling, how I wish I could! But starting right now, Kostis and the rest have me tied up in conferences practically every minute until we leave for location. They'll want you in on some of them, too."

"How shall I know—"

"I'll put a note in your mail box. That's a dear!"

She moved towards him, and Reith thought he was about to be kissed. But then she glanced down the hall, where several of the Cosmic crew were standing about chattering, and evidently thought better of the idea.

"Well," he said, "I wouldn't do this for any other woman. Até logo!"

A couple of hours later, Reith returned to Novorecife. A bag containing Alicia's possessions lay beside him on the seat of the gig. She was not in her room; but a note in his mailbox asked him please to attend a conference in Stavrakos's suite, beginning at the twelfth hour.

The next few days became a blur in his memory. Conference followed conference. Alicia was in the thick of it all, so that he had no chance to speak to her alone. He was called in on many conferences, mainly as a backup for Alicia when questions arose about Krishnan politics, topography, climate, and other matters where his knowledge surpassed hers.

By the time the meeting adjourned each night, Reith was glad to drive home, throw his clothes on the bedroom floor, and tumble into bed.

To entertain the Cosmic employees not included in the working sessions, Reith arranged for Timásh to take them on boat trips up the river to Rimbid and down to Qou. He hoped that, if they ever stopped chattering and admiring themselves long enough, they would learn something of the Krishnan countryside and its inhabitants.

During the first few conferences, Reith tried to lead the discussion around to things that he thought were wrong with the script and to suggest improvements. But Stavrakos, Fodor, and Motilal brushed all his objections aside.

Motilal said: "Perhaps you have not yet realized, Mr. Reith, not being of our profession, that we are not making a documentary. A number of cinematographers have already done this. What we are doing is pure entertainment. Do you understand the distinction?"

"Of course, but—"

"Then kindly leave to us the matters on which we are expert, and we shall likewise depend on you for information we lack. You understand?"

"I'm not a half-wit, Mr. Motilal. I understand, all right." *Nasty little man*, thought Reith; *why the hell should I give free advice to people who don't want it? Hereafter they can ask for it and pay extra.*

Reith's dislike of Motilal was somewhat softened when the assistant director, a stickler for authentic detail, took Reith's side in arguments over the film's veracity. One dispute concerned the color of the simulated blood to be shed in scenes of violence. Stavrakos insisted that the blood be red, since to a Terran audience blood was red by definition. The fact that Krishnan blood was blue-green, having a base of hemocyanin instead of hemoglobin, meant nothing to him. But Fodor, Motilal, Alicia, and Reith all objected so vehemently that Stavrakos gave in.

Four days after the arrival of the *São Paolo*, a train of vehicles appeared on the road from Qou: three of Mishé's omnibuses and four wagons, each drawn by a pair of ayas. Each omnibus bore, rising from the body, a wooden framework over which a canopy could be stretched in times of rain or excessive heat.

The whole Cosmic crew went out to examine the vehicles as they rattled into the compound. Reith heard grumbling, and Fodor said: "Is this the best you could do, Fergus? The people, they complain about the hard seats. These things will give a hell of a rough ride." (Actually he said: "Is dis de best. . . . De people, dey complain about de hard seats. Dese tings . . ." Fodor had never mastered the dental fricatives of English.)

"That's what we've got," said Reith. "Tell your people that Sívírd in the Outfitting shop will sell them seat cushions. If need be, he'll have some made."

Later, Reith ran into a grinning Kenneth Strachan, who said, "I'm working for Cosmic, too."

"Really? What as?"

"Set designer. The production designer thocht he wanted an engineer familiar with the local materials— strength in tension and compression and so forth—so he hired me. Says I could double as interpreter. You'll have to watch me and haul me awa' if I cast adulterous eyes on aucht female."

Reith sighed. As if, he thought, his list of problems were not long enough already!

The final conference broke up in late afternoon. It was agreed that all should leave Novorecife early the following morning, as soon as the vehicles could be loaded. Reith would drive his gig north to Rosid, to tell the Dasht of Ruz to assemble his five hundred warriors and to give him the authorization, signed by the Grand Master of the Knights of Qarar, to admit this armed band of foreigners to the Republic of Mikardand. This errand completed, Reith was to retrace his steps and join the shooting crew at Mishé.

Meanwhile the Cosmic crew would set out for Mishé, with Alicia and Strachan as guides and interpreters. In Mishé they would shoot the urban scenes and buy the equipment needed for camping out at Zinjaban.

Reith balked at the plan to send him to Rosid. Not wishing to say that he hated the thought of being separated from Alicia, especially with handsome lechers like Fairweather dancing attendance on her, he invented reasons for staying with the shooting crew. He feared, he said, that Dasht Gilan might suspect him of complicity in the disappearance of Princess Vázni and imprison him, or even shorten him by a head.

Stavrakos, however, waved the contract like a flag and threatened to withhold Reith's pay. Since nobody else was available to handle the task assigned to Reith, and since he prided himself on punctilious fulfillment of his obligations, Reith gave in.

As he rose to leave the conference room, Reith heard Fodor's bellow. "Hey, Fergus! Come here a minute!"

Although the blustering Fodor was not to Reith's taste, the tour guide came. The director boomed: "Now that the business is over, I am hosting a party in my rooms this evening. Come, and bring your money!"

"What sort of party?"

"Oh, some liquor, and a few hands of poker. We begin at half past twenty, Earth time, whatever the hell that would be here. Come! It will be a very select little party. I invite only my good friends."

Reith thought, *With Attila Fodor for a friend, who needs an enemy?* While he hesitated, Fodor slyly added: "Besides, your little yellow-haired Alicia, she is coming."

Reith was surprised; he had expected an all-male gathering. He was also concerned; although Alicia took pride in being able to take care of herself, she just might need her former husband's protection. After a moment he answered: "All right, thanks. I'll be there."

At the appointed hour, Reith found Cyril Ordway and two handsome young women, both dark and petite, in Fodor's suite in the Visitors' Building. The air was heavy with the smoke of huge Krishnan cigars, as Fodor rose with a cheerful roar.

"Come in Fergus! Have a drink. You've met my wife, Michelle." He nodded at one of the girls. "And my mistress, Nancy Boyce." He nodded at the other. "The rest will be here soon. Jack White is coming. Poor Jack always loses, but he can't keep away. I invited your friend Strachan, but he said he couldn't afford it. I guess he is like those Scotchmen in the stories, squeezing every pengö." He thrust a box of cigars at Reith, who declined.

Ordway remained seated, glass in hand, staring at Reith from bloodshot eyes as Fodor continued.

"You got no prejudice against playing with Krishnans, have you?"

"Of course not," said Reith. "I live among them."

"Good; we got one coming. Cyril here is a little touchy about those things; but I told him he could either be a good boy or get the hell out. Here's the guy, now!"

Tall and slender, Sivird, master of the Outfitting Shop, ducked under the door lintel, saying: "I am glad to see you, Mr. Reece."

"The reason I have invited him," said Fodor, "is he did such a good job getting those pillows made. He had all the whores in the place—what do you call it?—the Hamda', that's it. He had them all sewing and stuffing. Ah, here come the others. Hello, Jack; hello, Alicia! Come in, sit, have drinks. I pour."

White and Alicia, she in her topless dress, each accepted a glass of kvad and sipped cautiously as Fodor and Ordway stared at her with lustful fixation. White kept his eyes on his goblet, in patent embarrassment; but, as Reith noted with amusement, he rhythmically caressed the rounded curve of his drinking vessel.

"I was saying," continued their host, "that the reason people will flock to this movie is, they are sick and tired of too much civilization. They want a breath of clean, virile barbarism, which is after all the natural state of man. Now they got the Earth so damned civilized that you can't take a piss without filling out a form. So for a barbarian milieu, you got to come to Krishna."

Sivird gave the Krishnan version of a frown. "Mr. Fodor, I hope you will not take offense; but we Gozashtanduma do not consider ourselves barbarians. In fact, we are highly civilized."

"I suppose, compared to the Krishnans with tails, you are," said Fodor. "Compared to us decadent Earthmen, however, you are the noble savages—and all the better for it. Barbarism is the natural state of reasoning beings, and men always return to it the minute the restraints are off. Then we become *real men!*" Fodor thumped his chest with his fist. "Those who can't, die."

Alicia gave him a level stare. "You mean you'd prefer to live like those verminous nomads in Qaath, struggling to stay alive?"

Fodor nodded. "If I had been born a barbarian, I'd be twice the man I am. Why am I bald? Because no true barbarian would smear on his scalp the stuff that grows hair on a bowling ball."

White whispered to Reith, "The real reason is that he's allergic to the pilogen, like me."

Waving an arm like a knobby utility pole, Fodor orated, "I am barbarian swordsman at heart! Cut! Thrust! Slash! Blood running in the gutters! Heads rolling in the mud! If I could make a picture with *real* heads, *real* blood, that would be my great artistic triumph."

White snorted. "It's easy for you to talk about blood and gore. But when I saw those heads on spikes at Mishé, they almost made me shoot my cookies."

"Aw, hell!" said Fodor. "Your trouble, Jack, is your ancestors got civilized too long ago. The disease you call civilization only infected us Magyars in the last thousand years; so we haven't been so long going downhill. We still got a little of the old, manly barbarism."

Alicia said: "If the Qaathians were to spring one of their lightning invasions while you're shooting your picture, you wouldn't think them so romantic."

Reith added: "They may in fact be up to something. For moons they kept their borders closed."

Fodor snorted. "Just a couple of rabbity decadents, scared of your shadows. Now let's play. Jack, set up the table. Nancy, where the hell are the cards? Michelle, get out the chips. Fergus, you seem sober; you be banker. Straight draw, nothing wild. Poker with wild cards is degenerate."

"It's my lucky night," murmured White. "The astrologer told me so." His eyes held the glitter of a compulsive gambler about to indulge his addiction.

Reith took the money—Terran paper and a pile of silver coins from Sivird. There was a tedious wrangle about rates of exchange until Reith said: "Damn it, if I'm banker, I set the rates!"

Alicia said: "I didn't bring much cash. What'll you allow me on this?"

She unclasped a silver necklace, set with amethysts and rock crystal, and laid it on the table. With a start, Reith recognized the ornament as a souvenir from her long-ago days of wild adventure in the Khaldoni countries.

"What would you say, Sivird?" asked Reith.

The Krishnan picked up the bauble. "I would allow the lady five hundred karda."

"Good enough," said Reith, counting out chips.

"Hey!" bellowed Fodor. "Since we got so many beautiful ladies, let's play strip poker. Then we have a real game! How about?"

Michelle spoke with a French accent. "I do not sink so. On ze Riviera, perhaps. . . ."

"No!" said Nancy Boyce. "I will *not* take off my clothes in front of all these people!"

"It's against my religion," muttered White.

"Okay, okay," grumbled Fodor. "Cut the cards. Fergus, you deal first. Nancy bets."

Fodor pulled a new deck of cards from their box, ruffled them, and laid them before Reith, who saw that the backs bore a complex design centering on the monogram F.A.G.

"Are these your special cards, Attila?" Reith asked.

"Sure. I had them made."

"What does F.A.G. stand for?"

"Fodor Attilla Graf," growled Fodor. "In Magyar, we put the surname first, like the Chinese."

"Then is 'Graf' your middle name? It's German for 'count.' "

"It means 'count' on the cards, too. I'm a hereditary Hungarian count, or I would be if they hadn't abolished titles there long ago." He shrugged. "To use it makes me feel good; so why not?"

"No reason," said Reith. "I'll call you the Grand Khan of Tatary if you like."

"Ah, the Tatars!" exclaimed Fodor. "The last *real men*—"

"Let's play!" said Reith loudly, to cut off another monologue on the joys of barbarism.

For the first few hands, betting was cautious and stakes, low. Unfamiliar with their opponents, the players felt each other out. Reith lost a little through over-cautiously dropping out early; then he won a pot with three kings and more than recovered his losses.

White lost small sums. Then he plunged; Reith called his bluff, and White had to buy more chips. Fodor played in swashbuckling style, winning and losing substantial sums but coming out about even.

Ordway, now deep in his cups, leaned forward between hands to stare at Alicia's bosom. His playing was erratic; his words, surly.

To Reith's surprise, Alicia began steadily winning. Her face was as blank as when he had tried to talk about their joint future at Rimbid.

On Reith's left, Sivird played thoughtfully in a style much like that of Reith. He accumulated chips faster than Reith; but then Alicia beat him on a couple of hands and reduced his holdings almost to his starting stake. Fodor's women, who sat on either side of the director, played timidly, repeatedly dropping out before cards were called for.

Ordway, who had lost most of his chips, roused himself and began raising the limit. All dropped save Sivird, who kept raising until Ordway's pile had vanished. Ordway called. He showed a full house; Sivird laid down a flush.

For a long moment, Ordway blinked at the exposed hands as if he could not believe his eyes. Fodor said: "All right, Cyril! Shove them over!"

Ordway's stubble-bearded face turned an apoplectic red. "Goddamned if I'll let any fuckin' wog ramp me! Oo the hell does he fink—"

Ordway rose; his chair crashed to the floor. Instantly Fodor was on his feet, roaring: "Drunken son of a bitch!" With two strides he came around Michelle's chair and seized Ordway's arm. Ordway swung a fist at Fodor, but his short arms merely fanned the smoky air.

"Out!" yelled the director, whirling Ordway towards the door. He yanked it open and thrust the struggling inebriate through. Putting a large foot against Ordway's rump, he shoved, catapulting the production manager across the corridor, to crash into the wall on the far side.

Fodor slammed and locked the door and returned to

the table. "Sorry, folks," he growled. "Poor Cyril goes on these bats. Tomorrow he'll come crawling with apologies. Whose deal?"

Play continued. Then Fodor said he had a pat hand. Alicia took three cards and bet the limit; she raised him. Back and forth they went until Alicia's pile was almost exhausted and Fodor's completely so. At that point, Fodor dropped.

Reith hoped for a glimpse of the cards; but Alicia and Fodor both folded their hands, keeping the faces of the cards out of sight. Fodor pushed his pile to Alicia.

"You got to give me a chance to get even!" he said. "Fergus, I am broke, and I got no more cash. If I was a proper barbarian, I would just whack off a couple of heads and take back the chips. But as things are, let me give you Nancy as security for a loan, until I get to the bank tomorrow."

"Eh? What's that?" said Reith. "An I.O.U. would do—"

"No, no, you do like I say. I might be dead tomorrow, and then where would you be?"

"Now what," said Reith, "do you expect me to do with Nancy?"

"Good God! You have to ask? Take her to bed and ride her till she founders, natural!"

Reith looked around the table. "Does he really mean this?"

Nancy said, "Yes, he does! I've been through this before."

"He must be crazy," said Reith.

"I—we had a fight today," said Nancy, "and th-this is his way of g-getting even." She dissolved in tears, rose, and started for the door.

Michelle also rose, put an arm around Nancy, and went out with her, murmuring: "*Ma pauvre petite! Il est un sale bête, ce grand fripouille-là!*"

"We still got five," said Fodor. "Jack, it's your deal."

"I think I've had enough," said White.

Sivird said: "Excuse me, gentlemen, but I must get the shop open early tomorrow, for last-minute purchases by your cinema people." He rose, bowed, and pushed his chips forward for redemption.

Fodor sighed. "I guess the party is pooped. Help me collect the bottles and glasses. Fergus, pay the people off." He scooped up the cards, put them back in their box, and handed the box to Alicia, saying: "Take! They are your lucky cards, and they will remind you of Attila Fodor."

Walking Alicia back to her room, Reith said: "Hey, Wart Hog! There's more to this than meets the eye. What cards did you hold on that last hand?"

"You could have paid to see them."

"Oh, come off it! We're old co-conspirators."

"Well, then," she said, "I had three jacks."

"Not much, for a game and a pot of that size. Any idea of what the King of the Huns had?"

"I'm sure he was bluffing. Maybe king high or something."

"How on Krishna did you know that?"

"Because I'd been studying his style. Sivird would have cleaned out the Cosmic people, because they're not used to Krishnan facial expressions and body language. But I kept taking chips away from him almost as fast as he won them, because I'm used to Krishnans and Terrans both. Besides, you don't think I wore this dress just to look pretty, do you?"

"I've been wondering why. Hoped it was to please me."

Alicia smiled. "Besides, I knew the men from Cosmic weren't used to Krishnan styles and would spend more time gaping at my contours than studying cards. It didn't work with Cyril and Jack, because Cyril got too drunk and Jack has inhibitions. But it hit the shaihan's eye with Attila."

Reith chuckled. "You she-devil! That dress sure paid

for itself tonight. Where did you learn to play poker like an old pro?"

"In Montecito, with the movie people. After losing a month's salary, I learned the tricks. By the way, will you take charge of these cards Attila gave me? I really don't care for card games."

"From what I saw tonight, you could make a living gambling."

Alicia shrugged. "Not how I want to spend my life. I came only because Attila told me you'd be there."

"Son of a bitch! I came because he told me the same about you. Bet I know why he pulled that nutty stunt with his mistress. He thought if I was kept busy all night with her, I wouldn't be around to interfere while he turned tricks with you."

"Dear Fergus! With Fodor at large, I'd have been delighted to have you around to interfere."

They reached Alicia's door. Realizing that this would be his last chance for many days to ask his unfinished questions, Reith put his hands on Alicia's shoulders and turned her to face him. Holding her at arm's length, he drew a deep breath and said: "Dearest Lish, how would you like it if—"

"Ah, there you are!" A mellow actor's voice wafted lightly along the corridor. Randal Fairweather, as tall as Reith and much handsomer, approached with long strides. "Alicia darling! If I'd known you were wearing that dress, I'd have crashed Attila's party." He turned to Reith. "Hear you're going back to Ruz, Fergus. Is that right?"

"Yes," growled Reith.

"Well, keep your ass covered old boy. We can't afford to lose you. Say, is it true that you two were once married to each other?"

"It is," said Reith, wishing for some magical spell to make this charmer vanish in a puff of smoke.

"Reminds me of the time," Fairweather rattled on, "when I was married to Nadya O'Brien, who played the lead in *Sweat and Lust*. We stayed pals for years after we split. I was with the Loathsome Creatures—"

"You were *what*?" interrupted Reith.

"A Loathsome Creature. It was a dance band; I played the electronic banjo. You know, Fergus, you did the entire male sex a favor by breaking up. No one man should monopolize such a gorgeous woman."

"I'm not polyandrously inclined, Randal," said Alicia, "if that's what you're hinting at."

"You might give it a try, my fairy princess," said Fairweather. "Take my colleague, Gina Petrovsky. . . ."

As he chattered on, oozing charm, it became obvious that the actor was waiting for Reith to set out for his ranch, so that he could make a pitch for Alicia without competition. Reith stubbornly stood his ground, matching anecdote with anecdote and joke with joke, until Alicia, patting a yawn, said: "Good night, boys!" She closed her door firmly, and Reith heard the snick of the bolt.

Reith said: "Care to come out to the ranch, Randal? I have some good drinking kvad, and I can easily put you up."

"Thanks," said Fairweather, "but I think I'll turn in. We've got to be up with the aqebats tomorrow."

When Reith still did not move, Fairweather cast a look at the bolted door and laughed. "Okay, I'll come! We'd look pretty damned silly, standing here all night, each waiting for the other to go. Let me get my kit."

In the courtyard of the Visitors' Building, noisy confusion reigned. Climbing into the omnibuses, some Cosmic employees jostled one another for better seats. Others fretted lest any of their belongings be left behind.

On the pavement below them, Krishnan drivers and workmen shouted. Impatient ayas shook their horns, pawed the ground, and bleated. Valdez and Ordway yelled at the heavy-laden porters.

Reith stood moodily scowling with vexation at having

muffed another opportunity. He roused himself when he heard Ordway's voice, turning Cockney under stress.

"No, no, you've got it all wrong, mate! Hey, Strachan, can you explyne to this bloody wog that he's got to unload the wagon and start over?"

"And tell him," shouted Valdez, "that if he drops a camera, it will explode and blow us all to pieces!"

This, if an exaggeration, was not altogether untrue. While Interplanetary Council rules had been somewhat eased since the days when nobody might take any mechanism more complex than an abacus out of Novorecife, cameras and other advanced equipment were fitted with self-destruct mechanisms. If some inquisitive Krishnan tried to take one apart, either to discover Terran technical secrets or just to satisfy his curiosity, the machine would fly apart into hundreds of components, which no Krishnan could ever reassemble.

"Easy, easy," came Strachan's deep voice. "Ye'll frighten him so he'll drop something for sure." Strachan then spoke in Gozashtandou, and the reloading proceeded.

Reith saw that Ordway had recovered from his excesses, save for a pair of bloodshot eyes and a lump on his forehead. He had to admit that the Londoner was effective in bringing order out of chaos.

Roqir stood well up in the greenish sky when the last piece of freight had been checked aboard and the last passenger who had wandered off while waiting had been rounded up. Ordway swung up on the foremost wagon and stood looking aft. He called out: "I say, Alicia! Will you please for sweet Jesus's sake get aboard? You'll have time for that sort of thing at Zinjaban!"

"That sort of thing" was a parting embrace between Alicia and Reith. When they kissed, the passengers, leaning out to watch, sent up a ragged cheer. As he and Alicia pulled apart, Reith caught remarks amid the buzz.

"She's his ex-wife, you know."

"Hell, I wish my ex-wife would treat me like that!"

"She can be my ex, any time she likes!"

Ordway blew his whistle. The drivers cracked their whips, and the vehicles lurched, groaned, and rumbled into motion.

When the last wagon had swayed out through the gate in the compound wall, Reith turned to Timásh, who held the bridles of three ayas, one of them hitched between the shafts of Reith's gig. Reith climbed into the trap and, followed by Timásh riding one beast and leading another, guided his gig out the gate. Instead of taking the river road to Qou, however, he headed north towards Rosid.

VIII

THE DASHT OF RUZ

At Avord, the innkeeper Asteratun, he of the ragged antennae, said: "Hail, good Master Reef! Come ye with other *Ertsuma* this time?"

"No," said Reith. "Only my trusty Timásh, and I'll bunk with him."

"Then I'll give you Number Six, an that suit you."

Later, when Reith and Timásh sat in the common room nursing goblets of falat, Asteratun, having no other customers at the moment, joined them. Reith asked: "How go things in Ruz these days?"

"Well enough. Praise the divine stars, the Dasht hath rescinded that besotted ordinance calling for the bathhouse owners to divide their premises into compartments for male and female." Asteratun looked Reith in the eye. "Good my sir, last time we met, ye promised me an explication of the lady I took for your daughter. Now, since we're old friends and businessmates, I'll call in that note of hand. What's the tale?"

"She's the same one you met twenty years ago, who was then my wife."

"Master Reef, I know that, with your Terran medicines, ye live longer than do we human beings. In twenty years, forsooth, ye've aged a trifle; but less than

173

I during that time. Yet this pretty damsel seems no older than twenty years agone. Wherefore is that?"

"She's spent all but a couple of those years in space travel, that's why."

Asteratun stared down at the table. "Aye, I've heard of that space magic, that slows down time for him who partakes thereof, like unto the tales of a wight who goes to Fairyland for a day and returns to find a century gone by. A Terran once essayed to explain it to me, but I could make nought of't. Howsomever, ye said: 'was my wife.' Mean ye she no longer is?"

"That's right. We were divorced shortly after you met her."

"*Ohé*, so that's why ye insisted on her sleeping alone! Yet here ye were a while ago, traveling about together and acting like unto old friends and copemates, as if there'd never been a harsh word betwixt you. When one of us human beings is divorced, the reason is that one of the pair hath done some deed so foul that t'other would never again have aught to do with the wicked one."

"Neither of us did anything wicked," said Reith with a wry smile. "I suppose each of us craved to rule, and she couldn't endure the rivalry."

The old Krishnan shook his graying blue-green hair. "Aye, ye Terrans take your pairings and unpairings as lightly as do the promiscuous Knights of Qarar, who couple like unto the beasts of the wildwood. One, a Sir Khors, stopped here not long since. He had his new leman along and boasted of dropping his previous sweetling for the new—unless in sooth 'twas she who jettisoned him. He hinted that I ought to do the same with my old wife. 'Every man,' quotha, 'needs a new mate every few years.'

"I replied: 'The stars forbid! After spending forty year in learning to get along with a single mate, and getting her used to my crochets and indulgent of my faults, think ye I'd go back to the beginning and start over again? Think ye I'm moonstricken?'"

"Divorce is a matter of dispute on Terra, too," said Reith somberly, "with no final answer in view. But I find the subject like a knife in the liver; so let's talk of other things."

Arriving at Rosid the next day, Reith went directly to the palace. He asked one of the men-at-arms at the portal to find out when it would be convenient for the Dasht to receive him. The guard barked orders to another guard inside, who soon returned, praying Master Reith to accompany him forthwith. As Reith followed the usher up marble stairs, through huge bronze doors, and along a corridor lined with painted statues and other works of Krishnan art, he wondered why the noble should pay him this sudden honor.

Reith entered the audience chamber to find men with drawn swords suddenly surrounding him. By reflex his hand flew to his hilt; then he realized that resistance now would be suicide.

Before he could sheathe his half-drawn sword, however, a net whirled above his head and settled down upon him. A burly Gozashtandu gave him a violent push; unbalanced, he tripped on the net and went sprawling. Then the burly one and his assistant pulled the net together, binding Reith as firmly as a Terran fly wrapped in spider silk.

"What's this?" shouted the hapless Reith.

"Ye shall soon see," said one of the swordsmen. Several Ruzuma picked up the bundle containing Reith and bore it down three flights of stairs, through many wandering halls, and finally into the dungeon.

They laid Reith on the floor of the cell, unwrapped the net and, gripping his limbs to forestall resistance, relieved him of all his metallic possessions: sword, dagger, pocketknife, money, keys, pen, and pencil. They took his billfold with the letter from the Grand Master, inviting a regiment of Ruzuma to take part in the movie making in Mikardand. They ignored Reith's heated demands for an explanation.

While two of his captors held Reith's arms, a Krishnan in a uniform of different style came in, bearing a massive chain, on each end of which dangled a lock ring. The jailer fitted the larger ring around Reith's neck, adjusted it to size, and locked it shut. The smaller ring he attached to a fixture in the wall.

"There, now!" said the jailer. "Ye be not in discomfort, I trust, Master Reef?"

"I shall be more comfortable," growled Reith, "when I know what all this is about."

"As to that, ye must needs await the Dasht's return from Lusht, whither he hath gone for the wedding of the Pandr's daughter."

"When will he return?"

"Any day, now."

The soldiers filed out; but one remained in the corridor, looking through the bars.

Reith said to his jailer, "If His Altitude wished to see me, he had but to request. I have legitimate business, concerning which he and my clients have a written agreement. What is your name, my friend?"

"Herg bad-Yeshram. My people have been jailers to His Altitude for four generations."

"Since you know who I am, why treat me like a desperate criminal? Why chain me up as if I were the giant Damghan, who would otherwise run about slaying and devouring folk?"

Herg wagged his head. "The reason I know not. But the Dasht left orders that ye be kept beyond the remotest chance of evanishment. 'Tis known that ye be a slippery customer, who ere this hath escaped from bars and gyves. Now I go to fetch your supper."

There followed two days of unrelieved tedium for Fergus Reith. The jailer and his assistant did not treat him unkindly, and they took care of his basic needs. As Herg bad-Yeshram explained: "We've heard tales of you, Master Reef, and know ye be a wight of fair repute amongst the Terrans. I misdoubt not that, when the Dasht returns, he'll discover that he hath been the victim of a misapprehension and order you enlarged. Meanwhile, howsomever, we needs must do our duty."

One guard was always on sentry duty in the hall, watching him. It struck Reith that his present plight derived from his successes in previous adventures, for these very triumphs had endowed him with an inflated reputation for derring-do among the Krishnans.

On the second day, fumbling in his pockets for something that might help him to pass the weary hours, his fingers encountered a flat, rectangular box of pasteboard. This was the deck of playing cards that Fodor had given Alicia, which she had handed him. Ha! He thought. Sitting on his stool, he began dealing the cards out on the tiled floor, trying to remember the rules of solitaire.

On the third day, while engrossed in his eighteenth hand of this dull but time-consuming game, Reith heard a familiar voice, barking English with a distinctive Krishnan resonance. "Mr. Reith! What are you doing?"

Reith looked up. Outside the cell stood Gilan bad-Jám, Dasht of Ruz, wearing a silvered cuirass on which were superimposed figures of mythical beings. To his lip was glued a new mustache, with pomaded ends twisted into spikes. A pair of guards flanked his sides.

"Greetings, Your Altitude," said Reith with forced composure. "I'm playing solitaire."

"Eh? What's that? And why don't you stand up in my presence?"

"To answer your questions in order, my lord: solitaire is a game one plays with oneself by means of little rectangles of stiff paper, called 'cards.' One can also use these cards for other Terran games. As for your second question, your men have loaded me with a chain weighing, I estimate, thirty or forty Gozashtando pounds, which renders rising difficult."

"Yes, yes, I understand. I have seen playing cards. Now I wish you to answer certain questions."

"I'll try to, sir," said Reith.

"What was your part in the disappearance of my betrothed, the Princess Vázni bad-Dushta'en?"

"I had no part in it, sir. I first heard of it after the event."

After a thoughtful pause, the Dasht said: "Your Terran colleague, Mr. Strachan, went to Hershid with us but did not return. He vanished from our ken about the time the princess disappeared. Was there a connection between these events? Did they elope?"

Reith shrugged. "As far as I know, Kenneth Strachan is living happily with his Terran wife at Novo."

"When and how did you hear that the Princess Vázni had disappeared?"

Reith thought fast. Any lie should be one that the Dasht could not easily check out. "I heard it said in Novo, sir, that the princess had paused there on her way to join her daughter in Suruskand. I did not see the lady." After a pause, he added, "My informant—a local lady, I forget which—said the daughter had written, urging her mother to come to her and promising her a fine new husband."

"Damn it to Hell!" snorted the Dasht. "If she marries many more husbands, she'll be too shopworn to be *my* consort. Now, Reith! Answer truly!"

"Yes, sir?"

"What was your part in that forged letter from Dour Eqrar, which sent us off to Hershid on a wild-aqebat chase?"

"I know nothing about it, Your Altitude." Reith's heart thumped. He was determined at all costs to hide Alicia's part in the hoax, lest a vengeful Dasht send assassins after her.

"Nothing whatever?"

"Absolutely nothing, my lord."

"Can you imagine why anyone should play such a foolish, wasteful, tasteless, embarrassing jest?"

"Well, Your Altitude, I do have a tentative theory."

"Yes? Speak up, man, speak up! I'll not hurt you for bringing unwelcome news. *I* always keep my word!" Gilan slapped his cuirass so that it rang like a door knocker.

"My suspicion," said Reith carefully, "is that the letter was not a forgery after all."

"Impossible!"

Reith shrugged. "As you wish, sir. But it could be that the Regent Tashian made that request through his ambassador at Hershid. Then, after the Dour's secretary had written the princess, Tashian changed his mind. He may have decided to seize the throne himself, or to promote one of his own sons to royal rank. Why should he care whether he embarrasses Your Altitude?"

"If our lands lay adjacent," snarled Gilan, "my sharpest sword would soon teach him to care!"

"Another matter occurs to me as well, sir."

"Say on!"

"As I understand it, when a woman of your kind weds for the second time and conceives, it's widely believed hereabouts that the second husband merely raises up the seed of the first, which has lain dormant in her. The egg, it is thought, is as likely to be the offspring of the first husband as the second, though the first may have been years in his grave."

"That's the common belief," said the Dasht. "But Terran scientists, I am told, consider it mere folk superstition."

"Your Altitude has known Terrans to advance contradictory beliefs, have you not?"

"Yes, yes. We had the Reverend Trask claiming that the prophet of his sect was the son of his God, and the Reverend Muhammad Basri telling quite a different tale. But what has that to do with this case?"

"Just a suggestion, sir, that you don't accept any one Terran doctrine as necessarily true."

"Hm," said the Dasht. "Strange, to hear a Terran admitting that the all-wise aliens from his planet are not always right! Do you imply that the old belief about raising up the first husband's seed may be true after all?"

"I wouldn't know, Your Altitude. But the possibility might raise questions of the legitimacy of any heirs you begot on the lady in question."

"Oho! I hadn't thought of that, Mr. Reith. In Ruz, or course, my word is final. What *I* say is right by definition. But in case we should be called to wider responsibilities . . . You mean, any egg she laid might actually be sired by you or by the unfortunate Aslehán?"

"Not by me, sir. My sometime marriage to the Lady Vázni would not count, since we Terrans are never interfertile with your people. But she was married for years to Aslehán who, I am sure, performed his husbandly duties."

"I don't doubt that," said the Dasht. "She was a pretty thing."

"In any case," continued Reith, moistening his lips as he chose his words with care, "it seems to me that the chances of her ever becoming a significant factor in Duro politics is slight."

"Hmp!" the Dasht grunted. "You're hinting that I might find her, as wife, more liability than asset?"

"I would not presume to assert such a thing as fact, Your Altitude. I merely suggest that the possibility merits thought."

Gilan stroked his long nose. "Perhaps, perhaps. I'll think the matter over and consult my council."

"Another matter, my lord. What about the five hundred cavalry you promised for the motion picture?"

"They're ready to go, as soon as they know whither. Where is the work to be done?"

"Somewhere in western Mikardand," said Reith, deliberately vague. The more information he gave the Dasht, the fewer bargaining points he would have left to effect his release from the cell.

"How about our castles, which the Earthlings wished to rent?"

"I believe they chose a site in Mikardand."

"Putting us to all that trouble for nothing!" grumped the Dasht. "Well, less money is still money; so I'll command my cavalrymen to ride for western Mikardand. But how shall they gain admittance to that land? Without some arrangement, it would look like an invasion."

"That has been arranged, sir. The Grand Master gave me a letter to deliver to you, inviting your men into the Republic. I understand that he sent a confirmation to the commanding officer at Kolkh, instructing him to admit your regiment. Your soldiers took this letter."

The Dasht stood silently for a few breaths, looking fixedly at Reith through the bars. As the lamplight set little topaz highlights dancing in the Krishnan's eyes, Reith perceived Gilan's agile if erratic mind at work. Then the Dasht's antennae twitched.

"I must read this letter and think about it before taking further steps," said the Dasht. "I will not decide before consulting my council; I always follow a rational plan. This cannot be done before tomorrow."

"Your Altitude," said Reith, "did you ever learn who put one of my Terrans on a crazy aya?"

"We learned some things. This person gained access to the palace, passed himself off as a flunkey, and gave the horsemaster a message purportedly from me. Then he slipped out, went to the fair grounds, and began making speeches against you Terrans. When the fair-wardens made to arrest him, he disappeared."

"Was he one of Schlegel's gang?"

"Apparently not. We think he was a certain Nuchohr, once a follower of Schlegel but who, disaffected, started his own faction, with a much more extreme program. Where Schlegel merely would stop cultural interaction between Terrans and human beings, Nuchohr would kill or expel all Terrans from this world.

"But enough of that. I wish you to teach me some of those Terran games with cards, of which I have heard. I foresee increasing involvement with alien beings of your kind, and I shall have to learn their social customs in self-defense."

Reith smiled. "In the cell here?"

"Yes, yes; but you need not wear that burdensome chain." He shouted in his native tongue. "Herg! Come hither and remove this gyve from the prisoner. . . . Now fetch a table and two decent chairs. I, my good Herg, am about to learn the mysteries of Terran indoor games."

Reith, dropping easily into Gozashtandou, said: "I mind me of a game called 'poker.' "

"The word is familiar," said Gilan; "but methought it denoted an implement wherewith one manipulates a fire."

"It means that, also," said Reith. "As Your Altitude has doubtless observed, in my language one word may serve for several meanings. But as to poker: for a successful game one needs at least three players and a number of tokens, called 'chips.' These are disks of some common material, like unto coins but of little value. If a few hundred of your smallest coins be available . . ."

The Dasht spoke to one of his guards: "Fetch me a sack of arzuma from the Treasurer's office. Here's my seal ring to serve as authorization; be sure you return it with the coins! Herg, get us another chair! You shall play, also."

"*Me*, my lord?" said the jailer hesitantly.

"Aye, ye yourself. In a Terran game, there's no distinction of rank."

When the guard returned with a bag full of little bronze coins—the pennies of Gozashtand—he found Reith, the Dasht, and Herg sitting around the table, while Reith explained the values of the combinations of cards.

"I fear I be confused, my lord," said Herg. "I know not these little Terran symbols for numbers."

"You can count, can you not?" barked the Dasht.

"Then count these spots, which Master Reith calls hearts, spades, diamonds, and clubs, albeit they look like no hearts, shovels, gems, or cudgels that mine eyes have seen."

"I shall deal first, Your Altitude," said Reith. "Pray, hold your cards up, thus, so no other player can get a look at them. . . ."

Hours later, the Dasht rose. "My thanks, Mr. Reith," he said in English. "I fear I've been so engrossed in play that I forgot the dinner hour. Permit me to take your deck of cards with me; I have an idea for the evening's entertainment. Until tomorrow, then!"

"But, my lord!" exclaimed Reith. "How about letting me out—"

Heedless, the Dasht plunged out the cell door, slammed the bars shut, and strode away. Although he knew Gilan to be highly intelligent despite his eccentricities, Reith had been surprised by the speed with which the noble had mastered the game. Intelligence and a streak of zanyism, thought Reith, made a dangerous combination.

Later, Herg entered the cell to remove the remains of Reith's dinner. The jailer said: " 'Tis well, Master Reef, that we played but for arzuma, and they furnished by the Treasury. Otherwise the Dasht had reduced me to beggary."

Reith smiled. "You had done better, had you called his bluff betimes to keep him honest."

"Aye, that I once attempted, and marked how displeased he was. We his servants must needs attend to's moods. He liked it not when ye, as ye say, 'called' him."

The following afternoon, Herg unlocked the door and announced: "Ye are free, Master Reef! The Dasht hath sent word to enlarge you instanter. Ye shall, he saith, enjoy all the luxe his palace can afford."

Reith found Timásh patiently waiting before the palace, having taken a room locally for nights. Reith moved into the Dasht's guest suite. Hiding his resentment at the treatment accorded him, Reith dined with the Dasht and the weather-beaten Sir Bobir, commander of the detachment to be sent to Zinjaban.

Sir Bobir was full of questions about the part his five hundred knights were to play. "For look you, Master Reef. If we have five hundred of our men and five hundred Mikardanduma galloping about pretending to fight a battle, someone amongst the Mikardanduma will surely try to avenge the battle of Meozid by smiting the head from one of our folk. Then there'd be a general mêlée, with many slain and belike a war; albeit neither government lusts for such a brabble, with the Qaathian menace looming over all."

"We've thought of that," said Reith, speaking Gozashtandou like the others. "The motion-picture folk will furnish each warrior with a wooden sword covered with silver paint. Thus we hope to avoid injuries, save perhaps a few bruises."

"Bobir!" said the Dasht, beaming in a new uniform of bleached shaihan wool embellished with gold lace. "You are commanded to wait upon us here this even. I wish to teach you the fascinating game that Master Reith hath shown me. 'Tis called 'poker' in his Terran tongue. Last night I trounced the Treasurer and my secretary. For tonight, I've enlisted the Chamberlain. With you and the Earthman, we shall be four. And oh, ere I forget!" The Dasht pulled a small scroll from his sleeve. "Down on your knees, Master Reith! Behold your patent of knighthood!"

The Dasht slapped Reith's face with the scroll, then said, "Rise, Sir Fergus!" He seized Reith in a bear hug and kissed him on both cheeks. Reith blinked too late to keep his eye from being scrubbed by the boar's-tusk mustache.

"Your knighthood is a small token of my appreciation

for introducing me to so enthralling a game," said Gilan. "It hath military value as well, in case we should ever be compelled to draw our shining sword. Feint, bluff, and deception are necessary parts of the military art. I knew at first sight that you were one whose acquaintance would please me. By Qondyor's iron yard, *I* am never wrong in my judgment of men, whether Terran or human!"

"I thank Your Altitude," said Reith, wiping a tear from his assaulted eye. "By the way, my lord, you mentioned the Reverend Trask. How goes their enterprise?"

"I know not," snapped the Dasht. "They were expelled from the Dashtate a ten-day past, along with the other Terran missionaries—Christian, Buddhist, the whole lot."

"How so?"

"A band of the Trasks' fanatical followers seized upon my Chief Astrologer; knocked the old fellow down and broke his eyeglasses. I pay astrology small heed myself; but I cannot permit the abuse of my servants. Loyalty up; loyalty down."

"The Trasks told me they were devoted to non-violence," mused Reith.

"Indeed. They claimed to abhor the attack as much as I. But any movement of that ilk attracts unruly spirits, who grasp but the flimsiest pretext to assail and destroy. I allow no such turmoil in *my* realm! Given a choice between the peaceful security of my subjects and the Terrans' messages from the spirit world, I'll forgo the messages!"

Driving down the long road from Qou to Mishé, with Timásh riding a spare aya and leading another, Reith tried to sort out his feelings about Alicia. One part of his mind said forget the whole deal. If she wanted a permanent relationship with you, she would not have taken Sári so casually or questioned the girl in such a cold-bloodedly scientific spirit.

Meanwhile the other part of his mind missed Alicia with a poignancy that, a few moons before, he would not have believed possible. He had to restrain himself from winding the animals in his eagerness to see her again.

Being well-known in Mishé, Reith had no trouble at the city gate; but inside, he found the main avenue blocked by a growing crowd. By standing up in the gig, he could see over the Krishnans' heads.

A section of the avenue had been cordoned off by rows of Mikardando men-at-arms, their pikes held horizontally to keep the citizens back. In the cleared space beyond, he could see cameras mounted on wheeled scaffolds and a few actors, costumed as Krishnans, moving purposefully about.

Being too far away to hear, he hopped down from the gig, handed the reins to Timásh, and pushed through the crowd. Despite his apologies, the locals whom he elbowed aside looked angrily at him and muttered about mannerless alien barbarians as he squirmed past. When he reached the front row of spectators, further progress was halted by a soldier's pike. Reith said to the man-at-arms: "Let me pass, pray. I am with those Terran play-actors and must speak to them."

"Everyone hath some excuse for trespassing," sneered the trooper. "Orders are to keep all back, including you, alien!"

"But I am their official guide!" said Reith. "If you don't believe me, call one over."

Strachan's deep voice boomed out in Mikardandou. "Less noise, over there!! Whoever is babbling has ruined the sound for this scene, and we must start over."

"Now will ye get out?" snarled the soldier. "Or would ye liefer have your pate cracked by a spear shaft?"

With a sigh, Reith pushed back to the gig. By a roundabout way through back streets, he reached the consulate and found Fallon at his desk. Fallon told him: "They're all but one staying at Bosyár's Inn. Treasurer

Gashigi said it was out of the question to sleep all thirty-odd in the Citadel."

"I can guess the exception," said Reith. "Your fellow Briton."

"Of course. The Treasurer seems to have a fancy for him."

"Or for his capabilities. Have you a room reserved for me?"

"I'm pairing you with Doctor Dyckman," said Fallon.

"You *what?*" Reith bounced out of his chair. "Whose idea—I mean—did she—"

"Just joking," said Fallon with a satyrlike grin. "You've got a single, with a nice bed big enough for two. You can use it as you please so long as you don't break it in a transport of passion."

"My dear Tony," growled Reith, "your ideas of humor can be smelled a kilometer upwind."

"Sorry; I didn't mean to poke a sore nerve."

"By the way," said Reith with a wry smile, "you may call me 'Sir Fergus' is you like. I am now a knight of Ruz."

"Congratulations," said Fallon. "But you were already a knight of Dur. Should I call you Sir Sir Fergus? And what did His Pomposity honor you for?"

"For teaching him poker."

"By Qondyor's brazen balls, that's rich!" laughed Fallon. "Having been a king myself, I don't take titles seriously. But I shall want to see Ordway's face when he hears. He adores titles!"

"Poker's not just fun with Gilan," said Reith. "It's also a matter of money, lots of it."

"How do you mean?"

"Each night Gilan sends command invitations to some of his poor little bureaucrats and mulcts them of their salaries."

"I know that zany's clever, but is he such a marvelous player?"

"He doesn't have to be. You see, when he bluffs,

none of his underlings dares to call him, for fear of his august displeasure. So he rakes in pot after pot."

Fallon laughed again. "Fergus, old fish, the Dasht certainly owed you that knighthood. To do it right, he should have thrown in half the dashtate and a nubile daughter as well!"

Reith was sitting in a corner of Bosyár's lobby, toilsomely deciphering his way through a copy of the Miché *Defender*, when the shooting crew straggled in, chattering. A couple of them greeted Reith; the others failed to notice him. He told himself: when *she* comes, no extravagant gestures! She's just an old friend. (Then why, said another part of his mind, was he wearing his best Mikardando kilt and his sword?)

"Hello, Fergus!" said Alicia from the doorway. A dozen pairs of eyeballs swiveled towards them, patently expecting a repetition of their steamy parting at Novorecife. Aware of the curious stares, Reith merely said: "Hello, Alicia!" and shook her hand.

"How did you make out with the Dasht?" she asked.

"That's quite a story. Why don't we—you and I—go out to dinner? Baghál's Place is only a couple of blocks, and the food's good."

"Do they have dancing?"

"Some nights. And they often run a pretty good show—authentic Krishnan stuff instead of bad imitations of Terran performing arts."

"All right; give me a few minutes to wash up."

Alicia reappeared in a plain but attractive Terran street dress. As they walked arm in arm towards the tavern, words tumbled out. "One of the cameramen forgot to take off his lens cap today; ruined an hour's takes. . . ."

"Has Old Slimy been slithering up to you lately?"

"Cyril? No; he's been bunking up in the Citadel, where I guess Gashigi keeps him drained. But I've had to straight-arm Randal Fairweather more than once. The last time, he tried caveman tactics; so I hit him with my trusty handbag, with the coins. I will say he's a good sport; when he recovered consciousness he apologized. . . ."

". . . so His Pomposity chucked me into a dungeon dark and dank; but Fodor's deck of cards got me out. . . ."

". . . I had to give Ernesto Valdez the knee where it would do the most good, when he got grabby at the bathhouse the other day. Most of the crew have taken to Krishnan bath customs. . . ."

". . . so I taught that crazy autocrat to play poker. . . ."

". . . Randal's real name is Elmer Grotz, and he talks of nothing but the pictures he's been in. That's how they all are. Either they're bragging of past triumphs, or blaming someone for failures, or gossiping about who's screwing whom. . . ."

"I had a straight and was sure the Dasht was bluffing; but I didn't dare call him, because I'd already won as much as I thought safe. . . ."

". . . that horrid little Motilal made a nasty remark to Bennett Ames—you know, Cassie's big, dumb husband—about his wife's lovers, and Ames hit him, and then Attila hit Ames. . . ."

"Remember the Reverend Trask and his wife? They've been kicked out of Ruz. Some of their converts attacked Gilan's pet astrologer—"

"Poor things! And the Trasks mean so well, too!"

"Krishna is littered with the bones of Terrans who meant well. Somebody ought to tell the Trasks what happened to the Reverend Jensen."

"The one whose head arrived at Novo in a cask of salt? They probably know; and in any case, they might welcome martyrdom."

"At least, if we ever go back to Rosid, you can display your assets without fear of disapproval. . . ."

"When Attila isn't working, he's out touring the armorers' shops in Mishé. He has a famous collection of swords at Montecito; that's where his money goes. . . ."

At Baghál's, the manager, knowing Reith, gave him a table for two on the edge of the dance floor. A waiter in a black-and-white striped kilt came to take orders. Alicia said: "When I left Krishna, a few places were beginning to hire waiters, instead of making patrons give their orders to the cook and come to fetch their own meals. Is table service customary now?"

"It's spreading; but some of these waiters are still pretty new at the trade. So don't be surprised if one of them dumps a plate of *sodpá* soup in your lap."

"I'm glad I'm not wearing my best dress. I suppose this is an example of that Terran corruption of Krishnan culture that your enemy Schlegel deplores."

Reith shrugged. "He can deplore all he likes, so long as he doesn't interfere. Hey, do you see what I do, yonder? Fry my guts if that isn't Ordway, Gashigi, and a couple of locals!" Just then the production manager laughed with a bray like that of a lonesome donkey. "Hear that?" asked Reith.

"I hear them," said Alicia. "I also see that Cyril's sopping up the booze again. Here comes the band; how's your dancing?"

"Haven't had much practice lately, except for hauling overweight female tourists around the floor in line of duty. After dancing with you, they seemed like waltzing hippopotami."

"Then it's high time for a practice session," she said firmly. She paused to listen. "They're playing the Indian *tandava*, I think. Do you know it? It has those gymnastic arm movements. I'll show you!"

As they danced past the table occupied by Ordway and Gashigi, they paused and were introduced to two bureaucrats from the Knights' Treasury. Gashigi said: "I ba-rought Cyril here, Far-goose, because ze great singer Sotaru bad-Khors performs tonight."

"Isn't he the fellow who fights duels with rival singers?" asked Reith.

"So I hear. Isn't it exciting? If he finds a rival here—"

Reith said: "We'd better sit down, Lish, before he starts a fight with us."

Reith and Alicia were nearly through their dinner when Sotaru at last appeared. To the twang of a harp in the hands of one of the musicians, he sang three wailing Mikardando songs.

After the last of these, the singer bowed to the applause of cracking joints and retired. In the quiet that followed, Reith was startled to hear Ordway boom out; he proved to have an excellent singing voice as, beating time with an eating spear, he sang:

> *"Oh, some like to ride on the crest of the wave,*
> *And some like to ride on the billow;*
> *But what I like to ride*
> *Is a fair, blushing bride,*
> *With her arse propped up by a pillow!"*

At another time and place, Reith would have been amused; but now he worried. Alicia said: "Oh-oh, here comes the great Sotaru. He looks furious."

"Better be ready for trouble," said Reith grimly, reaching down to pick up his sword from beneath his chair and to loosen the peace wires.

The singer strode to Ordway's table, bowed stiffly, and went through the motions of introducing himself. Instead of assaulting Ordway, however, he pulled up an empty chair, seated himself, and plunged into earnest conversation, while Gashigi translated. Then Reith watched in astonishment as Ordway and Sotaru faced each other, beat time with outstretched fingers, and mouthed words that Reith could not hear over the background noise.

"By Bákh's toenails!" said Reith. "I believe Cyril's teaching him that song!"

After running through the verse a few times, Sotaru stood up, bowed to the assembly, and launched into Ordway's ditty:

"Oh, sam like to ride on ze ca-rest of ze vave. . . ."

Alicia murmured, "The Mikardando accent rather spoils the meter. So much for your authentic Krishnan performing arts!"

Reith sighed. "Sometimes I almost sympathize with Schlegel. Excuse me a moment."

When he returned, Reith was surprised to see his table empty and Alicia's weighted handbag lying on her chair. Thinking that she must have made a similar comfort stop, he sat patiently unconcerned for some minutes. When she did not reappear, he pushed past the dancing couples to Ordway's table.

"Cyril," he said, "did you see Alicia leave the hall?"

"Why yes, old boy," said Ordway. "Gashigi called my attention to it. A greenie came in and spoke to two chaps sitting at that corner table." He pointed. "Then the three hurried over to your table and talked to Alicia. They acted excited, as if there'd been some sort of disaster. Then she got up and went out with them. That's all."

Reith asked, "Can you add anything, Lady Gashigi?"

"No, Far-goose. We all sought it a little sa-trange; but I did not see any cause to interfere. She could have—"

Reith bolted out of Baghál's. The last twilight was fading as Mikardanduma went to and fro about their business. Everything seemed normal on the street, but there was no sign of Alicia. Reith strode up and down the block, looking in all directions.

At last he accosted the man-at-arms on point duty at the nearest crossing. "Have you seen a Terran woman come out of Baghál's?"

The trooper thought. "Aye, sir, that I did, but a short time since. She issued forth with three human beings, and all four got into a closed carriage and drove off. I should not have noticed but that the female alien had shining yellow hair, a thing whereof I have heard but have never witnessed."

"What can you tell me about the three with her?"

The trooper gave the equivalent of a shrug: "They seemed but ordinary citizens; nor was there aught strange about their carriage."

Further questions failed to elicit more facts, so Reith returned to Baghál's. On a last chance, he asked Gashigi to check the women's rest room. Still no Alicia.

"I say, cobber," said Ordway, "this has a fishy smell to me!"

"To both of us," said Reith.

"I'll do whatever I can to help."

"Thanks."

Reith next questioned the manager, who said: "They behaved themselves and paid their due; so I gave them little heed. Here's their waiter. Zalmánu! Tell Sir Fergus what ye know of the men with whom Doctor Dyckman departed."

The waiter wagged his head. "Nought out of the ordinary, sir. They wore common garb—one in gray, the other brown, methinks—but otherwise they ate their dinners, paid their scot, and went."

Reith asked "Was there anything in their speech or mannerisms to show their origin?"

"Nay, sir—but hold a bit. The little fellow with the purplish-red beard, who came in after the others, I took for a Khaldonian. He had the long smellers of's race and spake with the harsh Khaldoni accent."

"Good!" said Reith. "Here's something for your trouble; and where's my man with the bill?"

Having paid, Reith picked up Alicia's handbag. To Ordway and Gashigi he said: "I'm going back to Bosyár's, to see what I can learn."

"Do you sink zere has been an abduction?" said Gashigi.

"Just that," said Reith. "She wouldn't have left her handbag unless she thought she would soon return. You might alert your government. Good night!"

* * *

At the inn, Reith first knocked on Alicia's door. "Lish!"

There was no response, even when he knocked harder and called more loudly. He returned to the lobby and asked the innkeeper: "Have you seen Doctor Dyckman, the yellow-haired Terran woman?"

"Nay, sir; but a small human being, Khaldonian from his looks, came in and gave me this for you." He handed Reith a folded sheet. Reith read:

Dear Fergus:

Forgive my leaving so abruptly, but a representative of a powerful Krishnan nation has to me made an offer that I cannot refuse. I am leaving to take up a position of great authority, wherein I can do for this world the greatest possible good, When I am settled, I shall inform you of my location.

If you still entertain sentimental feelings towards me, forget them. Nothing would ever have worked for the pair of us. And fear not for the Cosmic project; you and Mr. Strachan can perform any tasks that would otherwise have fallen to me. Best wishes,

Alicia Dyckman, Ph. D.

IX

THE DOUR OF QIRIB

The message hit Reith like a punch in the gut. What had happened? Had he said something that so offended Alicia that she had left both him and her job with Cosmic Productions? That was hardly like the conscientious Alicia. Had she become fed up with his prolonged hesitation? Or had she concluded that, since she could do better elsewhere, she should seize the opportunity? Had some potentate really dangled an irresistible lure before her?

Reith reread the letter. He had not studied Alicia's handwriting; he had only a hazy recollection of the letters she had written in the brief interval between their first meeting and their marriage, two decades before. Although the writing did look familiar, he could make no exact comparison.

The stilted, formal tone of the letter, however, did not sound like her. However angry she might be with him, she would hardly refer to Strachan, an old friend of both, as "Mr. Strachan" instead of "Ken." Nor would she add "Ph.D." to her signature. Neither was the English completely idiomatic.

Reith was baffled. The "small Khaldonian" sounded like his secretary Minyev disguised by a crimson beard;

but how could Minyev have become involved? If Minyev
so idolized Alicia, why should he take part in a kidnapping project?"

He sought out the innkeeper. "Master Bosyár, our
companion Doctor Dyckman has disappeared. I suspect
that she did not leave voluntarily."

"Indeed, sir?" said the taverner.

"I wish to examine her room. You can let me in with
your passkey and stand by to make sure I respect her
rights of property."

Bosyár looked doubtful. "I know not, sir. . . . Who is
Mistress Dyckman's master? For whom doth she toil?"

"Oh, you want the approval of Master Stavrakos?"
Reith led the way to the producer's room. He found
Stavrakos lounging in a chair and Fodor sitting on the
bed. The two had been arguing but fell silent when
Reith strode in with the news.

Stavrakos shook his head. "That is bad. Still, I guess
we can manage, so long as you and Strachan stick with us."

Fodor remained silent, but Reith thought he de-
tected a glimmer of a smile. Fodor, he recalled, had
opposed the hiring of Alicia in the first place. Now
without opposition, the director would feel free to make
as silly a Krishnan movie as he liked.

"Sure, go ahead and examine her baggage," said
Stavrakos. "But what are you planning to do about it?"

"If I find a clue as to where she's gone—and I have
my suspicions—I'll go after her."

"Hey! You can't do that! You have a contract with
me, to stay with the crew until the movie's been shot.
After that, if you want to go chasing after some dame—"

Reith contained his temper with difficulty. "Look
here! I'm supposed to protect the whole lot of you.
She's part of your crew, too, and she's the one in
danger. The rest of you will do all right here in Mishé,
with Strachan to guide and interpret—"

"But your contract says you stay with us!" shouted
Stavrakos. "If you want to hire a private eye—"

"Don't talk rubbish! They don't have private detectives—"

"Kostis!" boomed Fodor. "Listen to reason! You know I'd be just as happy to shoot my picture without Alicia's interference; but everybody knows—"

"Traitor!" yelled Stavrakos. "Your first loyalty belongs to me—"

"Shut up!" bellowed Fodor. "Everybody knows those two were once married and are still soft about each other. My barbarian honor says if a man wants to go hunting for his woman, he's entitled—"

As the voices of the quarreling executives merged into an unintelligible roar, Fairweather and Cassie Norris appeared in the doorway, asking: "What's this about Alicia being kidnapped?"

News of the abduction spread through the crew as if by telepathy. Other heads appeared in the hall behind the acting leads, until most of the shooting crew had either crowded into the bedroom or blocked the doorway. Stavrakos said: "If this son of a bitch goes off on a wild-goose chase, he's broken his contract, and I won't pay him—"

"Oh, won't you?" said Ordway. "You just try something like that, and I'll jolly well walk out on you, too. That gel's worth a hundred greasy dagoes like you! We'll pull a strike!"

"You bet!" shrilled Cassie Norris.

"I'm with you, Cyril!" said Jacob White.

"Me, too!" called Ernesto Valdez.

When it became obvious that the entire crew was on Reith's side, Stavrakos grumbled, "Okay, okay. You're a bunch of lousy traitors and sentimental idiots; but I can't make a picture without a crew. So go on, Fergus; rescue your blond tornado, and try not to get yourself killed. If you do, I won't pay your estate one *lefta!*"

As Reith pushed out of the crowded room, Ordway said: "I say, Fergus! I want to go along with you and help out!"

"We'll discuss that later," said Reith, hastening back towards Alicia's room with the innkeeper in tow.

In her room, Reith found Alicia's clothes and toiletries scattered about; but she had always been untidy. Hanging from pegs on the wall, along with other clothing, were the topless lavender dress she had worn at Fodor's poker party and her crossbow-pistol, together with a leather case full of bolts. It looked as though Alicia had departed without taking a single possession other than the clothes she was wearing.

Reith appropriated the pistol and arranged with Bosyár to store Alicia's other effects until she could reclaim them.

"What the devil?" shouted Anthony Fallon in answer to Reith's knock. "Oh, it's you, Fergus. What brings you to my door at this time of night?" When Reith explained, Fallon said: "Oh! That's different. Come in, man. Do you need a drink?"

"No; I need information, and you're my best bet here in the outback."

They sat down in Fallon's living room, Fallon in an old green bathrobe and Reith in his dress Krishnan kilt and tunic. After discussion, Fallon asked: "What makes you so sure the note's a fake, and she didn't go voluntarily?"

"I'm not absolutely certain; but it's easier to believe she's been kidnapped than she'd leave without her favorite dress or even her toothbrushes." Reith paused. "Tony, when we were here last, you read us excerpts from the local newspaper. Wasn't there a feature called 'News of Royalty'?"

"Why, yes," said Fallon. "It's a gossip column about the ruling circles in the local kingdoms—though I daresay if the President of Suruskand ran off with the wife of the High Priest—"

"Have you a file of these papers?"

"My dear fellow, of course! Keeping up is my busi-

ness. Sorry; I should have realized you were in a hurry."
From a big filing cabinet, Fallon drew out a fistful of
large folded sheets of the Mishé *Defender*. "Here! The
one for the current ten-day is on top. You'll find the
royalty column on the second page."

Reith unfolded the topmost sheet, found the column,
and pored over it without result. In the preceding
issue, he found an item, which in a free translation
would read:

HOPEFUL MAMAS AGOG IN JAZMURIAN

We are informed that His bachelor Awesomeness, Dour Vizman of Qirib, hath the mothers of
marriageable girls in a swivet because of his pro-
jected sojourn in their bustling city, whither he will
shortly arrive from Ghulindé. Although royalty seldom gives out travel plans, a source close to the
throne hath revealed that a stay of a moon or more
is contemplated. The official report is that His Awesomeness wishes to familiarize himself with the
state of manufacturing and trade in Qirib's leading
commercial city, notwithstanding his oft-stated preference for life in the capital. We wonder if Jazmurian
hath not some attraction of a non-commercial sort. . . .

Reith looked up. "Have you a map covering the
country between here and Jazmurian?"

Fallon brought out a map from a drawer in his desk.
Reith pored over it, saying: "She could have been carried off to any of half a dozen countries. Qirib looks the
likeliest, since Vizman wrote inviting her to Ghulindé;
she put him off with excuses. If you were in Jazmurian
but had to travel to the borders of Mikardand to receive
a kidnapee, what would you choose as a transfer point?"

Bending over the map, Fallon pointed to a spot on
the shore of the Sadabao Sea. "Qa'la is on the border,
here. The roads from Mishé to Qa'la are at least fair."

"But," objected Reith, "Qa'la is a good three hundred kilometers from Jazmurian. That would mean a trip of at least six days each way."

"Here's another possibility," suggested Fallon, "a little town on the Zigros called Qantesr. It's just over the border from Qiribo territory and only thirty-odd kilometers from Jazmurian. With a fast aya, one can make it in a day by the river road."

"I know Qantesr," said Reith. "I'm off while it's still dark, before the aqebats begin to croak."

"Shouldn't you wait for me to send out inquiries, before you leap on your fiery aya and gallop off in all directions?"

"I count on your making inquiries, old man, and getting Castanhoso to do likewise. Meanwhile I'm off to the countryside; if any mysterious party has passed through, I'll have a good chance of picking up the trail, with the help of my native friends, while it's still hot. If I don't find any trace of my girl, I'll come back within a ten-day. Meanwhile you should have received answers to your questions."

"How do you expect to get her out of Vizman's grip, if that's what she's in? You couldn't cut your way single-handed through half the Qiribo army to rescue your lady—assuming she wants to be rescued."

"I don't think Vizman would bring half his army. I imagine he'll sneak quietly out of Jazmurian, ride up the Zigros with his personal guard, camp near the border, and wait for Alicia. If it turns out I'm wrong in any of these assumptions, I'll come back here to figure out my next move."

"Who's going with you?" asked Fallon, looking worried.

"Just my trusty Timásh. 'He travels the fastest who travels alone.' "

In midafternoon, six days after leaving Mishé, Reith and Timásh approached Qantesr. Each rode a sweat-damp aya, while the spare animal, saddled and bearing two small bags of personal gear, followed on a lead.

Reith took a dim view of Qantesr, because it was here, long ago, that Alicia had pushed him into the 'avval-infested river during a quarrel. Since the town was not really responsible, as Reith told himself, he compensated for his prejudice by being particularly pleasant to the townsfolk as he sought information.

Yes, they told him, everyone knew that the King of Balhib was camped a couple of hoda to the west, across the border. Yes, a carriage with window curtains drawn had, a few hours before, traveled eastward through the town with a pair of armed outriders. As soon as the vehicle cleared the village, its driver was seen whipping his ayas into a furious gallop. Reith smiled grimly to himself; his guess about Vizman must have been right!

Reith took a room for himself and Timásh, then wandered with elaborate nonchalance down the road towards the border. The border post had the usual cluster of shelters and storehouses. Before one of these a couple of bored soldiers lounged, dispiritedly playing games of chance while waiting for travelers to appear.

On each side of the border, a horizontal pole formed a barrier across the narrow road, while the forest on either side made detours impractical for mounted Krishnans or vehicles. Each pole was striped in the national colors; but whereas the green-and-purple pole on the Qiribo side was intact, the blue-and-orange pole on the Mikardando side had been broken off short. Looking at the splintered stump, Reith surmised the reason for the damage.

Two border guards on the Mikardando side were playing piza for small stakes. After watching for a while, Reith diffidently suggested that he join in. He allowed the guards to win a handful of arzuma, then engaged them in friendly chitchat.

"I hear rumors about a closed carriage, which lately came through the village headed for the border. Do you goodmen know anything about it?"

The soldiers exchanged glances. One said: "I know not that we should talk—"

"Oh, he seems a good fellow, for an alien," said the other. "Better he should hear the true tale from us than some fantastical rumor from another.

"Well, sir, we were standing here today, nigh unto noon, when these two bully-rooks rode up. One handed me a scroll, crying that it was authorization for his party to cross in haste, that the peace of our two nations depended upon it, and that we should raise the gate forthwith.

" 'A moment, good my sir,' said I, breaking the seal and unrolling the screed. Now, I can read a little; but this message was full of strange, long words, such as lawyers use. So I called Charvadir here to help decipher it. Whilst our heads were bent over this writing, the carriage came on at a dead run. The mounted man shouted: 'Ware, clumsy oafs!' We leaped out of the way and, ere we could blink, carriage, outriders, and all whirled through as if the fiends of Hishkak were in the saddle. Their animals struck the gate pole and broke it. Yon scrowles" (he indicated the two border guards on the other side) "had already raised their pole, so these runagates passed through without hindrance. When we protested, they did but laugh at us.

"Charvadir hunted up the Knight of the district, who berated us for failing to stop the carriage—what fancied he, that we should seize the galloping ayas' horns? —and promised to write to Mishé about the incident. The master capenter in Qantesr is making us a new pole."

With assumed indifference, Reith left the border post, strolled up the road until out of sight of the guards, then cut back through the woods to examine the border barrier. This proved to be a simple wooden picket fence, rotted and sagging.

Back in Qantesr, Reith hunted up the town's master carpenter and rented one of his saws. As Roqir set, he and Timásh rode towards the border, leading their spare animal. Before they reached the boundary, they dismounted and led their ayas through the woods to the section of fence that Reith had already inspected. As Reith set to work with his saw, Timásh said: "Sir Fergus, these beasts could easily jump this little barrier. Why do ye saw it up?"

"Because we may be returning in a hurry, and I shouldn't care to make the jump in the dark. . . . Come on!"

They led their beasts through the new gap in the fence and on towards Vizman's camp. A prowl through the trees brought them within sight of the clearing, where a dozen small, bulbous tents clustered around a very large one, like piglets around their dam.

"Stop here and tie up the animals," said Reith softly. From a small sack he dug out a handful of soot, which he applied to his face, ears, and neck until he seemed in the gloaming like a headless man. He treated his hands and wrists likewise and ordered Timásh to do the same. When this had been done, he said: "Now untie the ayas and hold their bridles. If I return, we shan't have time to fiddle with tethers. Keep your sword handy and remember: in a fight, one good thrust is worth half a dozen cuts. Where's that black cape of mine?"

For the next half-hour, as full darkness settled down beneath a blanket of cloud, Reith scouted the edges of the clearing, moving warily behind a screen of bushes and tree trunks. Lamps burned brightly in the main tent—doubtless the Dour's pavilion—and less assertively in the lesser tents. The animals were staked out in another, adjacent clearing; Reith could hear their restless stamping and smell their pungent odor.

Discernible by the light of a dying cook fire, Reith glimpsed two sentries pacing the periphery of the camp, walking in opposite directions. He stationed himself near the point where the two met, exchanged passwords, saluted, and continued on. As soon as both had their backs to him, he cocked and charged Alicia's crossbow-pistol and, crouching, stole into the camp. He slipped into one of the gaps between the small tents and lay prone, virtually invisible in his hooded cloak and soot. After the sentries had passed again, he wormed his way towards the pavilion, separated from the ring of smaller tents by several meters of grassy terrain.

For another quarter-hour, Reith lay still among the crumpled herbs. As he had expected, another sentry patrolled this area, circling round and round the big tent. By wriggling his way toward the entrance to the pavilion, he established that two more guards stood there. He retreated until the curve of the tent hid them from view.

Having no idea of the internal architecture of the pavilion, Reith could not guess in which compartment Alicia might be found. So he continued to lie prone and motionless, seeking a clue.

A faint pearly opalescence in the overcast sky told of the rising of one of the moons, which found Reith still immobile, watching and listening. Since he was learning nothing by his vigil outside the tent, he decided that, whatever the risk, he must get in. He tested the edge of his knife with his thumb. Satisfied, he picked up the pistol, rose, and took a step towards the pavilion.

A muffled exclamation, from around the curve of the big tent, caused Reith to turn. Tiptoeing towards the sound, he came in sight of the sentry, bending over something. By the faint light he perceived what looked like a giant larva hatching as it crawled from beneath the edge of the tent.

"Ha!" snorted the sentry. "Up to your Terran tricks, eh?" Reaching down, he hauled out a naked woman, clutching a bundle of clothing—a Terran woman whose blond hair shone even in that crepuscular light.

The woman fought gamely, but the sentry had a firm grip on her arms. Coming up behind the Krishnan on the run, Reith raised the crossbow-pistol within centimeters of the sentry's neck.

The bolt delivered its kiss with a smacking sound as it bored into the base of the soldier's skull. The sentry collapsed silently save for the muffled thud of his fall.

"Alicia?" whispered Reith.

"Who is it?" came the reply.

"It's Fergus."

"Sorry; seeing you all black . . ."

"Pick up your clothes and come."

Reith pulled Alicia across the open space into the sheltering circle of smaller tents. Here he stopped, whispering: "Better put some clothes on."

On hands and knees they crept towards the edge of the campsite and lay still, scarcely breathing, until both sentries were headed away from them. Then they rose and fled into the woods.

"Ye fetched her!" cried Timásh. "I knew ye—"

"Hush up, idiot, and hurry!" snapped Reith. "We'll each lead one aya to the border."

They set out afoot, feeling their way among the indiscernible trees. They were nearing the gap in the fence across their path to safety when, muffled by distance and foliage, a rising clamor wafted from Vizman's camp. Reith halted to listen. "What's going on, Lish? Have they just found the dead sentry?"

"It's more than that." Leaning closer, she whispered. "I killed Vizman."

"Oh-oh! We'd better mount. Hand up!"

She put her foot into Reith's clasped hands and mounted. They went at a fast walk, with their heads bowed against their ayas' necks. Branches still savagely scraped their faces, and thorns impeded their progress. At last they were through the fence and into Mikardando territory.

A half hour later, they pulled into the inn yard at Qantesr. Muffled in Reith's black cloak over her hiked-up dress, Alicia asked: "Are we stopping here, Fergus?"

"No; too close to the border. The Qiribuma will probably be running in circles; but it's barely possible they might try a quick raid to recapture you. Are you sure Vizman's dead?"

"I'm sure." She cast a glance at Timásh. "I'll tell you about it later. *Ton employé comprend l'anglais.*"

"I get it. We'll go on to Ghushang, as soon as I pay up and get our stuff."

Soon Reith emerged with the taverner's pot boy, each carrying a small duffel bag. When Reith and Timásh had strapped their bags behind their saddles, they remounted and jogged off into the night.

A Krishnan hour later, they reached Ghushang. Reith stopped at the first house identified as an inn by the conventional animal's cranium mounted above the entrance. The door was locked. Reith knocked until at last a spy hole opened and a pair of Krishnan eyes, obliquely illuminated by a candle or lamp, looked out. Reith began: "We are travelers—"

The Krishnan shrieked: "Aroint ye, fiends from Hishkak! Begone! In the name of Bákh and Varzai and Qondyor and Hoi and all the good gods and goddesses, get ye hence! We are folk of unsullied virtue—"

"I'm sure you are," interrupted Reith, "but we are not demons; merely two Terrans and a human being benighted on the road—"

"Sneck up, ye black devils! Vanish! If ye be mortal, we'll soon see if your sooty hides can stop a crossbow bolt! Kavir, fetch my arbalest, *byant-hao!*"

Reith hastily turned away, grumbling: "I'd forgotten we still have our war paint on. There's a public aya trough in the main square, where we can wash. Come on!"

They found the square dark and silent save for a pair of fading crimson fires in cressets affixed to walls. As they wearily dismounted, the exhausted Reith almost fell from his mount. He fumbled in his bag until he brought out his one clean undershirt. Dipping it into the watering trough, he and Timásh scrubbed from their hands and faces most of the deceiving soot.

Two patrolmen of the night watch appeared in a side street, tramping along with halberds over their shoulders. With arms at port, they hurried across the square as Reith and Timásh were finishing their cleanup.

"Who be ye?" demanded the taller of the two. "What business have ye abroad at this hour?"

"Belated travelers," said Reith, "and lost upon the road. I am Fergus Reith, the Terran tour guide."

"Foor-giss Reet," said the shorter watchman. "That sounds like unto the *Ertsu* who made a stir, years agone, by escaping the clutch of the late High Priestess in Jeshang. Be ye that yare alien runagate?"

"I am he," said Reith, smiling, "with a visitor from my native world. My people and I need shelter before we fall asleep upon your cobblestones. We should be most grateful if you found us clean quarters and assured the taverner that we are harmless folk."

"An honor to serve you, Sir Foorgiss! Follow me!"

When at last they found an inn with a willing innkeeper and two vacant bedrooms, Reith said to Alicia, "There's one single and one double. What's your preference?"

"I'll take the single. And oh, how I'd love some clean clothes! This dress is ruined."

"I can spare you my undershorts. Tomorrow we'll hunt up a proper riding outfit for you."

Reith followed Alicia into the smaller room and slumped on the edge of the bed. When she saw his haggard face in the lamplight, she exclaimed: "Fergus! I've never seen you look so exhausted!"

"Well, I haven't had much time for sleep lately. I've been on the go almost round the clock. But I'll sleep better if you tell me what happened."

"We don't want to start that now! Go to bed, for heaven's sake!"

"No, Lish. A little while ago I was so done in I almost fell asleep in the saddle. Now I'm so tired I'm wide awake."

"But you ought to—"

"Lish, if you won't tell me what happened, I'll lie awake all night imagining things. So you'd better talk."

"Are you sure you want to hear it? It's not a pretty story."

"I'm not looking for entertainment; but I want to know."

"Very well." She sat down beside him but remained silent until Reith pulled out the letter signed with her name, saying:

"By the way, did you write this?"

Alicia scanned it. "No! I never wrote anything remotely like—I hope you don't think I'd ever—ever—"

"It had a fishy smell, but I couldn't be absolutely sure. I think it's a forgery by Minyev." After another silence, he asked: "How did they get you away from Baghál's night club?"

"One of the Krishnans told me there had been an attempted murder; and the victim, a Terran, might die. But nobody could understand his speech, so they couldn't even find out who he was. They begged me to come along and interpret, assuring me they'd bring me back to Baghál's in a few minutes.

"I should of course have cleared it with you, or at least told Cyril and Gashigi where I was going; but they seemed so excited that I rushed out with them. That's what happens when you're caught by surprise."

"I know," murmured Reith; "even to smart people."

"Out in the street, they hustled me into a carriage. No sooner was I seated when one Krishnan grabbed me; another whipped a length of cloth around my face and twisted my arms to snap on some sort of handcuffs.

"When the carriage reached open country, they took off my gag but refused to answer questions. In the light of morning, I recognized the little fellow in the magenta beard on my left as Minyev. He wouldn't talk, either.

"There's not much to tell about the trip, except that I

never did get used to rest stops with a couple of Krishnans standing by to make sure I didn't bolt.

"Around midday today—I guess it's yesterday by now—we crossed the border into Qirib, and I was hustled into Vizman's tent. There they took off my bonds, let me wash up, and served me a meal. How did you ever catch up with us? As they say, a stern chase is a long chase."

"Timásh and I rode like hell, that's how. Go on; tell me everything."

After another moment of silence, Alicia resumed her tale. She had found herself in a compartment of the tent the size of an average bedroom, furnished with all the elegance of a room in a palace. There were two comfortable chairs, a dresser, a washstand, and a table, all decorated with Vizman's gilded royal symbol of a god astride a sea monster. In one corner stood a large bed with lace-trimmed bedding.

On the table reposed a three-dimensional colored photograph of Alicia, set in a silver-gilt frame emblazoned with rubies, emeralds, and sapphires. This picture, she reasoned, must have been bought or begged from some photographer in Novo, since native photography was still in the box-and-tripod, black-and-white picture stage.

After a servant in green-and-purple livery removed the food, Alicia curled up on the bed for a nap; but that nap turned into a sleep of exhaustion. When she awoke, darkness shrouded the compartment. Outside, nocturnal Krishnan creatures began their serenade of clicks, chirps, trills, and buzzes.

Abruptly the tentflap was lifted and Minyev, now without his crimson beard, slipped in, saying obsequiously in Mikardandou: "Ah, my lady! You slept well, I trust?"

"Minyev, what the devil is this about?"

"We shall discuss it presently. Do you wish a fresh repast?"

"No; the dinner they gave me sufficed. Now answer my question, damn it!"

"May I be seated, my lady?" he asked, promptly seating himself. "I said you should be a queen, and I meant it. You must pardon the extreme measures we have been compelled to take, to make you a queen in fact."

"Minyev!" cried Alicia. "What makes you think I want to be a queen?"

"All women, Terran as well as human, desire to be goddesses or royal consorts."

"You are mistaken, Minyev. I never wished to be a queen. If I had, I should long ago have accepted the proposal of King Ainkhist of Mutabwk. What has become of him, by the way?"

"An unknown murdered him." Minyev gave the equivalent of a shrug. "But to return: We have determined that for you to be Dour Vizman's queen would well serve Qirib and our world as well. We admire your superior abilities and commend your efforts to assure the common folk happiness and prosperity.

"King Vizman hath been besotted by his loss of you since you departed for the planet Terra. Never hath his passion wavered. If you but extend kindness to him, you will perceive his many splendid qualities and come to love him as he doth dote on you."

"You are entirely mad!" exclaimed Alicia. "Perhaps the women of your species react thus; but do not presume to predict how a Terran woman would feel, especially after having been snatched away from her friends by brute force. If your regard for me be anything like that which you profess, you must help me escape."

Minyev made the negative head motion. "Nay; our minds are set, and nought you say will change them. You shall receive His Awesomeness tonight in yonder bed; and your nuptials will be celebrated on your return to Jazmurian."

Alicia angrily tossed her golden hair. "And if I refuse to coöperate?"

"If you remain stubborn, His Awesomeness hath secret chambers in his palace, where intransigent subjects can meditate upon their faults. Unless he command their release, there they stay, unknown to the world, as if they had vanished into air."

"So you think you're doing me a favor by shutting me up for life?"

"Word it not so harshly, my lady," said Minyev. "We have only your ultimate best interests, as well as those of Qirib, upon our humble livers."

"Beware! My fellow Terrans will avenge me, as befell King Ainkhist."

"We have taken precautions, never fear," replied Minyev with a smugness that filled Alicia with grim desperation.

"What's your plan for tonight?"

"His Awesomeness is minded to give you pleasure in spite of your aloofness; and he is experienced in such matters. You were well-advised to bend with grace unto his will, lest he call in his minions to assist him. I do assure you, he will have his way.

"But let us speak of other things. For an aspirant diplomat, I have indeed been remiss in hospitality." Minyev went to a cupboard and returned with a bottle and two goblets. The goblets he filled with much ceremony and handed one to Alicia. "Let us drink to your future happiness as the beloved and noble consort of His Awesomeness. What joy that this delightful Terran custom of celebration hath reached this world!"

Taking a sip, Alicia found the kvad strong and of high quality. Minyev swallowed half his gobletful in one gulp, coughed, and wiped his mouth.

"By the way," said Minyev complacently, "should you entertain thoughts of fleeing Dour Vizman's custody to seek the arms of Sir Fergus Reit', let me assure you that my former employer will never marry you."

"What gives you that idea?" said Alicia sharply.

"I have been his confidant for years, have I not?"

"You'll never be that again, when he learns how you have betrayed his trust!"

"What objection will he have? I have done him no injury. Since he entertains no matrimonial designs upon you, your departure will cause him little grief. And, not wishing to leave Sir Fergus in an awkward predicament, I have asked my cousin Yinkham to take my place. He should soon reach Novo. Dear lady, as you see, I think of everything!"

"Oh, you're a monstrously clever fellow, all right. But what makes you positive that Mr. Reith will never wed me?"

"Dear madam, though you may be unaware, young Alister is much opposed. Sir Fergus hath promised not to wed without his son's approval."

Minyev finished a second goblet of kvad. Alicia sipped a drop at a time and sharply watched the Khaldonian. "Alister seemed to like me well enough, the few times we have met. I'm sure he would never force such a promise from his father."

"Ah, Lady Alicia, you do not grasp the youth's true feelings. He may admire you as a fellow Terran, but he is madly jealous of Sir Fergus's affections and unwilling to share them with another."

"I don't believe a word of this, Minyev. Why have you turned against your old employer?"

Minyev hiccuped. "My reasons are three: admiration for your superior qualities, sympathy for our lovelorn Dour, and a wish to bring together two spirits whom the gods plainly intend for one another."

"And besides, you are promised a substantial reward. Come now, old comrade, is it not so?" Alicia smiled disarmingly.

"Well, to tell the truth, Dour Vizman promises to finance my university degree, so that I can enter diplomatic service. Diplomats are a nation's first defense against the scourge of war; and I am devoted to the cause of peace."

Alicia continued. "And who are those others you call 'we'? Who abducted me?"

"Know you Enrique Schlegel?"

"Slightly. Are your accomplices active in his society?"

Minyev, taking a drink, made the affirmative head motion.

"And," continued Alicia, "doubtless the Dour has promised the society financial backing in return for me?"

"How clever you are, my lady! Much as we dislike distraining you against your will, you must see that we do but serve the greater good." Minyev drank deeply from his third goblet of strong liquor. "We commoners seldom taste so fine a beverage as this. Lady Alicia, you must surely be ready for a trifle more to wet your lovely lips!"

She shook her head. "You would not have me fail to give the Dour the welcome he desires. Do tell me more."

Minyev raised his goblet and swirled the golden liquid. "I perceive you have decided to take my sound advice. Some day you will be grateful to me. Now I must depart, ere His Awesomeness come to claim his royal rights." He downed the rest of his gobletful and set the vessel on the table with an air of finality.

"Oh, don't go yet!" said Alicia hastily. "Time enough when the Dour arrives. Tell me something of your personal life and your adventures."

"Well, I have a wife in a village near Sir Fergus's ranch, and a young son plus an egg in the incubator. The boy hath not, alas, inherited my splendid sensitive organs of smell. . . ." Minyev proudly fluttered the plumes of his own imposing antennae.

Two goblets more and several rambling reminiscences later, Minyev slumped back into his chair and closed his eyes. A faint snore escaped him.

Alicia sprang to her feet. When nudges failed to arouse the Khaldonian, she grasped him by his belt and dragged him into a corner. Then she drew his dagger, a sizable, needle-pointed weapon, from its sheath.

Next she pulled the coverlet from the bed and tossed it over Minyev's recumbent body, arranging it so that it looked as if carelessly discarded but still hid the Khaldonian completely. She hesitated before going on with the plan she had devised as she listened to Minyev's stories. Should she try to talk Vizman out of his intentions before taking extreme measures? She quickly dismissed the thought, knowing too much of the ways of Krishnan monarchs. If he was ruthless enough to have her dragged by force all the way from Mishé, he would not he balked at this late stage, either by piteous pleas or by rational reasoning.

Alicia slipped the dagger beneath her pillow, its pommel set to be within reach of her right hand when she lay supine. Then she turned down the lamp, stripped, and arranged herself upon the bed. After an intolerable wait, she heard the crunch of heavy footsteps outside. Vizman's voice called: "Minyev!"

"He's gone, but I am here," said Alicia, trying to feign eager anticipation.

The canvas flap rose; and in came Dour Vizman, a little heavier and a little slower than eighteen Krishnan years ago but otherwise the same bulky, middle-aged Krishnan politician. He wore the traditional Qiribo costume, a square of cloth pinned across one shoulder and under the opposing arm. At the sight of Alicia, Vizman paused with a gasp.

"Alicia!" he cried. "As beautiful as ever! My dear, I have dreamed of this moment for almost twenty years! Never hath my passion for your sweet self wavered by the thickness of a hair! I love you, and you shall love me, too."

Vizman cast off his exiguous garment and kicked off his slippers. "Ah, beloved, how I have yearned through the long years!" He ran a trembling hand along her thigh.

Her heart racing, Alicia forced her lips into an inviting smile. Vizman drew a long breath and threw himself upon her.

"Ah, Bákh!" he murmured. "What joy!" Then his body stiffened, his antennae quivered, and he tightly closed his eyes in ecstasy.

Gently, Alicia reached beneath the pillow, grasped the pommel of the dagger, and drew it forth. She raised her arms, embracing his massive torso, until she could grasp the dagger hilt with both hands while directing the point towards Vizman's back. While Vizman's breath came in gasps, Alicia suddenly pulled the weapon towards herself with a powerful thrust and drove the blade home.

As the dagger buried itself in the dour's body, Vizman's eyes snapped open. Disbelief distorted his heavy features before they relaxed in the expressionless calm of death.

Pinned beneath the Krishnan's huge, inert body, Alicia felt panic. Smothering an impulse to cry out, she managed to roll the cooling corpse aside and free herself. She hesitated over the dagger but decided to leave it protruding from the would-be lover's back. To be caught with the weapon in hand was a risk that she dared not take.

Blue-green blood made a slowly widening circle on the pristine sheet as Alicia shakily snatched up her dress and shoes, turned out the lamp, and sought a way out.

Moving catlike in the dark, she observed that three of the four walls glowed faintly, the canvas being illuminated by lights in the adjacent compartments. The remaining wall, black as the night, must, she inferred, mark the outer limits of the pavilion.

A cautious hand along the ground revealed that the loose canvas would permit an active person to squirm

under it. Lying prone and raising the tent edge by a
finger's breadth, Alicia peered out. At first she could
see only velvet dark, save for the crimson spark of a
luminous arthropod whirling past. As her eyes adjusted
to the overcast night, she made out the faint, colorless
bulge of a smaller tent several meters away.

Hearing nothing but the mating songs of Krishnan
arthropods, she decided that no guards were near. Well,
she thought, here goes. Still clutching her dress and
shoes, she squirmed forward on her elbows. She had
half emerged from the tent when a rough voice rumbled in the Qiribo dialect: "Well, fry my balls! What
have we here?"

Hard hands seized her arms and hauled her, kicking
and struggling, to the trampled herbage outside the
tent.

"Ha!" said the soldier. "Up to your old Terran tricks,
eh? The gods blind me, but if I weren't on duty I'd haul
you off in the bushes for a quick go myself!"

"And then you arrived," Alicia said to Reith. "You've
saved me once more from my own stupidity, though I
sure don't deserve it."

"Nonsense!" said Reith, affecting a heartiness he did
not feel. "You saved yourself. I merely happened along
at the last minute, more by good luck than good management. You're a heroine, like that woman who se-
duced a conqueror in order to kill him—Judith, that's
her name."

With eyes downcast, Alicia shook her head. "If I'd
been smart, I wouldn't have gotten into that fix in the
first place; and if you hadn't killed the sentry, the
Qiribuma would now be arguing over what lingering
death to give me."

Reith said "Tell me, Lish, could you ever have learned
to love Vizman?"

"Fergus! Sometimes you make me angry! Me, let a
medieval despot tell me what to do with my life? You

know me better than that." She paused. "Still, I can't help feeling a little sorry for him. He seems to have loved me, in his way."

"Don't blame yourself, darling! If I'd been there, I'd have scragged him, and done it much more painfully. He knew the risk he was running; he just pushed his luck too far. The one I'm sorry for is that sentry I shot; he may have been a decent fellow."

"I suppose they'll do something horrible to Minyev, finding him dead drunk and his dagger in the king's back."

"Don't waste your sympathy on that twerp. For all his high-flown talk about the kingdom's welfare, all he really wanted was the scholarship Vizman offered him. Let's be glad we got out of this mess as well as we did. Let's think of—"

"Fergus," she interrupted, "I can't talk about it any more. What I really want is a bath. I feel—unclean."

Reith sighed. "Okay, a bath it is. I'll drag the innkeeper out of bed to heat the water. He won't like it, but a bit of Stavrakos's gold should pacify him."

X
JACOB WHITE

Half a moon after the escape from Vizman, Reith's gig rolled along the road westward from Mishé. Alicia sat beside him, and Timásh followed, riding an aya with two others on the lead.

They trotted through the rolling countryside of western Mikardand, where a lessening rainfall caused the forest cover to thin out to occasional copses and gallery forests along the stream beds. Elsewhere, the stony ground was only sparsely covered by the Krishnan analogues of grasses, herbs, and scrub. The garish colors of the more easterly vegetation faded out to pastels. Farms tended to cluster in areas where water was readily available; deep wells for irrigation were beyond Krishnan technology. In the wide, unfenced uplands between the farms, occasional herds of Krishnan herbivores, some four-legged and others six-legged, looked up as the gig clattered by. If alarmed, they bounded away.

The relationship between Reith and Alicia, which had been on a warming trend before the kidnapping, had cooled down to polite impersonality. Ever since Reith and Alicia had first met, interaction between them had always been lively, whether in the form of lovemaking, quarreling, gossiping, or abstract discussion. On the journey back to Mishé from Qantesr, however, they had spoken but little, and then usually for merely mundane purposes.

Alicia seemed to have withdrawn into herself. Reith supposed that she was trying to sort out conflicting emotions, and that if he tried to pry her out of her shell he would only reopen old wounds and make her even unhappier than, he suspected, she was. So he treated her with wary respect, watching for signs that she would welcome a resumption of their old comradeship.

Now, approaching Zinjaban, they began little by little to warm towards each other. Reith said: "Stavrakos made a terrible fuss about my going off to find you. He actually expected me to stay with the crew until the movie was shot and then, if I liked, go searching. He talked of refusing to pay me, because I was breaking my contract."

"Sounds like the hog," said Alicia. "How'd you get around him?"

"Believe it or not, the rest of the crew—even Fodor and Ordway—took my side. Ordway would have gladly come along on the rescue if I'd let him; but he'd have been a liability. Anyway, the gang told Kostis that, if he tried to stop me from saving you, they'd pull a strike. So Kostis gave in."

A smile lit up her somber face. "Nice to know they think me worth saving. But I'm surprised Attila stood by you. He's always resented my position."

"He muttered about barbarian honor; and Cyril of course has been sweet on you all along. What's this mysterious magic you have, which works a spell on everyone?"

"Ha!" she said. "I don't try to fascinate anybody. All I want is to do my research, write my books, and leave the social sciences in better shape because of me. Hey, isn't that Zinjaban on that rise ahead of us?"

On the hither side of a row of distant mountains, two towers like oil-well rigs reared unlovely heads. As the gig rolled nearer, rows of tents came into view. The towers, it could now be seen, were built of wooden beams and braces supporting a network of stairs and ladders, which led to a series of platforms.

As the ayas toiled up the long slope, the landscape opened out. The village of Zinjaban lay off to the right of the tent city. On the left, in a fallow field, squadrons of cavalry practiced maneuvers, wheeling, charging, and rallying, while the low sun flashed ruby sparkles from their mail. Beyond the twin towers the ground dropped away towards the Khoruz, still out of sight below the curve of the ridge. Farther still, beyond the vale, the travelers saw the foothills and peaks of the Qe'bas.

The gig drew up at the edge of the tent city. Reith swung down and was looking for someone in authority, when he turned at a wild yell. "Hey, Fergus! You did it! By God's whiskers, you did it!"

Anthony Fallon hurried up, burbling: "Alicia! Thank Bákh you made it! It must be quite a story. When—how—"

"Go easy, Tony," said Reith. "She's had a rough time. Might have been rougher yet if Minyev hadn't quarreled with Vizman and murdered him."

"*What!*"

"Yep; struck a knife in his back. Alicia got away in the confusion, and I came along just in time to help."

"What happened to Minyev?"

"I suspect something lingering and humorous, with either boiling oil or melted lead. We didn't hang around to find out. Now tell me what you're doing here! By the time we got to Mishé, the crew had finished their shooting there."

"I came out with Gashigi. I thought, with such a mixed crowd of Terrans and Krishnans, the World Fed needed someone to keep an eye on things."

"Gashigi's here, too?"

"Yes; she wants to make sure the Republic isn't put to unnecessary expense, nor its people abused. See that big contraption over yonder, with all the gilding? That's her carriage."

"Where's Strachan? It's his job to find us quarters."

"He's over the river with the shooting crew, translating. I can tell you where you're going; he and I worked it out. You'll bunk with Colonel Bobir of the Gozashtando Regiment."

"And Alicia?"

"We'll put her in with Mary Hopkins, the wardrobe mistress. She's that severe-looking old prune you've met."

"Who's got the rooms at Manshu's?"

Fallon smiled wryly. "Rank has its privileges. Stavrakos and Gashigi have Manshu's two rooms."

"All to themselves?"

"Well, it's understood that Ordway visits the Treasurer more or less nightly; they seem to have a hot thing going. The joke on location is, if you feel the earth shake, it's not an earthquake; it's just Cyril and Gashigi having fun."

"And Stavrakos?"

"Far as I know, Kostis sleeps alone. Some say he's one of us girls; but I think it's only his moneybags he's in love with."

"What's that big tent over there?"

"That's the portable studio, for interiors. Come along, you two; I'll show you your tents and find your man a place among the Krishnans."

Reith met Mary Hopkins, saw Alicia's luggage stowed, and went on with Fallon to Bobir's tent.

An hour later, Reith was settled in. He had greeted Bobir, commander of the Gozashtanduma, whom he already knew, and was introduced to the colonel named Padras, who commanded the Mikardando regiment.

Reith was strolling about to orient himself when a bugle call drew his attention westward. A column of ayas, bearing both Terran and Mikardando riders, was fording the river. The water, now shadowed by the hills beyond, curled up around the shanks of the horned, six-legged mounts.

Reith picked out Fodor by his great stature and bald head. As the group plodded up the hither slope, Fodor spurred his aya to a gallop and swept past the tents, yelling "Hi-yah! Hi-yah!" Leaning as he banked a turn, the Hungarian, a magnificent rider, set his animal at the vehicle park and pounded straight for Reith's gig. When the beast seemed about to crash into the little vehicle, Fodor pulled his aya into a soaring leap and cleared the trap by a few centimeters. Although relieved to see his carriage unscathed, Reith was a little disappointed that Fodor's neck seemed equally intact.

The director galloped back, jerked his mount to a halt, and leaped down roaring welcomes. He grabbed Reith and boisterously kissed him on both cheeks.

"We got some first-class takes today!" he bellowed. "You must see the rushes! Now, what the hell have you been doing? The damn picture is three-quarters shot, castle scenes and all. All we got left to do is the long chase to Castle Kandakh, and then the big battle with your Gozashtanders. We do the long chase tomorrow, d.v. The battle will take several days, with rehearsals and all. Did you get Alicia? Is she all right? Where—"

"Here I am, Attila," said Alicia, who emerged from her tent to be promptly grabbed and kissed in her turn. "Thanks to Fergus, I'm still alive and in one piece."

"What happened?" roared Fodor. "Could we get a movie script out of the story?"

"I'm saving it for my next book of memoirs," answered Alicia.

As word of Alicia's arrival spread, the rest of the crew rushed up to congratulate her, wringing her hands, kissing her, and plying her with questions. She dampened down their exuberance and called: "Fergus!"

When she got him aside, she said: "A little bijar tells

me you could use something to restore your energy. I have a bottle hidden in Mary's tent."

"You wonder woman! Lead on."

Reith and Alicia were curled up in the tent, sipping falat and exchanging banter in a relaxed, low-keyed mode, when Alicia murmured: "By the way, thanks for the story you told Tony; I mean about Vizman's death."

Reith nodded. "That's the official version from now on. There's nobody to contradict it."

"How are you fixed for quarters?"

"The colonel's a good old soldier but a bit of a bore. If—oh, hello, Mary!"

Mary Hopkins came in. The wardrobe mistress declined a drink but listened eagerly to Reith's version of the rescue. Then she exclaimed: "There's the dinner gong!"

As they took their places in the chow line before the cook tent, Mary Hopkins said: "It's nice enough eating picnic style in good weather but miserable when it rains. Then we have to cover our plates and run back to our tents."

Dinner at the long tables over, Alicia took Reith to Manshu's tiny inn for a showing of the day's rushes. The common room was jammed, with people sitting on the floor and trying to see past one another's heads. The makeup artists, Reith thought, had done an excellent job on the Terran actors; it would take an expert to tell them from authentic Krishnans.

In one scene, Princess Ayala, played by the buxom Cassie Norris, was about to be burned at the stake. At the last minute Prince Karam, the actor Randal Fairweather sporting a short-sleeved, coarsely-knit sweater dipped in metallic paint to simulate chain mail without the real thing's weight, galloped up on an aya. Severing the princess's bonds with a slash of his sword, he caught her up and galloped off.

Cassie's complaining voice, high and sharp, rose above

the chatter in the crowded room. "I thought I'd gotten close enough to being fried; but Attila wanted more realism. So on the third take, he delayed the rescue till the damned fire burned my leg. The fuckin' thing still hurts, in spite of Doc Hamid's goo!"

Fodor growled: "You're lucky. It's my ambition to make a picture where somebody really *is* burned at the stake."

"Damned sadist!" said Cassie.

"Of course!" boomed Fodor cheerfully. "All barbarians are sadists at heart!"

"You can't do another take of that scene, anyway," Mary Hopkins put in. "That was the last of those white chemises she's supposed to wear."

"Then we get the local people to stitch us up some more and shoot the whole scene over. I don't like it the way it is. When Randal picks her up, her tits are supposed to pop out. The slips should be cut way down lower."

Groans filled the darkened room. Fodor said: "Okay, okay; I kid. Tomorrow we go on the long chase. The colonel at Castle Kandákh says we can stay all night at his fort. So bring your toothbrushes! He's moving his junior officers out of their rooms for us. Guess he hopes to stick his face in the camera and see his picture in the film."

Alicia and Reith sat their ayas in the foothills of the Qe'bas, watching cameramen struggle up rocky slopes sparsely covered with pink, mauve, and blue-gray herbage.

"One nice thing about making movies on Krishna," she said, "is the long days. Since it takes so much time to get everything set up and put away again, the extra daylight hours give us half again as much actual shooting time as on Terra."

"Lots of disadvantages, too, I suppose," suggested Reith.

"You just bet! No electric power, so we have to haul those super-storage batteries called 'hoarders' along. Oh, there's Attila waving at me. I have to go interpret for him. Don't fall off any cliffs!"

As he watched her receding back, Reith earnestly wished that he could get Alicia alone long enough to resolve the problem of their future. Even if her more-than-sisterly affection for him had been lessened by the Vizman episode, his feelings towards her burned brighter than ever. He felt a growing urge to "have it out" with her. But, in the hustle and bustle of cinematic work, there were scarcely five minutes when one or the other was not absorbed in some chore for Cosmic Productions.

Hour after hour, Reith watched from the sidelines as the chase sequence took form. The action was simple, if strenuous, for the actors involved. Prince Karam, holding a terrified Princess Ayala in the curve of his sturdy arm, galloped up the Balhib road with a dozen villains, played by Mikardando extras, in pursuit.

Over and over, as Fodor raised his bullhorn and bellowed: "Sound! Cameras! Action!" Prince Karam, clutching his leading lady, galloped past the cameras. Each time when Fodor yelled, "Cut!" Karam reined his aya down to a walk and guided it back to the starting point. After the shot had been repeated three or four times, Fairweather and Cassie were allowed to rest while the Krishnan pursuers were photographed galloping up the same stretch of road, again and again.

A short time later, the whole crew moved further up into the hills and repeated the process on another stretch of road. Alicia explained that such a sequence was technically called an alternating syntagma. Cassie's flimsy garment became shabbier by the hour.

Interested though Reith was, as the long day wore on, he found movie-making tediously repetitious. He was impressed by the time and the endless attention to detail that each take called for. A ten-second shot might require up to a quarter or even half an hour of repositioning the cameras, the sound equipment, and the sheets of silvered cardboard used to reflect light on the actors. Everyone, including Alicia, White, and Ordway, pitched in to move equipment.

Reith overheard an altercation between Cassie Norris and Attila Fodor. She screamed: "If you suckers weren't such cheapskates, you'd have brought doubles for the long shots. I'll be so worn out tomorrow, I won't be able to act for shit!" Reith was amused by the contrast between Cassie's raucous, inelegant everyday voice and the sweetly refined tones she used before the cameras.

A Krishnan aya-wrangler spoke to Alicia, who translated. "Attila, he says unless we take time out, we'll founder the mounts."

"Oh, hell, then we get some more ayas!"

"Don't be stupid!" said Randal Fairweather. "You want me to start the ride on a roan and end up on a gray, like when I played d'Artagnan in *Swords and Muskets?* I never did hear the last of that."

"You shut up!" roared Fodor. "Who's boss here? Anyway, it's time for lunch."

Roqir had disappeared behind the peaks when the fugitives reached Castle Kandakh ahead of their pursuers. Since the light was no longer strong enough for the last shots of the sequence, Fodor reluctantly called time and led the cast and crew into the fort. Those who could ride had ridden up from Zinjaban; those who could not had been ferried up in one of the omnibuses.

Inside the gate, Sir Litáhn's armored troops stood in a double line with drawn swords. As the Terrans approached, they raised their swords and shouted: "*Hao na Ertsumak!*"

Fodor called back over his shoulder. "Does that mean they welcome us or are going to cut us in pieces?"

"It's a cheer," said Alicia. "Go on in."

"This guy wants to make sure he gets a bit part," growled Fodor. "We'll let him make a cameo appearance." He strode in, grasped thumbs with Sir Litáhn, and made himself agreeable. The others followed.

In what appeared to be an officers' club, a tidied and refreshed film crew assembled for drinks. Reith, Alicia, and Fallon were kept busy interpreting the pleasantries between Earthmen and Krishnans. Ordway came up to Reith, his round face disarmingly respectful. He exclaimed: "I say, Sir Fergus, Tony just told me about your new title. Isn't that splendid?"

"I hope I don't let it go to my head."

"Oh, surely not!" said Ordway, completely missing Reith's irony. "We all know you're a man of sound character. May I shake your hand? And will you do me the honor of having a drink with me?"

Reith smiled at Ordway's infatuation with titles. He let Ordway press a drink of kvad upon him, then another.

Lady Gashigi appeared, crying: "Ah, my two fah-vo—fay-vah-rite Earsmans! How I loov ze Terrans! Get me a da-rink, pa-lease, Cyril."

Reith was congratulated again on his knighthood, and more drinks were thrust at him. He would have liked to stay close to Alicia; but she was surrounded by junior officers and seemed to be enjoying herself.

Sir Litáhn came up with more congratulations and another brimming goblet. By the time a silver trumpet sang the call to dinner, Reith's head was spinning. He started determinedly for Alicia, intending to escort her into the mess and seat her beside him. But an officer buttonholed him to discuss Terran military history. When at last he escaped, he saw that Randal Fairweather had pushed through the circle of Krishnan admirers and captured Alicia's arm. The tall actor was now attentively escorting her into the mess.

Reith arrived at the long table to find all the places near Alicia occupied. He had to take a seat well away from the clump of Terrans that included Bennett Ames, the assistant grip, his wife Cassie Norris, Randal Fair-

weather, and Jacob White. Alicia sat between Fairweather and White, facing a row of Krishnan officers of
various ranks.

Cassie Norris, wearing a fishnet dress and nothing
beneath, kept trying to invite Randal Fairweather's attention. (She must, thought Reith, have forehandedly
sent that dress up ahead; most of the Terrans were still
in the outdoor clothing they had worn through the day.)
But the actor, ignoring Cassie's spectacularly displayed
charms, devoted himself to Alicia, detailing his adventures as he played the title rôle in *Sir Francis Drake*.
On Cassie's other side, Bennett Ames scowled. Jacob
White, frowning in concentration, tried his rudimen-
tary Mikardandou on a Krishnan neighbor. On Reith's
side of the table, a well-liquored Cyril Ordway, waving
a piece of roast shaihan on an eating spear, declaimed:
"One thing I like about this bloody planet is, plenty of
beef, even if the cow had six legs. Back home, a steak
the size of your thumb costs the national debt. . . ."

Reith scarcely tasted his food. Afterwards, during a
showing of the day's rushes, he fell asleep in the darkened room until Fallon nudged him awake.

"Pull up your socks, old boy!" whispered the consul.
"You're snoring."

Reith looked up blearily as an officer went around
lighting candles set in mirrored sconces on the wall.
Then he felt Fodor's large, hairy hand on his arm.

"Fergus!" said Fodor. "I am having anudder party,
very exclusive. You and the little Alicia, both come
along!"

When Reith's head cleared enough for him to remember anything, he was seated on a divan in a large
room, occupied by seven others. Looking about, he
wondered if the commandant had turned over his private
quarters to Fodor; for the room was sumptuously
appointed, with fur rugs on the polished floor and pic-

tures of battle scenes on the walls. Two open doors led to bedrooms.

Silently, Reith berated himself because he, usually one of the most self-disciplined of men, had lowered his guard long enough to get tight—something that had not befallen him a dozen times in an active life. When he managed clearly to focus his eyes, he saw that the other men, besides his host, were Anthony Fallon and Jacob White. The females were Alicia, Gashigi, and Fodor's two women. Reith turned to Michelle.

"How did you get here, Mrs. Fodor? I didn't see you during the shooting."

"*La Madame* Gashigi, she brought us up in her carriage," said Michelle with a charming smile.

"It is time," said Gashigi, "zat I visited zis pa-lace for ze gov—governam—for ze Ga-rand Master. So I sought it would be nice to ba-ring ze gir-rals to zeir man."

"Anudder round!" shouted Fodor to the Krishnan steward. "Now we sing! I lead!"

Fodor had been drinking two goblets to Reith's one, but the drink seemed merely to make the director more boisterously self-assertive. He bellowed songs in five languages and tried to lead the others. Reith, a mediocre singer, followed a couple of ditties in French and German, but Magyar baffled him.

"Now we dance!" cried Fodor, producing a violin and kicking back a rug with such force as to hurl it into a heap in a corner. Rising, Alicia asked: "What dances do you play, Attila?"

"All kinds! What you like? Waltz? Fox-trot? Khopak? Zulu?"

"How about a tango?"

"Sure, I know a hundred!"

"That would be just divine! Fergus dances a splendid tango." Turning, she grasped Reith's wrist and pulled. "Come on, Fergus! Let's show them!"

"Out of practice," he mumbled. "Besides, I'm afraid I've drunk more than I should have."

"Oh, come on! You'll do fine!"

He got unsteadily to his feet and followed her to the cleared space. Fodor played Jacob Gade's *Jalousie* and followed it with one of Carlos Gardel's tangos. Reith did not know whether his reflexes took over, or whether Alicia was so good a dancer that she could follow the most inept partner. But he managed the *corte*, the Argentine cross, and the double flare without bumping anyone, losing his balance, or treading on Alicia's toes.

Reith became aware that Fallon was dancing with Nancy. He glimpsed Gashigi and Michelle trying to haul Jacob White to his feet, despite White's protest that he had never learned to dance.

When Fodor stopped, Reith sank back on his sofa. Fodor pressed another drink upon him. Being overheated with exertion, he drank most of it before he realized his precarious state. Then he set down the goblet and stared glassily at the others, feeling sweat bead his forehead as he fought to keep control.

"Now I show you a dance!" boomed Fodor. "Who else plays the fiddle?"

"I learned as a boy," said White, staring shyly at his hands. "I'll give it a try."

"Know any Gypsy dances? That's what I do!"

"Matter of fact, I had to practice one of them, day after day. Here goes!"

White sailed into *Tzigane*, by the twenty-first century composer Milescu. Fodor danced solo, stamping and whirling. When White ended the piece, Fodor clapped him on the back with a force that nearly felled him; then put away the violin, gulped another drink, and roared: "Now for the game!"

Fodor whipped out another deck of cards backed by the cipher "F. A. G." and said, "We don't got a table, so we sit on the floor in a circle. Come on!"

He collected an armful of cushions from the sofa and spread them on the floor. "You sit there, Jack! You there, Fergus! You there, Tony! You girls, take the places between."

"Where's Cyril?" asked White.

"He got drunk and is somewhere sleeping it off," roared Fodor. "So in his place I got Tony here, even though the Limey party-pooper don't drink!

"Now, my friends, we will have a orgy. A real orgy. You know what that is? I bet none of you ever had one. So you will remember this night as long as you live. If anyone don't want this kind of fun, he better get the hell out! Okay?

"First, we play strip poker, like I said the other time at Novo. Any objections?"

Reith glanced about, expecting Fodor's women to object again; but only Nancy uttered a timid squeak of: "Well, I don't know. . . ." Fodor ignored her. White mumbled something about its being against his religion; Fallon grinned in anticipation. Alicia, silent, had donned her poker face.

"Everybody knows the rules?" said Fodor. "You, Gashigi?"

"I haff pa-layed it only one time," she replied. "I sink I know ze rules."

"Fine; maybe we strip you first. The unit of betting is one garment, represented by one chip. Once off, the garment stays off. Straight draw, nossing wild. Here, Fergus, cut!"

Fallon spoke. "But what's the point, Attila? Mere nudity means nothing on this world, especially when we've all been bathing together in the river. Everyone knows what the others look like."

"I know, but I haven't finished. To add a pinch of pepper to the party, I make a new rule. When one of you strips a player of the odder sex, they drop out and screw, right then and there!"

The other players traded startled glances, showing various degrees of apprehension and anticipation. White, looking around like a beast in a trap, mumbled: "Where?"

"Anywhere—on the rug, on the sofa, or you can go in the bedroom."

White muttered: "I may fornicate in the sight of the God of Israel, but I'm damned if I'll do it in the sight of all you reprobates!"

"Attila, really—" began Alicia, but Fodor cut her off with a bellow. "Oh, come on! You're the smartest poker player here, so you can strip any man you like. Besides, is nossing like a orgy to stimulate interest. This will wake you up! Okay, here we go! I deal. You open, Nancy."

Reith felt that something was terribly wrong; that he should have interfered or objected. What if one of these characters stripped Alicia? What would he do? Why didn't she refuse, or better yet rise indignantly and walk out?

If he could only summon the energy to get to his feet, take her hand, and lead her out. . . . But she might refuse, or explode in a temper tantrum, as she would have twenty years ago. Somebody should do something, Reith felt; but a curious lethargy gripped them all. The combination of liquor, fatigue, and Fodor's intimidating physical presence seemed to have reduced everyone to helpless acquiescence.

Reith opened his mouth to raise an objection; but under the baleful glare of steel-cold eyes beneath Fodor's shaggy brows, the words died in his throat. As Fodor dealt cards, however, Reith became suddenly aware that Alicia was on her feet. Lithe as an eel, from sitting cross-legged she had smoothly risen erect without apparent effort, like a khaki-clad goddess manifesting herself. She took a step towards the door.

"Hey!" said Fodor, also rising. "Where you going?"

"Out," she said. "Sorry, but your game is too full-flavored for me. Give Cassie my place, if you like."

Fodor stepped in front of Alicia. "No, you don't!"

"What do you mean? I'll go where I please!"

She tried to dodge around Fodor, but the director

spread orangutanian arms to block her. "If you don't want to play, you should have said so sooner. Now it's too late. I promise myself I win *you*! I pay you back for telling me how to make my movie!"

"Get out of my way!" said Alicia through set teeth, attempting an end run.

Fodor's long arm shot out and grabbed Alicia's wrist, so tightly as to bring a small cry of pain. Fodor shouted "Like hell—*ow*!"

Reith saw one of Alicia's boots leave the floor and heard the solid thump of a kick. The cards in Fodor's left hand went flying.

"*Ördög! Teufelin!*" yelled Fodor, gathering Alicia into a smothering embrace.

Up to that moment, Reith, still in the grip of alcoholic lethargy, had stared bemused, as if witnessing a stage play. Now a surge of fury brought him to his feet. He did not consciously plan his next acts; it was as if some outside agency had taken control of his body.

Before he realized what he was doing, he stepped forward, seized the slack of Fodor's jacket, and wrenched the director around. Alicia squirmed out of Fodor's grasp, and Reith drove his fist into Fodor's belly. As the director, eyes wide with surprise, doubled over, Reith landed two furious punches on his jaw. Fodor staggered back; Reith followed, sinking punch after punch, until Fodor crashed to the floor and lay with limbs twitching like a wounded insect.

"Come on, Lish," said Reith. Wordlessly she grasped the hand he held out. Hand in hand they left the room and walked down the hall to the bedroom assigned to Alicia.

In the bedroom, Alicia spoke. "Fergus, your poor knuckles are bleeding! Let me get my kit to bandage them!"

"Must have hit that blug harder than I realized."

"I never knew you to be so fierce with your fists."

"I'm not, darling. As a kid, I couldn't punch my way out of a paper bag. I guess the sight of that brigand hauling on your arm gave me an extra shot of adrenalin. Besides, he was pretty drunk, or he'd have made hamburger of me."

"There you go, being modest!"

"Not modest; realistic."

"Sometimes you're too realistic for your own good. Why did you do it?"

"Why? You of all people ask why? First, because you obviously didn't want to play. So, what man's going to sit quietly while the girl he—"

The door burst open, and in the doorway stood Attila Fodor with a Krishnan sword in his hand. "Ha!" he said, and strode purposefully towards Reith, a slit-eyed grin on his face.

"Attila! Please!" cried Alicia, throwing herself in front of Reith. "I'll give you what you want, but leave Fergus alone—"

"Out of the way, Alicia!" growled Fodor. "You want to fuck, fine; but after I kill this guy. Nobody beats up Attila Fodor and lives!"

Reith glanced around, but his sword was in the room he shared with Ordway. The only weapon Reith could see was a light chair. He snatched it up. As Fodor went into a fencing stance, Reith wondered if he could parry a lunge.

Alicia whipped the bedspread off the bed, whirled, and threw the heavy cloth so that it settled over Fodor's head and shoulders. The director ripped out a Magyar curse as he struggled with the fabric. While his attacker was still blinded by the spread, Reith swung his chair and smote the swathed form with such force as to break the two front legs of the improvised weapon.

The blow staggered Fodor, who threw off the bedspread just as Reith struck his knees in a football tackle. Both men crashed to the floor. Fodor squirmed over on his back and tried to bring the sword into play, while his free hand clawed at Reith's face.

Clutching fiercely at Fodor's sword arm, Reith got a grip on a finger and bent it back, his muscles quivering with strain. Something cracked, and Fodor yelped. Alicia circled around the struggling pair with her crossbow pistol cocked.

At last Reith wrested the sword out of Fodor's grasp. With all his strength, he brought the pommel down on Fodor's head, again and again. After several blows, the director lay inert.

Reith looked up to see the doorway crowded with staring spectators, including White with his arm around Gashigi, and both of them nude. White's narrow face bore an unhappy look. Reith recognized Hamid Mas'udi, the shooting crew's physician, and called: "Hey, doc! Will you take charge of this clown? Patch him up and tell him next time I won't let him off so easily."

"Are you all right, Mr. Reith?" said the physician.

"Nothing a little washing and bandaging won't fix." Reith rose to his feet. Mas'udi and Fallon hauled Fodor up and staggered out, each with one of Fodor's arms around his neck. The others dispersed. Reith closed and bolted the door, saying: "Stupid of me not to have done that sooner."

"Oh, Fergus, sit down and let me clean you up!" said Alicia, setting down her crossbow pistol and going to the washstand. "Your face is all bloody."

"The bleep was trying to gouge an eye; so I got a few scratches."

A quarter-hour of washing, disinfecting, and bandaging left Reith sore but functional. He said: "Thanks, Lish darling. You've saved my life for the umpteenth time. He'd have drilled me for certain."

She put a hand on each side of his bandaged head and gently kissed him. "Well, you saved me once more. While you two were thrashing around on the floor, I'd have killed him if I could have gotten a clear shot. But what were you about to say when that dreadful man burst in?"

Reith rose, wincing, and paced. "Let me think. . . . Oh, yes. I was saying, what real man would sit by and watch the girl he loves being manhandled?"

"Fergus! Do you mean that—that—"

Reith took a deep breath. "Of course I mean that. I love you!"

Alicia's smile was like the sun breaking through a leaden overcast. Then, assuming a sober mien, she continued. "Are your intentions honorable or otherwise, sir?"

"I'm just another retarded flatworm! Alicia, will you marry me?"

"Fergus!" She threw her arms around him. "I wondered and wondered when you'd make up your mind! I was determined not to ask again."

"Well, will you or won't you?"

"Will I or won't I what? Ask you?"

"No, silly; marry me."

"You just—but wait a minute. What would Alister say? Minyev said the boy is absolutely opposed."

"Minyev was lying." Reith pulled out the folded note from his son. "As you can see for yourself, he's a hundred percent for it."

Alicia glanced at the note and smiled. "Well, that's a relief! I didn't want to take on the rôle of a wicked stepmother."

"What made you believe Minyev, without asking me?"

"I—I thought you were just being polite to me, and I'd better end the whole thing."

"Whatever gave you that idea?"

"Oh, various things, like seeing how Sári adores you."

Reith grinned. "And I thought you weren't serious about me because you seemed so indifferent to my affair with Sári."

"I was jealous as all Hishkak," said Alicia with a spark of her old fire, "but I wasn't going to let you know."

"Good; so let's get back to basics. Will you marry me?"

"You just bet! The sooner the better; I don't want you wriggling off the hook. On the trip back to Krishna, I kept telling myself: When you see Fergus, be friendly but businesslike. Don't daydream of a romantic reconciliation, because he probably won't be available. When I found that you were free and still seemed to like me, it was hard to remember my good resolutions."

"Just as well I didn't know," said Reith. "By the time we reached Zinjaban, I was in love again—or still, after all those years."

"I never stopped loving you," murmured Alicia. "When I got that final decree from a messenger in Katai-Jhogorai, I knew I'd made the ghastliest mistake of my life. But I never could figure how to unmake it. I have been dropping hints; but you were never very sharp about picking them up."

"Oh, I got the message all right! I just wanted to make sure there was water in the pool before I dove in." He gave her a squeeze. "Let's forget all that. At Zinjaban, I was prepared to go to the mat with you—"

"Don't you mean the mattress?"

"Of course, I—" Both burst into laughter, hugging each other until the merriment subsided. Reith continued. "It would have been the mattress, if Cyril hadn't stuck his fat face out and given me a nasty, knowing grin."

As Alicia laid her golden head on his shoulder, Reith asked himself: Would her new gentleness prove lasting? Or might her violent temper surface again? Well, the die was cast; he would have to take his chances, as lovers have done for ages.

Reith smothered a yawn. He did not ask to spend the night with her, nor did she invite him. They simply began casually, like an old married couple, to undress. She took off her shirt and turned her back, saying,

"Fergus, will you unhook my bra? This one always gives me trouble."

Reith complied. "Lish, have you a spare toothbrush, to save me from a trip down the hall?"

Later, passion spent, they lay close and relaxed. Reaching out to turn down the bedside lamp, Alicia gave a long sigh. "I don't mean to give you a swelled head, darling; but I've been dreaming of a night like this ever since you saw me off on the *Juruá.*"

"I've thought a lot about it, too," he said sleepily. "We should have started that first night at the ranch. Everybody thinks we've been at it all along."

To Reith's surprise, Alicia sat up. "Oh! I almost forgot." She slipped out of bed, dug into her baggage, and extracted her notebook. Among the pages she found a loose sheet of paper, which she handed over with a cryptic smile. Reith looked at it, puzzled, then realized that it was the missing dedication page from *Pirates, Priests, and Potentates.* He read: "To my one true love, Fergus MacDonald Reith."

Alicia said: "I almost dedicated the book to 'My Once and Future Husband.' "

"Why didn't you? Then I'd have *had* to make an honest woman of you."

"What if I'd arrived to find you dead, or happily married? Then wouldn't I have looked silly!"

"I don't know. If I'd been dead, you could say we planned to meet in Heaven."

"And suppose Elizabeth had been smart enough to hang on to you? I wouldn't steal another woman's husband, even if you were stealable—and you're too conscientious for such monkeyshines."

"Darling, forget Elizabeth. You've won fair and square. Come back to bed and I'll prove it!" Laughing, he pulled her down beside him.

"You mean—again, after all you've been through?"

"Absolutely. My strength is as the strength of ten, if not for Sir Galahad's reason."

"Good heavens, that's one part of you that hasn't aged a bit!"

At dawn, an unshaven Reith opened the door of Alicia's room a crack, then strode out in his riding clothes. As he did so, Jacob White emerged from another doorway, halted at the sight of Reith, and said: "Oh, hell! I lost it again!"

Reith turned on him. "You lost what, Jack?"

After an uncomfortable pause, White replied. "Fallon organized a pool, betting how long it would take the pair of you—" (he glanced at Alicia's door) "—to—uh—get together. We've been watching, and I guess Cyril wins. Say, Kostis wants to see you at breakfast!"

"What about?"

"About Attila. It's urgent."

"How is he?" asked Reith.

"In bed with a severe concussion and a broken finger. Doc Hamid says he'll keep him there for at least a few days. They had to hide his clothes to prevent him from going hunting for you, Fergus."

As they walked down the hall towards the mess, Reith asked: "What happened last night after Alicia and I left?"

"We pulled Attila up on a chair, and Fallon tried to get the game going again. I suppose he figured that, being sober, he'd clean up; but nobody had the heart for cards. We had another round of drinks, and then Gashigi asked to speak to me privately in one of the bedrooms.

"When we were alone, she explained that I was to service her in Cyril's place. Good God!"

"Well, how did you make out?"

"I just couldn't. Boy, was she disappointed!"

"Hm," said Reith. "What was your trouble?"

White paused to think. "I guess you'd call it mental—or

maybe I should say, moral. You see, I've never had intercourse with anyone except my wife—my former wife, that is."

"How come, 'former'?"

"Because of the gambling."

"They can cure that nowadays," said Reith. "My Alicia had one of those personality lifts back on Terra. It seems to work."

"I know," said White. "She told me about it. But I don't *want* to be cured! Gambling's my one great pleasure in life."

"I find shepherding Terran tourists through half-civilized countries quite enough of a gamble," mused Reith.

White ignored the comment. "Alicia would have argued some more, but when I said: 'Doctor Dyckman, don't be a yental' she shut up."

Thoughtfully, Reith said, "The Moritzian treatment must have worked wonders on Alicia. In the old days, she'd have gone after you hammer and tongs, until you either reformed or fled the country."

"I'm just not cut out for screwing around," said White with a touch of pathos. "My father's a Conservative rabbi, and I was brought up strict. Whether Gashigi's human or not, it's a sin either way. If she's human—a kind of super-shiksa—it's fornication. If not, it says in Exodus that, 'Whosoever lieth with a beast shall surely be put to death.' I guess I'm not sorry I failed, though it's hard on the ego."

"What else went on—I mean, in the living room?"

"I don't know; by the time I gave up with Gashigi, the others were gone. I suppose that when Attila came to, he borrowed the general's spare sword and went looking for you. What are you and Alicia going to do, Fergus?"

Reith smiled. "Lish and I mean to make it official, that's all."

"You mean . . ."

"Yep, we're engaged, betrothed, plighted, and affianced."

"Congratulations! When two forceful people like you
team up, nothing short of murder can stop you!"'

When Reith and White entered the mess hall, they
found Stavrakos seated at one of the long tables. He
mumbled a greeting with his mouth full of scrambled
bijar egg.

"How did you get here, boss?" asked Reith, who had
visions of the rotund Stravrakos bouncing perilously on
the back of an aya.

"Took one of the omnibuses," grunted Stavrakos. "I
heard about your fracas—oh, hello, Alicia! Sit down and
have a bite. Fodor swears to kill you, Fergus. Says he'll
challenge you to a duel. If you won't fight him with
swords, he'll chop you down whenever he sees you."

The sleepy smile with which Alicia had entered the
mess disappeared. She leaned forward tensely.

"What am I supposed to do about it?" said Reith.

"We want you to go away for a while," said the
producer.

"You mean cut and run? I'm not afraid of that bastard! I'll meet him—"

"Fergus!" said Alicia. "Listen to reason. We can go
visit that rancher friend of yours across the mountains."

Angrily, Reith began: "I'm damned if I'll let an oversized ego chase me out—"

Alicia laid a hand on his arm. "Please! Who loves to
lecture me on taking foolish risks? And we need a
break—"

"But, damn it—"

"Shut up, Reith!" said Stavrakos. "You listen to me!
In the first place, if you fight him, he'll probably kill
you. He's a one-time saber-fencing champion of Hungary.
If you got killed, I'd be sorry, but I could bear it. But if
you killed him by chance, it would raise holy hell with
our production. Millions would go down the drain, and

it's *my money!* So take your buggy and amble over to that ranch and stay there until we send word to come back."

As Reith opened his mouth to protest, Stavrakos barked: "That's an order! And if you don't think I have the authority to make you go, read your contract! If you refuse, you've broken the contract, and I won't pay you one of those little brass Krishnan coins—what do they call 'em?"

"An arzu. All right, I'll make you a deal. You've owed me the first half of the payment on that contract ever since you arrived, but you've put me off with excuses. Pay up, and I'll go to that ranch with Alicia, who's—"

"Hey! We need her here, to interpret!"

"I'll lend you my tour assistant in her place. Timásh's English is pretty good; and besides, you have Strachan and Fallon. Alicia is my fiancée, and where I go, she goes."

"Oh," said Stavrakos, scratching himself.

"If you don't pay up," continued Reith, "I'll do my best to kill Fodor, and to hell with your movie!"

Stavrakos stared and chewed his lip. Then he gave a sour little smile. "Now that's what I call a sensible man! Liquor and sex and titles are all very nice, but money is the real *arithmos enas*—number one to you." He brought out his wallet. "Will you take a draft on the Novorecife bank?"

"Okay." Reith shrugged and turned to White. "Do me a favor, Jack. Find Timásh and tell him to get the gig and the animals ready."

With the draft in his pocket, Reith returned to his room to pack. He found Ordway sitting up and stretching. "I say, Sir Fergus, whither away?"

Reith explained. "Thanks to Kostis, we're taking a kind of pre-honeymoon."

"Mean you're really going to . . ."

"Yep. Soon as we can get to the proper authority—oh, good morning, Tony."

Fallon appeared in the doorway. "Alicia told me you two were outward bound," he said.

"That's right. Could you, as a Terran consul, marry the two of us, right now?"

"Wow, what a question! Let me think. No; it would be legal only if performed in the consulate at Mishé, with the necessary papers all signed."

"Then it'll have to be honeymoon first, wedding second."

"But I say! If you regard her as a sister, as you claimed, isn't that a bit incestuous?"

Reith smiled. With fawning deference, Ordway said: "I shan't say it doesn't cost me a pang, Sir Fergus. But if I've got to lose the bird, I couldn't lose her to a better man. Of course there's a disadvantage to such a ripping attractive wife."

"Yes?"

"There'll always be other men dangling after her. If she ever gives you the boot again, she'll have plenty of other choices."

Reith chuckled. "I'll take my chances. So long, you two!"

Reith shouldered his bag, picked up Alicia and her luggage, and soon was driving his gig up the long slope of a winding road through the mountains, with the spare aya trotting behind. Alicia nestled close beside him, enjoying the view of the rugged mountain tops emerging from the morning mist. At last she broke the spell.

"Do you know what that lunatic wanted to do?"

"Which lunatic?"

"Attila Fodor, of course. He thought he'd have a more realistic battle if he allowed the Mikardanduma to use real weapons, while the Gozashtanduma fought with wooden ones. Then there'd be plenty of gore and severed heads all over. By the time the survivors of Gilan's men got back to Ruz to complain, as he figured it, he and his crew would be on their way to Terra and beyond Krishnan vengeance. What would happen to you and the other Krishnanders didn't matter."

"So that's why our Scourge of God was so keen on having the fake Krishnan blood just the right color! He couldn't have Lord Whozis bleed red when he gets his throat cut, and then have those poor Ruzo knights bleed green on the battlefield. What stopped him?"

"One of Attila's women thought it a terrible idea and leaked it to me. So I rounded up Ken and Jack and Tony and bullied them into going to Kostis to protest. I tried to get Cyril to come with us, but he'd only help for a price. You can guess what fee he named."

Reith made a fist and inspected his knuckles. "One of these days . . ."

Alicia smiled fondly and went on. "Luckily the four of us worked Kostis round. He wanted to let Attila's plan go thrugh, until we convinced him it would cost him a fortune in the long run. The story would get back to Earth; and he'd be fined millions and his company grounded. No more space movies for him!"

"Darling," said Reith, sliding an arm around Alicia and giving her a squeeze, "being married to a super-woman will be a more fantastic adventure than anything Kostis's script writers could think up!"

XI

PERCY MJIPA

Days later, Fergus Reith and Alicia Dyckman returned from a long morning's ride and tied their animals to a post beside Yekar's watering trough. As they mounted the steps to the ranchhouse porch, singing "Git along, little dogies!" Reith said to their hostess, "Hail, Mistress Bashti! Where's Yekar?"

She replied, "He hath gone across the mountains to Zinjaban, to buy supplies. Ye twain are overly heated!"

"We were out with your herders, chasing stray shaihans," said Reith.

"And," added Alicia eagerly, "Fergus showed he could rope a calf as well as any. Your ranch hands couldn't believe their eyes. One said: 'Tis a thing impossible, that an *Ertsu* should have this skill!' "

"So now," said Bashti smiling, "your sweat-soaked garments cling to you as bark to tree. I'll wager ye crave baths; and after that a generous repast."

"You read Terran minds," said Alicia. "But you must let us help with lunch—"

"Nay, I suffer no guests to toil in my kitchen. By the time ye've soaked and dried, my board shall await you. And—I almost forgot. Whilst ye were out, your man Timásh came by with a letter for Master Reit'. Here 'tis!"

247

Reith opened the letter and read:

Dear Fergus:

I have received reports on the abduction of Doctor Dyckman, her escape with your help, and the
death of King Vizman at the hands of your former
secretary—at least, that is the official story. I should
have given much to take fresh fingerprints from the
knife handle. Before he died, Minyev told a tale
different from the official one; but there is no way
now to settle the matter.

According to another report received, Schlegel is
by no means reconciled to accepting the failure of
his kidnapping plan as the workings of inscrutable
fate. You have not, he has been heard to say, seen
the last of him.

Yours most attentively,
Herculeu Castanhoso Souza

"What should we do about Schlegel?" asked Alicia,
frowning.

Reith shrugged. "Nothing much we can do before we
get back to Novo. We'll just have to keep our eyes and
ears open and our weapons handy, and not go wandering off alone."

After lunch, Reith and Alicia retired to the guest
room for well-earned naps. Alicia murmured drowsily:
"This has been simply heavenly. If it could only go
on. . . ."

"We'd get itchy," said Reith practically. "Matter of
fact, we ought to be on our way back to Zinjaban right
now. I figure they're ready to shoot the big battle
scene."

Alicia ran her fingers across Reith's lips. "Don't be
impatient, darling. The last time Timásh came over, he
said there was no change in the standing orders."

"You're right. We can't expect more news for a cou-

ple of days, unless Fodor takes time off to come looking
for us."

"He might, at that," said Alicia. "Instead of ideas,
that man has obsessions. After you beat him up twice,
he'll be in no mood to hand you a lollipop."

"So let's enjoy ourselves while we can." Reith smiled
slyly and opened his arms.

Just then came a knock on the door, and Bashti's
voice called, "Master Fergus!"

"Yes?"

"A strange *Ertsu* hath come, asking for Yekar. When
I told him my man was away, but ye were here, he
demanded to see you. Pray come! He's a terrifying
creature, as black as a demon from Hishkak!"

Reith sighed as they swung out of bed and reached
for their clothes. "Sounds like Percy Mjipa."

Percy Mjipa, Oxon., a native of Botswana and now
Terran consul at Zanid, was over 190 centimeters tall;
lean but iron-muscled; dark of skin and frizzy of hair. As
Fergus and Alicia emerged from the front door, in
impeccable British English Mjipa boomed: "Hello, old
man! What the devil are you doing here? And with
Alicia, too!"

"My fiancée and I," said Reith with an embarrassed
grin, "are taking a leave of absence from our jobs with
Cosmic Productions, over in Zinjaban."

Mjipa goggled. "It's too bloody much to take in all at
once. Look here, butties, I'm delighted and all that rot;
but we haven't time for amenities. I've galloped all the
way from Zanid to tell the people hereabout that
Kamoran Ghuur and his Qaathian hordes are on the
move. You can expect a major nomad invasion of Zinjaban
Province, if not tomorrow, then the day after." To the
uncomprehending Bashti, Mjipa repeated the last sentence in Mikardandou.

Bashti gave a little shriek before regaining a measure
of composure. "I must needs inform the herders, so

they can begin to move our stock to the hills. When Yekar returns, he and I and our egg shall follow. We know a secluded valley. Alas, that they should burn our dear little house!"

She ran towards the stables. Mjipa said: "I learned of this, through my connections, three days ago. For the last two, I've been on the road, eating in the saddle."

"Where's Vicky?" asked Alicia.

"I sent Victoria to Novo with the carriage a ten-day ago. My information is that the Qaathians will cross the Khoruz at Zinjaban; but they could change their minds. So I've come this way to warn my friends here. I'll tip off Litáhn at Port Kandakh. What's this about a cinema crew, making a flick in the Qe'bas?"

Reith outlined the Cosmic Productions project. Mjipa said: "Good thing I came along; I'll warn them, too. No, wait. If I stop at Zinjaban to explain things to your movie gaffers, they'll pass me around like a bloody medicine ball, and I shall waste hours of precious time. If I warn Litáhn and go straight on to Novo, will you inform your Californian lunatics?"

Reith smiled. "It's a prejudice to call all Californians crazy; I once knew a sane one. But I'll do what I can."

"Fergus!" cried Alicia. "How shall we warn them if, as soon as we appear, Fodor comes out and kills you?"

"I'll have my sword handy. Anyway, he won't hurt *you.*"

"I couldn't bear to lose you now. . . ." Alicia bit her lip and blinked in a not entirely successful effort to keep from crying.

"I know, darling," said Reith gently, "but sometimes we have to take chances."

"Right-o!" said Mjipa. "That'll give me time to tip off the fort at Kolkh."

"How come, Percy?" said Reith. "I thought you consuls always remained strictly neutral."

"Between civilized Krishnan nations, we do; but these barbarians are a common enemy of mankind—well, of

Krishnan kind. Ghuur doesn't give a damn for diplomatic immunity; I learned he was planning to have me assassinated. Wanted to make sure I didn't spread the alarm, like that American chap who rode all night crying: 'The British are coming!' What was his name? Buffalo Bill?"

"No, Paul Revere," said Reith.

"Anyway," Mjipa continued, "it is my business to warn Terrans in the path of the invasion. If in so doing I help the Mikardanduma to mobilize, I'm damned if I find that out of line.

"You should see what these noble savages have done to Balhib. Pyramids of heads piled up in the marketplace! Not that all these natives are my dish of tea; but Ghuur of Uriiq regards all civilized folk as vermin to be exterminated. Well, I'm on my way. Cheer-o!"

Mjipa bounded down the porch steps and ran to his tethered ayas. Off he galloped, leading his spare mount.

"Oh, dear!" said Alicia as she waved farewell to the towering black Terran. "It was such a lovely prehoneymoon, too."

"Sure, but all good things—even for Mr. and Mrs. Reith . . . Let's pack."

Alicia drove the gig, while Reith bestrode the spare aya as they neared Castle Kandakh. Presently Reith caught a twinkle of sun on armor and glimpsed a band of Krishnans working on the road, where it passed through a narrow defile below the fortress.

Coming closer, he perceived that the Krishnans were soldiers from the garrison. A sweating score, stripped to loin cloths, were constructing a stone wall across the highway, while others in armor stood guard against a surprise attack. Reith dismounted, walked forward, and hailed the officer in command.

"Ohé, Sir Chomaku!"

"What would ye, Sir Fergus?"

"I beg that you move a few of your stones, so that Doctor Dyckman and I can pass."

"Aye, aye." The knight barked an order. "Your fellow Terran, the black man, warned us of the Qaathians."

Reith asked, "Does Sir Litáhn plan to stop the invaders here?"

"For a while, albeit we could not hold such a barrier for ay. They'll charge us mounted. When enough have been stricken by our missiles, they'll pull back, dismount, and attack afoot, scaling the walls of the gorge to come at us. Then we'll retreat into the castle.

"If they lay siege, 'twill delay their invasion, and we can hold for a moon, giving time for relief. If they essay to run past, we'll slay a mort of 'em with catapults and crossbows along this road. 'Tis the best we can do with what we have."

Reith thanked the officer and helped to manhandle the gig's wheels past the obstacle. They rode on, down the long slope as the road snaked its descending way out of the eastern flanks of the mountains. When the downgrade became steep, Reith said: "Lish! Do you need any help on the brake?"

"No; I'll manage," she muttered through set lips, as she held the reins in one hand and strained against the brake handle with the other.

When the road leveled off in flatter terrain, they urged their beasts to a canter. At the ford of the Khoruz, Reith said: "Better change places, darling. It's a little ticklish, guiding the trap through the water."

Reith had been giving Alicia lessons in driving, but her hold on the reins was still uncertain. She mounted the spare aya, while Reith drove the draft animal into the broad, shallow stream. He clucked soothingly at the nervous beast but tickled it with his whip whenever it tried to balk or turn back.

The gig rocked dangerously as one wheel or the other went over a rock and water curled up around the aya's legs and the half-submerged wheels. At last they reached the Zinjaban side. Beyond the gentle swell of the river bank, the travelers glimpsed the skeletal shapes of Fodor's two observation towers for photographic use.

When they topped the rise, Reith observed a crowd milling around the base of one tower. He picked Fodor and his massive aya out of the throng. The director was arguing with two Krishnan knights, while Timásh interpreted. Coming closer, Reith recognized the knights as Sir Bobir, the Gozashtando commander, and Sir Padras, leader of the Mikardanduma.

When the travelers neared the outskirts of the crowd, expectant faces turned towards them. Tensely, Reith gripped his scabbarded sword. Leaning from her saddle, Alicia said: "Please, Fergus, pull up here and wait! I think I know how to handle the terrible Hun."

Alicia spurred her aya towards the group and trotted up to Fodor. Soon the pair were walking their mounts away from the crowd in earnest conversation. Then they turned their ayas and trotted to Reith, waiting uncomfortably in the gig. As he approached, Fodor held up his right hand in a gesture of peaceful intent. One finger was still splinted and bandaged.

"Hey, Fergus!" he roared, grinning through his mustache. "Good thing you came back! The battle takes begin tomorrow, and we need all the translators we can get.

"Alicia tells me what really happened. I guess I owe apology. If I'd known you two was going to get married again, I'd have said: 'No play! Out! Take my bed and bust the springs!' I got the barbarian sense of honor!" He thumped his chest.

"I owe an apology, too," said Reith. "We should have told you, but we'd celebrated our engagement with too much kvad to think clearly."

"So no hard feelings? Good!" Fodor extended his left hand. "Got to shake this one, until the ozzer heals. What's a little fight between friends?"

"You're going to have a real battle on your hands," said Reith. "I've got to talk to you and Kostis, right away. There's a full-scale invasion heading this way, and we're right in its path."

"A real fight? *Wunderbar! Csodálotos!* Who we fighting?"

"The Qaathian nomads. Their Kamoran—I guess on Earth we'd call him a Great Khan—has decided to add Mikardand to his empire."

"You go stow your stuff. I'll get the boss and see you at the inn right away after."

As Reith helped Alicia to move her gear into the tent she shared with Mary Hopkins, he whispered: "You little liar! You fibbed to save my gore."

"Hardly a real prevarication," said Alicia complacently. "Merely a slight confusion in the order of events. I moved your proposal up a couple of hours. Any psychologist will explain that the human memory plays tricks with time. Anyway, if it came to a fight, I'm sure you'd have bested him."

Reith grinned. "Flattery will get you everywhere. Since we're sleeping apart tonight, give me a nice, big—"

"Oh, excuse me," said Mary Hopkins, entering the tent. "I'll come back later."

"No, no, Mary!" said Alicia laughing at the older woman's embarrassment. "Everything's okay. We're properly engaged, you know."

"Really? You mean you're going to have flowers and bridesmaids and all the trimmings?"

"I don't know that we'll go that far," said Reith, "but we do figure on a proper wedding. Now we've got to go see the big shots at the inn. Come on, Alicia."

Stavrakos swallowed a bite of sandwich and frowned in concentration. "Fergus, seems to me the only thing is for us—the shooting crew—to run like hell for Novorecife."

"No, no!" said Fodor, pounding the table. "Are we cowards or fools? If there's a battle, we can shoot the whole thing from the towers. Think, man! With a little rewriting of the script, we can use all the meterage in *Swords.*"

"You're nuts, Attila!" said Stavrakos, turning to Reith. "How many of these nomads are on the march?"

Reith shrugged. "At least a few thousand."

"And we've got only a thousand knights and men-at-arms, assuming we can get those two gangs to work together. Plus a few hundred in the garrison at Kandakh. Resistance would be as loony an idea as any they had in old Hollywood, before the earthquake. We've got to make a run for it."

"We don't have that option," said Reith. "These Qaathians ride like bats out of Hell; each trooper travels with remounts. If you started your people off right now, and the nomads arrived tomorrow, they'd catch you on the road."

"Tell me about Qaath," said Fodor, ignoring the peril, "so I get a feel about Krishnan history."

"Qaath is a big steppe country west of Jo'ol and Balhib," said Alicia. "Culturally, the people living there are like Earth's Mongols and Tatars."

"Real men!" growled Fodor.

"All very fine," said Reith, "unless one of them decides to decorate his harness with your scalp. Usually they're split into warring tribes, cheerfully slaughtering one another. But once in a while, an effective leader welds them into a single fighting machine. Then he sets out to see which of his neighbors he can most easily rob and slaughter. Ghuur of Uriiq, the Kamoran of Qaath, is such a leader.

"Because the Varasto nations have been too busy quarreling among themselves to unite against the outside menace, Ghuur has been picking them off, one by one. Now he has his eye on Mikardand, which is stronger than his earlier conquests. He's getting on in years and, I suppose, wants to lead one more grand conquest while he can."

"Any idea how these Qaathians operate?" asked Fodor more soberly. His euphoria at the thought of a battle had been replaced by grim calculation.

"I have an idea," said Reith. "They'll send ahead several thousand light ayas. If they don't meet much resistance, they'll go right on, killing and burning, clear to Mishé. If they encounter strong opposition, they'll recoil against the forces coming up behind them. This main army will move slowly, because the foot soldiers from the tributary states can't travel more than twenty-five or thirty kilometers a day."

"So if we—I mean if our Krishnan extras—smash this advance force, it might stop the whole invasion?"

Reith shrugged. "I don't know Ghuur's precise intentions; but at least it would buy time for Mikardand."

"I think we'd be crazy not to run—" began Stavrakos; but Fodor cut him off with a roar.

"Get hold of the colonels, you two!" He addressed both Reith and Alicia. "I don't care what Kostis says. I'm going to have this battle in my movie!"

"I'll fire you!" shouted Stavrakos.

"You can't! Read the contract! What I say goes for details of the picture, and I say the battle is part of the picture! Go find those colonels!"

"Read the contract yourself!" yelled Stavrakos. "Clause twenty-three gives me the final say on all expenditures. . . ."

Reith and Alicia left them shouting like angry schoolboys. While Alicia was searching the Gozashtando encampment, Reith found the Krishnan officers relaxing on a bench among the Mikardando tents, sharing a bottle of falat. When Reith told them of the imminent invasion, they sprang to their feet.

"The living-picture folk are discussing what to do," said Reith. "Will you please join them, so we can form a plan?"

Bobir, the older colonel, whispered in Padras's ear, and the Mikardandu departed at a run. Bobir said: "He'll join us presently, Sir Fergus."

Reith and Bobir found the two motion-picture executives still in dispute. From Fodor's glum expression,

Reith surmised that the producer had all but won the argument.

Stavrakos said: "Fergus, I convinced Hungary's Revenge here—" He waved a pudgy hand at Fodor. "—that we'd be crazy to stay for a battle. All the crew will take to their heels anyway, when they hear what's up. So as soon as we can pack our gear, we'll make a run for it, even if it's in the middle of the night."

"What saith he?" asked Bobir.

Reith translated. Bobir shook his head. "*Iyá!* So thinks he, belike. Pray, tell him that Sir Padras and I have seized all the ayas, for we shall need every animal to face the invaders. Moreover, all able-bodied male Terrans *in situ* are conscripted into the army of Mikardand, and any attempt to flee will be punished by instant execution.

"The Terran women may do as they like. I can, howsomever, promise that if they set out on foot, and the Qaathians win the battle, these females will be caught on the road by the nomads, raped, and slain."

Again Reith translated. Stavrakos went pale, while Fodor chewed his mustache. Sir Padras came in. "The guards are now posted over the ayas and around the camp, Sir Bobir."

Stavrakos pleaded. "Look, I'm not able-bodied. I'm an old man. I'm overweight, and I've never ridden an aya or handled a sword in my life."

"Then you shall learn," said Bobir complacently when this had been translated. "Sir Fergus, assemble all the male Terrans at those wooden towers Master Fodor hath built. Padras and I shall compel them to learn to fight. You've had experience with riding and swording; so have Masters Fodor, Strachan, Fallon, and that actor fellow, Master Fairwedder. The four of you shall be drill instructors. No argument, Master Stav—whatever your name is! To dispute a lawful order of a Knight of Qarar is grounds for execution."

When Reith, going through the Terran tents, told the

Cosmic crew what impended, he was met with shrieks of fear, anger, and outrage. There were cries of "I'm leaving this place in spite of their guards!"

"It's not fair!"

"I'll sue 'em!"

"Actor's Equity will hear about this!"

"It's all your fault, Fergus Reith!"

"Wait till I get hold of my agent!"

"I'll appeal to the Terran consul!"

"Won't do you any good," said Reith. "Tony Fallon's been drafted, too. He's to be one of your drill instructors."

"Huh!" exclaimed Cassie Norris. "Not a man with balls in the whole friggin' lot! If you can find a breast-plate with bulges to fit mine, I'll get out there with a sword and show you!"

"Thanks, Cassie," smiled Reith. "You're the best man of the lot. The rest of you, follow me!"

Roqir, hanging low in the sky, saw actors, camera-men, and other members of the shooting crew learning, with grunts and groans, to mount an aya, guide the animal with reins and heels, and tie the beast up prop-erly. Alicia acted as a translator; Reith, as a general trouble shooter.

After a brief dinner break, the conscripts were di-vided into five squads and assigned to the drill instruc-tors to learn sword-play. Issuing the silver-painted wooden swords intended for the battle scene, Reith lined up the five assigned to him. Fodor was put in charge of Stavrakos, and Reith observed that the direc-tor took sadistic pleasure in beating his boss black and blue in the guise of teaching him saber-fencing technique.

Reith told his pupils, "First we'll learn the normal guard position for fighting without a shield. Place your feet in line with your opponent, right foot forward. . . ."

When he had reduced his charges to exhaustion, Reith sent them to bed. Ordway, passing Reith on the way to his tent, muttered: "By God, Sir Fergus, the Lady G. will jolly well have to do without me tonight.

I'm so whacked, I couldn't make love to Helen of Troy, Cleopatra, and the Queen of Sheba rolled into one!"

The groans of the shooting crew the evening before were nothing compared to the chorus of outcries and complaints that rose the next morning. "Oh, God, Fergus, I can't move! Between those damned animals and that fencing footwork. . . ."

"I'm so stiff that if I bend, I'll break in two."

"Damn it, why can't they give us noncombatant jobs, like stretcher bearing? We're no warriors!"

"You'll loosen up with exercise," said Reith implacably. "Come on!"

Although the Terran recruits needed moons of practice to make them passable riders and swordsmen, Bobir and Padras decided that, for lack of time, they would be put through mounted drills. On the field chosen for the cinematic battle, two dozen Terrans tried to maneuver in formation. They succeeded only in caroming into one another, causing their ayas to run away with them, and otherwise earning their instructors' curses.

During a rest period, Reith noticed a little knot of women and cameramen around Attila Fodor. When he walked over to investigate, Fodor exulted: "Didn't I say we'd have this battle on film?"

"What are you doing?" asked Reith.

"Teaching the girls to use the cameras. When the Qaathians come, the women will go up the towers with the cameras and shoot the action."

Reith said: "If the Qaathians win, your girls will be trapped up there. The nomads will either climb up after them or burn down the towers."

"Sure; but what else can they do? If they run away on foot, the nomads will catch them, with the same results. So on the chance that we win, we might as well get something out of it. I'll change the script to fit later."

Reith looked around. "Where's Gashigi?"

"Oh, she took off in her carriage last night. Said duty called her back to Mishé. The colonels let her and her driver go, but they kept her bodyguards for soldiers. Most of the camp followers sneaked away, too."

"I thought the colonels had posted guards on the perimeter?"

Fodor smiled and spread his hands. "Imagine you're one of these soldiers, Fergus, and during the night your woman comes up and whispers: 'Let me through, love, so I'm not killed if the nomads break through! If we live, I'll meet you back home.' Are you going to turn her back?"

"Hm," Reith pondered. "Who's got Gashigi's room at the inn?"

"I have it, natural, with my two girls."

"Then your tent's empty. Any reason why—uh—"

Fodor dealt Reith one of his bone-breaking back-slaps. "Go ahead, move in with her! You two are so near married, it don't make no difference."

Reith had his squad lined up and stretching their leg tendons by practicing the lunge, when a Gozashtando soldier galloped up, flung himself off his aya, and demanded to see Colonel Bobir.

"Over there!" Reith pointed. The soldier ran, leading his mount.

Reith told his men to stand at ease and followed the soldier, whom he found talking earnestly with both colonels.

"Ah, Sir Fergus!" said Bobir. "This trooper is one of the scouts we sent to watch the approaches. The foe come not by the Qe'ba road but swing wide about the southern end of the range. Now they hasten along the farther bank of the Khoruz, approaching yonder ford."

"How near?" asked Reith.

"With's own eyes, Trooper Arum hath seen, not the veritable Qaathians, but only the vast cloud of dust they raise. Belike, we have an hour ere they arrive."

"What's your plan?"

"Why, to meet them in mid-stream and smite them sore!"

"Look, Sir Bobir, they'll outnumber us at least two to one. Shouldn't we let part of their force cross unopposed and then charge them? That way, we shall have the advantage of numbers at the point of contact."

Padras asked: "How shall we hide our intentions from the oncomers?"

"If we form here, below the towers, they won't see us while crossing because of the swell of the ground. Then someone in the towers can signal when the first thousand or so have crossed, and we can charge down on them. They're light-armed, with little or no armor, and their beasts are small."

"A clever plan for a civilian *Ertsu*," said Bobir. "But we are old, experienced warriors, and natives of this world to boot. Think not that I mean aught of unpraise, Sir Fergus; but 'tis our responsibility—"

"Hold ye one moment, Bobir," said Padras. "Come aside and speak privily."

Reith and the trooper fidgeted while the two officers conferred in low tones. When they turned back, Bobir said, "We've devised our own plan, Sir Fergus. True, it hath a few features like unto yours; still and all 'tis ours. We'll mass our men betwixt these towers. Then, when we're signaled . . ."

Colonel Bobir described a plan exactly like Reith's; but Reith thought it inexpedient to comment on the fact.

"Who shall be our signalman?" said Padras. "I mislike to waste a single fighter."

Reith said: "Give the job to the Terrans' leading actress, Mistress Norris. She has more guts than any of the men. By the bye, the commander at Kandakh expects an attack through the mountains. His men will be staring westward over their wall when they should be galloping eastward, towards the river, to surprise the Qaathians from the rear. We should send him a message."

"That would mean detaching another warrior," said Bobir uncertainly. "We must not disperse our meager strenth—"

"I can furnish you a non-combatant rider," said Reith. "Give her your fastest aya and she'll beat any of your soldiers, since she's lighter than they." He looked up at the towers. Sighting Alicia's shining hair, he shouted "Hey, Lish! A-*lish*-a!" When he caught her attention, he beckoned.

Bobir and Padras were arguing over the best aya for the job. Reith heard: ". . . and you're ever bragging of that beast of yours hight 'Thunder.' 'Tis time we put your boasts to the test!"

"But she'll ruin the animal, spurring it uphill—"

"She's an experienced rider," interjected Reith. "And at the worst, it'll be ruined in a good cause."

While horns blew, ayas squealed, and armored men clattered about, Alicia swung into Thunder's saddle. She trotted to the river, picked her way across, and spurred to a canter up the mountain road. Reith breathed a sigh of relief. She, at least, would survive.

"Sir Fergus," said Bobir, "worthy though your Terrans be in other ways, as untrained warriors they'd be worth no more than a herd of unhas. So we'd best not put them in the fore. I trust they'll not be insulted?"

Knowing how desirous the Terrans were of missing the battle altogether, Reith hid a smile. "I'll explain it to them, and I'm sure they'll understand."

"We intend," continued Bobir, "to hold them back as our reserve. If—may the divine stars forbid—the Qaathians break through our lines, we'll send the Terrans against them at that point."

Fodor, his huge frame outfitted in a mail shirt too small to be properly laced at one side, had elected himself commander of the Terran contingent, and none disputed the choice. He named Reith, Fairweather,

Strachan, and Fallon as his junior officers, saying: "As a born barbarian, I ought to be fighting on the ozzer side. But I will give the Knights of Qarar good mercenary service, like the barbarian Stilicho did the Romans."

The Krishnan units had too few spare weapons to equip all the Terrans, so Attila Fodor made up the difference, handing out the souvenir swords he had bought in Mishé until all the men were armed. About half the Terrans received mailshirts; a few wore Krishnan helmets.

The braver women waited in the towers beside their cameras. Others hid in the shrubbery with food and water and such makeshift weapons as they could find, mostly knives from the cook tent. Cassie Norris, wearing a saucepan for a helmet, stood with flag in hand on the topmost story of one of the openwork towers. She cried, loudly enough to be heard below: "If those gooks burn this tower down, they'll make me a second Joan of Arc, like when I played her two years ago. If you've got to go, I say go in style!"

The long wait began. As Roqir slid slowly down the turquoise sky, quiet descended on the scene, broken only by the whir of flying arthropods, the furtive whispers of the defenders, and the snarls of officers ordering their troops to silence.

At last Reith saw the flag—a square of white cloth on the end of a spear—float outward from the tower and wave horizontally to signal "enemy in sight."

Sir Bobir shouted "Mount!" The clatter of weapons and the creak of harness shattered the silence. Stavrakos had to be boosted into the saddle by two of his squad.

Reith relayed the command to his men and badgered them into the proper stance. "Matthews, you've got your reins twisted!" "Saito, press your knees in!"

A quarter-hour later, Cassie waved the flag in a circle, to indicate that the Qaathians were crossing the ford.

At last a vertical wave ended the weary wait. The

colonels passed commands, and the long double line of cavalry advanced, slowly at first, then faster.

Fodor raised his sword in his left hand, seemingly unhindered by the substitution. Standing in his stirrups, he craned his neck to look up at the women manning cameras and bellowed: "Sound! Cameras! Action!" To his company he cried: "Forward at a walk! Trot!"

Reith and the other junior officers tried to keep their men in line; but to Reith the advance was the most ragged and unsoldierly he had seen. The ayas disobeyed their riders' unskilled commands. In trying to straighten out their line, riders drove their beasts into one another. One reluctant warrior was hooked in the leg by a horn. Two of the animals started a fight. When one tyro pricked his neighbor's aya with his sword, the animal bucked its rider off. The fallen man got up and limped after his mount, which trotted ahead just out of reach.

At last, behind the Krishnan force, the Terrans trotted raggedly over the sheltering bulge. Down the long slope, the Krishnan soldiery were now traveling at a canter, with lances in the front rank and drawn swords in the second. Before them, the Qaathian nomads who had crossed the river churned in a dark mass. Others were splashing through the ford, while still others awaited their turn on the far side of the stream.

The knights met the enemy with a thunderous crash. Reith could see nothing but the armored backs of knights and men-at-arms, obscured by a thickening cloud of dust. War-cries, screams, and cheers mingled with the clatter of swords against shields and mail.

Little by little, the nomads were pressed back. The line of knights formed a crescent, trapping the Qaathians against the banks of the river.

A knot of Qaathians broke through the lines, and a desperate score of them swirled up the slope. As they approached, Reith picked out their fur caps and baggy garments of shaihan wool, and the short, curved swords held in dirty, olive-brown fists. They clustered about a Qaathian whose towering stature was augmented by a tall helmet with gilded decorations.

"Come on!" shouted Fodor. "The colonel says to kill those guys! Charge!"

Arrows, shot at a high angle by the Qaathians at the ford, began to rain down on the Terrans. Precipitately, Fodor spurred ahead. Some of the shooting crew tried to keep pace with him; others, less heroic, hesitated lest they be the first to collide with the foe. Two wheeled their animals about and galloped back up the slope.

Roaring a Magyar war cry, Fodor drew farther and farther ahead of his Terran companions, until he was charging the enemy alone. He headed straight for the leader in the gilded helmet. There was an anvil-like hammering of blade on blade, and the gilded helmet disappeared. Then the fallen one's comrades surrounded Fodor, hacking and thrusting.

Seconds later, Reith confronted a Qaathian. With upraised sword, the fellow rode directly at him. Reith heeled his aya at the nomad and, as the animals came into contact, thrust out his blade at arm's length. He felt the point bite through cloth and flesh. The slash that the Qaathian had aimed at Reith's head wavered and missed as the attacker, run through the body, pitched out of his saddle.

Then Reith faced another nomad. Since his mount had lost momentum, he could not this time use his sword as a lance. He parried two wild slashes and then thrust home through the Qaathian's cloth coat. He felt his point pierce meat, before he had to jerk the blade back to parry a furious backhand. Reith caught the blow—and his sword broke a few centimeters from the hilt. Before he could react, a second cut descended on his head, slicing through the helmet and into his scalp. He saw stars, felt the ground come up and hit him, and knew no more.

* * *

Reith awoke with a pounding headache and found a bandage around his head. He lay on a camp cot in a large tent among other wounded, some of whose bandages were stained with blue-green Krishnan blood. A Krishnan whom Reith recognized as the Mikardando army surgeon spoke to him as from a distance.

"How feel ye, Sir Fergus?"

"Not so well as yesterday. Who won?"

"We did, good my sir. Had we not, ye were dead. The fall of the Kamoran—"

"You mean we killed the old savage?"

"Aye; 'twas the Terran, Master Fodor, who slew him."

"And Fodor?"

"Slain, too, alas. But he took a parcel of barbarians to Hishkak with him. That, together with the charge of the garrison from Kandakh at the nomads' rear, broke their spirit. Many were slain, and the rest fled like leaves before the blast. Thanks to our armor, we lost but twain besides your Master Fodor."

Reith sighed. "Poor Fodor! Always talking of the glories of barbaric battle. He got more than he bargained for; but perhaps he died happy. Any other hurts among the Terrans?"

"Master Ames hath sustained a wrenched shoulder in falling off his mount, while Master Strachan suffered a grievous leg wound. Your Terran physician, that Doctor Mas'udi, hath removed him to's own tent."

"What day is this?" asked Reith.

" 'Tis the even of the battle, at the thirteenth hour. Excuse me, pray, whilst I fetch your Terran leech. I dare not treat you, for that your organs internal differ from ours."

Mas'udi opined: "Fergus, I want you to stay quiet in bed another day; you may have a concussion. You've had nine stitches."

Reith gingerly felt his scalp through the bandages. Then he sat up purposefully. "No, doc, I feel pretty good. If I get woozy, I'll come back. Right now I want to find my—my—"

"Your friend—your fiancée, Doctor Dyckman. She's been in and out of the tent ever since we put you here, waiting for you to wake. At last I told her to get out and stay out; she needs some rest, too."

"Okay, where are my clothes?"

Mas'udi clucked and argued, but Reith was determined despite his throbbing head. He hurriedly dressed and left the hospital tent. Night had fallen; but the camp was well lit by cookfires, torches, and two of the three Krishnan moons.

Sounds of an altercation drew Reith's attention. Pushing through a gathering crowd, he saw Anthony Fallon in heated discussion with the two colonels. Nearby he preceived two kneeling men: Stavrakos and another Terran, the gasser or lighting manager Olson. Both were stripped to the waist, with hands bound behind them. Over them stood a Krishnan trooper leaning on a broad-bladed, two-handed sword.

Reith ran, even though the movement sent shooting pains through his skull. "Hold everything! What's up?" he shouted.

Fallon said: "Fergus! Our commanders here want to cut off a couple of heads: the blokes who galloped away from the fighting. Can't say I blame the colonels—cowardice in the face of the enemy—but we can't have that sort of thing done to our fellow Earthlings if we can help it."

"Will they take money for compensation? Stavrakos has plenty."

"No. They say it would ruin discipline, if anybody would buy his way out of a charge."

"I have an idea," said Reith. He came close to the colonels and spoke in low tones. The officers walked off a little way, conferring and arguing. At last they came back, making the affirmative head motion and breaking into smiles. Reith walked slowly towards the culprits, looking grave; he did not intend to let them off too easily.

"Please, Fergus!" cried Stavrakos, his voice a terrified squeak. "Get me out of this! I'll do anything for you! Come to Montecito, and I'll get you money, broads, dope, anything you want!"

"I may be able to get you off, on one condition," said Reith.

"Anything! What condition?"

"They'll let you and Olson go—for the time being anyway—on condition that you give both colonels significant parts in the movie. Motilal can change the script tonight. You can run off takes in a few says and dub in the dialogue back on Earth. Okay?"

"Yes, yes, that's wonderful!" gasped Stavrakos. "Just have 'em cut these damned ropes, will you? How much do I pay you, personally?"

"*What?*" exclaimed Reith, incredulously.

"I said, how much must I give you, for yourself, for springing me?"

"Gods of Krishna!" said Reith. "Did you think I'd extort money as the price of your worthless life?"

"Well—ah—it's what I'd do in your place."

"You mercenary son of a bitch! You think I'm the same sort of louse you are?" He spoke to the headsman. "Cut their ropes."

Stavrakos rose with a grunt, rubbing arms scored by rope marks. He shook his head in a puzzled way. "Well—ah—I thought you were a practical man."

"You and I look at things differently," snapped Reith, turning away. He started for Fodor's former tent, into which he and Alicia had moved their things. As he neared the tent, however, a singular sight assailed his eyes.

Cyril Ordway, wearing only a khaki shirt and slippers, ran out of the tent, pursued by Alicia Dyckman, clad in riding breeches and shirt but barefoot, and swinging a sword. Being faster than the bulky Ordway, she caught up with him, tripped him, and stood over him as he sprawled prone.

"You lie there," Alicia cried in her clear soprano, "or I'll cut your damned head off!"

With the point of the sword, she raised the tail of Ordway's shirt, exposing his fat buttocks. Then she swung the sword in both hands and brought the flat of the blade down on Ordway's fundament.

Ordway grunted. Up went the sword, and down again. At the third blow, Ordway uttered a little cry. At the sixth, he began whimper: "Alicia! That hurts! Please! I'll never bother you again!"

Alicia continued her merciless bastinado until Ordway's buttocks were red in the firelight and oozing blood. "Now get up and get out!" she snapped.

Ordway crawled a few paces, then rose and hobbled towards his tent.

"Darling!" said Reith. "My Valkyrie!"

Alicia gave him a hug. Reaching their new quarters, Reith sat down, rested his chin on his fist, and asked: "What the hell did that two-legged cockroach do?"

"When Doc Hamid chased me away from your bedside, I came back here, meaning to snatch some sleep," she explained. "I was bushed after that breakneck ride to the fort. I'd just taken off my boots when Old Repulsive came in wearing that sword the Krishnans lent him for the battle. I suppose he thought it made him look heroic; though from what I hear, you, Ken, Randal, Tony, and Attila were the only ones who actually crossed swords with the invaders. Randal killed one of the Kamoran's bodyguards, and Tony says he cut another one but doesn't know how much harm he did in the confusion. After Attila drilled the Kamoran, his people's one thought was to get him away, since they didn't know whether he was wounded or dead.

"Anyway, Cyril sat down and poured sweet talk over me like syrup on a waffle. I was his ideal of womanhood, and why hadn't he met me sooner—his same old line. He insisted on calling me 'Lady Alicia'; you know how he is about titles. Then he unbuckled his sword and slithered up close, if you can imagine a stuffed pigeon like Cyril slithering.

"He said he knew I was yours; but he loved me, too; and soon he'd never see me again, and I could make him the happiest man in the world, and it was such a small parting gift to ask, and it wasn't as if I were a virgin, and how marvelous he was at rogering, as he calls it. I kept pushing his hands away.

"Then he did an incredible thing. He slipped off his pants, and he wasn't wearing underwear. I suppose he thought the sight of his—uh—capabilities would so inflame my passions that I'd throw myself across the bed crying: 'Take me! I am yours!' As you saw, it didn't quite work out that way."

Reith had gone into a laughing jag, rocking helplessly back and forth on the bed. When he caught his breath, he said: "I—I ought to beat the sh—stuffing out of Cyril. But the sight of him eating standing up for days, with everybody kidding him, is revenge enough. And it's all happened for the best, in a way."

"What do you mean?" Alicia asked, suspiciously.

"Since you got back to Krishna, I've been afraid that the Moritzian therapy, besides curing your compulsions, might have taken the spunk out of you. I see now that I needn't have worried!"

XII

ENRIQUE SCHLEGEL

Another moon had passed since the rout of the nomad horde. Reith had presided over makeshift rites for
the fallen Krishnan soldiers and the rash Fodor, who
had died like the hardy barbarian he had always yearned
to be. Dutifully, Reith had consoled the late director's
widow and mistress, although he sensed ambivalent
feelings in both.

Reith sent Timásh to Novorecife via Kolkh, to pick
up the accumulated mail and to return with Zerré. He
thought that an extra subordinate, loyal to him, might
be useful on the journey home.

While Alicia and several women from the shooting
crew assisted the Krishnan army surgeon in tending the
wounded, a subdued motion-picture company, under
Hari Motilal's fussy direction, completed the final takes.
The script had been revised to make the most of the
battle; and Krishnan knights and men-at-arms, some
clad in garments from the Qaathian corpses, reënacted
scenes from the fight. The Krishnans grumbled about
the stench of the nomads' filthy attire and the heat of
the heavy woollens under a blazing sun.

Sobered by genuine battle and death, the shooting
crew, anxious to finish and begone, completed their

work with dispatch. One day when the sky clouded over and a brisk rain fell, the actors and the crew spent the time in the studio tent, making blue-screen shots and voice-overs. To pass the afternoon, Reith wandered among the forest of stands bearing lights and reflectors and picked his way over a floor cluttered with coils and loops of cable. He overheard Olson the gasser saying to Motilal: "Number three hoarder is getting weak. If she goes, with number four dead, we'll be up the well-known creek."

"A couple of inkies will do for this shot," replied Motilal. "It's a night scene." He turned to Fairweather. "Now, Randal, go back to 'How could I have doubted you?' and run through it again. Try to sound more British! American audiences think it's more aristocratic, the way a prince ought to sound. Speak as I do."

"You mean with a Hindi accent?" said Fairweather with ostentatious innocence.

Motilal hurled his roll of script to the floor. "No, damn it! I am speaking perpect Oxpord English! I mean—oh, devil take you!" Quivering with rage, the little man mastered his passions. "My good *Mister* Pair—Fairweather, will you be so kind as to go through that scene again, beginning at 'How could I—'?"

After an hour of watching, Reith returned to the tent he now shared with Alicia and buried his nose in a grammar of the language of Katai-Jhogorai.

Atop the long slope to the river, in the village of Zinjaban, the folk went about their daily tasks. When they could steal time from work, they and their children gathered to gape at the aliens' movie-making. Some shyly offered edibles as thanks for their deliverance from the nomad horde.

Timásh returned from Novorecife, bringing with him Zerré and a young Khaldonian, who introduced himself as Minyev's cousin Yinkham. He had, he said, received word that Minyev was leaving his post with Reith and was recommending Yinkham for the job.

"My God, what effrontery!" exclaimed Reith in English to Alicia.

"We'd better learn what he knows about the Vizman business," said Alicia. "He may be entirely innocent."

"Maybe," said Reith grimly, "but he'll have to work like a beaver to convince me of that. You'd better ask the questions, since you speak better Khaldonian than I."

Alicia began the interrogation. Yinkham gave his place and date of birth and his relationship with Minyev. Then he asked: "Madam, be ye not the Doctor Dyckman whereof I have heard my cousin speak?"

"Yes. What had he to say about me?"

"Oh, he always spoke in terms of the most lavish praise. He said that ye ought to be the queen of a Krishman kingdom; if it was ever within his power to do so, he would try to bring that event to pass."

An hour's rigorous questioning convinced Reith that Yinkham knew nothing of Alicia's abduction, and Alicia agreed with this conclusion. The Khaldonian, however, revealed several limitations. He was not fully mature, and like Minyev he was small and slight. Moreover, he had only a smattering of Mikardandou and knew no Terran tongues at all.

"He's got a long way to go," said Reith. "I don't know that it's worth my while to try to teach him all he needs to know, or whether I'd do better to pick some promising local boy."

"Are you going to send him packing?"

"I might, if we were back at the ranch. I won't fire him now, but keep him with us on the way home to see how fast he learns and how willing he is to turn a hand to tasks we ask him to do."

At last the final takes were in the can. The Krishnan cavalry regiments struck their tents and packed their gear. As an afternoon sun danced on the rippling Khoruz, the two long columns of armored ayamen, like silver serpents, took to the dusty roads, the Ruzuma moving north towards Kolkh and the Mikardanduma east towards Mishé, their standards languidly waving in a lazy breeze.

For the return to Novorecife, Reith had intended to lead the Cosmic crew to Kolkh and thence along the Pichidé via Rimbid to the spaceport. But Motilal, now director, insisted on going back by way of Mishé to film some street and temple scenes that Fodor had deleted from the original script.

Reith would not have minded the change of plan if he could have kept Alicia with him; but this proved impracticable. The small, infrequent wayside inns along the road to Mishé dictated that the Cosmic crew be split amebawise into halves and travel a day apart. The first half would reach a designated inn, fill it to capacity, and depart the following morning. By dusk, the second contingent would arrive to occupy the abandoned quarters. Timásh would ride ahead of the lead party to reserve accommodations, and Zerré would bring up the rear to collect stragglers and unremembered belongings. Each section of the cosmic crew required a competent guide; and since Strachan's wound was not sufficiently healed, and Fallon had left days before, Reith and Alicia must each shepherd a moiety.

On the day before the first group's departure, having sent Timásh on his way with Minyev's young cousin, Reith ordered the Cosmic personnel to gather at the mess tent. Cyril Ordway was not present. Unable to bear the ridicule that had dogged him after his public thrashing, Ordway had already left camp despite Stavrakos's threat to fire him for desertion. Having found that it is easier to give gibes than to receive them, he had hired a local farmer to drive him in a light wagon all the way to Novorecife. Reith asked: "Who wants to go in the first group with me?"

"I go with you," said Kostis Stavrakos.

"And I," said Hari Motilal.

"Me, too!" said Cassie Norris.

When sixteen had volunteered, Reith called a halt. "The rest of you will leave two days hence, with Alicia."

Next morning, amid the usual bustle, clatter, and confusion, two omnibuses and one wagon were loaded. Stavrakos insisted that the canisters containing the exposed film and the costlier cameras be placed in the first wagon, where he could keep an eye on them. Doctor Mas'udi helped a hobbling Strachan aboard the second omnibus and sat beside him.

Just as Reith put a foot in the stirrup of Fodor's huge aya, Jengis, Cassie Norris rushed up. "Fergus! I want to go with the second party."

"Why? Accommodations are too tight for any more shifting around."

"It's that!" she said, pointing an accusatory finger.

Reith saw Fairweather and Valdez standing close to Alicia, vehemently arguing in low, tense voices, and realized that both had chosen to travel with the second group in hopes of a chance to be alone with Alicia.

Reith grinned. "You don't want Randal making a pitch for Alicia, eh?"

"No! I'll snatch her bald—"

"Calm down! I don't like that scenario, either. I'll see what I can do."

Reith strolled over to the disputants, leading his mount. As he approached, the men fell silent.

"Lish!" he said, crooking a finger.

They walked off together, leaving the two admirers glaring at each other. Out of earshot, Reith asked, "What's their argument?"

"Both want to ride in the gig with me," she replied. "I kept saying I'd pick my own passenger, but they refused to quit bickering."

"How about if we decide you haven't had enough carriage-driving, and we change places? You ride Jengis at the head of the first group while I drive the gig with the second. I don't think those lechers will quarrel over the privilege of riding with *me!*"

"What if they demand to go with the first group?"

"Too late! We already have as many in that lot as the smaller inns will hold. We won't announce it. Just climb aboard Jengis here and take off! By the time those jerks catch on, it'll be too late."

Reith made a stirrup of his hands. Alicia placed a toe in his cupped hands and swung into the saddle. She leaned down, smiling. "Give me a kiss for remembrance, Fearless . . . See you in Mishé!"

She trotted the animal to the head of the column, raised an arm, and cried "Go!" The drivers cracked whips, and the vehicles lurched into motion.

Grinning, Reith strolled back to Fairweather and Valdez, who stood openmouthed. "We had a last-minute change. I hear both you fellows are hot to ride in the gig. You can flip a coin, or you can take turns enjoying my company."

Valdez sputtered "You—you—*animalejo baboso!*"

Reith laughed. *"No quisiera ser cabrón!* See you all here tomorrow at this hour."

Four days later, at Vasabád, Reith settled his people in the inn. As he finished assigning rooms, the taverner stopped him. "You are Sir Fergus Reit'? He who slew that ging of rogues in the temple of Bákh? Methought I espied a familiar face, notwithstanding that many oft maintain that all Terrans look alike."

"I am he," said Reith. "Is aught amiss? Your magistrate cleared me of wrongdoing."

"Nay, sir, he not concerned! Pray hide ye here; I'll return instanter."

The Krishnan departed at a run, leaving Reith to wonder whether the taverner had gone to raise a mob against him. Presently he heard a shout from the street: *"Ohé,* Sir Fergus! come ye forth!"

Reith drew a deep breath and, displaying a mien of

more self-confidence than he felt, strode out the front
door.

A swarm of townspeople had gathered before the
entrance to the inn. Moment by moment their numbers
grew.

In the front rank, Reith recognized the magistrate,
his friend the priest of Bákh, and the mayor. "Well,
sirs, why this assemblage?" asked Reith, concealing his
trepidation as best he could. Hearing the commotion,
members of the shooting crew crowded the common
room behind Reith.

The mayor swelled visibly as he stepped forward.
"Sir Fergus, we have gathered here, suspending our
workaday tasks, to pay condign homage to the savior of
our fair land. Though ye be a alien from a far, fantastical
world, yet we know you for a true human being at
liver. . . ."

The speech went on until, when the mayor paused
for breath, Reith interjected: "Pardon, Your Honor, but
I do not understand. Why think you I saved your
country?"

"Ah, good my sir! When your fellow Terrans of the
living-picture folk passed here last night, one, who
spake our tongue, told us how ye devised the plan for
the vanquishment of the barbarous riders of Qaath,
against great odds, and how ye bravely fought and
sustained a grievous wound in the battle."

He must mean Ken Strachan, thought Reith.

The major continued. "So we besought this *Ertsu* to
tell us how we might do just honor to your esteemed
self when ye in turn reached our splendid city, as this
Master Satrakhan said ye would erelong. This Terran
graciously vouchsafed to us that, in his world, a city
would betimes give up one whom they wished thus to
adulate a key to the city. Since our gates be secured by
wooden beams, there is no such Key; but Master
Satrakhan explained that any large key would serve as a

symbol. So the worthy blacksmith, Master Hangra, working the night through, hath forged one for you."

The mayor raised a hand. Thereupon a burly Krishnan stepped forward with a huge iron key, having a stem the size of a baseball bat and a bit as large as a dinner plate.

"Sir Fergus Reef," said the mayor, "I have the inexpressible honor and ineffable pleasure to present to your surpassingly worthy self this minuscule token of our undying esteem!"

The blacksmith thrust the key into Reith's hands. The unexpected weight of twenty-odd kilos almost overbalanced him. He staggered, almost dropped the object, and recovered, as the mayor and the other Vasabáduma stared expectantly.

Reith, with the muscles of his lean arms taut, carefully lowered one end of the monster key to the ground. Knowing the Krishnan passion for fustian oratory, he launched into a speech that he had delivered on many formal occasions on Krishna.

"Dear friends! I have come to you from a distance so vast that the minds of mere mortals like unto us cannot truly grasp its magnitude; yet here, amongst folk of vastly different internal anatomy, I have found respect, friendship, and love. Verily, I have learned to regard your world as my true spiritual home. . . ."

After a quarter-hour, Reith ran out of clichés. He ended his speech with, "Last night, when the first group sojourned here, you beheld my affianced bride, Dr. Alicia Dyckman. In consequence of her breakneck ride to fetch reinforcements, her part in the victory was every bit as vital as my own. Since we shall soon wed, one key will suffice for the twain of us."

Reith paused to allow a ripple of Krishnan laughter. "In any case, my beloved and I offer our heartfelt thanks!"

The Krishnans whooped, cracked their thumb points,

and hoisted Reith to their shoulders for an impromptu parade.

Roqir had set, and a gaggle of townsfolk were escorting Reith back to his inn, when a clatter of hooves interrupted the merrymaking. A lathered aya rounded a corner and staggered to a halt. The rider, Reith was astonished to see, was Jacob White, reeling in his saddle and gray with fatigue.

"Jack! What the devil?" exclaimed Reith, breaking away from his companions. White got a foot free, but instead of dismounting normally he collapsed in a heap on the cobblestones. Reith leaped forward and helped him up. White gasped: "They've kidnapped Alicia and Cassie!"

"*What?* Not again!" Fear knotted Reith's stomach, though he showed no sign save a tightening of his mouth. He dismissed his escort with a brief good night and turned back to White. "Who are 'they'?"

"Those Krishnan culture people. Schlegel."

Reith half led and half dragged the exhausted White into the common room of the inn and ordered a goblet of kvad for him. He himself took nothing, to avoid dulling his wits. In a low voice he asked: "What for? Ransom?"

White gulped the liquid and coughed. He whispered "No, not ransom—I mean, not the usual kind. Not money."

"What, then? Come on, pull yourself together!"

"Please, I'm trying!" White took a deep breath. "Schlegel demands all the photographic equipment be turned over to him—every last camera, reflector, jar of developer, and scrap of film."

"What on earth for? Schlegel isn't going into the movie business, is he?"

"No. He wants to destroy *Swords Under Three Moons*—totally." White took another gulp of kvad.

"Go easy," warned Reith. "You're not a two-fisted

drinker like Cyril. Why does Schlegel want to destroy our equipment?"

"He says the movie would show Krishnan culture in an unflattering light. It would increase Terrans' contempt for Krishnans. He'll destroy the cameras and stuff to make sure we don't reshoot the film while we're on this planet."

"He may be right about giving Krishna a poor image; but that's not my concern. I sighed on to protect you people and your property, whatever you do. Where are the girls being held?

"Somewhere in the big forest east of Gishing."

"Durchab Forest. Tell me, how did Schlegel nab them?"

"We don't know. I heard Cassie ask Alicia's advice on how to keep Bennett and Randal happy when she's sleeping with both. I guess they decided to walk down the road a ways, because that little inn is so crowded you can't say a private word. When they didn't come back by dark, Doc Hamid and I decided to go look for them. Just then an arrow with a message rolled around the shaft came whistling out of the woods and struck the front door of the inn. Here's the message!"

White handed Reith a small, torn sheet of native paper. Reith read:

TO THE OBERHAUPT OF THE CINEMA COMPANY: I HAVE YOUR WOMEN WHERE YOU SHALL FIND THEM NOT. I SHALL RETURN THEM UNHARMED WHEN YOU TO ME HAVE GIVEN ALL PHOTOGRAPHISCH EQUIPMENT FOR WELL-SERVED DESTRUCTION, A CRIME AGAINST KRISHNAN CULTURE TO PREVENT. WRAP YOUR REPLY AROUND THIS ARROW AND STAND IT UPRIGHT UPON THE ROAD. ATTEMPTS AT RESCUE OR TO ALERT KRISHNAN OFFICIALS WILL THE INSTANT DEATH OF THE WOMEN CAUSE.

SCHLEGEL

"Why did Stavrakos pick you to bring the news?"

White shrugged. "We tried to get one of the drivers to do it, with Strachan interpreting. But they wouldn't get involved in a quarrel among Earthmen. Strachan didn't trust any of them to deliver the message anyway. I'm not much of a rider; but I've had more experience than any of the others except Strachan, and he's not up to riding yet. What are you going to do?"

"Have to think," muttered Reith. "What did Stavrakos make of the kidnapping?"

"Said he'd rather let the whole company be slaughtered than give up the film."

"I might have guessed. But I wouldn't trust Schlegel to deliver his part of the bargain, either."

"Say, Fergus, why was that crowd of Krishnans carrying you back to the hotel?"

"They had a banquet for me at the town hall. Now I've got to make an announcement to my party. Help me to get them together."

The news caused consternation and an outburst of protests. Reith studied his fourteen Terrans. When the chatter died down, he beckoned to Fairweather and Valdez. He led them into the street, saying: "Are you two up to trying a rescue? We may all get killed; but you two are the only ones here who look as if you'd stand up to a fight to save Alicia and Cassie."

Fairweather grinned. "Hell, yes! I've rescued so many damsels in distress in my movies, I'd like to try the real thing once!"

"You, Ernesto?" said Reith.

"I will be a good soldier. It would, of course, lend extra courage if I thought the lady would express her gratitude in—in a suitable manner afterwards."

Reith scowled. "Damn it, if you think you're going to screw my fiancée as a reward—"

"No, no, Fergus; I was only joking. You do not understand the Latin sense of humor. I will be as brave as a lion."

"Okay. I want you two in bed early and up before dawn. We'll have to get some bows, even if we've got to rout the armorer out of bed. When we go after Schlegel, I'm your captain; whatever I say goes. Is it agreed?"

The two men mumbled assent.

As Roqir incarnadined the farmlands around Vasabád, Reith stood on the edge of a freshly-plowed field, teaching his companions to use the Krishnan crossbow.

"Hey!" said Fairweather. "This thing has sights. None of the crossbows in my medieval movies ever had 'em!"

Reith explained. "A Terran named Hasselborg introduced them around thirty years ago. Came out alive in a duel because of them. There was some stink about his violating the technological blockade, but all crossbows have sights now.

"To cock the weapon, put the muzzle end on the ground and stick your toe through the stirrup. Take the cocking lever in your right hand . . ."

Reith had offered White a place in the enterprise; but the location manager begged off, saying he was done in by his all-day ride. Seeing him lying drawn and pale in bed, Reith admitted that nothing more could be expected of him for the time being. Reith had also sounded out the three Krishnan riders in charge of the remuda of spare ayas. But, like the drivers at Gishing, they refused to take part in a quarrel among Terrans.

So an hour later, the three rescuers were on the road to Gishing, Fairweather and Valdez mounted on ayas from the pool and Reith driving his gig. Beside Reith a half-dozen newly purchased crossbows were stowed, along with several swords left adrift after the battle at Zinjaban.

Fairweather and Valdez wanted to gallop the entire distance; but Reith insisted on leading the way in order to pace the beasts, varying their gaits from walk to trot to canter and back. His companions grumbled that he was wasting time.

"Damn it!" he burst out. "I've been riding and driving these critters for twenty-odd years, and I know what they can and cannot do. We won't get to Gishing a second later than I can help."

Arriving in midafternoon, the rescue party went to the little inn at the edge of the unwalled village. Before the inn stood the wagon that had accompanied the first group. The photographic equipment still lay under its tarpaulin, but on top of this, Olson the gasser and two other Cosmic employees were piling hay. The party's hand luggage stood in a neat row on the ground beside the vehicle.

The remaining crew members excitedly rushed out of the inn and surrounded the newcomers, yammering: "Hey, Reith, what are you going to do?" "How'll you get us out of this fix?" "Why didn't you foresee this kidnapping, if you know this world so well?" "If anything happens to us, we'll sue you!"

"What's this?" demanded Reith, indicating the activity on the wagon.

"Ask Kostis," snapped Olson. "We're just following orders." Olson had been disagreeable to Reith ever since Reith had saved him from beheading. He was the sort of person who can never forgive one who does him a favor.

Reith found Stavrakos in his room, thumbing papers. When Reith repeated his question, Stavrakos explained: "I'm just getting ready in case we have to run for it. We're putting hay on the wagon and baggage on the hay, so if we're stopped, we'll say the photographic stuff is with the second group; this is just baggage. I hope that, at night in the dark, they won't look under the tarp."

"You mean you're planning to beat it, leaving the girls at Schlegel's mercy? Why, you—"

"Now, now, don't get angry, Fergus! I wouldn't do that unless I absolutely had to. But be practical! Ken Strachan tells me this Schlegel would as lief kill you as spit. The worst of it is, he's some kind of idealist, who thinks he's serving a cause. They're the worst kind of nut; you can't bribe 'em."

Reith growled: "He's a con man who's come to believe his own line of crap."

Stavrakos continued: "Ken says that, even if we give up the film and stuff, there's no assurance Schlegel would turn over the dames. Both have probably been raped to a fare-thee-well, and he's liable to kill them to make sure they don't testify against him some day."

Reith winced.

"But look at the bright side," continued Stavrakos. "I'd be sorry to see you lose your fiancée, if that's what you call her; and Cassie's a hot movie property. But if she gets killed, think what it would do for the box office! Millions would go to see Cassie Norris's last film who otherwise wouldn't bother."

Holding a hammerlock on his temper, Reith said dryly: "Nobody's ever accused you of lack of business acumen. What have you heard from Schlegel since Jack left yesterday?"

"Oh, several of these damned arrows, back and forth. I sent word that if he'd loose the girls, I'd turn over my stuff. Of course I'd hide the cans of developed film; I'd tape 'em under the wagons or something. But he says no. He wants us to drive out on the Mishé road till his men stop us. We're to line up and strip while he goes through our clothes and baggage before sending us on. Then, when he gets word we're on our way back to Earth, he releases the dames. I said no to that."

"Good," said Reith. "Keep the argument going, in oriental-bazaar style, while I see what I can do."

"What you got in mind, Fergus? A rescue?"

"Maybe. What about it?"

"Okay! Either you win, in which case the dames are

free and Schlegel's dead; or he wins, and you and the girls are dead. Either way, there's nothing to stop the rest of us from lighting out. But how will you find them? We don't even know where in that forest they hang out; and we don't have bloodhounds."

Reith peered at Stavrakos through narrowed eyes. "You may not know it, Kostis, but I think you've solved our problem."

Reith found the Krishnan in charge of the spare ayas. For a generous fee, the wrangler agreed to take two of the animals, so that he could ride them alternately, and travel all night, reaching Mishé the following midday. There he would deliver to the Terran consul, Anthony Fallon, a letter from Reith about the kidnapping.

Fallon had left Zinjaban ahead of the Cosmic crew; and Timásh and Yinkham had been instructed, on arriving at Mishé, to get in touch with him. Reith asked that the consul order both hands to ride to Gishing forthwith.

The messenger clattered off into the night with Reith's precious message tucked into his glove. As Reith reentered the inn, the Cosmic people clustered around, asking: "Hey, Fearless, what now?" "Are you gonna try a rescue?" "When can we be on our way home?"

Bennett Ames growled. "Say, Fergus, if you're going to have a crack at those bastards, I want in. Cassie's my wife, after all."

"Good!" said Reith. "Any more volunteers?"

None spoke. Looking them over, Reith was not displeased. Of the males, all but Ames were too slight, too fat, too old, or too querulous. Reith shrugged aside further questions, saying: "Sorry, folks, but I've been on the go since dawn, and I'm half starved. See you in the morning!"

The sinking sun saw Reith teaching his volunteers swordplay and crossbow shooting in the backlot behind the inn. For fencing, he used the wooden swords designed for the battle scene of *Swords Under Three*

Moons. He improvised protective gear and borrowed the shatterproof goggles owned by members of the crew.

He added a local hunter named Shedan to his band as a mercenary, promising the Krishnan more money than he normally saw in a year, because of his knowledge of Durchab Forest.

Ames grumbled: "Why all this practice, Fergus? They may be killing our girls right now!"

"So they may. But if we go stumbling around Durchab Forest like a herd of shaihans, they'll hear us coming and either ambush us or scram. So I'm waiting for my bloodhound."

"Your *what?*"

"I'm getting a bloodhound from Mishé, to help us locate Schlegel's gang. Now let's see that stop-thrust again!"

Zerré arrived in the late afternoon. During the night, Reith was awakened by the arrival of Timásh and Yinkham. He sent them to bed but routed them and the volunteers out before dawn. He bullied them into dressing and eating a hasty breakfast, and led them out on the Mishé road as the sky was beginning to lighten above the morning mist.

"Why this ungodly hour?" complained Valdez. "I am not a human being before noon!"

"Keep your voice down!" snapped Reith. "Schlegel has people in the woods watching us. If we set out in daylight, they'll see us for sure."

"Where are we going?"

"We'll leave the main road soon. Shedan knows the secondary roads and trails."

Ames mumbled, "Where's this bloodhound you're getting?"

"It's Yinkham here. See his extra-long antennae? He's a Khaldonian, which means he has a keener sense of smell than Krishnans of other races. When the wind was right, my former secretary could not only detect the approach of visitors half a kilometer away but even tell which species they belonged to." To Yinkham he said in Mikardandou: "Do you smell anything?"

"Only that people and animals have passed this way. I do not smell Terrans except those with you."

They walked in silence as the mists melted away. Reith unfolded a map and conferred in low tones with Shedan, tracing dotted lines on the sheet with his finger.

"This way," said Reith. He walked straight into the wall of vegetation bordering the road. Once past the screen of shrubs and saplings, they found themselves on an abandoned secondary road, invaded by seedling trees. The growing light brought out the brilliant colors— azure, ruby, emerald, and gold—of the trunks of the Krishnan trees; it also illuminated the stealthy passage of the eight invaders.

A dawn breeze rustled the leaves. The squad tramped on, trading one road or trail for another. The sun was high when Yinkham at last held up a hand and whispered: "I smell human beings upwind, with a trace of Terrans."

"How many?" asked Reith.

"I cannot tell at this distance. I think several."

Reith got out the map and, with Shedan's help, located the point where they now stood. He drew an arrow through that point showing the wind direction. After conferring with Shedan, he went on. Another hour passed, and Yinkham said: "The wind hath shifted, sir. Now I smell them that way!" He pointed.

Again Reith marked the map, explaining in a whisper: "Their camp is probably near where those lines cross—at least, within a few hundred meters of it."

"How far?" breathed Fairweather.

"As a rough guess, another half-hour's hike."

They resumed their march, zigzagging on old overgrown trails. Reith hissed at them to make less noise in moving.

"How the hell can I help it, with all these damned

bushes and things?" said Ames, after a twig beneath his foot snapped with a crack like a pistol shot.

"Watch Shedan." Reith nodded at the hunter, gliding noiselessly ahead of them.

Time passed. Yinkham held up a hand. "I smell them strongly. I think they are over yonder, too far to see. They have Terrans with them."

Reith unslung his crossbow and pulled the cocking lever from his belt. "Load!" he whispered.

Soon seven of the rescuers, bent over their cocked crossbows, stole ahead, with Shedan in the lead and Reith next behind him. As Yinkham worked his way through the underbrush, being too small to handle a full-sized crossbow effectively, he cradled Alicia's little crossbow pistol, which Reith had found in her room at the inn.

Suddenly a crossbow snapped, and a bolt whistled past Reith's ear. He spun around, furious, and hissed, "Who's trying to kill me?"

"I—I'm awfully sorry," mumbled Bennett Ames, looking reproachfully at his discharged crossbow. "Didn't know these things were on such a hair trigger."

When Ames had recharged his weapon, the eight moved on, until Shedan again held up a hand. Reith whispered: "Spread out and get down on your bellies. Pick your targets, but don't shoot until I give the word." To Shedan he added: "You know which you're to shoot?"

"Aye; the fellow at the door when the fight begins."

Reith surmised that Schlegel would post one of his band inside, to guard the captives and to kill them if need be. Therefore he had asked the hunter, as the best arbalester, to hold his shot until a Preservationist appeared in the doorway of the hut, and then shoot to kill. Reith also gambled that, orders or no orders, the Krishnan in question would come to the door to see what the noise outside betokened.

As they wriggled forward on bent elbows, pushing their crossbows ahead of them, the Preservationists' camp came into full view. Centered on a small clearing, they saw a dilapidated hut with its roof half fallen in. About a dozen persons, some armed, squatted or stood around a small fire, eating. The huge Schlegel, their leader, stood facing the oncomers.

Ignoring a many-legged arthropod that had crawled inside his shirt, Reith crept forward a few meters more. When he had a clear view of the site through the crowding, many-colored vegetation, he eased his crossbow forward into position, sighted on Schlegel's midriff, and in a low but clear voice said: "Shoot!"

Six crossbows went off with loud, flat snaps, as if someone had knifed all the strings of a musical instrument with one slash. The quarrels thrummed and thumped home. Reith enjoyed a moment's ferocity as Schlegel staggered back; dismay replaced blood lust as, with a roar, the man jerked the bolt out of his midriff and threw it away. Then Shedan shot in his turn.

"Up and at 'em!" Reith shouted. Dropping his crossbow, he ran towards the clearing, drawing as he came. He faintly heard the tramplings and voices of his squad, half drowned by the shouts and clatter of the foe.

Although his attention was fixed on Schlegel, Reith was peripherally aware of one Krishnan kidnapper writhing on the ground, another lying in contorted quiet, and a third turning to flee. By the time Reith reached the clearing, Schlegel had his sword in hand. Reith bored in; but Schlegel beat off his lunge. Save for a timely parry, the cultist would have taken Reith's head off with a fast return cut.

As they lunged, hacked, and parried, Reith half-heard other clashes around him. Someone screamed as a blade thrust home. Now Schlegel's left hand, instead of being extended in a fencing position, was pressed against his belly. Blood seeped out between his fingers, but the wound did not slow the man's competent swordplay. The belt buckle and the mailshirt worn under Schlegel's clothes had limited the penetration of Reith's crossbow bolt; so that the wound, while serious, was not immediately disabling.

Sweating, Reith lunged again but was beaten back. Schlegel launched a running attack, whirling his blade in a tight circle to throw Reith's sword out of line. The more agile of the two, Reith dodged to one side as Schlegel pounded past. He made a solid thrust into Schlegel's sword arm; his blade pierced the biceps and came out the other side.

Schlegel wrenched his arm free, tearing out the sword and enlarging the wound. As he turned to glare defiance at Reith, the sword fell from his lax fingers. When Reith's companions converged on the pair, blades ready, all of Schlegel's Krishnans were either down or running away.

Reith placed his point at the base of Schlegel's neck, above the edge of the mail shirt. Schlegel sank to one knee, pressing his left hand to his abdominal wound. Apprehension furrowed his forehead.

"Mercy!" cried Schlegel. "I am helpless, wounded, disarmed. You cannot kill a man in my condition; it would dishonorable be!"

"Randal," ordered Reith, "see if the girls are in the cabin."

Fairweather grasped the ankle of the Krishnan lying dead in the doorway and dragged the body aside. Then he entered the hut and presently came out with Cassie and Alicia, both rubbing wrists raw from rope bindings.

Reith called, "Are you hurt, Lish?"

"Nothing serious, darling."

"And you, Cassie? Did this *zeft* mistreat either of you? Aside from the kidnapping, that is."

"No, except for tying us up," said Alicia.

"You're sure? He didn't *do* anything to you?"

"No, Fergus; though he promised us some interesting experiences if he didn't get the movie materials."

"What shall I do with him?"

"Kill him!" said Alicia, always the ruthless realist.

"You know what happened when you let Warren Foltz go."

"Mercy!" wailed Schlegel. "I have not injured your women or inflicted indignities on them! I acted only for the common welfare of Krishna—for the preservation of its collective soul—for the integrity of its culture."

"I'll be merciful," said Reith grimly. As Schlegel broke into a feeble smile, he added: "I mean, you won't be tortured, even though you laid hands on my wife."

With that, Reith thrust his sword into Schlegel's neck until the point struck the neck vertebrae. He twisted the blade and withdrew it. With a choking sound, Schlegel sank down into a sitting position. Like a massive tree, he slowly toppled over, to lie with blood spurting from both mouth and neck.

Satisfying himself that his foe was dead, Reith wiped his blade and sighed. Neither so ruthless nor so realistic as Alicia, he never found the taking of life something to do lightly. He looked around.

Besides Schlegel, five of his band lay dead. Valdez sat on the ground, holding a wounded arm and muttering a stream of Spanish obscenities. Then Reith spied Yinkham, sprawled with a sword through his body. "What happened here?"

Fairweather explained, "The little Krishnan, your new secretary, ran up to this guy, who was just about to let you have it from behind. With that little pistol thing, he shot the fellow in the ribs from about a meter's distance. The Krishnan, before he collapsed, whirled around and ran Yinkham through. So both ended up dead."

"Damn," muttered Reith. "The little guy might have made a first-class secretary, if he hadn't decided to play the hero. He was a better man than a lot of Terrans. Girls, will you bandage Ernesto before he bleeds to death?"

* * *

In Alicia's room at the inn, Alicia took off her shirt and examined her shapely torso in the mirror. "A couple of bruises," she said, "but nothing like the shellacking they gave me on the temple roof. I was an idiot to go walking with Cassie without you to watch out for me. And thanks a million!" She grasped Reith's shoulders and gave him a long, lush kiss.

"Thanks for what?" asked Reith. "For the rescue? But—"

"Not exactly. That kiss was for calling me your wife, even when I'm not."

"Oh. To quote the late Attila Fodor, we're so nearly married it doesn't matter." He paused.

"Fergus!" cried Alicia. "You look pale all of a sudden. Are you sure you're not wounded?"

Reith sat down heavily on the bed. "I'm okay. It's just that—well, I'm no berserker. When I have to kill or be killed, I kill. It doesn't bother me at the time; but afterwards a reaction hits me. My leg bones turn to an inferior brand of jelly."

Alicia sat down and put an arm around him. After a silence, Reith said: "You know, Lish, there's much to be said for preserving native Krishnan culture. It's too bad the movement got into the hands of a nut like Schlegel."

"He meant well in his way," said Alicia.

"Sure, like the Trasks. Hundred-percent villains are as rare as hundred-percent heroes. But you've seen how Terra has become homogenized—arts, customs, costumes, everything—and I see the same process starting here."

"But darling," said Alicia, "when two cultures meet, there's always mutual acculturation."

"Eh? What's that?"

"They borrow traits from each other. If one is more advanced, the other does most of the borrowing. When Europeans conquered the Terran tropics, the native peoples began to imitate the Europeans—as by wearing clothes—not for rational reasons but because the Europeans had all the power and prestige. When Terran culture meets Krishnan, the same thing is bound to happen. And if, as twenty-second-century Americans, we believe in individual freedoms, why shouldn't the Krishnans have the same right to copy Terran culture traits all they want?"

Reith yawned. "Too complex for my simple mind. Dearest Wart Hog, can we please go to bed now? I'm all in."

XIII

RAM KESHAVACHANDRA

The rest of the journey brought Reith no worse perils and pains than being dragged by Alicia through half the shops of Mishé, while the Cosmic crew shot the street scenes demanded by Motilal. When the crew was once more settled in the Visitors' Building at Novorecife, to await the arrival of the space ship *Ceará*, Reith and Alicia went to see Stavrakos, to ask what further services might be required.

The producer waved them away. "We don't need you. Just stay in the neighborhood, so we can find you if anything comes up."

"I'd like to get the balance due me," said Reith.

Alicia added, "And my salary for the last two weeks?"

"Oh, for God's sake!" shouted Stavrakos. "I'm being driven nuts, between temperamental actors, a sorehead new director, your finicky head cop at this stupid compound, and a mountain of paper work. Don't you two start on me! I'll get to your checks as quick as I can. Why don't you go off to that ranch of yours for another honeymoon?"

So Reith moved Alicia's possessions to the ranch. He also took home the monster key to the city of Vasabád. The following morning saw Reith and his groundsman, each holding one end of the key against the masonry of Reith's main fireplace, while Alicia gave directions: "A little more to my left. . . . No, you've got it too high. Down a couple of centimeters. . . . Fergus, your end's higher than Khudmet's. . . . Now it's lower. . . ."

"My arms are giving out," grumbled Reith.

"It won't be long now." At last she stepped forward and made pencil marks on the stones. "When we go in to Novo, you can order a pair of hooks from the blacksmith, and Khudmet can drill holes for them."

Reith visited the compound more or less daily. He tried several times to reach Stavrakos; but the producer was always in conference. When Reith encountered other members of the crew, they smiled vaguely, as if he were someone they had met but could not quite remember.

After twenty-odd years on Krishna, Reith had become too important a personage to angle for gratuities at the end of a tour. Nonetheless, he was used to having his tourists express their appreciation by clubbing together to buy him a gift or giving a party in his honor. As far as the Cosmic people were concerned, though, he seemed to have become invisible. Reith accepted this neglect philosophically, but it made Alicia furious.

"After all the work you did and the risks you ran!" she fumed. "They're the world's most self-absorbed narcissists! I'd never have stayed with them after the first month, if the job hadn't given me a chance to get back to Krishna and find you."

Reith smiled. "Don't give them a second thought. After all, I've got you. Wouldn't trade you in for all of Cosmic Productions—properties, rights, and people, including Cassie and Fodor's pair of cuties."

Driving to Novorecife the next morning, with Alicia curled up beside him in the gig, Reith said: "If that bastard doesn't ante up today, I'll begin to think he's trying to take off without paying what he owes us. If you ever have to jump into a river to rescue a drowning person, don't hand Kostis your wallet to hold while you do it."

Ahead, they glimpsed the silver spire of the *Ocará* above the sand-colored wall of the settlement. Alicia frowned. "Amazing luck, that the crew gets back to Novo to find a ship ready for takeoff a ten-day later. What's Kostis doing about the people that the ship won't have room for?"

"Doing?" said Reith. "Nothing. Kostis Stavrakos and Hari Motilal grabbed two berths and let the rest of the crew scramble. Cassie made it; the rumor is that she offered the port captain certain—uh—inducements. Those left behind will have to wait. Meanwhile Stavrakos and his new director will be back on Terra, editing the rough cut and adding special effects."

Reith and Alicia hurried to the Customs and Security Building as soon as they had stabled their aya. They found people rushing about, standing in line, shuffling papers, inspecting luggage, loading supplies, and going through all the manifold preparations for an interstellar flight.

Reith and Alicia looked around for familiar faces and sighted Michelle Fodor, relaxing in a lounge chair behind the pages of a book.

Alicia hailed her. "Why, Michelle! Are you one of the unlucky ones left behind?"

Michelle smiled. "No, I am ze lucky one. I decided to stay on Krishna. Mr. Castanhoso, he says he will process my permit as soon as ze ship takes off."

"My goodness! Why?"

Michelle shrugged. "Wiss Attila dead, I have no husband. So I look around. I see zere are many more men zan women here. Some would be glad to get a wife who know how to make zem 'appy. I have one picked, but of course I do not tell him. I only hope he will turn out a more conventional man zan Fodor, who was very difficult. Nancy and I were friends, *en quelque façon*; but ze arrangement still made for—how you say—a bit of strain."

There's your practical Frenchwoman, thought Reith. "Good luck, Michelle! Have you seen Kostis?"

"No; not today."

Reith and Alicia wandered about, watching for the producer as they bade farewells to the travelers. After half a Krishnan hour, Reith said: "Lish, how would it be if I stayed here, while you go back to the Visitors' Building and bang on Stavrakos's door? He can't be wearing a helmet of invisibility!"

"Okay," said Alicia and vanished into the crowd.

Reith waited. The first bell sounded, warning passengers to board. There was a stampede towards the gate, where Assistant Security Officer João Matos stood checking papers and calling, "Get in line! *Em fila de pessoas! Não empurrão!* No pushing! You there, go back to the end, or you shan't board today!"

The would-be queue jumper was Cyril Ordway, who slunk back to the end of the line with his lower lip thrust out and coat collar turned up. Since his arrival at Novorecife, he had kept out of sight. He and Reith ignored each other.

Reith shook hands with Randal Fairweather, who playfully punched Reith's shoulder, saying: "You lucky bastard! You know, my shrink warned me against remarrying any of my exes; said such reunions usually don't work. If he's right, and you and Alicia break up again, let me know and I'll come running!"

"It's a deal," said Reith, who found that he liked the actor in spite of himself. "But don't hold your breath in the meantime!"

Reith was seized and avidly kissed by Cassie Norris, who employed her tongue like an anteater raiding a termite nest. She whispered: "If I was gonna be here longer, boy, what I'd show you!"

Next, he shook the left hand of Ernesto Valdez, whose right arm was still in a sling. The last passengers were passing through the gate when Stavrakos and Motilal bustled up, documents in hand. Reith caught Stavrakos's arm. "Hey! Where have you been?"

"Little argument over spaceport fees," said the producer, "in the head cop's office. G'bye, Fergus—"

"Wait! You haven't paid the second half of my fee. I've been trying to catch you—"

"Don't worry, old pal. I deposited a draft to your account in the bank on my way here. I'm no deadbeat; your money's safe."

Although the producer's words had the ring of sincerity, Reith turned and walked rapidly out of the building. Outside, he broke into a run.

At the bank, Reith found a queue leading to the teller's cage, and he realized this was pay day. He took his place at the end of the line and fidgeted while the customers transacted their business with agonizing slowness. For a while, his inhibitions held him back from bulling his way to the head of the line. He had just worked up the courage to demand attention out of turn when a familiar, thin-lipped face appeared in the doorway behind the teller.

Reith yelled: "Hey, Pierce!"

The Bostonian accents of Pierce Angioletti, the Comptroller, replied: "What is it, Fergus?"

"Look, this is urgent. Could you find out if Stavrakos deposited a draft or check to my account this morning?"

"Okay," said Angioletti. "Come on around."

The Comptroller seated Reith in his office and went out. Soon he returned, saying: "No, no deposit. Yesterday he drew out all the liquid funds he had with us, and he hasn't put anything in since."

Reith sprang to his feet. "The son of a bitch bamboozled me! If they haven't lifted off—" He departed at a run.

Reith was entering the Customs and Security Building just as the warning siren sounded. He dashed to the passenger gate but found it closed and locked. No officials were visible.

Another blast of the siren, and the floor shook with the familiar rumble of a ship blasting off. A voice behind Reith said: "Fergus! We have been looking all over for you."

It was Herculeu Castanhoso. When he got his breath, Reith explained Stavrakos's trick.

"I suspected something," said the security officer. "He and that little Indian director and the man White were in my office to straighten out a dispute. They wanted to cheat the Viagens of the spaceport fees for their equipment.

"As they went out, I overheard an argument between Stavrakos and the American. Senhor White was saying: 'But it's *wrong!* Especially after he saved your life. . . .' And Stavrakos said: 'Forget it, Jack! He broke the contract when he went off to hunt for his girl friend. If he wants his money, let him come to Earth and sue me.' It struck me that they might be talking about you. So I sent João to look for you, but without success."

"I was waiting in line at the bank," growled Reith, clenching his fists in frustration. "Where did White go? I didn't see him board."

"He is one of those left behind, to await the next ship."

Reith grunted. "That guy's a born loser. The *fraco* could have tipped me off—but I suppose that's too much to expect. Oh, God damn them all to Hishkak!" Reith's voice rose to a shout as he pounded his palm with his fist. He picked up a light chair as if to throw it across the empty waiting room.

"Do not assault Senhor White if you meet him!" said Castanhoso sharply. "I warn you, Fergus!"

Reith got his rage under control and set down the

chair. "Don't worry. While he's no hero, he at least made an effort to keep Stavrakos honest."

"In fact, he is thinking of—"

"Darling!" cried Alicia, running towards them. "Where have you been? I couldn't find Kortis. . . ."

Reith explained the contretemps. Castanhoso added, "Senhor White, as I was saying, is talking of staying on here and becoming a Krishnander."

"He might make it," said Alicia. "He has adapted himself much better than Sexy Cyril did."

"My friend," said Castanhoso to Reith, "you look as if you needed a drink. I, myself, do not drink on duty; but I have a bottle secreted for emergencies."

Reith shook his head. "I don't want a drink, thanks; but I'd like to sit down somewhere quiet for a bit."

In Castanhoso's office, Reith looked bleakly at Alicia. His anger had given way to a mood of morose discouragement. "Lish, are you sure you want to marry an ineffectual wimp like me? You needn't, if you've changed your mind."

"Don't be silly, Fearless! With the money they did pay you, we're rich by Krishnan standards. Anyway, I'd still want you if you were flat broke. And you're *not* a wimp."

"Oh, yes I am; a mere bug tossed on a chip on the sea of life. A loser, like Jack White. Not to mention weary, flat, stale, and unprofitable."

She gave him a little shake. "Stop it, you dear idiot! Anybody can have a run of bad luck—even Fearless Fergus!"

"She is right," said Castanhoso. "With a quarter-hour's leeway, I could have put a hold on their equipment until he paid up. But . . ." He shrugged. "These things happen. I do not see what you could have done differently, unless you had that extra-sensory perception they talk about. I hardly suppose you would go back to Terra in pursuit of your second payment?"

"Great Bákh, no!" said Reith. "They've got more money to hire gonifs in Montecito then I could ever beg, borrow, or steal. If I sued, they'd keep me mucking around with courts and lawyers until I died of old age. I have better things to do with my life, I hope." His eyes narrowed and he doubled a fist. "But if Stavrakos ever comes back here . . ."

Castanhoso headed off another outburst by changing the subject. "When will be this wedding of which we have heard?"

"In four days. I wanted to splice the halyard as soon as we reached Mishé—"

"But," said Alicia, "I thought it only fair that Fergus's friends have a chance to wish him well."

"Ah, *as mulheres!*" said Castanhoso. "The women always hope that the bigger the ceremony, the more secure the knot. Perhaps it works that way. At least, I shall be there!"

Reith had hoped to marry Alicia before Anthony Fallon in his consulate, sign the proper papers, hear the necessary words, and get the formalities out of the way. To make a big event of the occasion, he thought, would be in doubtful taste for someone already thrice married. But as so often in the past, Alicia had her way; although nowadays, Reith observed, she got it by subtle suggestion instead of imperious demand.

On the appointed day, Reith and Alicia, in their best, stood in a packed courtroom. The magistrate, a small, slight man with a fringe of white curls around his bare, brown scalp, beamed upon the wedding party. Alister Reith was his father's best man, while Masako Ishimoto was Alicia's attendant. For a flower child, they had drafted the youngest daughter of Li Guoching, the communications officer; but in lieu of Terran flowers, the little girl carried a bunch of multicolored local herbs.

After questions were answered and a final pronouncement made them once more husband and wife, Judge Keshavachandra raised his hands and solemnly intoned: "*Isvâr bhagvân tumhâre sâdh haim!*"

The ceremony over, the spectators rose and filed past the reweds, showering congratulations. Castanhoso cried: "*Parabens!*"

Masanobu Ishimoto murmured: "*Omedetō gozaimas'!*"
Juanita Strachan said: "*Felicitaciones!*"
Percy Mjipa boomed: "*A re itumêleng!*"
The new comandante, Jules Planquette, bowed over the bride's hand. "*Je vous an fais mes compliments!*"
Prince Ferrian of Sotaspé called out: "*Hao na zan-shihoraka!*"

And Juana Rincón and Michelle Fodor burst into tears. Hands were wrung, backs slapped, cheeks kissed. Meilung Guan lined up the wedding party for photographs. Nobody was so tactless as to mention the couple's previous intimacies, within and without the bond of matrimony. At last Reith raised a hand for silence and said: "Alicia and I are grateful for your friendship; and now we invite you to a small party at the Nova Iorque!"

As they walked from the Law Building to the cocktail lounge, an ecstatic Alicia was surrounded by a gaggle of women, who chattered about houses, furniture, and clothes. Strachan and Castanhoso carried their instruments, bagpipes and a recorder, to furnish dance music. Reith found himself paired with Ram Keshavachandra. The magistrate asked: "Do you plan a wedding trip?"

"No," said Reith. "We're just going back to the ranch to help dig a swimming pool. Then we'll sit around with our feet up, enjoying the simple life until my next group of tourists arrives.

"By the way, Ram," continued Reith, "Hindi is not a language I know. What was that sentence you uttered so impressively at the end of the ceremony? A Hindu blessing?"

"Well—not exactly. I merely said—the nearest English idiom would be: 'Better luck this time around!' "

A Krishnan year later, four friends sat under the tree, which grew beside a handsome swimming pool. They were Fergus Reith; a very pregnant Alicia Dyckman Reith; Percy Mjipa, now Terran consul at Majbur; and his massive wife Victoria, almost as tall and just as black as he. Mjipa was saying, ". . . the office in Majbur has gone to pot since ibn-Ayub got himself murdered. He *would* try to mingle with natives of all classes on a familiar basis. Some Krishnans are fine people; but you'd jolly well better keep a little distance from them. If you don't . . ." Mjipa drew a finger across his throat.

Victoria hastily changed the subject as Reith's new Krishnan secretary appeared, bearing a tray of refreshments. "And where's your son? I haven't seen him around."

Reith answered, "Alister's running a tour, all on his own. His clients are three rich Mexican widows."

Mjipa commented: "Shouldn't think so small a party would prove profitable."

"It isn't; but the boy needed to start somewhere. Guiding on this planet takes special skills and resourcefulness, which can only be developed by experience."

Alicia added: "You should see how Fergus trained him for this tour! He and Juanita Strachan and I would sit facing Alister and all scream outrageous complaints and demands in Spanish. Then we'd rate the lad on how adroitly he handled each one."

"Actually," said Reith, "Alister's three widows seem to be nice old ladies who won't give him trouble. Most tourists are easy enough to manage; and with a bit of luck Alister and Timásh will be able to handle all my tour groups during the next few months, while I stay home to help with the blessed event."

"Lish, my dear," said Mjipa, "I seem to remember that in Zhamanak, you said you were married to your career and didn't want a husband or children knocking holes in your work schedule."

Alicia, beaming with the smug satisfaction of mothers-to-be, raised her chin with a touch of her old arrogance. "Don't you go thinking I've given up my researches just because I'm a wife and mother! In fact, I've just sent off the manuscript of my latest book, and I'll go back to professional work full-time when the kids are grown."

"What book is this?" asked Victoria Mjipa.

"On the marriage system in the republic of Katai-Jhogorai, where all husbands and wives are expected to take lovers and show no jealousy. Next comes my ghosting of Tony Fallon's memoirs."

"Don't whitewash him!" said Mjipa.

"Indeed not! He knows I won't write the book unless he confesses his whole rascally past."

Reith said: "Speaking of the past, Lish and I have a peculiar problem."

"Yes?" said the Mjipas in unison.

"It'll soon be twenty-five Terran years since Lish and I were married for the first time. Now, do you think we should celebrate our silver wedding anniversary next year? Or should we count the years we were divorced as time out, and celebrate—oh, about twenty-three Terran years hence? Or should we go by the Krishnan calendar—twenty-five local years from the beginning, whether or not we called time out?"

"That's not all," said Alicia, laughing. "Fergus, being a self-centered male, thinks only of things from *his* point of view. To me, because of my space-shuttling, we were first married about four and a half Terran years ago."

"Great Bákh!" exclaimed Mjipa. "I can see at least eight possible dates for your silver wedding anniversary! Why not celebrate all eight? Think of all the gifts you could cadge!"

"That's an idea," said Reith, grinning. "If we counted

all the possible anniversaries—crystal, china, and so forth—and figured eight dates for each, we could celebrate nearly every moon from now on."

"I'm surprised you keep track of such things, Fergus," said Victoria Mjipa, "since so few Americans nowadays get past their tenth year with the same spouse."

Percy Mjipa lit his pipe. "Trouble with you Americans is, you think your Declaration of Independence promised you happiness. It doesn't, of course; merely the pursuit thereof. So when the pink fog thins and your spouse shows the normal quota of faults and foibles, you feel cheated. Then your average American dumps his or her mate, picks another, and goes through the same dreary charade over and over.

"Oh, hell, I oughtn't to run on this way, like a bloody moralist. Besides, I've let my pipe go out again."

"What's wrong with moralists?" said Alicia. "We need them to balance the hedonists."

"Hm!" said Mjipa. "Maybe you've got something there." He turned to the others. "When we get our Novocife college off the pad, Lish and I might give a course in cultural relativism."

"I'd like that!" said Alicia. Eagerly she asked, "Think I might get a full professorship?"

"Better yet," said Mjipa. "The Committee wants you to head the Sociology Department, as soon as family responsibilities allow." He looked at his watch, a native Krishnan timepiece, thumb-thick and saucer-sized, with a single hand and a loud tick. "Must be going. Thanks for a wonderful visit."

Victoria added her thanks as her husband handed her into his trap. He touched the aya with his whip, and the little vehicle wheeled down Reith's driveway.

Out of hearing, Victoria Mjipa said: "Alicia has changed, and I don't think it's just the pregnancy."

"Certainly she's changed," said Mjipa. "Had to if she didn't want all that fancy psychotherapy to be a swindle."

"Somehow I found her more likable but less interesting. She's never dull; but she's lost some of the fire that used to fascinate people but make them a little afraid of her, too."

Mjipa blew a smoke ring. "True, my dear. Alicia's old fiery self lit the romance of the century under Fergus and then burned it to ashes. If, by giving up that volcanic temperament, she can now live in loving domesticity with her man, I'd say she's made a sound trade. And that's about the best that anyone can expect out of life."

ADDENDUM

While the reader may pronounce the Krishnan names in the story as he likes, we have the following renditions in mind: *a* and *á* as in "add" and "wad" respectively; other vowels as in Spanish. The acute accent on the *ó* at the ends of words is put there merely to indicate that the letter is not silent, as it often is in English. Among the consonants, *k* and *q* are sounded as in "keep" and "quote"; *gh*-French uvular *r*; *kh* = German *ch* in *uch*; ' = a glottal stop or cough. Words ending in a consonant or a diphthong are stressed on the last syllable; others usually on the next to the last. Examples: Qirib = "keer-EEB" (with a guttural *k*); Mishé = "MEE-sheh"; Khoruz = "khaw-ROOZ"; Qou = "KO"; Vázni = "VOZ-nee."

Portuguese, like French, has nasal vowels, indicated here by a line over the letter. Herculeu Castanhoso = "air-koo-LEH-oo kush-TAH-nyew-soo"; João Matos = ZHWOW MAH-toosh; Viagens Inter-planetarias = "vee-AH-zhaysh ee-tair-pla-neh-TAH-ree-ush."

Paksenarrion, a simple sheepfarmer's daughter, yearns for a life of adventure and glory, such as the heroes in songs and story. At age seventeen she runs away from home to join a mercenary company, and begins her epic life . . .

ELIZABETH MOON

THE DEED OF PAKSENARRION

"This is the first work of high heroic fantasy I've seen, that has taken the work of Tolkien, assimilated it totally and deeply and absolutely, and produced something altogether new and yet incontestably based on the master. . . . This is the real thing. Worldbuilding in the grand tradition, background thought out to the last detail, by someone who knows absolutely whereof she speaks. . . . Her military knowledge is impressive, her picture of life in a mercenary company most convincing."—**Judith Tarr**

About the author: Elizabeth Moon joined the U.S. Marine Corps in 1968 and completed both Officers Candidate School and Basic School, reaching the rank of 1st Lieutenant during active duty. Her background in military training and discipline imbue The Deed of Paksenarrion with a gritty realism that is all too rare in most current fantasy.

Fantasy: The Golden Age
Only at Baen